Other titles from BackHouse Books:

What's a Knucka?

We'll Get Back to You

Where'd You Park Your Spaceship?

An Interplanetary Tale of Love, Loss, and Bread

Rob Bell

BackHouse Books
California, 2023

Paperback ISBN: 979-8-9869960-4-2
E-book ISBN: 979-8-9869960-5-9

First printing edition 2023

robbell.com

TABLE OF CONTENTS

PART 1 THIS IS THE OUT   3

PART 2 YORCH   92

PART 3 PIDDLE PIDDLE PIDDLE   163

PART 4 I BET YOU HAVE A GUN   344

PART 1 THIS IS THE OUT

The earth didn't make it.

It got BROWNBALLED.
Literally.
It turned brown.
Ma'am Kirti told us this as she paced back and forth in front of our class, reminding us that to understand BEGINNINGS we had to understand ENDINGS. It was the first day of EARTH UNIT and right there, on the first page of our textbook, was this picture of a BROWNBALL floating in space.

That had apparently once been green.
And blue.
But was now brown.
How did she think we'd respond?
She said the word *brown* followed by the word *ball* to a room full of-what were we at the time-eleven, twelve laps old?
We looked around at each other. *Are we allowed to laugh at this?*
And then we did. We lost it.
BROWNBALL.
Could there be a more glorious word for a room full of prepubescent boys?
This kid named Eppers raised his hand. *Was this the only time?*
Ma'am Kirti looked confused. *The only time this happened to the earth?*

Eppers shook his head. *No, did this happen to any planets other than the-*

And then we saw it. What he was doing. The trap he was setting. And the best part? She didn't see it. She actually thought he was asking a question because he wanted to know the answer. But we knew what he was doing-all earnest and serious-pretending like he cared. She considered his question. *No, this is the only known case of a planet getting BROWNBALLED.*

Boom. The room erupted. Again. The sheer, unadulterated ecstasy of hearing our teacher say those two words over and over. Brown. Ball.

Ma'am Kirti was an intense woman, all elbows and angles, constantly moving around the room gesticulating with great flourish, as if the sheer physicality of her teaching was enough to convince us that this-whatever it was she was talking about-THIS was the most compelling subject in the universe. I have no idea how old she was-her hair was white but not OLD WHITE-more like ELECTRIC WHITE, MADE YOU WONDER IF IT WAS ON PURPOSE WHITE-and she wore severely red lipstick and thick blue glasses. Like if a clown had a mother. And she wore platform shoes that made this distinct clicking and clacking noise as she moved among us. It was the sound of learning.

Of course I'd seen that image before. That BROWNBALL floating in space. It was everywhere. It still is. Public buildings, stores, little plaques you come across in the park. A constant reminder that THIS is what happens when you don't take care of things.

I remember so clearly sitting in that class, watching Eppers ask her that question, all of us looking around at each other like we shared an unspoken volcanic secret, my body tensing in anticipation of the riotous explosion of laughter that would soon be ours. It's a strange and elusive thing, memory. So bendy and stretchy. There are entire years from my 20's that I can barely recall and then there's that one day in that one class and that one kid Eppers-he was something. He wore orange everyday. A sweater, a hat, socks-at least one item of orange clothing every single day. Sometimes he'd be wearing an orange tee shirt under his jacket with the word ORANGE in big letters across the front. Eppers was fully committed to the bit. Of course the other lads caught on and endlessly shredded him for it. One day at lunch a kid named Koolie Hilbers asked him, *What's the deal with you and orange?*
We all got quiet. This should be good. Eppers leaned over his food and got really close to Koolie's face and said, *I've proven I'm willing to kill for my tribe.*

Please. We were merciless. He couldn't live that one down. Like he'd tried to flex and everybody saw right through it. Plus. He didn't have a dad. Every day when class was over all the dads would be lined up on the berm out in front of the school. Except for him. There was nobody waiting for him. He'd walk home alone. He always said that his dad was traveling. That he was involved in something. That he wasn't there after school because of matters he was attending to.
He actually said that.
Matters my father is attending to.
Super fishy and evasive.
Clearly lying.

Until one day we walked out and there, standing behind the other dads, was this massive man. Just huge. Like a cartoon had come to life. He had a giant beard that appeared to be its own ecosystem connecting his face to the rest of his body. And he was smoking a pipe. And he had a dog-a large dog with white spots and a gray tongue hanging out-in a canvas bag slung over his shoulder. And he was using a steel pole as a walking stick. Absolutely terrifying this man. And he was wearing an ORANGE jacket. He made the other dads look like boys.
Like he was the father of the other dads.
And Eppers, he didn't say a word. He casually walked up to this man like he does this every day and hugged him. WITH HIS ARMS. For a while. They just stood there hugging each other. In public. In front of all of us. And then they turned and walked home together. We stood there gobsmacked next to our tiny little dads.

That was the day everything changed for Eppers. Like a switch had been flipped. He came to school the next day transformed into EPPERS OUR FEARLESS LEADER.
So when he started asking Ma'am Kirti about what happened to the earth and whether this was unique blah blah blah we immediately knew something was up. He was going somewhere with this. We were in the hands of a master.
And then she said it: *BROWNBALLED.* And then she delivered the coup de grace by uttering this sentence:
The EARTH is the only recorded instance of a BROWNBALLING.
We couldn't get enough. She'd handed us the stickiest phrase we could ever imagine and it just wouldn't leave our lips.

Ma'am Kirti went on to explain that farming did it.
Farming? Farmers? Farmers killed the earth?
So could you say that they were the original
BROWNBALLERS?
Anything to get her to say it out loud.
On it went.
Forget what she was trying to teach us. BROWNBALL
BROWNBALL BROWNBALL.

Although the farmer thing, that stuck. That was new. There were people called farmers then? We could not wrap our heads around that. Farmers-as opposed to other people? Because everybody grows food. That's basic. It's not like there are some people who do and some people who don't. And yet, Ma'am Kirti insisted that was how the earth was arranged. A certain group of people grew the food that everybody else ate-everybody who didn't grow food.
History.
EARTH UNIT.
So strange.

*

The plow.
That was the problem, according to Ma'am Kirti. I remember that because it was on page 2 of our textbook. A picture of a plow. A curved metal blade used to carve up the surface of the earth so they could plant seeds. Over time, all that systematic slicing of the soil turned the ground to dust. Of course it would. And you can't grow anything in dust. That dust began to affect the weather. The earth got drier. And hotter, obviously. And as the weather changed, everything changed.

Did nobody see that coming?
As a kid I sat there thinking
Am I missing something?
Romzi asked Ma'am Kirti
Were people less intelligent then?
She jumped on that one.
We don't rank such things.
Right.
She went on. *There were farmers who didn't use plows to cut open the ground, but there weren't that many of them. And the people who were in charge of the earth only paid the people who used plows.*
When you're a kid you barely know anything, but you know that's insane.
EARTH UNIT.
Of course they got BROWNBALLED.
They had it coming.
They deserved it.

*

My mother hit her head when I was 7. We were playing Forky. You take a fork from the kitchen-the bigger, the better. One of those large wooden ones for salad? Perfect. You place a basket in the middle of the table. First person places the fork in front of them, handle towards the basket, and then you slam your forehead down on the tongs of the fork. That's the trick of it. You hit it just right, the fork flies up in the air, hopefully does a flip or two, and then lands in the basket.
Score.
You get a point.
See what I mean?

The best. I loved that game.

The three of us would play every night after dinner. Round after round. My mother was so good at Forky. The challenge wasn't just to score, but to hit the fork with your forehead without your forehead hitting the table too hard. Which is what happened. I didn't catch it. Neither did my dad.

Until later that evening, when my mother was sitting on the floor of the kitchen, leaning up against the stove. She asked me, *Is plaid a color?*

Huh?

My dad came in. She pointed out the window. *Yon, is clear a color?*

My dad was thrown by that. He got down on the floor with her. *What do you mean?*

Her eyes rolled back and then forward. She placed a hand on his chest. *Yon Chambroy Gru-Bares, tell me my love: Is warm a color?*

When you're seven, your mother is a rock. The calm, enduring presence that holds your world together. A sun by which all the other planets warm themselves.

Her not making sense? Devastating.

Why is she calling my dad by his full name? Why does she keep asking these questions that don't have answers? What is happening?

She asked me to sit on her lap, there on the floor in front of the stove. She held me close. And then she turned my shoulders so that we were face to face. She looked me in the eyes and said, *Heen, my love, is night a color?*

We took her to the THRIVAL in our CIRCLE that night.

They put us in an examination room. People came and went, checking on her, doing tests. Lots of hushed voices. I heard the word *concussion*. A word you don't understand when you're 7.

She didn't get better.
She made less and less sense.
At my 10th lap party all my friends sang me the usual birth song.

How many laps have you done around the SUNS?
One?
MORE!!!!!
Two?
MORE!!!!!
Three?
MORE!!!!!...

While they were singing to me, I watched my mom sitting in the corner, mumbling in an endless sing-song loop *10, 10, 10, 10, 10, 10...*

My friend Moogee Fallers asked me, *What is the deal with your mom?*
I was so used to it by then.
I answered. *She hit her head.*

It wrecked my dad.
He'd bring home these thick binders he'd found at the library. I called them his brain books. He'd pile them high on the table, reading way into the night. As if he studied enough he'd find some way to fix her. As if there was some secret buried way down deep in one of those books,

10

a secret that if he just kept digging he'd eventually uncover it and he could bring my mother back. That's a very vivid memory for me, saying goodnight to him in our dark house, him all hunched over another tome, me putting myself to bed. Sometimes, when I didn't have school, he'd pack enough food for a day and we'd start walking, ending up at the house of somebody he'd heard about who had been through something similar. We would walk home so much slower than we walked there.

I'd seen pictures of people working on space stations, tethered to the side, fixing whatever needed fixing. It always used to give me a shudder. All that empty space around them, and only that little rope preventing them from floating away.

My mother wasn't tethered.
And she floated away from us.

*

Sir Pong.
What a teacher.
We'd heard about him for years.
Everybody said Sir Pong was the best.
I learned so much from Ma'am Kirti, but Sir Pong, that guy shaped me. On our first day, he announced EARTH UNIT 2. We opened our books to page 1. A picture of a sun. Not a particularly unusual or unique sun, just your average flaming hot yellow sphere. You've seen one, you've seen most of them. He told us that for almost the entire time people lived on earth they believed that the earth was the

center of their solar system and everything revolved around it. Around *them*.

Seriously?

I raised my hand. *Were their brains smaller than ours?*

He'd heard that one before. *No, not that we're aware of.*

He went on. A few hundred LAPS from the end, someone invented the telescope. Which showed them that their planet wasn't the center, their sun was. Their planet, they learned, was just one more ball orbiting a much larger ball, inhabiting a galaxy filled with them.

What would that do to your brain?

He let the question hang there.

What would happen to your mind if you found out that the entire way you understood the universe was wrong?

Sir Pong did this all the time. He taught us something, and then he'd pause, and then he'd ask a question that suddenly connected that world with our world.

One day he led us out into the field beside our school and then he told us to lay down and look up at the sky. I can picture us so clearly-13 boys, on our backs out there in the open. He told us to feel the surface of Lunlay beneath us, the gravity holding us there. His voice was so hypnotic. He showed us how to become aware of the exact places where our bodies made contact with our planet. He told us to imagine ourselves lifting up, off the ground, away.

There were no tests in his class, only experiences.

He pointed out that we understood the sky to be up, and the ground to be down.

Yes, that's correct.

He then told us to picture ourselves lying on the ground on the exact opposite side of Lunlay. I'd never been to the other side of our planet. I'd seen pictures. Desolate, barren. Cold. I saw myself lying there in my school jacket, out in the midst of all that unexplored wild.

He told us to imagine ourselves there looking up at the sky.

He asked us *Which one is up?*

Whoa.

Which UP is the true UP? The up in the sky you're imagining while you lay there on the ground on the exact opposite side of Lunlay or the up that you can open your eyes right now and see above you?

That hurt my brain.

Which up is the true up? he asked. *Can they both be up and yet be in totally different directions?*

Sir Pong.

What a teacher.

*

One morning I complained about having to wear my school jacket. I hated wearing that jacket. It was gray with white piping around the edges and a crest on the front pocket.

I yanked it off and threw it on the floor.

And then continued eating my breakfast.

My dad calmly picked up my jacket, folded it neatly over the back of my chair, and then pulled up a chair next to me.

You know why your school requires you to wear a jacket?

I didn't. And I knew he would sit there until I said something.

No, I don't.

I could feel a story coming on.

When I was your age, the world was different.
I started to roll my eyes, then caught myself. The sooner I
let him go on, the sooner it would be over.
Everybody carried a camera with them everywhere.
I had a camera. But I only took it with me when I wanted to
take pictures. *Everywhere?*
He had hooked me and he knew it.
Yes, everywhere. And they constantly took pictures.
I hadn't heard any this before. *Of what?*
Themselves, he said, *themselves.*
As if I'd understand that.
*And what they ate for breakfast and what they were wearing
and their hair and their muscles and their dog…and they'd
send those photographs they'd taken of themselves to their
friends and also strangers who wanted those photographs
sent to them.*
I stopped him.
You're making this up…
He was insistent. *No, I'm not. Some kids spent all their
time on these photographs. Making comments about their
photographs. Making comments about other people's
photographs. Sending their friends photographs
taken by people they didn't know.*
He paused, like he was about to make a big point.
*By the time we got to school we'd already been bombarded
by hundreds of photographs THAT WEREN'T REALLY
ANYTHING WE COULD DO ANYTHING WITH.*
Do you know what I mean?
Uhhhh, no, but I nodded for him to keep going.
*Our heads were so full of stuff-comments, clips, bits and
fragments-but it wasn't anything of any substance. Some of
it was funny and some of it was clever and once in a while it
was compelling or informative but there was just so much of*

14

it you couldn't really keep up, even if you wanted to...

It's funny now, to think of my dad trying to explain all this to someone who'd only done 10 LAPS. Points for effort.

He went on. *So THE CHAIRS changed it. No more broadcasting all the time. They officially called it THE RETURN TO DIGNITY.*

He said this in an announcer's voice, like it was a bit much. But also respect there.

They said that there is a DIGNITY to being HUMAN, and it was time to reclaim that DIGNITY. No more sharing everything all the time. No more endless broadcasting of every last little detail. We had to start wearing jackets to school and calling our teachers Ma'am and Sir and Ma'ir. It was a huge deal. Some people were so furious-your mother's parents were angry enough they kept her out of school for a year.

I hadn't heard this. *They did?*

Oh yeah, people said they were having their voice taken away, that this was a basic human right that was being infringed upon etc, etc, that you have to be free to express whatever you want to. Which only showed how addicted everyone was. All I remember was having to wear the jacket.

I knew it. I knew he was going somewhere with this.

You hated the jacket too?

So much-at first.

Then what?

I grew to like it. You may, too.

*

Sir Pong told us to turn to page 3. On the left was a picture of a stick figure person. Above them was a yellow ball. The stick figure head was looking up at that yellow ball.

A very simple drawing.

I could have drawn that.

He told us to *take it in.*

Take it in? What does that mean?

Let your heart take a picture of this drawing he said.

Huh?

He went on. *The people on earth didn't know about other SUNS. They thought theirs was the only one. They actually called their sun THE Sun.*

We had a very difficult time processing that.

THE Sun?

They thought theirs was the only one?

Sir Pong was just getting started. *Now turn your attention to the drawing on the right hand page.*

That same stick figure drawing. Only on this page there was at least ten yellow balls over that stick figure's head.

Yeah, of course.

Obvious.

There are lots of suns.

Who doesn't know that?

Except them, way back then.

Sir Pong held up his hand, with his palm straight up and down and the thumb side towards his nose, motioning for us to do the same.

Now, place your hand on the seam in the middle between the two pages-between the two drawings.

We did it. He looked at me. *Tell me, Heen, how did we get from the one page to the other-from one understanding to the other?*

I had no idea what to say.

Jirby G raised his hand. *We learned.*

Sir Pong nodded. *Yes, we did.*

I spoke up. *We studied, we explored, we expanded...*

I let it hang there, that word *expanded.*

Yes we did! Sir Pong clapped. *And what did that require?*

It was so quiet.

He had that effect on us.

Boys. Deep in thought. A rare thing.

You didn't want to stick your neck out there and miss the point in front of everybody. And yet you wanted to get it.

Open.

He said the word gently. Like it was a baby bird he was holding in his hands.

How many of you find it hard to comprehend how they could have been so limited in their thinking?

Every hand went up.

How do you know our thinking isn't just as limited? How do we know we aren't just as ignorant? Who's to say we aren't about to discover something that will change everything forever?

Oh man.

That was intense.

He did it again.

We'd be feeling so superior, working our way through the EARTH UNIT, thinking we were so much more advanced than them, and then he'd pull the rug out from under us.

Like this.

And he wasn't done.

Now turn the page.

We did.

Across the following two pages was a drawing of more stick figures and above them in the sky more yellow balls. Lots of stick figures, lots of yellow balls.

I took it in.

Sir Pong asked *Who knows what else is out there?*
He asked it again, with a lilt in his voice.
Who knows what else is out there?
He asked it again, like it was a line from a song.
Who knows what else is out there?
I felt like I was starting to get it.
He told us to turn the page again.

On the next page in big letters we saw two words:
PATTERN RECOGNITION.
That is some ADULT WORDING right there. We were going
to need some help with that one. Sir Pong explained. *We do
EARTH UNIT because we're looking for patterns. People
used to see their world one way. And then they learned and
grew and their understanding expanded. And then it
happened again. And then it happened again. And THAT,
gentlemen-*
He never called us gentlemen, I kind of liked it.
*THAT is a pattern. And you're learning to recognize them.
Because once you understand one expansion, you can
understand them all. You learn to spot the pattern, and
you'll spot it again. And again. And again.*

*

I lost my dad as well.
I see that now.
People regularly told me how sad they were for what
happened to my mother.
I get it.
But no one ever mentioned my dad.
He was obsessed with helping her. Fixing her. Curing her.
Undoing what had been done.

Then he grew weary.
And then he gave up.
It took a while, but gradually he floated away too.

*

My life changed the day the Yegs started digging.
There's a distinct sound a Moler makes as it rolls along.
I heard it while I was still in bed.
I ran out front.
Everybody did.
Big day.
Lunlay is one of the warmer planets, at least our half is.
There's no humidity, the water in the lake is warm
year-round. I didn't own a coat growing up.

That heat can be brutal on houses. When Lunlay was first
landed, they built houses like they had on other planets,
only to discover that they baked in the SUNS, dried up,
and fell apart within a lap or two.
So they went down, into the ground.
At first they dug by hand.
Which took a while.
And then the first Moler arrived and suddenly one person
could dig out a home in a day or two. What a machine, the
Moler. Four wheels, a seat, and a drill the size of a large
person. Hills, mountains, cliffs, slopes, that gradual incline
out by the trail to Tonpers. Pretty much any incline
anywhere could become a home. The slightest angle could
be Molered.

A typical home had several bedrooms at the back-no
windows so no SUNS light coming in when you're trying

to sleep. And it's cooler back there. Then a bathroom in the center that had a compost system running under the house and out front where it was used to fertilize the flowers. Everyone had a garden in front. Most homes were like ours with one main window and skylight in the central room of the house which had the kitchen and table and couch and all that. The kitchen had it's own compost system that flowed out to the part of the garden where the food was grown. That's where we spent most of our time. In among all those plants and flowers. When people walked by you could see them and they'd stop and talk, maybe they'd sit for a while. I'd run off with the kids while the parents chatted away.

We lived on The Thiru, a long and steep hill that had 60 or 70 homes dug into it. My dad Molered ours when I was a kid. I remember the sound of all that dirt as it came flying out of the hole. At one point, I stood directly behind it so I'd be sprayed with the dirt. That smell of fresh soil. I loved it.
People did all sorts of things with the dirt that had previously occupied the space they turned into their home. Some had it hauled away. Others built seating, walls, terraces-one family near us made their front yard look like a miniature castle.
What you did with that dirt told us so much about who you are. You'd hear that sound of a Moler coming and know that today someone new was joining The Thiru.
And the Yegs, they were unlike anything we'd ever seen. There were 9 of them. Two parents and seven of the loudest human beings ever to walk a planet. When I ran out in front of our home, they were following the Moler up the path, singing and dancing. One of them was wearing

a large hat with fake birds on it. Another had a dog on a leash. The dog was painted purple and had wings strapped to its sides.

And they were my age.

At least a few them.

I stood there staring.

I don't even think I waved, I was so transfixed.

One of them, a girl, ran up to me and grabbed my hand and yanked me into their procession.

That about sums it up.

I was yanked into their family.

Our home was so quiet by then. The three of us, sitting around that table. My mother murmuring to herself in a string of words we had stopped trying to translate. My dad doing his best to hold it together, but so weary. Just a shell of a man.

There is a stillness and silence that actually has sound. You can't hear it at first, but over time it gradually becomes all you can hear. It's a quiet so quiet it's loud. It's the noise that absence makes, the aural aftermath of loss and departure. It's what it sounds like when what you once had is gone and nothing has arrived to take its place.

But the Yegs, good gods, they made such a ruckus. I ate there, played there, yelled and sang and ran and came back from a day at the lake to there.

Nord was my age.

This is how close Nord and I were: Nord stuttered when he got excited. At least when he was young. I didn't have a stutter. Until the Yegs moved in. And then I began to stutter.

We were that close.

One day me and Nord were at the top of the Greven, a medium-size peak near The Thiru. We had taken these old tarps and built wooden supports to stretch them across, like sails on a boat. We were convinced we could fly if we strapped them to our backs and then got enough speed and jumped at the top of a certain steep section of incline. His was blue, mine was red. We were obsessed with flying. We'd been working for ages to get our ships-that's what we called them, our ships-just right. I painted a giant eyeball on my wings, he painted an elbow on his. I have no idea why. We strapped ourselves in.
We were ready.
All we had to do was run and jump and we'd know if our wings actually worked. It was the moment before the moment, both of us panting and sweating from the hike up, from carrying our ships on our backs.
He turned to me. *Let's do this brother.*
I got a lump in my throat.
Brother.
The thrill of that, him saying brother, eclipsed everything else in that moment. He crashed immediately, for the record. I flew all the way down.
But that. *Brother.*
He had 3 brothers!
He had enough.
But he didn't.
He made me one his of brothers.
That was the Yegs right there.
Such large hearts. They just scooped me up. One night I stayed for dinner like I usually did and when we all sat down Rooty The Mother placed a pot in the middle of the table so

large I swear I could have climbed in and gone swimming in whatever was in that pot. None of us knew what it was. Soup? Stew? Broth? Whatever it was, she'd never made it before. She announced with a grand flourish, *Heen said that potatoes are his favorite food, so I decided to make potato soup!*

I immediately jumped up from the table and said I forgot to wash my hands. I ran into the bathroom, closed the door, and sat down on the floor and cried. Rooty had 7 kids and she remembered what I had once said about potatoes.

We walked to school together.
We played the beautiful game together.
We made up contests involving sticks and mud and birds we caught.
We paddled across rivers on rafts we made from branches we found in the woods.
We stood on the edge of cliffs and tried to see who could pee the farthest.
One night I sat at our table, watching my dad cut his birthday cake. He served my mother a slice, knowing she'd take one bite and then drift off. He served me a slice. He thanked me for the cake. He opened his gift. I'd carved him a sculpture. I don't know if that's the word for it-I'd taken a stone and a branch and some little crystals I'd found in one of the fjords and I'd painted them different metallic colors. I was in my arty phase. I assume I was trying to say something about technology and nature and the symbiotic relationship between the two-the kind of thing you think about the first time you take an art class. He opened it and examined it, turning it around in his hands, doing that thing dads do when they admire

something simply because you made it. And then he set it down on the table. And then he took another bite of his cake.

I was swallowed up in that moment with an aching emptiness, a realization that the celebration was over. He'd take another bite of cake, I would too. He'd thank me again later for the gift, I'd tell him I was glad we could have a party. I saw the rest of the evening play out before us. I knew exactly how it would go. That was the part that was so crushing-knowing that by then the script had been written, the story told ahead of time. It made the universe feel like a very sad place. The three of us in that house, going through those motions, but without whatever it is that makes your life together feel like a life together.

And then someone pounded on the door. We all jumped. It sounded violent. And then the door flung open and in came the Yegs, in a line, youngest to oldest. They were singing.

Yon Chambroy Gru-Bares
we know that on this night
IT'S YOUR BIG DAY
Don't put up a fight!!!
You're going to dance with us,
you're going to SSSIIINNNNNGGG!
Because today we are your subjects
and you're the lap day king...

They sang it like a march, with formal accents, like it was as old as the world, like people had been singing this song for hundreds of laps. They stomped their feet on the big words-DAY! FIGHT! DANCE! SING! KING!-they sang like it was the only thing left to do in the worlds. I knew they'd made that song up that day, probably on the way over, they were that good. But the passion, the way they barged in like this was always how it was going to go. They were such a force, such goodness to me, that for a few brief verses of that song I was able to forget that noiseless, aching abyss that had slowly been engulfing my family.

They formed a circle around the three of us, banging on lids and blowing horns they'd made out of tubes of paper-the youngest boy Soony was wearing a monster head he made out of strips of bark and he kept inflating this yellow balloon and letting the air out slowly so it sounded like someone had stepped on a cat. It was so loud and cacophonous and Rooty was wearing a sarong with a turban and Nord kept yelling *BOOTAH! BOOTAH!* at random intervals.
None of it made any sense and it was perfect.
My mom smiled.
Everybody saw it.
She smiled.
That's how indomitable the Yegs were.
Try to keep them at a distance. You will fail.
Everybody got sucked into their vortex.
Eventually, they all quieted down a little and Duque The Dad cleared his throat like he was going to give a speech. He straightened up his spine, puffed out his chest and clasped his hands in front him.

We have an age old tradition in our clan, Yon, that when a man reaches your age-
Goja interrupted him. She was two years younger than me. *Dad, what are you talking about?!! What tradition?*
We all laughed.

Duque gave up. *You're right, we don't have a specific tradition for when a man turns your age, Yon, other than banging down the front door and invading your home with noise and love.*

Noise and love.

And Goja.

Nord's little sister. Always trailing behind, trying to keep up. Slower, younger. A girl.

That night was the start of it.

I saw her strength. Her power.

Had I missed something?

Because suddenly Goja was everything.

I couldn't stop thinking about her.

Nord was the first to notice.

We were hiking a peak about a half day from The Thiru, almost to the top when he said

You and my sister.

He let it hang there between us.

Not really a question, not really a statement.

I forgot about getting to the top.

I thought about it.

Yeah I said.

And then I repeated it. *Yeah.*

He nodded. *Yeah.*

*

One day we walked into Sir Pong's classroom and there were thin, rectangular metal sheets about the size of my arm hanging from the ceiling by clear strings. One over each of our desks. And on our desks were these wooden sticks with cloth covered knobs on the ends. I think they're called mallets.

26

Sir Pong watched us take this all in with great pleasure.
He loved it, being a step ahead of us.
I struck the piece of metal above my head with my mallet.
That sound.
It was so clear and it rang out while it vibrated there above
my head. The only drawback was that everyone was doing
what I was doing and that made it unbearable.
So loud.
And clangy.
I could hear that there was something different about each
piece. They made different sounds.
Notes Sir Pong said.
We stopped whacking away with our mallets, the combined
cacophony of all that noise gently fading.
I could hear myself think again.
They're called notes, Sir Pong explained, *and you each
have a different note above your head. That's why they
sound different from each other.*
I'm sure the boys around me who played instruments knew
this already but it was new to me. I didn't know anything
about how music works.

There wasn't any music in my home.

Once again, Sir Pong was up to something. *I am now going
to give you an assignment. It is a group assignment. The
entire class is the group.*
We looked around at each other.
We're the group?
He went on. *Your assignment is to make a song. You have
2 hours. I will return at that time.*
And then he walked out of the room.
Instantly we were seized with a low grade panic.

Create a song?
What does that even mean?
Silence. And then pandemonium.

Boys can be very emotional.

This kid Maury Ipnow sat next to me. I watched him turn
red and then frantically begin repeating *We're going to be
fine we're going to be fine we're going to be fine* in such a
way that it was clear he did not in any, way, shape or form
believe that we were going to be fine.
Bozra Hominary? That obnoxious kid by the window who
always acted like he knew what he was talking about and
once ate an ant off the floor? He got up from his desk and
began pacing around the outside of the room, as if he
could walk this assignment into existence.

We adored Sir Pong. And not just adored, respected.
It was so important to us what he thought of us. We
desperately wanted to impress him. But those of us who
weren't musical, we had absolutely no idea what to do.

And then Ackas Fath stood up on his chair, calmly hit his
note three times, and solemnly proclaimed *Bretheren. I
beseech thee.*
What a moment.
Ackas Fath was born old. Sometimes he wore this silk
knot thing that he tied around his neck. He called it an
ascot. On a regular basis he would speak with a particular
accent for the entire day. You'd ask him who he was
imitating and he'd say,
The Golden People of the Southern Basin
or

Our ancestors from the north who were known to don the burlap kaftan.

That sort of thing.

It's not that we didn't like him or he didn't fit in, it's like he was with us but he was also somewhere else, in his head or in history or in some drama he was writing that only he knew about.

And he was short.

And skinny. Wiry is a better word for it.

And he had kind of bulgy eyes and a large nose that sort of…I don't know…hooked? That's the best I can come up with-hooked.

Unexpectedly enough, his *Brethren, I beseech thee* stopped everyone dead in their tracks. We were desperate for some leadership. And then he sang out in a startlingly clear voice *Let us now create a song together for music is the soothing balm of life.*

He held out the word *together* for a while.

I believe *vibrato* is the word for it.

It was awesome.

Ackas Fath can sing?

He stayed up there on his chair. *We can do this!*

He said it with authority. He punched his fist into the palm of his other hand. Man that felt good. He was just warming up.

So first, everyone, back to your seats.

We did it. Quickly.

Now it is clear to me that some of you have a bit of background in music and some of you don't.

He said this like he'd said it before, like it was a speech that he'd written out and memorized and rehearsed ahead of time.

So we will take this slowly and will sort ourselves out and in no time we will have ourselves a song.

Eppers clapped and shouted *Yeaahhhhh boooyyyy let's do this!*

That was key for Ackas, getting Eppers on board early. Ackas went to the writing wall, like he was Sir Pong, and began to draw a series of rectangles in a row from left to right, lecturing as he drew. *Notes function in a twelve note scale. The 13th note begins the scale all over again, only higher. That 13th note is called the octave. There are 13 of us in this room.*

Albie Pastens raised his hand. *Do you think Sir Pong knew that?*

Knew what? Maury Ipnow asked.

Ackas did a dramatic exhale, like their questions were important and deserved a significant amount of pondering. Well played by him, especially for those of us who were intimidated by anything involving music. It made us feel like our questions weren't that stupid.

Yes, I think he knew exactly what he was doing. I was tipped off to this when I first heard you each hitting your note. Ahhh, I thought to myself, these don't all make the same sound. And then it hit me: there are 13 of us. My guess was that each of us has one of the notes of the scale plus, of course, the octave. We'll test my theory and if it's true then we'll simply figure out who has what note. Make sense?

A few heads nodded.

I kind of got it.

Jirby G, the roundest human you've ever seen, raised his hand. Like Ackas Fath was Sir Pong. And to top that, Ackas didn't flinch. He called on Jirby G as if it was just another question on just another day in HIS classroom.

Yes Jirby G, what is the nature of your query?
Jirby G said cautiously *I know you're working a plan here Ackas, and of course I'm all in…Can I make a suggestion?*
Please do Ackas said. Casually. What a pro.
How about we go around the room one by one and we try to find the lowest and highest notes? That'll at least get us started.
Ackas responded *Brilliant. That's our plan.*
Around we went. At first it all sounded the same to me, one sustained clang after another. But then, ever so gradually, I became aware of subtleties, tones, slight variations. And then, out of that, I could identify what Jirby called *higher and lower.*

This is music? What a mysterious new world opening up right there in front of me. Above me.

Fifteen minutes in, we had identified who was what note. Bozra-who was the octave-took it upon himself to write each of our names on our note on the board. Turns out I was a C sharp. I had no idea what that meant. But I held that C sharp down with everything I had. Ackas had been moving around the room, listening very intently. He now got back up on his chair.
Excellent, now let's write some lyrics. And then we'll give those lyrics a melody. And then we'll find that melody here in the room. And then we'll have ourselves a song.
He said it like it was doable. Like it was within reach.
I understood about half of what he said BUT THE CONFIDENCE. That I got.
Maury squinted. *Are lyrics words?*
A few muted laughs. People caught themselves though, because we were all in this together.

Can't slag a man for asking.

Ackas answered. *Yes, Maury, lyrics are words. And the thing with lyrics is to start with a word or phrase or image that grabs you. That stands out. That pops. Anybody got anything for us?*

Koolie Hilbers raised his hand. That just killed me. Dudes raising their hands. And Ackas calling on them. *Yes Koolie.* Koolie just went for it. *I've got a word, it's actually two words: bun cakes.*

So fantastic. I don't know if it was the relief in the room because our panic had subsided with Ackas in charge or it was the sheer joy of hearing BUN CAKES spoken by one of our colleagues but the euphoria was explosive. BUN CAKES.

Albie Pastens, who was not the most talkative fella, raised his hand. *All due respect to BUN CAKES, but I'd like to one up BUN CAKES with this word: BUTTOCKS.*

Again, fantastic.

Fellas were really finding their form here.

Ackas smiled just a bit. Like a master teacher, he acknowledged the tomfoolery but knew he had to keep us focused on the task at hand. *Clearly you all are exquisite lyricists and we could go all day wordsmithing deft and poignant verses, but we have a song to write here. So let's go with BUTTOCKS. I can't believe I just said that. Allow me to sing it.*

And then he puffed up his chest and sang
My buttocks are mighty…

What a marvel. We gave him a standing ovation. He took that word someone threw out trying to be funny and he made it into a line in a song that he sang like it already existed.

He sang it like it was an actual song.

It was like a magic trick hiding in plain sight.

You can do that?

You can conjure up an actual song out of thin air?

Because we just watched him do it. With a little help from us. We were speechless, we were entertained, we were inspired. We were making a song.

Ackas was all business. *All right then, moving right along, someone give me a word that relates to the word BUTTOCKS. Once again, I can't believe I just said that last sentence.*

Ackas was learning on the fly that sometimes being a good leader means holding your nose.

Eppers was on it. *Jowls.*

Ackas winced. *Jowls? For the next line?*

Eppers nodded. *Yep.*

Well that was settled. Jowls.

Jirby G was puzzled. *What are jowls?*

Ackas waved it off. *Not important. What's important is that they anchor the next line-*

Eppers interrupted. *And they're related to your buttocks.*

Ackas took a big breath. And then he sang

My buttocks are mighty
And these jowls are strong.

He made *strong* sound different than *mighty*-lower, fuller, heftier.

Again, amazing. What he just did.

Eppers raised his hand. *Loins.*

Perfect said Ackas. And then he sang it all the way through, but he shifted the pronouns.

Our buttocks are mighty
And our jowls are strong
These loins are ready
To sing our new song!

Maury jumped out of his seat and ran up to the board and wrote out the lyrics. We were cheering, pounding our fists on our desks, singing bits and fragments of what we'd just heard. Ackas went with it, directing us from the top as we all sang it together. We were swooped up in an unstoppable force, belting those four lines out at the top of our lungs. At one point I became aware that I had stretched out both of my arms as far and wide as I could. I looked over at Eppers who was tilting his head back so far it looked like he was going to fall over backwards. Jirby G's eyes were closed and he was swaying back and forth, lost in a hymn of our own making.
We sang it again.
And again.
And again.

It was rapturous and transcendent, the depths of its nonsense equaled only by it's miraculous existence forged out of thin air mere moments earlier.

Ackas signaled us to pause. *Gentlemen, one more thing: We need to sort out the notes. So listen to this first one-* And then he sang that first word. *MY.*
Who has that note?
He pointed to one of us, and then another, and then another. He sang that one note again. Another mallet strike. Nothing. He pointed to me. I hit my note.
It was me!

I HAD THE FIRST NOTE.

What a glorious rush of recognition.

All right, Heen, you'll be starting us.

45 minutes ago I didn't know a thing about music, and now I WAS THE FIRST NOTE.

He went quickly around the room, moving to the next word, the next note-we were locked in, fused as one. Racing against time. Sucked up in a vortex of creation.

Ackas asked *Does everybody know the words?*

A general nodding of heads.

Good, because now I'm going to wipe the board. Can't let Sir Pong see what's coming.

He winked.

Ackas Fath.

Two steps ahead.

Legend.

Sir Pong returned.

We sang him our song.

He loved our song.

We sang it over and over and over.

We hit our notes. And hit our notes again. We sang them with passion. Sir Pong walked in among us as we sang our song, soaking it up like it was the most beautiful song he had ever heard. Eventually, after I can't begin to count how many rounds of that same verse, he arrived at the front of the room and sang our song with us. I could have sworn his voice was louder than all of ours put together and clear and deep and strong. He added hand motions and he pumped his fists and held the last note until his face started to turn blue and we clapped and yelled and hooted and hollered and then collapsed into our chairs completely spent.

I was hoarse.

I looked over at Maury, who's shirt was soaked from perspiration.

It had been three hours since Sir Pong gave us that assignment and then walked out.

We'd missed lunch.

We didn't care.

We sat quietly at our desks, resting in the triumph.

Exalting in what we had just accomplished.

Wallace Froomzin raised his hand. How does he have the energy to ask a question right now?

You have a question W? Sir Pong always called him W.
Sir Pong, what does this have to do the EARTH UNIT?

You could feel the collective *Huh* in the room. A few murmurs of agreement. What a great question. We perked up. Because Sir Pong always had an angle. *W, allow ME to ask YOU: What happened just now?*

Classic Sir Pong. Responding to a question with a question.

Wallace jumped in. *You gave us an assignment and a number of us immediately shatcaked our pants because we didn't have the slightest idea where to begin to make a song and then OUR BROTHER Ackas Fath stepped up and led us to victory. Because that fella has music in his bones!*

Ackas managed a dignified bow, sitting there in his seat.

Sir Pong had more. *And what would you have done, W, if Ackas hadn't stepped up and led the way?*

Wallace thought about that one for beat. *It would have gotten ugly. We were in trouble. That would have been one nasty song.*

Heads nodded. Truth.

Another question for you, W: What if one of your classmates had stepped forward and tried to lead you but they didn't know anything about writing a song?
Wallace shook his head. *Same thing, only worse. Total disaster. Some of us would have gotten angry. Heads would have rolled.*
We were all nodding along, we agreed.

Sir Pong told us to turn in our textbooks to the next page. There, at the top of the page, were two words:

DEMOCRACY FAILED.
He went on to explain that the earth was arranged in a very particular way with everyone having a vote.
What's a vote?
And why did everyone have one?
We had so many questions.
We were so confused.

We grew up with THE CHAIRS. They run everything. And things run just fine. Why complicate it?

But EARTH-everybody had a vote, and they could vote for whoever they wanted to vote for? And the winners got to be in charge of the earth?

Sir Pong showed us pictures of flags and buildings with domes on top and crowds gathered to hear someone speaking on a stage about how they would run things if they won the voting. He explained that pretty much anyone could try to get votes. And they didn't have to have any experience being in charge of anybody or anything in order for people to vote for them to be in charge of everybody.

He had us, right there, again, in that familiar place. Bewildered. Curious. Waiting for him to tie it all together. I couldn't wait any longer. *But what does any of this have to do with our song?*

I could tell he knew this question was coming. *Excellent question, Heen. Now turn to the next page.*

We did, and there it was: The BROWNBALL. Ahhhhhh, now we could see where he was headed with all this. He then explained that everyone agreed that the end of the earth and the failure of democracy were pretty much the same thing. The people who won the voting-the people in charge of the arrangements-were unable to do something as simple as TAKE CARE OF THE EARTH. And if you can't do something as basic as that, well then you have to ask more important questions about the entire ARRANGEMENT itself.

Sir Pong had more to say. *They often referred to democracy as an experiment. Well, some experiments fail. Because you have to have someone in charge who actually knows what they're doing. If you leave it to chance, if you leave it up to the shallow whims and fleeting preferences of the masses, who knows who may end up in charge? They may not know what they're doing. Those leaders may not have any idea what people truly need-and that could lead to the end of your world. That is what happened on Earth. Who wants to hear that song?*

*

One time Nord handed me a stack of papers.
What's this?
My play he said.

Your play?

Yeah, I wrote a play.

Conversations with Nord were often like this. Whatever it was he'd just done he'd act like he'd done it a thousand times.

He once told me his life philosophy was: *Act like you've been there.*

Been where? I wanted to know.

I was often a half step behind.

He clarified. *The THERE is anywhere you find yourself.*

Nord. What a head scratcher.

His play was called WHAT'S A KNUCKA? It was about four mountain climbers who'd all reached the top of a mountain that had never been climbed at the same time. He watched me while I read the whole thing in one setting.

I loved it.

I didn't know Nord knew how to write a play.

Had he ever even been to a play?

He said *Do you want to be the narrator?*

I didn't understand the question. *Where?*

Again, a half step behind.

I'm going to stage my play at the theatre in CIRCLE 4 and I want you to read the NARRATOR parts.

Suddenly I had nerves. *On a stage? In front of people?*

Yes, he said, *a real live performance.*

Then he told me we had to go to CIRCLE 8 for CASTING.

Why? There's no lake in CIRCLE 8...

Nord looked at me patiently and sighed. *Not FISHING CASTING, CASTING CASTING. For my play.*

That was Nord in peak form, acting like we do this all the time.

I heard there's a kid there who can cry on command. I

want to audition him for one of the lead parts.

There were a number of things in that sentence I didn't understand. But there's a kid who can cry on command? I was in.

It occurred to me *How will we find this kid?*

Nord wasn't phased in the slightest.

We'll ask around.

That was his plan. Ask around.

Which we did. We arrived in the CENTER and started walking. Nord went up to the first kid he saw and asked *Do you know anyone who can cry on command?*

This kid was a gangly chap, standing there in the path before us, sporting a plaid green sweater vest. Not a swerve you would have seen a kid out our way make. He eyed us suspiciously. *Are you talking about Pabbi Apsar?*

Nord looked at me with a *DID YOU DOUBT ME BROTHER* look. Then he turned back to the gangly chap as if all of this was going according to plan.

Yeah, good old Pabbi. I got some business with him-can you point us in the direction of his digs?

And just like that, we were standing on Pabbi Apsar's front steps. Nord knocked. The door opened. There stood a kid about our age.

You Pabbi?

Nord said it like he was in the midst of very important dealings and couldn't be bothered with long, drawn out formalities.

…Yeah… There was a fair bit of hesitation on Pabbi's part. It came out more like a question than an affirmation. I don't blame him. Nord had a habit of coming in hot.

Nord Yegs here, this is my associate director of content development Heen Gru-Bares.

Wait. I'm what? I looked at him in disbelief-*Development...?*
Nord pressed on. *We'd like to talk to you about auditioning
for one of the lead roles in my newest production WHAT'S
A KNUCKA?*

I'll point out here that there's one word in that sentence
that tells you all you need to know about Nord: *newest.*
If you weren't paying attention, and you didn't have all the
context, that one would fly in under the radar, undetected.
But if you were me standing there on those steps, you'd nod
to yourself knowingly because he'd done it again. Taken the
facts and tweaked them just a touch in his favor without
technically changing anything. *Newest?* Yes, it was his
newest production. It was also his first production. His
ONLY production. But Pabbi, Pabbi didn't know this
standing there in his fuzzy yellow socks, nibbling on a
Jabbo jelly sandwich-probably made by his mommy-holding
his frizzy white toy poodle in the other hand. Of course that
kid could act. He was wearing a shirt that said *I DON'T
LOVE THE DRAMA, THE DRAMA LOVES ME.*

Pabbi Apsar stared at Nord like he had three heads. I
actually found this to be a sport unto itself-watching
people size up Nord upon first encountering his obtuse
charms.
Okay then, WHAT is it?
Nord hesitated. *What is what?*
You didn't see that much.
Pabbi straightened up just a touch. Stood a little taller.
He'd figured out that Nord needed him. The power dynamic
shifted.
What IS a Knucka? That's my question.
That was a good one. Letting Nord know you've got him in

your sights. The dog, I noticed, had no teeth. Its tongue drooped flaccidly out the side of its mouth. Like it didn't know where it was supposed to go. Pabbi scratched the dog's chin. The dog enjoyed it.

Nord rolled his eyes. *Well, it's not like I can just tell you what a Knucka is-*

Nord may have overplayed his hand there. Pabbi was all over it.

Unacceptable. Why would I audition for a role in a play when I don't even know what it's about?

He started to close the door.

Wow. That kid was not mucking about.

Turning the screws on Nord from the get go.

Until that moment I had only ever seen Nord bowl people over. He would come on so strong and undaunted and people would get caught up in the momentum of it and go along with all kinds of things he'd cooked up.

But there, on Pabbi Apsar's front porch, he'd met his match.

It was delightful to watch.

The two of them sparring like that.

Another kid joined Pabbi in the doorway. He was older, taller, bigger-but the look in his eyes. Not right. Something was off about that one.

He mumbled something in our direction, his eyes glued to the floor. It sounded like he said *toads got sunburn.*

Pabbi looked mortified.

*This is my brother Babak-*and then he pushed Babak away-*WHO IS NOW LEAVING!*

He was so harsh with his brother. No love there. Babak shuffled away.

Nord and I didn't know what to do with that.

Pabbi rallied very quickly.

I'm in. Where do you want me and when?

Nord started to pump his fists in triumph but held himself back.

Next day? CIRCLE 6? After school. At the theater.

You got it. See you then.

We turned to leave but I stopped.

I had a question.

Is it true you can cry on command?

To come all this way and not ask-I had to.

Pabbi's face completely changed. He looked offended, shocked, outraged, hurt-all at once. All these motions were racing across his face in rapid succession, like thunder clouds in the sky. It was fairly disturbing to witness. His shoulders lurched forward. His eyes rolled back. He twitched up one side of his body, then down the other. Was he having a spasm? Or a seizure of some sort? How did my question set him off so violently? I kept wondering if we should call for an adult. He grabbed his stomach. He heaved. His bottom lip quivered. Giant sobs began to rack his entire body. Tears poured out of his eyes. He placed a hand on the frame of the door to steady himself. Every square inch of his body was dominated by some deep sorrow that had risen up from the depths of the worlds. Nord and I watched this all unfold before us, stunned speechless with this staggering spectacle. And then Pabbi Apsar stood up straight, wiped his eyes, scratched that dogs chin, and smiled.

That answer your question?

*

Nord's play was a hit.

Such a hit that we did it 6 nights in a row.

People loved his play like I did.

After the last show we had a party. Nord and I had recently discovered this drink called a Penicillin. It involved fresh ginger and lemon and something from the planet Moriba called scratch. And a large square ice cube. We loved that drink. We had way too many Penicillins at that party and walked home together as the suns rose, singing and repeating our favorite things people had said about the play. I woke up late, immediately panicking because I hadn't gotten my mother her breakfast. I raced out into the kitchen. It was empty. And then I saw, through the window, my mother and Goja. They were sitting in the garden, side by side, watching the birds in the tree above them.

They were holding hands.

Goja was saying something to her.

I watched them for a while.

Goja.

*

I played the beautiful game almost every day growing up. We'd hear about a game happening at a certain pitch at a certain time and we'd be there. I had heard some fellas say that CIRCLE 6 had the best pitch on Lunlay and, you know, you have to see those kinds of things for yourself. CIRCLE 6 was high up on a steppe-the whole area was flat with these very steep drop offs. Beautiful, windy, extreme-I was constantly struck with how different the CIRCLES were from each other. And the people, too.

Was the land different and it shaped the people in a

particular way, or were the people different and they just happened to find themselves together on the same land?

And that pitch. If you kicked it too far it looked like the ball would roll down that slope for miles. They'd attached nets to these giant boulders that surrounded the pitch. It was like playing a game on top of the world. Or a moon. It actually was the best pitch on Lunlay. Fair play to them. We were well into the game when I sensed I was being watched. But in a good way. My mind countered that sense with *Who would be watching you? You don't know anybody out here!*
I turned and saw that someone had climbed up on one of those huge boulders.
Goja.
And she was wearing my favorite sweater.
What? She went into my closet?
How wonderful.
I was flooded with a swimmy, floaty bliss.
I stopped right there in the middle of the game and stood still.
I looked her in the eyes, from kind of far away.
And then I put my hand on my heart.
She did, too.
And then I kept playing.

*

I remember Sir Pong going on about this word CULTURE. Normally, that would be another case of ADULT WORDING that we could not care less about. But it was Sir Pong, so we listened. And besides, Sir Pong was from The Degs. The Degs were legendary. Eleven planets way, way out past the

Elt and the Eln. You had to be seriously tough to survive out there. None of us had ever been there, obviously, or even met someone from The Degs. Until Sir Pong showed up at our school in his long green tunic with silver wave lines on his arms. He wasn't that tall, but his hair stood straight up in the middle of his head and he shaved the sides. Whatever image we had of someone from The Degs, he lived up to it.

CULTURE. That was a very important word to him. He had us turn the page to a picture of a lion eating a man. The man-and the lion-were on the floor of a massive bowl, and there were people-lots of people, thousands of people, sitting in staggered rows on the inside of the bowl, watching the lion eat the man. No one in the picture was trying to stop the lion from eating the man. They appeared to be enjoying it.

On the opposite page was a picture taken in a similar bowl. Same size crowd, it looked to me to be earlier than the first photo, judging by how they were dressed. There was no lion in that picture, only men. They were wearing tight pants and helmets, and they were grabbing each other as they ran into each other head first. One of the men was carrying a ball that had something wrong with it. Like it had been damaged and lost its shape.

I raised my hand. *Is he carrying a ball?*

Yes he is, Sir Pong said, *that's a Tackle ball.*

I didn't understand. *It doesn't look like it would roll.*

Sir Pong was waiting for this. *Exactly. It makes no sense, right? A ball that doesn't really roll...*

The class agreed.

That's what a CULTURE is-a complex, interrelated web of structures and codes and customs people create together that sometimes makes sense and sometimes doesn't.

Earth fascinated me. I raised my hand and said *It looks dangerous.*

Sir Pong nodded. *Oh it was. Incredibly dangerous. A ton of people died. But they kept doing it, for generations. The lion eating the man was dangerous, too.*

*

It had always been me and Nord. And then suddenly it was me and Nord and Goja.

We were exploring on the ridge north of the Almanar when we came across a group of people standing out in a flat area overlooking the ravine below. They were studying charts and graphs they'd laid out on a table they'd set up. One of them had a meter machine in her hand she was using to measure something. It all looked rather official and serious. Nord walked right up to them and asked *What is the nature of your business here?*

The nature of your business.

That's what he asked a group of adults.

Peak Nord right there.

I was assuming they'd tell us to get lost. But they didn't. They laughed. Nord had that effect on people. The woman holding that meter thing said

You want to see what we're doing? She held up her chart. *We're planning CIRCLE 9.*

The first 10,000 people to land on a planet create the first CIRCLE, called CIRCLE 1. That circle has everything those first 10,000 need to live. The stores and schools and theaters and pitch to play the beautiful game on are in the CENTER of that CIRCLE. A CIRCLE is set up so that everyone can walk everywhere. If you want to go to another CIRCLE there are GLIDES that connect all the CENTERS of the CIRCLES. All of it planned, organized, thought through from that first moment when those first LANDERS set foot on that new planet.

On Lunlay, CIRCLE 1 was on the west side of the Lake. When the 10,001st person arrived, they began planning CIRCLE 2 so that as those second 10,000 people landed they could each participate in the creation of CIRCLE 2. On it went.
Because, well, the BROWNBALL.
If you don't go slowly, and think sustainably and plan intentionally with everyone involved it could all fall apart.
And then you'd have to leave.
And that would be heartbreaking.
Who would ever want to leave home?
I knew about CENTERS and CIRCLES, obviously. But it had never occurred to me that someone somewhere had to actually pick a place to make the next one.
That's the thing about being a kid.
Adults have the world sorted, you just live in it.
It doesn't occur to you that it ever…wasn't.
Or what it took to set it up.
What it takes to run it.
It just is. It was always there.

It's like when you're a kid and you see your teacher at the market. He eats? They buy things? She has…a life?
It can be a shocking idea that your teacher is a human like everyone else.

The three of us were captivated by those planners out past the Almanar planning the next CIRCLE.

What a revelation.

It brought the world closer.

It was like going behind a curtain.

What we had always known to be how it is is actually something that people created.

And Goja, she was so into it. She studied their maps like she knew what she was seeing. She asked them questions. She held that meter and tested whatever it tested. A couple of times she asked follow-up questions and I had no idea what she was talking about. At one point she commented on the *topographical aesthetics* of the area. Where did she learn all that? I was missing things right and left, but the spirit of it, making a new CIRCLE. That was intoxicating.

We were buzzing as we left them.

Goja was quiet for most of the hike home.

As The Thiru came into view, she said *Someday I'm going to do that.*

*

Jirby G was the first to spread the news. Someone had painted CHUBBS LOVES CHEESE on the side of the library in CIRCLE 8 in big PURPLE letters.

We couldn't stop talking about it.

Who is Chubbs? And what is their deal with cheese? AND WHY PURPLE? Albie was panic stricken.

It was the mystery of it that sucked us in. The intrigue.

Not to mention the danger.

Ackas informed us *It's called vandalism. From the root word vandal, a reference to an ancient earth tribe of marauding destroyers.*

Well there you go. There's a word for it. Ackas went on *It's also referred to as the MALICIOUS DESTRUCTION OF*

PROPERTY. This was all new to us, somebody painting something on the side of a building. Shocking, really. Someone just did that? Without something happening to them?

A few days later Jirby G reported that his sister had a friend whose mother had a sister in CIRCLE 8 whose dog had gone missing. They searched and searched and searched for that dog until they found it hanging upside down from a tree in the woods. Dead. Jirby G was emphatic about it-THAT DOG WAS HANGING THERE DEAD.

Strange things afoot in CIRCLE 8. The only thing I knew about that CIRCLE was my one trip with Nord to see Pabbi Apsar.

I told Nord what I'd been hearing.

I feel for Chubbs loving cheese like that.

That's the first thing he said. Followed by

Let's investigate. Gather a team.

I reported back to the lads at school. Nord was a year older than us and adored by everybody.

Nord is putting together an investigation team? Bozra was clearly already on board.

Yes, we both are. Had to give myself some credit.

Ackas was on it. *I'd be happy to take care of logistics.*

I had no idea what that meant.

Then I'll put you in charge of that.

I had learned a lot about leadership from Ackas. Take the energy and go with it.

We went a few days later, six of us. We figured the first place to start was Pabbi Apsar's house-Nord said he'd be our fixer. We all nodded confidently.

Fixer. Yeah. Of course. Gotta have one of those.

We get there, Pabbi opens the door, surveys the six of us

standing there on his porch, and says *It was Babak.*
Who? Jirby G wanted to know.
My brother. Nord and Heen met him the first time they came here. It was him.
I realized in that moment there wasn't much left to investigate.
He painted CHUBBS LOVES CHEESE on your library?
Nord asks this formally, like he's an adult, filling out an official form.
Yep. And the dog.
Pabbi doesn't flinch a bit when he says this. Like he's telling you what he had for lunch.
Your brother killed that poor little helpless dog? Ackas's voice cracks as he asks, like he's going to cry. Or throw up. Nord motions for us to quiet ourselves. Like he's got this.
Well gentlemen, we can be on our way, Pabbi has answered our questions.
Not really Jirby G protested. *We still don't know who Chubbs is.*
Pabbi had clearly heard that one. He threw up his hands.
Doesn't everybody want to know! Here's the thing: there is NO Chubbs-
Albie let out a squeak. *Does that mean there's no cheese?*
And that means there is no cheese Pabbi stated with finality. *My brother isn't right. He's got a chip missing. Always has. And now he's gone.*
He paused while we took that in.

He's gone, gone? I repeated.
Gone, gone. He left. They're going to help him.
We had no idea what that meant.

*

I remember the last page of our textbook. Sir Pong said it was the most important page. It was a picture of a plane and on the side of the plane was written F14 in big letters. It was a very primitive looking plane-like someone who did not know much about flying made it-and it was flying over a group of people. The people on the ground were celebrating something important. In the picture, the plane had just dropped a bomb. It was going to land in the middle of the group. All of the people on the ground were smiling.

Sir Pong had us sit and look at that picture, imagining what was happening in it. The story. That's what he kept repeating: *What is the story here?*
We didn't have a clue.
He explained that CULTURES always make EXCHANGES. That's the line that stuck with me. And that new word EXCHANGES.
He went on to say that the people with that old plane thought that someone there on the ground had attacked them earlier and so they were going to take him out to get him back for what he did. And in the process, of course, send a message to anyone else who might be thinking about attacking them.
I raised my hand. *But what about all of the people on the ground who didn't have anything to do with the attack?*
Sir Pong knew that question was coming.
He always did.
That's what I mean by exchanges he replied. *If a few innocent people die, the people with that old plane believed, that was unfortunate but necessary to properly protect them from future attacks.*

I distinctly recall how quiet we all were, hearing this.
I had another question. *Why didn't the people who paid for the plane object to this? Didn't they know this was going on?*
They knew, he answered, *but they chose not to know.*
Huh?
He nodded and said
EXCHANGES.

*

One day I was coming back from a game when I saw the top of a long wooden pole with what looked like fabric or some strange sheet clumped around it, staggering slowly along the path. And then I realized
It's Goja.
Whatever it was, she was having a beast of a time carrying it. I ran over and grabbed one end.
What is this?
She clenched her teeth. *My final project.*
I looked closely at what I thought at first was fabric but then realized were leaves.
Are these leaves?
Yes, she said, *from that Hanggi tree between our house and yours. Do you know the one?*
I desperately want to appear like I knew the one, but I didn't.
There's a tree that makes leaves that look like this?
She looked at me patiently. *They turn this color once they've fallen and spent about three days on the ground.*
I was starting to get it.
You collected these off the ground?
I did.

For how long?

The last two LAPS.

Oh man, that was intense. Her discipline.

And then I cataloged them by texture, color, thickness, etc.

I was trying to get my head around just how long this took her. *Did you know what you were going to make when you first started collecting them?*

I felt like I was interviewing her, and I loved it.

No, I had no idea what I would use them for-I saw how they reflected light, and I knew that would lead me somewhere...

I hesitated before I asked the next question.

What is it?

She took her end and set it down, then she took my end from me and pulled it straight so that the whole thing was laid out flat on the ground.

You hang it on the wall with the pole at the top?

The power of it. I was doing my best to take it all in.

You could put it on a wall...I guess...for the show I hung it from the beams in the ceiling so that you could walk around it.

It's incredible. I was serious when I said this. There were these variations in color from leaf to leaf that created this glistening, shimmering effect.

I was enthralled. *I don't understand how they got this... shiny? Is that the word-shiny?*

I didn't really know how to talk about art.

Oh that, yeah. I kept experimenting with different varnishes-I wanted to create a clear varnish that would preserve the leaves and give it that reflective appearance, like they were permanently wet-

You MADE a varnish? Once again, I must have sounded so simple.

She didn't seem to care. *Some pastes I came up with made the leaves too brittle, others were so sticky they were a nightmare to deal with. You know that Imaldi plant in your garden? I used the sap from that to try something thicker but the smell was unbearable.*

I could have stood there all day and listened to her talk about saps and varnishes. I never imagined in a thousand laps that someone using the phrase THE SMELL WAS UNBEARABLE would be the sexiest thing in the WORLDS to me.

Eventually I tried mixing the aloe from that Densran plant near the top of The Thiru with the foam that forms on the east end of the Lake on a windy day and then I heated it with some sugar from that cane we walked by that one day we were hiking near Greven and WAHLAH!! I found what I was searching for…

I was listening to her explanation and nodding along as I took in the scope of what she'd done there.

And then you figured out how to attach these leaves to each other?

That was the hardest part she said.

That was the hardest part? I laughed. *That?*

She held up her hand.

She was laughing as well.

Okay, okay-good point. The whole thing has taken so much-so much everything.

A flash of weariness. And bitterness.

It didn't go how you wanted it to?

She sighed.

I just thought it would be more of a moment, the unveiling …All that work and then the space I was assigned to display was down a back hall because it was too big for the main gallery and the lighting wasn't right-way too bright in some spots, too dull in others-and then Simona-you know who she is?

I did.

She made this bright pink dress with lights and speakers and a voice-activated playlist and everybody gathered around her and-

I could picture it. *She stole the show?*

She did. She stole the show.

We carried it home together. I asked her if I could display it. She agreed, but for a limited time. I think she knew I had a plan.

I then went door to door in The Thiru, inviting every single family to come to our garden the following day to see the latest installation from local artist Goja Yegs.

They came.

All of them.

They gathered around her, asking questions. She stood there for the entire day, talking about her project. She called the piece Aperture. She explained that you adjust the aperture on your camera depending on how much light you want to let in. We'd all walked by that tree, many of us our entire lives, and we'd never noticed its leaves. And it had never crossed our minds to make something with them.

*

Ma'ir Dobie was next level.

Ma'am Kirti was all about the facts, making sure that we knew WHO did WHAT and WHAT happened WHEN.

Sir Pong was about the experiences-laying out in that field, showing us pictures that upended what we thought we knew. GRAVITY and CULTURE and EXCHANGES and all that.

And then there was Ma'ir Dobie. They wore a dress everyday. A bright dress, usually with a pattern that if you focused too hard on it you'd get dizzy. And always black boots. And over that dress a fishing vest, with pockets all over the front. Pockets that often stored things they would pull out at just the right moment to make a point. We were doing a unit on HOW THINGS GROW and they showed us a picture of a CIVET. Not that interesting of an animal. We'd seen stranger creatures on Lunlay-have you ever seen a knucka? But then they explained how that animal eats coffee beans, poops them out and then people pay more for coffee made from those beans...and just when we were so grossed out we thought our heads were going to explode they opened one of those pockets in their vest and pulled out a handful of those beans, winked at us, and said *Coffee anyone?*

The theater of it, the surprise, the planning, the timing. Brilliant.

You never knew what was in those pockets.

Oh, and the hair.

They wore 2 ponytails.

Every day.

I remember my dad telling me that during the RETURN TO DIGNITY the CHAIRS excused half of all teachers.

Excused? I didn't know what that meant.

Yep, he said, *FIRED is another word for it. In one day. Suddenly half of our teachers were gone.*

Where'd they go?

I have no idea, he went on, *one day they just weren't there. The CHAIRS changed it all around. Starting then, to be a teacher you had to be THE BEST OF THE BEST. That's the phrase they used. And they announced that teachers would be paid three times as much as before,*

and that no class would ever be bigger than 13 students.
Ahhh, that sounded familiar. Above the door of every class
I'd ever been in was that number 13.
My dad did his usual intense stare. *It didn't use to be like this.*
He lost me. *Like this?*
Yes, like it is for you.
Still lost me. *How it is for me?*
He answered my question with a question. *Are you ever bored at school, Heen?*
I thought about it. *No.*
That's what I mean.
I see now what he was getting at. All I'd ever known about
school was learning and curiosity and head scratching
and everybody engaged and our teacher pulling poop
beans out of their fishing vest. School was a good word
to me. Surprising. Dangerous. You never knew what was
coming next.

Our first assignment in Ma'ir Dobie's class was to keep a
DREAM JOURNAL. For the entire lap. Our instructions
were to keep that notebook by the side of our bed and
first thing in the morning write down everything we
remembered from our sleep.
That got weird.
Fast.
I had no idea just how much my mind was making up while
I slept.
At the end of that first week Ma'ir Dobie asked *Who
would like to read one of their entries out loud?*
Out loud??!!
No way.
We were terrified. I didn't think anyone would do it.

I wasn't going to.
But then Albie Pastens volunteered to go first. We all exhaled with relief. Whew.

Albie Pastens hadn't said ten words all year. He sat on the far left side in his green pants and velcro shoes and stared straight ahead. Albie Pastens. About to go where no man had gone before. He opened his DREAM JOURNAL and started reading about how Voltara summoned him to appear before the Exchequers Grand Council to present his BLOOD Package and he was flanked by Xon The Craft Master of Poison Butter and his sister LADY STANKWEED who had a four-headed dog on a leash made of pasta and he was sinking in to the chunky soup filled with GORFAN horse intestines when his neighbor Ricardo poured out a bucket filled with Monkeyface fish-
Albie Pastens, we didn't know you had it in you! We were hanging on his every word, so happy someone went first and blown away that this kid had even stranger things happening in his sleep than we did.

That's how compelling Ma'ir Dobie was-we did it. We kept that journal, we read out loud. We went all these places and did all these things we wouldn't normally do. That was their genius right there-they didn't explain why we were doing this. They simply acted like a DREAM JOURNAL was a perfectly reasonable and interesting thing to keep. And we went along with it. Astonishing.

And then, at the end of that lap, Ma'ir Dobie asked *What are your dreams made of?*
What a question.
I hadn't ever thought about that.

Ideas? Thoughts? Images?

What is the SUBSTANCE of your dreams? they asked.

Substance?

Huh?

Dreams, they said, *are created in our minds.*

Yes, that's true, I could see that.

So whatever it is they're made of, they're created OUT OF thoughts BY our minds.

I could follow that. Kind of.

So whatever is happening in your dream-trees and warlords and neighbors and soup and animal intestines- they all appear to be separate people and places and things in the dream but they are, in fact, all made of the same substance.

Ma'ir Dobie paused.

Whoa.

I had to think about that.

And then came the banger: *What appear to be separate objects in your dream are in fact made of the same substance.*

I can still remember that feeling, sitting there in that class, something opening up inside me.

All that separateness is in fact an illusion. All that appears to be separate is in fact one substance.

We were what? 17 at that point-18 laps old?

And we were being taught that?

And we were grasping it, kind of, as much as we could.

What a teacher.

Ma'ir Dobie explained that on earth before it BROWNBALLED-smile from all of us for that callback-they had lost this awareness. Their view of the universe had become so saturated in separateness-I loved that phrase, *saturated in separateness*-that they had lost their grasp of the unity and one substance that is how things truly are…

*

I skipped the FOLLOWS.
Why wouldn't I? I knew what I wanted to do.
There was a way it usually worked. You finish school, you approach someone who is doing work that you want to do, you ask them if you can follow them around, they usually say *Yes.* Hopefully that led to more permanent work. If you followed them around and realized that work wasn't for you, you thanked them and found someone else to follow around. Everybody did it that way. That's how work worked. No pressure. No rush. You kept trying until something clicked. And then if you did that for a while and then it came to an end, you tried something else.

But I knew.
Ever since that day out past the Almanar when Goja and Nord and I had come across those PLANNERS, I knew that's what I'd be doing.
They made me a STAKER.
And I loved it.
The best job ever. Even though I hadn't ever had any other.
I had a quiver full of wooden stakes on my back that I had made and then painted different colors. I carried a small sledgehammer with me to drive them into the ground. It was surprisingly empowering, carrying that hammer around with me everywhere, those stakes sticking up out of my quiver behind my head. After they'd measured where a building or a trail or path was going to go, I'd put stakes in the ground

and then connect them with string to help the PLANNERS visualize what it would all look like. The head PLANNER was this woman named Spy V, she was always saying that it wasn't just how it LOOKED or whether it WORKED, it was about how it FELT. I'd stake a trail and the structures along that trail and maybe a path or two leading out from the CENTER and then she'd spend hours walking it one way, then turning around and walking it the other way. Often she'd ask me to move a stake a pace or two. I made thousands of these adjustments for her. Sometimes she'd sit in a chair in the the middle of where we'd staked a path and she'd get really, really still and just sit there. For hours. Listening. Watching. Sometimes she'd do long stretches without any movement. She had a method, I know she did. But it often appeared from the outside like she wasn't doing anything.

One time I staked a library-it was the biggest building I'd done up to that point. Libraries are always the largest structures in the CENTER of a CIRCLE, obviously. It had taken me an entire day to connect those stakes with string. I was standing there, surveying my work with great satisfaction when she strolled up, shook her head, and asked, *Could you please use red string instead of blue?*
Red string?
All right, then.
I found a coil of red string three CIRCLES away.
That alone took half a day to find.
I restrung the entire thing.
Which took another day.
Which I didn't mind. That was all part of it.
And then she returned and took it all in.
She tilted her head, the way I'd often seen her do. And

then she motioned for me to come stand next to her.

I did, and I was flabbergasted.

It looked totally different with the red string. Bigger, wider, more-I don't know what the word is…presence? Suddenly I could feel the library. It wasn't there, it hadn't been built, it was just stakes and string and yet…I was aware of it. I know that's not how people talk about libraries that don't exist yet, but Spy V-she was a master of whatever THAT is. Everybody looked to her every step of the way. There was a guy whose speciality was construction and another who was all about water and waste and compost and there was this old lady named See who was an expert in the psychology of color. They had a language between them that had evolved over time that only they spoke. An understanding of what they were trying to do, something elusive they were going for that they knew when they had achieved it and they knew when they hadn't. And when they'd hadn't, they just kept trying. Thousands and thousands of small tweaks and adjustments, day after day. Move a stake here, move one there. Change the color of the string.

When I first became a STAKER they were planning CIRCLE 11, which was out past the Merr and Murr, in the middle of nowhere. There was a river there, and they had endless discussions about which side of the river to put the CENTER.
This side? That would affect how the CENTER received the reflected light of the SUNS off the water.
That side? Better for the GLIDES coming and going, but not as good for the compost flow-there was a slight incline

going the wrong direction.

See suggested having the center on both sides, with the river running right through the middle. No one had ever done that. This fella ChaChi, who had a squeaky voice and always wore a fuzzy mauve cardigan with a koala bear stitched across the back, drew up a plan to divert the river into two streams, forming a circle of water with the CENTER in the center of that CIRCLE.

That got a huge laugh.

ChaChi, that guy.

What a dumb idea.

Way too convoluted. Even I knew that.

Almost like the PLANNERS were showing off.

But then I watched over time as the other proposals just wouldn't come together and that CENTER in the CENTER idea with the river going around on both sides just wouldn't go away.

They brought in a guy whose specialty was water flow. His name was Chuck. I'd never seen that before, a man with his name stitched on a patch on the front of his shirt. He had pens in his front pocket and wore cropped brown pants. What an unusual man. He said he was a hydrologist. You can have that be your job? Water? He showed up carrying a curved stick. Engraved on the stick was the name DIANE.

Chuck greeted each of us, and then kindly asked us to step back and give him some room. He stood along the river and took a series of deep breaths. He moved so slowly. Then he walked up above on the ridge and looked down at all those stakes I'd put in. He studied the drawings and maps that Spy V and her people had made. He held his stick above his head, then swung it down and tapped the ground with it in certain places.

I asked him *What are you looking for Chuck?*
He answered. *I don't know. I'll know when I find it. Or I won't.*
And then he took off his shirt.
Right there in front of me.
And his shoes.
And his pants.
Whew, this guy.
On his own wavelength.
He folded his shirt and pants and placed them neatly next to his shoes. He carefully tucked the laces inside his shoes. And then he got in the river.
Chuck in the river.
All of us on the bank, watching him.
He swam underwater. He floated on his back for a while. He gulped a large amount of water and then gurgled it for a while in his mouth. And then he spit it out like he was a fountain. He floated face down in the water, without any movement, like he was dead. He submerged so just his toes were sticking out of the water.
None of us said a word.
We just stood there watching CHUCK IN THE RIVER.
After forever he swam over to us, lying in about a foot of water. He propped himself up on his elbows, there in his underwear. He looked at each of us as he said
Sometimes you have to get in and see what it's saying to you.
The river? See what the river is saying to you? This fella Chuck was throwing me for a loop.
Spy V loved that one. *I totally know what you mean.*
Eventually Chuck got out of the water, dried himself off with his shirt, put his pants back on, and then declared
It's a brilliant idea. A CENTER in a CIRCLE that actually IS

the CENTER of a CIRCLE. Surrounded by water. I love it.
And then he put his wet shirt on, said goodbye to each one
of us by name, and then walked away.

Word spread fast.
CIRCLE 11 was going to be something different. Something
new. The river was going to be split, the CENTER would
essentially be an island, and there would be bridges, lots of
them, at least 5 or 6, connecting the CENTER with the rest
of the CIRCLE. People started coming out to see the
progress. They'd stop us and ask questions, some of them
very detailed and technical. I was part STAKER, part TOUR
GUIDE. At first I was irritated, complaining to Spy V *They
act like I have all the time in the world, as if I don't have a
job to do here-*
She stopped me. *That's your problem right there.*
It is my problem! I was quite cranked up about this.
Turn it around. She said it calmly, like it was obvious.
Turn what around?
*The things they say to you. Don't see it as a problem, or a
distraction. See it as help. They're helping us.*
*But it's not help!!! They're not helping-they make it harder
to do my job. They're in the way!!*
She motioned for me to sit down on some flat rocks
nearby. *Heen, what is your job?*
Uhhhh, staker. Staking. Right?
Hmmm. That's interesting.
That's all she said. *That's interesting.*
It was very unsettling.
I'm not a staker? I was clearly missing something.
*That's part of it. A little bit. But this staking you do, what is
it in the service of?*
I literally scratched my head at that one.

Building? Making a CIRCLE?

I was grasping here.

Yes, it is. We're creating space here, new space, space that we want people to thrive in. So yes, it's buildings and paths and lighting and shade-but it all forms something much larger.

It was all a bit humbling. Sitting there listening to her put me in my place.

See those birds over there? She pointed to some swallows that often circled above the river. See how they fly as a group?

I nodded. Where is she going with this?

Who decides where the flock goes?

I had no idea. *The lead bird?* I said.

No, Heen.

The bird in charge?

No Heen. There is no lead bird. And there is no bird in charge.

I was getting worked over. Answering questions about birds. I was terrible at this.

Each of the birds has a brain, Heen. But if you were to study their individual brains, you would not find a part that decides where the flock is going to fly.

Spy V knows about bird brains?

When birds fly in a flock, a group brain emerges in their midst. You cannot locate this brain in any one of the birds, it only exists when they fly together.

Bird minds were blowing my mind right then.

You add those birds together and something appears that is not present in any of the birds individually.

It clicked.

Like if one plus one equaled 12. Or 9. Or 37?

Exactly, Heen.

And this has what to do with me being a staker?
I had to ask. I knew there's a connection because Sir Pong was always with me.
A CIRCLE isn't just a path connecting a row of houses to a store to a library to a park-
I interrupted *You put them together and all those parts create something bigger and more than all those parts.*
She nodded.
For the first time I understood why she spent so much time sitting in those spaces appearing to do nothing but actually doing the most important thing.
She wasn't finished. *So when people come out to see what we're creating and they stand there next to you while you're staking, talking your ear off about water and noise and wind and when their kid goes to school and where they get their bread and what happens when it rains and where they walk their dog and it sounds like they're just prattling on about the details of their lives, they're actually giving you data. About how they live. About what works and what doesn't. About how spaces function, about how people live with each other. About what they love. How they thrive.*
Okay, that was a really good speech.
So you're telling me to turn it around...
Yes, exactly. Don't fight it, listen. Pay attention. Think of it like this: They're creating this with us.
Spy V, another of my teachers. One in a long line.
It's all data.
That's what she said that struck me the most. It's all data.
Listen, pay attention, people are giving you information all the time-about themselves, about the worlds, how it all works. Don't fight it, don't ignore it, take it in. Notice.

*

Goja would often visit me after school-she'd skipped a year and was finishing early. She always had questions for Spy V and the others. One day she stood over their maps and asked *Why aren't the bridges set like hands?*
ChaChi loved that one. *Like hands? With fingers?*
No Goja replied.
This is one of the thousand things I loved about her. She was a kid, a student, not even out of her parents house yet, and she was acting like she was the design director. And when someone like ChaChi who was twice her age challenged her in just the slightest way she didn't hesitate a bit. Just absolutely fearless-
Not like hands with fingers, hands on a clock. There are 20 hours in a day, why not have 4 bridges, placed on the quarter hours? Or 10, one every 2 hours? Make it symmetrical, something in alignment with how a clock looks. Different bridges could be different times, in essence. How cool would that be?
ChaChi looked at her in disbelief. *It's a little cute isn't it?*
Goja wasn't having any of it. *Well, how DID you decide on the current bridge placement?*
That was actually a good question.
I had no idea.
And I had been there from the beginning.
ChaChi hesitated. *Uhhhh, well, it's about ease of entry and exit from the center.*
Goja smiled. *In other words: random. Am I right?*
ChaChi choked on that.
Because ease and exit are not an explanation. They're an excuse for poor design.
Oh she went there.
Cha Chi looked over at Spy V for help. *Why DO we have the bridges where we have them?*

Spy V laughed. *It IS totally random at the moment. We haven't given it any thought yet. I actually like Goja's idea.* It wasn't long before they offered Goja a spot when she was done with school. She'd show up at the end of the day, walk around and see what we'd done, and then eventually we'd walk back to The Thiru, or take a GLIDE if it was late or we weren't up for that long of a walk. Sometimes we'd be gliding along, and the SUNS would be setting out across the plain, and Goja would put her head on my shoulder and everything would be perfect.

I heard someone say once that the best songs are the ones that when you hear them you feel like they've existed forever, it just took someone to finally bring them into the worlds.
That's how it felt with Goja and me.
Like we'd always existed.
Like we were inevitable.

*

Of course we'd zimzum.
Goja and me.
People were asking us about it all the time.
It was that obvious.
You start to create a life with someone and that creates space between you that exists nowhere else in the universe but between the two of you-that's a zimzum.
And in our world, you marked that. You celebrated it. You invited all your family and friends to a party and you acknowledged that something new was being created in the worlds between you. And through you. And around you.

We'd found a spot on The Thiru that was perfect for us, a small section of hill on the north end. We couldn't afford a Moler, so we dug it ourselves after work. Sometimes Nord helped us, or Goja's other brothers and sisters. One time my dad showed up and helped. It was nowhere near finished, but we loved it. We had a stove and sink and some chairs around a table and our bed in the back. Goja had such an eye. She would take scraps of lumber and fabric she'd found here and there and suddenly our place would feel a little bit more like home. It worked for us. It was ours.

*

It happened on the third day of the week.
I used to love the number 3. I was born at 3:33 in the morning. I used to see 3's everywhere.
We had the day off.
I had our lunch in a pack on my back. We were hiking our favorite peak, a few hours from The Thiru. We had just found out that Goja was pregnant.
Could a human being be any happier?
I don't know how many times I'd hiked this peak over the course of my life. I knew it so well. There's a dip there, some loose gravel on that switchback, a rock on the curve of that spine that you can rest on and see all the way to the lake.
I don't remember what we were talking about.
It's all a bit blurry.
And I haven't ever talked to anyone about it.
That day.
Goja stepped off the trail to pick a flower.
I do remember that.

A flower.

Yellow maybe? Orange?

It all goes opaque if I try and recall details like that.

She slipped.

I was preoccupied-rummaging through my pack trying to get my camera out before she actually picked the flower so I could get a photo.

Her picking a flower. That was Goja.

I loved taking photos of her.

It wasn't even that steep of an incline, or that dangerous of a hike.

Just enough.

She slipped.

And fell.

And tumbled.

Down.

And down.

And down.

I could see her and then I couldn't.

I didn't know what to do.

I could hurl myself down after her and hope.

I could run back down the trail, and hope.

Two options.

But no hope.

Not that day.

I wasn't the first to her.

Some other hikers heard her and-

From there it goes dark.

I'll skip the rest.

In the CENTER of a CIRCLE is a CHARIS. A CHARIS is a stone slab, like an elevated bed. When someone dies, all the people who knew them gather around that CHARIS.

Wood is stacked all around that slab. Everybody holds hands in a giant circle around the person lying there on that CHARIS. Everybody has a chance to say something about the person they've lost.
You light the fire.
I grew up with this.
That smoke.
Going to get bread in the CENTER and seeing people holding hands in a circle around that CHARIS. Knowing someone had died. And they were letting them go.

Sir Pong had explained to us that in the beginning, people were born in tents. As a child, your brothers and sisters were born right there. A few feet away. And then, when your grandparents were old, they would lie down in that same tent and eventually stop breathing. All those comings and goings that are so central to the experience of being human, they happened right in the midst of life.
You saw them.
They were close.
Happy, sad, tragic, euphoric-all of it a natural part of life. Sir Pong said that ever so gradually these comings and goings began to take place farther and farther away from the everyday flow of life-in places he called hospitals and nursing homes and institutions-buildings removed from where people actually lived. This REMOVAL-that's what he called it, the GREAT REMOVAL-was so extensive that it got to the point where a lot of people walking around on EARTH had never witnessed a birth. Or a death.
Lots of humans had never experienced a coming or a going up close.
Can you imagine? he asked.
No we said. *We can't.*

I thought I knew where he was headed. I was right.

And so, of course, death became something to be feared. That's always what happens with the UNFAMILIAR and the UNKNOWN. And then he had us all say: AND THE UNKNOWN ALWAYS RUNS THE SHOW.

Next to every CHARIS in every center is a MARY. I have no idea where the name MARY came from, but a MARY is where you go when you're having a baby. It's a building shaped like a cone, and they're always white, and there are usually people milling around outside on the benches that surround it, waiting for a baby to be born. They set up a CHARIS and a MARY in every CENTER so that the comings and goings would happen right in the midst of ordinary life. So that entries and exits wouldn't be foreign or unfamiliar, but as natural as breathing. So that boys like me would be walking to get bread and we'd see the smoke and we would know that someone had left and we'd see the people gathered outside the MARY and we'd know that someone was about to arrive.

*

We gathered.
All of us who loved Goja.
We gathered around that CHARIS.
To let Goja go.
I was numb all over. Alive but dead. Present but absent. I distinctly remember not being able to speak. When it came time to talk about Goja, I couldn't find words. I just stood there, holding hands with my mother on my left and my father on my right.

I know my heart was beating because I was still alive, but

it wasn't *beating* beating.

After everybody had spoken, Duque and Rooty each took
a torch and began to walk towards the CHARIS.
They took their time.
They were about to light the CHARIS when Nord let go of
the hands he was holding. Everybody saw it. He stepped
forward from across the circle and looked at me.
His eyes were so cold and distant and severe.
You.
That's how he started. One word.
You.
He said it again. His voice shook.
This is on you.
I saw one of his brothers drop the hands he had been
holding and turn his back to me. Then one of their sisters
turned her back to me as well.
I started shaking.
Nord's fists were clenched.
*YOU DIDN'T KEEP HER SAFE. THAT'S ALL YOU HAD TO
DO. AND YOU DIDN'T DO IT.*
Where was this coming from?
Is this what death feels like but you're still alive?
My throat burned.
Please, somebody. Anybody.
SET ME ON FIRE, NOT HER.
Another sister turned her back.
They planned this?
Nobody said anything.
I felt my mother's hand tighten on mine.
My dad. His tears.
Nord took another step forward.
I blame you.

He said it like he had been chewing on nails and he was now spitting them out.

He was my brother.

It was him and me before it was Goja and me.

This was my family. My family *family.*

And Duque and Rooty weren't stopping him.

They just stood there holding their torches.

They all agreed on this?

My mind was racing as it stood still with grief.

Everybody around the circle was looking at me.

Accident.

That's all I could cough up.

That one word.

It felt so thin. So brittle.

That's all I could do. That was my defense.

He wasn't having any of it. He wasn't finished.

You are no longer my brother.

I stood there and shook.

Duque and Rooty lit the wood, the last act of heartbroken parents. And then they and their kids locked arms, turned as one, and walked home.

They left us standing there, staring at those flames.

Me holding hands with my mother on one side, my father on the other, an island of desolation in a sea of obliterating grief.

*

I don't know if Ma'ir Dobie was right.

About dreams.

About the oneness and unity of all things.

About how all separation is in fact an illusion.

They would often say that all experience of PARTS takes

place within the WHOLE.
That blew my mind when I first heard it.
It made sense. It explained things. I felt it.
Until then.
Until that moment at the CHARIS.
The parts.
The separation.
The death.
THAT is real.
If it's an illusion, it's a real illusion.
A real accident.
A real CHARIS.
Real flames.

A real space in our bed where she used to sleep.

*

Everywhere I went on Lunlay I could feel the eyes.
That's him.
That's the guy.
The one who lost his love.
Everybody knew what happened.
It was so lonely, to be known, and seen, and recognized.
For that.
It was a darkness that hovered just over my skin and heart,
that I could not slough off, with soap or sobs.
Nothing meant anything.
There was a trap door beneath my feet.
It had opened.
I fell through.
I stopped going to work.
I stopped seeing people.

I left the house once a day.
To get bread.
My mother and I had our favorite bakery in the CENTER.
I'd go late morning when I knew the least amount of
people would be out.
Sourdough with rosemary.
It was the only connection left with my mother.
It became our daily ritual.
I'd get us a small loaf.
We'd eat it together.
In the garden.
Me hoping that no one would walk by.
Her sitting there quietly.
And then we'd go back into the house and I'd wait for dark
and the end of the day.
Nothing about the present or the future had any magnetic
pull. It was only the moment and it's enduring agony.

*

I was standing in line at the bakery, there for my daily
sourdough with rosemary. The man in front of me was
talking way too loudly to his friend. I heard him say the
words CHAIRS and INTERVIEWS and LIBRARY.
Excuse me? I tapped him on the shoulder. *I didn't mean
to eavesdrop. The CHAIRS are interviewing?*
That's actually impossible. I knew that. No one knew who
the CHAIRS even were. They were obviously not at the
library. The absurdity is what hooked me.
Yeah, the guy said, *that's what I heard.* And then he turned
around and kept talking to his friend.
I forgot about the bread.
I walked straight to the library.

There was a small, temporary sign out front that read INTERVIEWS THIS WAY. You'd only notice it if you were looking. I followed it through the entrance, down a hall to another sign sending me around the corner. There. On the right. Another sign, with an arrow pointing left.

An office.

I went in.

A man and woman were sitting on one side of a desk, an empty chair on the other. It felt so secretive, and yet it was all happening right there in the open. In the CENTER. In the library. Where I'd come thousands of times as a kid. Where everybody could see us.

They both looked up.

The man had buttons down the front of his shirt. And a tie around his neck. I'd only seen that in pictures.

And he had a mustache. Once again, hadn't seen that in real life. He had hair growing around the sides of his head, but none on top. And he had shaved that hair on the sides. Again, not something I'd seen before.

Heen? he asked. *Heen Gru-Bares?*

Wait. What? He knew my name.

The woman leaned forward. She was beautiful.

Your friends-mom-beautiful, that kind of beautiful.

Like she was so beautiful she could hold the worlds together.

Or is it Gru-BARES?

She put the emphasis more on the *Bares*, less on the *Gru*, like most people do.

Yeah, that's it.

The guy sat up straighter.

Well, all right, then. Where would you like to begin?

HE was asking ME a question. I placed both hands palms

down on the table.

Where would I like to begin? I have no idea what I'm doing here. A guy in the bakery mentioned that-wait, wait, just wait.

I took a deep breath.

How do you know my name?

The woman held up a screen in her hand. A screen. I had only seen a few of those.

There's a camera over that door.

She pointed to the door behind me.

You just walked through it. That camera is linked to very basic facial recognition software that is connected to a database of all the citizens of Lunlay. Your name and face-and address and school and family-popped up before you even sat down. Does that answer your question?

I just sat there.

Yeah, I guess it does.

Then it was the man's turn.

No real magic there, son, as you can see.

He set his pencil down on the table.

Depends on what you mean by magic I said.

They looked at each other and smiled. The man said

What we're curious about is your curiosity.

Not a question, that. I didn't know whether to answer it or let it sit there.

Curious about my curiosity.

I was starting to get my bearings. Calming down. Less overwhelmed.

What is this?

I laughed out loud. It came out before I'd even thought about it. I had't laughed since before-it had been a long time since I'd laughed.

The woman cleared her throat. They had some sort of tag

team thing between them. I bet they had done this a thousand times.

You were at the bakery?

She knew the answer to that.

How do you know that? Have you been following me?

I was twitchy, itchy. On edge.

She laughed. *You told us. About two minutes ago. When you first sat down.*

I blushed. How embarrassing.

Good point.

I was trying to rally. Save some face.

I was at the bakery. We have established that.

I smiled, like we were friends and we were messing around with each other. There is nothing like pure, unfiltered humiliation to break the ice.

The woman was wearing two silver bracelets that clinked together when her arm slid across the edge of the desk.

I noted that sound. I enjoyed it. She rescued me.

Who owns the bakery?

Finally, a straightforward question.

The Schoof's. I've known them since…forever. I went to school with Mette, their son.

How often do you get bread there?

Pretty much every day.

And what would you do if they closed down their bakery?

Well, I'd be bummed.

Why?

Because, their bread is the best. And it sometimes feels like it's all my mother and I have left.

She doesn't acknowledge the pain in what I just said.

Would you stop eating bread if they closed their bakery?

These questions.

I'd probably start going to another bakery.

Because bread is good. She stated it very matter of factly.
Yes, bread is good. I have no idea where you're going with this.
She shrugged.
They bake the bread, you enjoy it. It's a family business, but it's also a gift they give. To everybody who enjoys their bread.
I hadn't thought of it like that.
Yeah, I see your point. I was starting to get bored.
I don't mean to bore you with these questions-
She said it like she had been reading a printout of my thoughts.
Man, she was good. She kept going.
It's important to point out how we each contribute something to our life together.
A twinge of recognition. I'd heard something like that before. School. Ma'am Kirti. That's it. The CHAIRS.
Everybody does their part.
That was reaching way back right there. That was a TRUNK. Ma'am Kirti taught us that the CHAIRS arranged the worlds according to truths they called TRUNKS. Like TRUNKS on a tree. *Living sources of truth and guidance that are constantly growing and providing life to the branches.* Or something like that. Amazing what you remember. We memorized a number of them in class.
Exactly, everybody does their part. Well said. I thought she was impressed.
Where are you going with this? I didn't want to sound rude but we'd been going on about bread and the rest for a bit now. And I was in a room at the library with a man who had a mustache.
I like that, Heen, you want to get to the point. Here it is: We all do our part. Some people bake bread. Other people

help make the worlds run smoothly. That's us. And every once in a while we have openings…

Jobs?

Yes, jobs. And so we go out and we look for people who might be well aligned with our open positions.

You're recruiters for the CHAIRS?

That brought the fella to life.

Well, now, I don't know if we'd say it exactly like that…but yes, we're interviewing.

This is an interview? Because if it is you all could tighten up your game a bit. I have no idea why I said that. I sat up a little straighter. It occurred to me that I had nothing to lose in that moment. Why would I defer to people who hadn't even given me their names?

So I asked. *What are your names?*

They both smiled in a way that avoided the question.

It was the woman's turn.

Oh we will get to those and other crucial questions shortly. What's most important is that we get a read on where you're at with all this. Would you like to know more about these open positions we have?

My bottom lip quivered. It does this when I don't know what to say. Or I'm about to cry.

I slumped in my chair.

A long, languishing exhale.

I could see right then that I had been desperate for something for a while. Something new, something different. It hits me.

A way out.

That's what I'd been craving.

I didn't want to be home anymore. Hiding out in my house. Shunned and blamed by the Yegs, the only real family I'd ever known in the only place I'd ever known.

Those people. That planet.
Suddenly my planet felt claustrophobic.
Like my heart couldn't get enough of whatever the oxygen
is that the heart needs to breath. And knowing that
everywhere I went everybody knew who I was and they
were talking about me.
Heen. He's the one who...

And then I saw.
My chance had arrived.
The door had opened.
A way out.
Yes, I said with clarity, *I would like to know more about
these open positions you have.*
I sensed movement behind me.
I turned and there in the doorway was a tall man also
wearing a shirt and tie. And cowboy boots. I had never seen
cowboy boots in real life. Only in pictures. There was a
cactus stitched on each side. His belt had a large buckle. It
shined. Like a mini little sun right there on his waist. This
man appeared to be wearing this get up without any irony.

It was unexpectedly inspiring.

I turned back to see the woman tap something on her
screen as Mustache Man wrote something in the notebook
in front of him. He looked up.
All right. This is Wade. You can go with him.
Wade turned and started to walk away. I was torn. I actually
liked those people. Who I had known for 7 minutes.
Especially that woman. I would have liked to know more.
About what-I had no idea. I stood up and leaned over the
desk and offered my hand. They each shook it. The woman

smelled like all the good I had ever experienced before it all went away.

The man squeezed my hand a little too tightly. I assume it had something to do with the mustache.

I turned toward the door and then stopped.

I sat back down.

I asked them *Why me?*

The woman responded

Why you?

She asked this in exactly the tone I asked her.

As if she had the same question.

It was quite clever, the way she did it so quickly.

I steadied myself.

Why did you choose me?

Mustache Man leaned back in his chair.

Hold on. You chose us.

No I didn't, you just told me to follow Wade, which means you think I can do whatever it is you people do. Why do you think that?

She really was lovely. I would have liked to sit in her lap. I know how that sounds, and I'm okay with it. But I just know Mustache Man would have objected.

You're here because you overheard some words in a bakery, correct?

Easy question.

Yes, that's what happened.

These people knew how to take a conversation in unexpected directions. She continued.

That's interesting.

All I could think of to say was *I was interested.*

THAT'S WHY YOU. She said it like it was so obvious.

That's why ME? Because I heard those words and came and found you here?

Mustache Man exhaled loudly, like he was really satisfied.
Yep. You got it.
She turned to him, then turned back to me.
Curiosity. That's most of it right there.

I followed Wade, who immediately made a sharp turn and
opened a door. A nondescript door in a back hallway that I
would never have noticed in a thousand laps. I went
through and saw stairs heading down. I was aware we were
on the first floor. Now we were heading below the library?
At the bottom of the stairs was a tube. In the tube was a
GLIDE. I'd ridden GLIDES my entire life. They usually sat 6
or 8. I once saw one that seated 12. They run off the SUNS.
There's a pad on the outside. You enter the number of the
CIRCLE you want to go to and you get in and off you go.
About as simple as that. But that GLIDE.
It was underground. In a tunnel. And there was no pad. And
it seated 2. And it was down a stairway under the library.
Wade and I got in.
He stared straight ahead.
Hang on.
That Wade wasn't much of a talker.
I then learned why Wade said *Hang on*. That GLIDE flew.
Like a rocket. Twice or three times as fast as any GLIDE I'd
ever been on. In a tunnel. It struck me that the sense of
speed may have been an illusion-we may have been going
the exact same speed all GLIDES go, it was just the tunnel
flying by a few feet away that made it seem faster.

We rounded a bend in the tunnel and passed through an
opening. For a split second I saw a man in that opening.
The man was wearing a green matching outfit with white
stripes on the sides of his pants and the tops of his

shoulders. He was sitting on a stool. He had a rifle slung over his shoulder. I had never seen a gun in person in my entire life.

And he was eating a sandwich.

A large sandwich.

So big he had to hold it with both hands.

By the time I'd seen that guy we were through that opening and back in the tunnel.

There's a tunnel under the LIBRARY?

And in that tunnel sits a man with a gun?

And he's eating a sandwich?

Wade reached under his seat and pulled a metal bottle out of a drawer. He handed it to me.

Hydrate.

Wade. That guy. 3 words at that point.

I decided it was my job to loosen this chap up.

Thank you Wade. Where are we going?

He grinned. *That's the best part.*

Wade Grinner just doubled his word count.

Is it far? Are we almost there? Do you know where we're going?

Wade grabbed the end of his tie and tucked it neatly in between two of the buttons on the middle of his shirt.

Which, of course, I had never seen someone do.

We will arrive in just the right place at just the right time.

He turned to me as he said this, deadpan.

Sound good?

It was as if a still small voice somewhere far inside me was asking *You wanted out?*

I put my feet up on the dash.

All right, let's do this.

I said it like I'm a cowboy. Or how I imagined a cowboy would say it.

*

You can do one, but not two.

My mom hit her head, and it fundamentally altered how I understood the universe. It's not safe. It's not looking out for you. It's not good. It's not rigged in our favor. At least not in mine. It doesn't have my best interests in mind. And things do not magically work themselves out in the end.
And then the Yegs moved in.
And there were my teachers.
And friends.
And hiking and exploring and Nord's play and us building and flying those winged glider ship things.
It all helped me survive what happened to my mom.
Enough good seeped in that I could keep going.
The balance tilted ever so slightly.

And then Goja.
And our life together.
And a baby coming.
I was almost back.
You can endure one, but not two.
One tragedy, and you can recover.
I knew that. I had lived that.
It took a while.
But I was almost there.
And then that.
I did one.
But two.
You can't do two.
No.
It can't be done.

No bringing that back into shape.
No coming back from that.
The heart can't do it.

*

The GLIDE came to a silent stop.
Wade pulled out a fob and clicked it.
A light came on in the tunnel above us.
A door. Flush with the wall. You would never know it was there. Unless you were with a man named Wade who had a fob. He got out. I followed. He clicked the fob again. The door was a sliding door. A WOOSH of air. Stairs. We went up and out the door at the top. We were in a barren field. The ground was black. And hard. Like lava. I could see a mountain in the distance.
It didn't look familiar.
We're on Lunlay, right?
As I heard this question come out of my mouth I knew how pointless it was. But talking, hearing the words, narrating for myself helped me remember that I was me, and that was happening.
I thought I knew my home planet, but that didn't look like anywhere I'd ever been.
I heard a beep.
I turned around and saw a spaceship, about 100 paces away.
Is that a spaceship?
That's what I asked Wade.
Is that a spaceship?
What a noob.
Wade took his time answering, like it was a trick question.
That's what everybody asks.

Once again, just a few words from Wade and I had a
thousand questions.
Another beep.
They're ready for you.
Was that an instruction? Who is THEY? Why did he act like
I should know what to do?
Wade.
That guy.
I just stood there.
*I'm going to leave Lunlay? Right now? Can I? Should I tell
someone? Should someone be informed that this is
happening?*
I had a thought as those questions came pouring out of me:
What is THIS that is currently happening? And who is them?

That's what killed me.
Who would I have told?
My dad? He was just as checked out as my mother.
My friends? I hadn't seen most of them since the…

And what would I tell them? That I'm leaving because the
CHAIRS need me? Because I have a job interview on
another planet?

I was swimming in my own head, drowning in questions
and fragments, when Wade placed his hands on my
shoulders.
He was very still.
He spoke to me slowly.
THIS. IS. IT. HEEN.
There was kindness in his eyes.
NOW.
He squeezed my shoulders gently.

You have wanted an out. THIS. IS. THE. OUT.

He took a breath.

TAKE IT.

And then he turned me towards the ship and gave me a little push.

PART 2 YORCH

I looked up.
There were purple swirls in the sky.
The Swirls?
I'd heard of those. We studied them with Ma'am Kirti.
Certain times of the year under certain conditions-when Sil
Ray is ascendent, Meebs is on the cusp, there's a grand
trine with the Pegs and Nalee's in retrograde-purple swirls
appear in the sky. Miles and miles from the CENTERS of
Lunlay. We'd read about them, studied them, discussed
them-but I'd never seen them, they happened somewhere
else.
Which was there. Right above me. Wherever that was.
I was transfixed by these swirling, shifting, oscillating
shapes up above me.
A bang.
I flinched.
A door slammed.
I turned around.
Wade was gone, down those stairs we just came up. I was
all alone in a wide open plain, purple swirls above me, a
spaceship straight ahead.

An hour before that I had been standing in line for bread.
I heard that beep I heard earlier.
I was trembling all over.
From lots of things, among them conviction.
I had been engulfed in despair.
For a while.
Sitting there day after day in our garden, eating that bread

with my mother, essentially hiding from Nord and the Yegs.
And my friends. And everybody else. The world.
Weary from being seen like that.
And talked about like that.
Discussed. Analyzed. Accused.
Standing at a distance from my own existence.
Trying to make it go away.
I hadn't just lost my love, I'd lost my life.
The grief was relentless in its expansion, devouring me
from the inside.
I understood why people end their lives.
I hadn't until then.
But then I did.

And then the bakery.
Fragments from that conversation. That room in the
library. Those questions. Mustache. Wade.
He was right.
That was the out.
I had been looking for that, waiting for it, aching for it
without knowing I was.
That's the conviction I trembled with.
A deep knowing.
This.
I started walking towards the ship.

*

My dad had a brother.
His brother had a box he carried around with him. He called
it a suitcase.
I hadn't seen that before.

His brother was obsessed with our kumquat tree. It wasn't that big of tree but it produced an astonishing amount of kumquats. Like it was showing off. He'd pack them in his suitcase until there was juice coming out the sides.

He was a sweaty man.

With a blotchy face.

He wore shirts that were too tight.

And he was always in a rush.

I asked him once why he only visited us for a few hours.

He said he didn't want to stay too long in a backwater like ours. I hadn't heard that word before.

Backwater.

He'd be down on his knees in our garden, surrounded by kumquats, frantically packing them in his suitcase, telling me with a frightening level of intensity,

YOU REALLY GOT TO JAM THEM IN THERE, HEEN, YOU JUST HAVE TO JAM AS MANY AS YOU CAN IN THERE!!!

His name was Dir.

Uncle Dir.

*

I'd gone as a kid with my dad to the port in CIRCLE 4 to see spaceships take off and land. But then you grow up and that's not interesting anymore. You stop going to the port.

No one I knew had been in a spaceship. No one in my world could afford to do something like that, and if you could, where would you go?

Why would you leave home?

It just wasn't a part of my life.

It had never crossed my mind that I'd ever be anywhere

near a spaceship.
Why would it?
Let alone board one.
But there it was.
A spaceship.
Right in front of me.
Beeping.
Occasionally.

*

Ma'am Kirti had us turn to the end of our textbook.
Last week of school.
Last pages.
Last lesson.
On the left page was a drawing of that BROWNBALL.
Going up and out from the BROWNBALL were little
curved arrows. At the end of each of those curved arrows
were spaceships and in each of those spaceships were
stick figure people.
The drawing, Ma'am Kirti explained, *was about the end of
the earth. Sometimes it's simply called THE END. Other
times it's called PHASE ONE.* That seemed like a bit of a
gloss to us, trying to make it appear like that was all part
of some grand plan. The Departure. The Exodus. The
Final Days. The Great Escape. THE LEAVING.
*There were lots of names for it. The earth was no longer
livable and so people got on spaceships and left.*
Then she told us to turn the page.
On the next page, on the left, was that same drawing only
the arrows and spaceships had been drawn much, much
smaller. And something had been added.
People.

Little stick figure drawings of people standing there on the surface of that ball that was browning.
While the other people flew away on spaceships.
Such a simple drawing.
And so, so devastating.
Ma'am Kirti explained to us that towards the end of the earth a split arose between people who had more and more money and people who had less and less money.
She told us about how some people had a difficult time finding enough money to eat while people living a few minutes walk from those people owned multiple houses.
We had no idea what she was talking about.
Multiple houses?
What?
People did that?
Why?

She might as well have told us that we should jam our pencils into our eye sockets because that's fun.
It just made no sense.

She told us story after story, she gave us facts and numbers and statistics, she explained how lots of people were paid X amount for their work while the person they worked for was paid 100 TIMES that amount for their work.
And it kept increasing.
That gap.
Did people know about this gap? we asked.
Yes, they did she replied.
We had so many questions.
Why didn't they stop this?
Ma'am Kirti explained that the people who had the most money controlled the ARRANGEMENTS. So they

continually tilted things in their favor.

Tilted things?

Yes she said. *Laws, markets, banks, rules, brackets, loopholes, rates, taxes, codes-*

We got it.

Apparently there were a lot of things that could be tilted. She drew our attention back to that drawing. As we'd seen again and again, there was always a point. Always somewhere the drawings were taking us.

The BROWNBALLING of the earth exposed this growing gap in a way no one saw coming.

I could see that, right there in the drawing. I knew where she was going with this…

In the end, it all came down to spaceships. Some people could afford to get on one and leave, and some people couldn't.

I raised my hand. *So the gap turned out to be bigger than anyone thought it was?*

Exactly, Heen, it turned out to be the difference between who survived and who didn't. Which was, of course, the difference between life and death.

We took that in for a minute.

It struck me as so primitive, so archaic.

What a horrible world to call home.

She then pointed us to the right side of the page.

Another drawing.

This one may be the most simple we'd ever seen.

A row of stick figure people of all shapes and sizes, above them a horizontal line, below them a horizontal line.

She then wrote these words on the wall:

THE TRAUMA THAT TRANSFORMS.

She explained that the people who were on those spaceships-who flew away seeing all those people they were leaving behind down there on the ground-they couldn't stop thinking about what had happened. As fortunate as they were to have survived, they did not live like they were grateful to be alive. They endlessly relived those moments when the people still on EARTH watched them fly away.

It stayed with them.

It haunted them.

And then, gradually, they began to be transformed by it.

We didn't really know what Ma'am Kirti meant with that word transform-but we hung in there.

The CHAIRS were established to run the new worlds, and one of their first priorities was to make sure nothing like that ever happened again. So they released this drawing, the one in front of us. They announced what they called THE CEILING AND THE FLOOR. They plastered this image all over the galaxies.

THE CEILING AND THE FLOOR.

No one, they declared, *would ever lack enough money to take care of their basic needs.* They called this THE FLOOR. Everybody would get a FLOOR CHECK three times a LAP just to make sure that everyone had their basic needs met.

And no one would ever be allowed to endlessly stockpile their money. There would be a limit to how much one person could have. And you couldn't go over it. They called this THE CEILING. If you went above that amount, you wrote a CEILING CHECK that was then converted into a FLOOR CHECK for someone else.

Ma'am Kirti asked us, *Does it work? Look around you-*

*do you know anyone who doesn't have a house and food
and clothes and all that?*
No one said anything.
We didn't.

*

That beep.
Again.
The spaceship was right in front of me.

It was the longest walk of my life.

Another beep.
It wasn't an irritating beep. I noted this. The beep was
reassuring. Soothing even.
The tone. The duration.
It was just a beep. But it was more than a beep. It was like a
voice saying
I'm here. We're good. You're doing great. Keep coming.
How a sonic pulse like that could convey so much in just
one beep is beyond me.
A lot, at that moment, was beyond me.
I was 20 paces away.
A ramp dropped down.
Exactly like you picture it happening. If you were to
picture yourself boarding a spaceship. In the middle of
nowhere. Under a swirling purple sky.

The ship was silver and white, and curved, with wings.
There were lights on the underside. It had a cockpit. I'm
aware that is the most bland description ever. And of course
now I could go on for days about the various features and

details and design elements. But then, way back then on that day, before I knew what I know now, it was just a spaceship, and I was getting on it.

I walked up the ramp into an open space shaped in a circle. A woman was standing there in a charcoal tunic. It was made of linen or canvas or some fabric that reminded me of a weaving or a tapestry. I was struck by the organic nature of that fabric in sharp contrast to the sleek, carbon fiber and glass, glistening, spotlessly synthetic steel space-ship all around us. There was a silver pin on her left chest. Her hair was short. And pushed forward into a peak.
Hello.
It was a soothing voice, at once kind and totally in command.
Welcome.
She put me at ease.
You must be Heen. I am Vo. We are so glad to have you join us.
I still hadn't said anything.
It is okay, it can be a little overwhelming at first.
So true.
The others are right this way.
She motioned behind me. Which I think was the back of the ship. I turned and walked down a short hall. There were no buttons or levers or doors or anything really in that hall. Smooth metal everywhere I turned. More like a rectangular tube pretending to be a hall. A door-with no visible latch or handle-opened in front of me. I stepped through into a room shaped like a circle. A large couch lined the wall. There were five people on it. They each had a small table in front of them. Behind them was a window.
Broseph, you must try these pears!

I have dark skin. I hadn't ever met someone with skin darker than mine. Until that guy. He stood up and shook my hand. He had very clear blue eyes. That's the first thing that struck me about him.

I heard Vo behind me.

This is Florent, and as you can see, he loves the pears.

The others laughed.

And this is Duda.

A woman offered me a fist bump. She appeared to be carved from rock, all tight muscles and coiled energy. Her hair was bleached blonde-there was no way that is how it actually grew out of her head-and she was wearing coveralls.

It took me a beat to realize they were all wearing coveralls. Light gray. With pockets on the chest. And shoes I hadn't ever seen before. Ankle high. With just a few eyelets for the laces but you could definitely run in them. They may even have been waterproof.

Hi Duda, I'm Heen. Finally, I was able to speak.

Yeah Heen, we've been expecting you.

She said it with a glint in her eye, like we were all in on a joke together.

A tall, pale fella sprang out of his seat, offered his hand and then pulled me in for a hug.

AS IF ANY OF THIS COULD BE EXPECTED!!! WHO KNEW WE'D ALL BE HERE NOW DOING THIS TOGETHER!!!!

And this is Stilitz Vo said.

Florent laughed. *This one goes to eleven, know what I mean?*

I had heard that phrase before. I had no idea where it

came from. It's what you say when something-or somebody-has extra volume. Or presence. Or energy. It was a welcome burst of familiarity in the midst of the Stilitz onslaught.

Vo keeps telling us you're the last one and then we go, you know, we go...

Stilitz came on strong and wobbly, all jittery nerves and jerky hand motions-but then he trailed off.

Duda fake punched my arm. *I think what Stilitz is getting at is the vertigo, am I right? We don't quite know how we got here or what we're in for-it messes with your head, yeah?*

I nodded. *Yes. Exactly.*

I just did not have many words for those people.

You can sit here.

A lovely young woman gestured to the space on the couch next to her. Her hair was long and springy. Like coils. Or spirals. Sitting next to her was another young woman who looked just like her. Twins.

Vo said *And this is Corta. And her sister Zoma.*

I extended my hand so we could shake. They dismissed this as they stood up and each kissed me once on either cheek. Stilitz loved that. *Isn't that cool? How they greet you with a kiss? We DO NOT DO THAT where I'm from.*

I sat down.

Florent offered me a pear. It was as good as advertised.

Corta poured me a drink. Pomegranate juice, I think.

Duda put her feet up on her table.

And where's that? I asked Stilitz. *Where are you from?*

Nims he said.

Oh. That's all I had for Stilitz and his Nims. Oh. I didn't know the first thing about Nims.

Duda did. *Is it true there are no pets on Nims?*

Stilitz was so thrilled someone had asked him a question. *That was true for a while. People used to breed their cats. For size. And those cats-YESIREE BOB!!!-they just kept getting bigger and bigger. Our neighbors, the Donkmoores had a 150 pound cat. In their house! That thing had its own room…*

Florent had a question. *At what point-or more precisely what weight-does a cat stop being a house cat and start being a lion?*

Zoma came to life at that. *Or a panther? Or a cougar? Or a jaguar?*

Corta rolled her eyes. *My sister is really into large cats. You have no idea how much she's enjoying this story.*

Stilitz lit up. *Well, yeah, that's the thing. It ate our other neighbor's-The Lutens-it ATE their dog… They had this great dane named Horace that they bred with a hot dog, so it was the longest-*

He said the word LONGEST with great drama-

THE LONGEST DOG you have ever seen. Three small children could ride it at once. They had a saddle made for it. Three saddles actually, in a row. Their kid Nathil-who I went to school with, not the best athlete but man could that lad play a mean trombone-Nathil would sit out by the trail on holidays and charge money for rides. He made stacks of quan off that long ass giant mutant great horse dog.

Stilitz was kind of annoying, but that story. Didn't see that coming. A glimpse of life on Nims.

Corta jumped in her seat. *Wait! The cat ate the dog? Is that where this story is going?*

She was indignant.

You got it, MISSY!!! he exclaimed. Man, he was brutal. Just missing the social cues right and left.

Florent pointed like he had something important to ask. *The cat/lion ate the dog?*

Stilitz corrected him. *Actually, it only ate part of the dog. Mostly the head and shoulders. The lower half it dragged around for a few hours-its entrails and organs and few dangling ribs were bouncing along after it on the ground-it went past a school during recess. Kids were screaming and crying and trying to shield their eyes and throwing up...a teacher from the school ran out and jumped on it, pinned it down, and yanked that formerly alive long ass hot great dane dog carcass out of its mouth.*

Stilitz was so proud of himself. He appeared quite confident that he had wowed everyone with this story. However, the twins were utterly repulsed.

Zoma shook her head. *That is the most vile story I have ever heard.*

Stilitz wasn't phased. *You should have seen the teacher afterwards.*

Corta almost gagged. *Ohhhhh...was he okay?*

She asked this with a wounded look on her face, bracing herself for the worst.

Stilitz's eyes got huge. *SHE! The teacher was a SHE!!! Magor Fondy...*

He savored the saying of her name.

Duda was so inspired. *Yeah Magor! Go get it, girlfriend.*

Florent found this all very amusing. *Nims. What a planet.*

Corta agreed. *What a story.*

But Stilitz wasn't finished. *Oh that's nothing, there was this other family, they had a cow that-*

Vo appeared and interrupted him. *A small order of business. Heen, one more thing before we go. Through this door on the left is a changing room. You will see a shelf. On that shelf are your clothes. You can leave what you are currently wearing on the shelf.*

I went into the changing room. I saw the shelf. On it was a gray folded pile. As I picked it up it dropped to full length. Coveralls, just like the others. I moved slowly. The simplest task of unzipping the front took all my powers of concentration. Pulling those new socks on required massive effort. It was overwhelming.

I could not avoid the symbolism of it.

I told myself putting on new clothes should't be this intense-but I was in new territory. SHOULD did not have the same power it used to have.

I returned to the circle couch room.

I hesitated before I sat down.

They were all watching me.

I had a lump in my throat.

Florent leaned forward. *Same thing happened to me, broseph.*

I exhaled. The solidarity was wonderful. I sat down.

Corta sighed. *That changing room is a like a portal.*

Zoma nodded. *You enter one person, you leave another…*

Duda stretched out her arms. *Totally. Not to be all dramatic but I felt like I was saying goodbye to who I've been…*

Florent laughed. *I was feeling all those feels in there putting on my fresh gray threads.*

Yes, that was it exactly. That perfectly captured it.

I liked those people.

Then Vo appeared. *Strap up. We are leaving.*

Strap up?

The others reached below them in the cushions, pulling up straps. Zoma grabbed mine for me and hooked it over my shoulders.

It was awkward the first time, then it gets easier.
She said this and then she winked.
I liked her.

I felt the low rumble first in the bones of my heels. Barely discernible. My feet hummed. Then my legs. A subtle vibration rose up through the floor. As if my body was a tuning fork. It made its way vertically up my spine. My thighs were gradually pressed against the seat.
Up we went.
Straight up.
What-50 feet? 100 feet?
And then-
Boom? Not boom. It wasn't loud.
Whoosh? Kind of. But there was no rushing wind sound.
ZShhhuupe? Closer. Definitely. But that word doesn't capture the absence of…

Any word I would use here sounds silly, inadequate, the very nature of the sensation limiting my vocabulary. More than that. It shrinks what words can even do.
We were there, hovering above the ground.
And then we aren't.
We were weightless.
Not here OR there.
On the way.
It was so smooth, so effortless.
For all of your life you're in a particular place.
And then you move and you are in another place.
But that. That thing that happened to me when the spaceship took off.
It was something other.
I was nowhere specific.

I was not in any one place.
The motion, the movement, the speed was so all
consuming that a sense of place dissolved.
Fleeting. Beyond.
See? Words don't work here.
A thousand lifetimes and I will not be able to describe it. I
looked out that window behind us and I couldn't see Lunlay.
In the time it occurred to me to look out that window we had
left the only planet I had ever known.
Home was gone.

*

Once Ma'ir Dobie had us turn to the middle of our textbook.
On the left was a drawing of a planet. Standing on that
planet was a stick figure drawing of a person. They were
standing next to the letter A. Next to that letter A was an
arrow leading to another spot on that planet where there
was also a stick figure drawing of that same person,
standing next to the letter B.
Ma'ir Dobie told us to study that drawing in silence for
two minutes.
Which we did. We knew by now-we'd had laps of
practice with our teachers-that there was a world of depth
and insight in these simple drawings in our textbooks.
We knew not to skim it, but to let it sink in. That's why I
remember so much of it to this day. Ma'ir Dobie called it
THE SIMPLICITY AFTER COMPLEXITY. Sometimes we'd
spend weeks and weeks exploring the depths of just one
of those drawings. Turning it over, coming at it from yet
another angle, discussing yet another layer of meaning.
And so it happened again.

We turned the page to discover another of these drawings-this one of a person in one location-A-moving to another location-B.

So simple.

We knew that we were just getting started.

Ma'ir Dobie drew our attention to the opposite page. Here was that same stick figure person, standing in the center of the page. To the left was that same planet, only smaller, with the letter A in the same spot as the other drawing. To the right of that planet was an arrow leading across to the right of the stick figure person, where there was another drawing of that same planet, with that same letter B on it.

We took that drawing in. We were ready.

Ma'ir Dobie explained that people used to see location in only one way:

You're

here

and then you go

there.

They went on to say that geography, locations, and places were understood to be fixed points in the universe and you as a person traveled from

one

to the

other.

The locations stayed put, you did the moving.

You're either

here

or

there.

Ma'ir Dobie said those words with great emphasis

Here,

There,

One,
The other,
Locations,
YOU…
Then they explained that things shifted. EXPANDED is the better word for it. People began to understand location in a more EXPANDED way. Instead of a person moving from place to place, they began to understand you could see it another way:

Different places come and go from you.

That's how they said it.
I had a question. *Instead of me going from place to place, places come and go within me?*
Yes, that's what they were saying.
I stay put?
Yes, Heen, that's another way of seeing it.
I could tell this was stretching a lot of us in the class past what we could grasp. Bruman Fostels raised his hand. Bruman was a fiesty, confrontational kid, with spongey hair and large calves. He was always trying to show how much more he knew than the rest of us. And he had sideburns that he'd grown down to his jawline. So there's that.
He piped up. *Prove it.*
Ma'ir Dobie loved it when we challenged them.
I'd be happy to prove it, Bruman. What is the name of the location that you have always been in?
I swear he went cross-eyed.
What? I've been in lots of different locations in my life.
Maybe. Ma'ir Dobie shrugged. *Maybe not.*
We were in the deep weeds. I had no idea where that was going.

Bruman, answer me this: Are you here in the front of the class teaching or are you sitting there at your desk listening to me?

What an odd question.

It was so obvious I knew it was a trap.

Bruman thought about it, looking for the same glitch the rest of us were looking for. He couldn't find it either, because he replied *I'm here.*

Ma'ir Dobie made a mock display of pondering his response, like it was really profound.

Okay, let's go with that answer: HERE. Now, let's imagine tonight that I show up at your house while you're eating dinner with your family-

WELL THERE IS AN IMAGE FOR YOU.

Ma'ir Dobie showing up at your house!!! I pictured my dad. All mellow and quiet, sitting there with his brain books, trying to absorb the radiant presence of Ma'ir Dobie. Offering them tea, trying to make them feel comfortable in his house. What a scenario. Ma'ir Dobie in your house-

And what if I ask you this question while you're sitting there with your family: Bruman, are you sitting in class listening to me teach right now or are you sitting at home eating dinner-are you here or there?

Those questions. So obtuse.

Bruman held his ground. *I'd answer you: I'm here.*

You would, wouldn't you?

It wasn't said as an accusation, but an affirmation.

Here, not there.

You could always tell when Ma'ir Dobie was about to make a big point and bring together a bunch of loose threads because they'd slow things down, like they were building to a moment. We were moments from that moment, I just knew it.

So wherever you are throughout your life, whatever that place is called, whatever the name of that location is, the word that you use for wherever you ever are is HERE. You have only ever been HERE!!!

And then they punched the air like they'd just won the game. Which they kind of had.

I raised my hand.

So the only place we ever are is HERE, and locations come and go from HERE?

Yes, Heen, that's another way of saying it.

I loved it when Ma'ir Dobie told me I was doing a good job. They then told us how this expansion of understanding regarding location happened as the earth was BROWNBALLING. All that pain and loss actually catalyzed all kinds of new awareness and expansion, as people began to realize how limited they had been in their thinking about how to travel around the galaxies.

*

My drink sat there on the table in front of me.

Undisturbed.

Florent still had his row of pears. Neatly arranged in front of him.

We were fine.

Flying through space, as though we were sitting on a blanket in the park having a picnic.

Duda pumped her fist above her head.

Yeah, Heen.

She gave me a knowing glance.

Yeah is right.

I pumped my fist right back at her.

First time? she asked.

Oh my yes. I sounded like an old woman. *Oh my.*
A nod of recognition from her. *I was the first one on so this is my fifth takeoff. But each time is the first time, know what I mean?*
I could only imagine.
Stilitz coudn't hold back any longer. *My balls drop like stones every time we takeoff!!! Just the HEAVIEST METAL IN A SACK ATTACK you have ever beheld.*
We traded glances among us. The twins were slack jawed.
Florent inquired. *Is that how they talk on Nims?*
How what? Stilitz squinted. His innocence was actually quite refreshing. Charming even. He just said what he was thinking. No edit button. I was slightly envious. Of that. But not the reaction he got from the twins. Florent turned to me.
Frank is the word that comes to mind. Explicit. Blunt.
Florent had a certain refinement to him. I liked it.
Duda held her drink up and motioned to Stilitz. *Man tells it like he sees it, BALLS AND ALL. Respect.*

I had never imagined I'd be on a spaceship. So I'd never imagined who I would be on a spaceship with. Or what they'd be like. Or what we'd talk about.
Vo reappeared again.
She was gone? She left? Where did she go? Who is she?
What do you do? I asked her.
I asked her the same thing! Corta exclaimed.
And she kind of avoids it, watch Zoma said.
Vo laughed. *Yes, I have been a little evasive. But now you are all here. So I can say more.*
Ahhhhh, that was interesting.
Something about the six of us.
She had our attention.
Duda's feet hit the floor.

Florent put his current pear down.

The twins' hands were folded on their laps.

Stilitz rested his chin on the palm of his hand.

I am your STAGE 1 Vo began. *I will be your STAGE 1 throughout the SESSIONS. Anything you need, you tell me-*

Corta interrupted. *How long will this be?*

Vo looked at her. *I do not know.*

Corta's eyebrows lowered. *You don't know? Does anyone know?*

No.

So...

There was a poetry in their interaction I found fascinating, a sort of sing songy cadence that carried it along.

No one knows. Allow me to continue-

She smiled as she said it. She was kind and considerate but also made of steel. And so firm.

We have been doing this for a long time. You are not the first SERIES 5's and you will not be the last-

Duda interrupted. *What's a SERIES 5?*

Stilitz jumped on that. *Because there's 6 of us.*

That's actually a good point. Shout out to Stilitz.

Vo was completely unphased. *THAT is what you are going to discover.*

It hit me. Vo didn't use contractions. As in *Vo does not use contractions.* No *you'res* or *won'ts*. I suddenly saw how much clarity and force this brought to her speech. It was crisp. Like she was in no rush, but somehow her speech created an acute urgency that demanded you pay attention. Interesting, all that.

I am confident that you are going to see that we have

thought of everything. You have each said YES. Because of this-

Stilitz threw up his hands. *When did I say YES?*

He glanced around at us nervously, looking for some confirmation. *I don't remember saying YES...At least in any official capacity-do any of you remember saying YES?*

Vo stopped him. *If at any point you would like to return home, just tell me. It is as simple as that. Within moments you will board a ship and you will be home, back where you started, as quickly as you find yourselves here, now. Are you each clear on this?*

Duda let out an *AHHHHHH. So that's why you're so evasive about the length-you truly don't know how long it will be! Some of us might bail.*

Zoma looked concerned. *Does that ever happen?*

Florent leaned forward. *Has anyone ever experienced take off and then said THAT'S IT!! I AM DONE! TAKE ME BACK! NO MORE OF THIS!!*

We thought that was hilarious.

Vo laughed as well. *I have seen it all.*

That was her answer.

I have seen it all.

That woman.

She was something.

Suddenly I was back in class. Ma'am Kirti, Sir Pong, Ma'ir Dobie-young again, taking my cues from the person in charge, following along, seeing where it goes. Something very innocent and pure opened up within me, some ache to get it. To understand. To do it right.

She looked me in the eyes. I nodded *Yes.* She then looked at Corta. *Yes.* She went around the circle and got a *Yes* from each of us, one by one. She took her time.

There was something solemn and profound about it. Like a

ceremony. Or an oath of some kind. Each *Yes* brought me visceral relief. I had gone from skeptical and hesitant to committed and invested in about the time it takes to board a spaceship and take off.

Vo had more to say. *We are headed to Yorch. It is not far. It will not take very long. When we land, I will lead you off the ship. I will not give you much more information than that because we have learned over time that too much information can easily feel like overload-*

Zoma agreed. *First ride on a spaceship is enough for me for one day.*

Vo nodded. *Absolutely. Now, a small detail about time. We picked you up all over the galaxy, which means you are all coming from different CLOCK SPACES. You are about to go through these SESSIONS together, and it is very important that you are all in the SAME CLOCK SPACE as far as your bodies are concerned. To help with this, in about ten seconds you will begin to feel quite relaxed as you gradually doze…*

*

I woke up.

I heard a beep. That beep.

Muffled sounds of people talking somewhere in the distance.

The others were stirring as well.

I felt so good. I was just waking up but I was AWAKE.

Duda felt it as well. *Now that's what I'm talking about!*

Corta did a little shake with her body. *Whew!*

Vitalized. That was the word for it.

That was the deepest sleep ever Florent said as he stretched his arms out wide. Zoma did the same. Their hands touched for a second.

Stilitz joined us. *Yhew!!! LET'S GO!*

He clapped loudly. So spastic that guy.

I asked *How long were we out for?*

The door opened.

Vo appeared. *Long enough to land on Yorch. Welcome.*

Yorch? I knew nothing of Yorch.

Zoma squinted. *Did you drug us?* It sounded like an accusation. Which it was.

Vo was not even slightly thrown. *It depends on what you mean by the word drug. It was all natural. Nothing you could not find within a mile or so of your house. You breathed it in. It relaxed you so much you fell asleep.*

Corta was so suspicious. *Are you allowed to do that?*

That struck me as a fairly surreal question. There were rules? Here? On a spaceship in…space? On Yorch? Doing whatever it is we were doing there-flying across the galaxy and landing on a planet we'd never been to? Rules?

Zoma was with her sister. *Okay, yeah, that may have been all natural, whatever-but we all woke up AT THE EXACT SAME TIME! Does that strike any of you as being a little-*

Stilitz had a lot to say about that. *WE DID!! AT THE SAME TIME!! ISN'T THAT AN AMAZING COINCIDENCE??? WHAT ARE THE ODDS OF THAT?? IT MAKES A GUY'S HEAD SPIN!!*

I had the urge to tell Stilitz to pump the brakes, but I knew he would look at me and say *What are those?*

Zoma kept going. *I get that we breathed in whatever that was together but waking up at the same time is a little suspicious-okay-A LOT suspicious.*

Vo tilted her head. *You can see the air vents above your heads. We sent some new air in here. Once again, ALL natural, nothing you could not find within a stones throw of where you live.*

Vo said this casually. And very persuasively. With a particular blend of authority and ease. I was struck in that moment with how ignorant we must appear to her. She'd been doing this for who knows how long and after a few hours we had concerns and questions that we presented like we had some ground to stand on. Was there one thing we could have said or asked that she hadn't heard who knows how many times before?

Right this way.

We followed her off the ship.

Flat.
I was immediately struck with how flat it was.
Yorch. Yorch felt like Yorch sounds.

Our ship-*our* ship…there was nothing first person plural about that ship…*that* ship had landed in a circle of grass. Lining the perimeter of the circle were cylinders. Tall cylinders the size of buildings. There were lots of them. Some right along the edge of the circle, others staggered a bit further back. A circle of circular buildings, surrounding a circle of grass. It appeared that there was a pattern to how they were arranged, although the distances varied between them. Whatever the intention behind the design was, it eluded me at that moment.

The buildings were white, a few of them had windows. One had what appeared to be a crane on the roof. Beyond those cylinders-that-are-buildings there was nothing.

Not a mountain or hill or trees.

Not even a tree.

Just flat, flat, flat.

I turned around.

There was a sun low on the horizon. Just one. Tulare? Sil Sy?

I couldn't tell which one. A light breeze came through. Not too hot, not too cool.

A single bird flew over our heads.

Vo was on the move, heading towards one of the buildings. We followed. A door opened just before she got to it. I was last, and as the first one after Vo-that was Duda-went through the door I heard her yell *YES!*

And then I entered and I saw why.

There were trampolines, everywhere.

They covered the entire floor.

They were red. The walls were light blue. The effect of those colors together was strangely energizing. Every kind of trampoline in every direction. Round ones, square ones, there was a row of them set at various angles facing a foam pit.

Have fun Vo said. And she left.

We all looked at each other. *WHAT?*

And then it was a race to see who could get their shoes off the fastest. Zoma won, and she was jumping on the closest trampoline in seconds. And laughing. And taunting us with how slow we were to join her. Three minutes in I was wheezing, bent over in the corner trying to catch my breath. My calves burned.

There was a platform in the middle, about twice a person's height. Hooked to it was a thick rope with a knot at the bottom that hung from a beam that ran from one side of the building to the other. Across from that platform was a trampoline on its side, up against the wall.

I assumed it was broken.

But Duda had climbed up on the platform and was holding the rope in her hands.

Florent loved it. *Yes, of course, try it!* He shouted.

Try what?

Ohhhhhhh. I got it, just as she swung off the platform on the rope. It was a sideways trampoline. She hit it shoulder and hip first and then bounced out, away from the wall. Still on the rope. And then she swung back in, and back out.

There was a mad scramble to get up on that platform. Everyone wanted to try it. I was slightly terrified. I tried it anyway. It was as exhilarating as it looked. I saw Corta and Zoma on matching trampolines. They'd leap, passing each other in the air doing some sort of hand clapping thing, landing on each other's trampolines and then repeating the same thing backwards. It was mesmerizing. I watched them do this over and over again.

It took me a bit to realize why the walls were light blue. When you jumped it looked like you were up in the sky, way higher than you actually were. Soaring. Flying.

There was a lightness to each of them.

I noticed this with a pang of jealousy. They were jumping and pointing at each other and trying new things. Gravity did not seem to have the same hold on them as it did on me. Not the gravity of physics, the gravity of grief. There was a sadness deep in my bones that was always with me. I had left my home, my people, my planet-and yet that grief was still with me. In some ways at that moment more than ever. Something about those trampolines accentuated this sense I had that the ache within me could not be left behind. I could jump with them and swing from that rope and hurl myself into that foam pit, but there was something forced to it.

A weight I could not get out from under.

Eventually we tired, making our way to the biggest trampoline in the center where we sat in a circle. Turns out Stilitz was a gymnast, Duda a track star, Zoma and Corta had a trampoline in their backyard, and Florent had never been on a trampoline until that day.
Then we heard that door sound.
Vo entered.
I trust you have enjoyed yourselves?
We were like school children, recounting for her who did what and how. We got our shoes on and followed her as soon as she headed for the door. From there we left the trampoline cylinder and headed for another.
What are these called? I asked her.
TUBES she answered. *That was TUBE 10, we are now headed to TUBE 4.* She pointed ahead. There were numbers just above the doors. TUBE 4 was smaller.
The door opened.
Did Vo ever have to actually open a door? Or did all doors see her coming and respond accordingly?
We entered.
There were six tables, laid out in a circle in the middle of the room. They each had a small hole at the end towards the center. There was a metal circular ring hanging from the ceiling about 8 or 9 feet above the floor, running across

the centers of the tables. Metal rods bisected that circular ring, with curtains on them pushed up against the wall.
Vo stood in the center.
You will see that your name is on one of the tables, please find which one.
The door opened.
Six people came through the door. They were wearing jackets made out of what I can only guess was some sort of gauze. They were short, and they glowed.
I'm serious.
Those people. They radiated. I don't know what exactly it was that they radiated-Health? Blood flow? Youth? A few of them were way older than any of us.

They each grabbed a curtain and pulled it towards the center.
Their movements were synchronized.
None of us said a word.
My guy pulled the curtain past me and then turned it right. Which the person next to him did as well, forming a little curtain room.
Hello he said. *I am Keeth.*
Hi Keeth.
Keeth? That's a name? It sounded like a weapon. Or the sound something metal makes when it breaks. Keeth.
Keeth and Heen he said, smiling. Like that's all that needed to be said.
He knew my name-how did he know my name?
Oh yes.
It was written on a card on the end of my bed.
Now, if you could take off your coveralls and lie face down, we can begin.
I did it.

Right away.

That is what had happened to me in just a few hours.

A man named Keeth on the planet Yorch kindly asked me to remove most of my clothing AND I DID IT WITHOUT HESITATION.

I heard the others doing the same.

Whatever that was, I had company.

Ohhhhh I realized. That's what the hole was for-my face.

Vo was right.

These people had thought of everything.

I heard Keeth bend down and then jump up.

Wait…what is he…?

His feet landed on the table between my knees.

And then he stepped on my shoulder blades.

WOW I shouted.

I heard the others making similar noises.

Keeth giggled.

Funny at first, right? he said.

Was that a question? It was so unexpected. And jarring. A grown man was on my back. His toes were moving back and forth, up and down. I heard his hands sliding around on the metal bar.

If someone had ever described someone doing this to them I would have instantly asked them *AND YOU LET THEM????*

I let him.

Keeth.

It felt so good.

Things were cracking and popping back there. Loosening up.

That man's toes worked wonders.

I remembered again Ma'am Kirti reading us one of those
TRUNKS from the CHAIRS about how EVERYONE DOES
THEIR PART.
Keeth.
Doing his part.
With his toes.
I heard Duda squawk. But with joy.
Corta shouted *YES!* like she was having sex.
Florent quietly mumbled. *Broseph you have no idea...*
There seemed to be no end to the contortions and
movements Keeth was able to do on my back, my calves,
that bone on the top of my shoulder. At one point his heel
pressed on the back of my skull which made my elbow
tingle.

I could swear that my body was having a conversation with
itself. He stepped on my shoulder and my gut made a
noise, he dug the ball of his foot into the small of my back
and my neck relaxed.
Did he do this on purpose because he was aware of all
those connections?
Or did he just randomly walk around and see what
happened?
I found myself sinking into the table. Looser, looser, looser.
Waves of release moved through my body.
I lost all track of time.

And then I heard six sets of feet hit the floor simultaneously.
It was over.
I lifted my head out of the head hole as Keeth put his palms
together in front of his heart and bowed towards me.
He quietly said *Thank you Heen.*
HE thanked ME.

And then he walked out with the others.

Door noise. They were gone.

I sat there on that table in that little temporary room made of curtains, woozy with bliss. My face felt flush.

Vo, who somehow managed to enter silently and made her way to the center-Didn't the curtain rooms go all the way around? How did she do that? And why do I fixate on details like this?-Vo spoke softly. *If you will get dressed and meet me outside, we will proceed.*

I wanted to lie back down and put my face back in that hole in the table and dissolve into the bowels of Yorch.

I heard the others putting on their coveralls.

I moved so slowly.

A few groans. A sigh.

Florent moaned through the curtain. *I feel like a puddle with arms and legs.*

We shuffled outside.

The suns had set.

We discovered that there were small white lights all over the TUBES. Hundreds of them, thousands of them. They were pulsing brighter and then fainter and then brighter at irregular intervals. Like the TUBES were having a chat among themselves, like they were neighbors who'd gotten together for drinks after work, standing in a circle exchanging the latest news about who's been up to what.

We paused there outside TUBE 4, taking it all in.

It was beautiful.

And calming.

So calming.

Vo put her index finger to her lips, that universal sign to cease your speech. She started walking. We followed. We passed a TUBE, then another, then another. We went to the left around one, then to the right around another. The ground was a blend of decomposed granite and thick, short grass. It was soft and springy and wonderful to walk on. We made almost no noise as we ever so gradually made our way around this large circle of circles out in the middle of a vast nowhere. Nothing to our left, the green circle of grass we landed on to our right.

Vo was in no rush, neither were we.

It struck me that this was the perfect thing to do after the day that we'd had.

No one talked.

*

We returned to where we began, to the TUBE next to the Keeth TUBE.

That's funny. The KEETH TUBE. THE KEETH'S TOES TUBE.

The door opened.

We entered to GREEN. Green everywhere. Floor. Walls. That TUBE was smaller. In the center was a large circular table. Of course it was circular, isn't everything? Fascinating how I was starting to think in circles, expect circles, see in circles.

I counted the plates set on the table.

12 plates.

There were red flowers in glass jars on the table, placed above every other plate.

Vo gave us instructions. *If you will take a seat at a plate with a red flower in front of it, dinner will be served in just a moment.*

We sat down.

The door opened.

Vo left. Six people entered in a single file line. I had never seen people like these people. Their clothes, their hair, their skin, their…demeanor? Is that the word for it? One of them was an old man. Really, really old. He was wearing a cream-colored dress, with question marks all over it. And sandals. With little smiling frogs on the straps. Behind him they diverged from their single file as they spread out to sit down. One of them was a woman younger than us, by at least 5 laps or so. But then she said *HELLO* and her voice was so deep and full and I stared at her and then I could see that she was way older than us. How did she do that?

They sat down among us. Florent started shaking their hands, introducing himself. The rest of us followed. Those people had the strangest names:
Firpo and
Lax, and
Imaltaneous Arphaxad-
I wanted to write them down as we introduced ourselves to each other just so that I could say them out loud later.
Savoring them, remembering them.
And they were from planets I'd only heard about-
Engar and
Changmin and
Godofe and
Puwa and
Roohi.
It was so much to take in.

People entered with food. Some of the dishes I had never seen before, others were ones my mother used to make. It was new and familiar, strange and comforting. One dish came around that I had no interest in until Firpo exclaimed

My mother made this when I was a child! You must try it!
I did.
Long, soft purple tubes with little blue chips in a mustard colored sauce…
It was delicious.
I had no idea what it was.

Duda slid her plate forward at one point and arm wrestled the man next to her. Stilitz happened to sit next to a woman who knew his father from their home planet. He was absolutely over a moon about this and let us all know *WHAT A SMALL GALAXY IT IS!!!*

I grew up in a very small world.

That truth quietly pierced my center sitting there at that meal with those strangers.

The worlds are many, and varied, and I hadn't seen anything, really. We ate and talked and ate some more and asked questions and answered questions and learned and told stories-I had no idea that it rains twice a lap on Engar, on the exact same two days. Or that Godofe was landed by seven women whose ship broke down, forcing them to eject and land by parachute. With no food or water or supplies. Or that on Roohi the beautiful game lasts ninety minutes, not the usual hundred.

The color, the depth, the shade, the nuance-in just one dinner with a few strangers. How much more is out there?

Eventually Vo showed up, telling us to say our goodbyes. I hugged those strangers, aware that they had been like

doors for me into new worlds.
They left us.

We were all glowing, like we'd just encountered whatever it
is that makes everything hum.

Vo walked among us. *We have come to the end of the
day. Please follow me.*
We left the dinner TUBE and headed to TUBE 9.
Is this where we sleep?
We entered.
Oohhhhhhhhhh. This is…this is…
Home?
Vo said *This is your new home.*
All right then.
It was a lot to take it in.
The floor of the TUBE was wild. Grasses and trees and
plants and flowers. Some of them head high. A few
higher.
It was like outdoors invaded indoors.
We looked up.
That TUBE-our home TUBE-was open to the sky. And
attached to the inside walls were…what is the word here…
pods? Half circle containers? Birds' nests but people
sized? They reminded me of tree houses. Probably 15 feet
by 15 feet. Although they fit the curved shape of the wall.
And they were placed at irregular heights. And they
each had their own set of stairs.
Vo pointed to the one closest to us. *Duda, that is your
NEST. Florent that is yours…*
She pointed to the next one.
We each have our own NEST? This was obvious, but I said
it anyway.

Yes Heen Vo smiled again. *And yours is that one.* She pointed. *You all will see that your NEST has everything you need. You will sleep now. You will know when it is time to wake up.*

Door sound.

She left.

We mumbled good night to each other. We were spent.

What a day.

I climbed the stairs to my NEST.

Amazing how a word can be introduced to you and within moments you're using it naturally, like you've always used it. NEST. My nest.

There was a thick jute rug on the floor. A bed against the wall, with a cover made of something very soft and springy. There was a door open at one end, to a bathroom. I dropped down on the bed.

And then I saw it.

I saw them.

On Lunlay, in The Thiru, we slept in the ground. My room was dark, and cool. That's all I'd ever known.

But there, when I lay down, I could see the sky.

The roof of my NEST was clear. Glass. Or something like it. This was entirely new to me.

I noticed a large switch to my left. I flipped it.

Instantly the glass turned dark.

Ohhhhhh. Nice. They had thought of everything.

I flipped the switch back.

The stars returned.

I looked to my right and laughed. A small closet. In it were nine-I counted them-nine coveralls, each in a different color. I had a hunch.

I checked it.

Yes.

My hunch was correct.

Each coverall had a number on the inside tag.

One for each day of the week.

I checked the tag on the coveralls I was wearing.

Number one.

There were drawers below. One had boxers, one had shirts, one had socks. All in my size.

Like they knew I was coming.

*

I have only ever heard my dad tell one joke. Someone told him that someone in CIRCLE 6 had a wife who hit her head. We were doing what we always did on these excursions: trying to find help. It took half a day of walking to get there. I sat in the front garden while my dad went in and asked his usual questions. He had a notebook he carried with him everywhere he went.

Sometimes he would sit in our garden and hold it against his heart. For hours.

That notebook was his love for her in paper form. But sometimes it struck me as just, well, kind of pathetic.

A reminder of his failure to make peace with what is.

Eventually he came out of that house, like he always did.

Only this time he was laughing. And the man he was visiting was laughing as well.

My dad never laughed.

They shook hands, him and the man.

And then my dad said *Want to hear a joke, before I go?*

My dad knows a joke?

Sure! the man said.

All right, here we go, said my dad.

He never talked like that.

These two guys meet up at a bar on Hackle.

Hackle? My dad opened his joke in a bar in Hackle? Hackle was the most well known planet on the outer, outer edges of the 9's, which were the outer, outer edges of… everything. What does my dad know about Hackle?

One of them is wearing a bright green coat. Just the brightest, greenest coat you have ever seen. They have a drink, they go their separate ways.

My dad paused.

Please tell me there's more. Because that is not a joke right there.

The man on the porch was listening intently.

I realize now that my dad was savoring the moment. I missed that at the time. My dad didn't savor much of anything.

He kept going. *One day 30 LAPS LATER these two men both happen to be passing through Hackle. They see each other in that bar and they remember meeting all those years ago. The first guy says HEY, DIDN'T WE MEET ABOUT 30 LAPS AGO RIGHT HERE IN THIS BAR? The other says YES! WE DID! I REMEMBER YOU! The first guy says I REMEMBER YOU WERE WEARING THE BRIGHTEST, GREENEST COAT THAT DAY! And the other guy says OH YES I WAS! AND DO YOU WANT TO KNOW WHY I WAS WEARING THAT COAT THAT DAY? And the first guy says YES-I'D LOVE TO KNOW! And the other guy says I WORE THAT COAT THAT DAY SO THAT WE COULD TALK ABOUT IT NOW!!!*

My dad delivered that last line with a bang.

He stomped his foot on that man's porch.

He clapped his hands.

He and that man laughed so hard.

That man thought that joke my dad just told was the funniest thing he'd ever heard. I can only assume he had not heard that many jokes. I sat there on that porch trying to work out why they found that joke funny.

My dad stood there on that porch glowing. Like he'd been carrying around a large piece of gold and he finally got to take it out of his bag and show it to someone. He glanced over at me sitting there on that porch, a look of triumph on his face.

*

I heard horse music. At least that's what I think it's called. Ancient music, earth music, I've heard it called string music. Wood music. Apparently the bow that moves across the strings of those kind of instruments is made from the tail of a horse.

Horse music.

I woke up. In my NEST. The sky above me was blue. I have never woken up to the sky. I was in the exact position I was in when I first laid down on my bed.

Still in the coveralls from the day before.

The music was wonderful. So relaxing.

I spotted the speaker in the far corner of the ceiling. There was a small table next to my bed. On it was a large glass filled with a thick, green liquid. I tasted it. It was delicious. What a drink.

Wait. Someone came in while I was sleeping?

I cleaned up. I checked the coveralls in the closet, choosing the one for today.

I was pretty sure it was as obvious as that.

Two.

They were blue.

Two is blue.

Excellent.

I left my NEST.

Duda was waiting on the ground, which I was assuming was called the FIELD. A few others were coming down their stairs. All wearing blue coveralls. Interesting how we all sorted that one out.

I felt a tremendous bond with those people. I did not understand how I could feel so close to people I had known for barely a day. There was something about the intensity and newness of the experience we were having together that connected me to them far more than people I had spent my entire life with. I noted this.

Vo appeared.

She was wearing silver that day. A long, flowing silver blanket with arm holes. That she could walk in. With an orange stripe across the front.

Zoma said to her *Vo I love what you're wearing. After two days I'm beginning to think that you can pull anything off. You are entirely correct Zoma* Vo replied. *And the same is true for you: We can pull off whatever we believe we can pull off.*

You believe that? Florent laughed as he asked.

Vo was resolute. *Absolutely. Anybody can wear anything. You think that what you wear is about the outside. But that is merely the outer and last layer of the expression-*

The outer and last layer of the expression. That's what Vo called clothing-

What you wear begins with how you see yourself. If you decide that you can wear whatever you want to wear then you can wear whatever you want to wear.

I was beginning to wonder if Vo was the most unusual
person I had ever met. It was the way she carried herself, a
flow inherent in her presence. Powerful. But restrained.
Understated. Subtle. Like what she said there about
clothes. That is profound that bit about pulling off
whatever you believe you can pull off. But the way she
said it, like it was just a toss off comment, a stray thought
she pulled out of the air on the way to saying something
else. That sense of ease and command, together.
Effortless.
By then we were all together in the FIELD.
Stilitz jumped off his stairs. *Vo is this called the FIELD?
Because it feels like a FIELD!!!*
Vo smiled. *It is now.*
We did this thing with tennis balls. There were lines on the
floor, dividing the floor up into spaces that had numbers
written in them, which corresponded to points you got for
getting the balls into those spaces. There were cups used to
move the balls. And we could only stand in certain spaces.
And there were these three sticks that had velcro on the
end so you could move a ball without using a cup or
standing in that space. Because the number on the space
was added to the number on the ball and then divided by
the number of people in that space.
It was really complicated.
We had to move from space to space, pairing up with
different partners-we were each given a number based on
the order we were picked up yesterday-WAS THAT
YESTERDAY???!!!-Trying to keep our running score above
a certain number which flashed on the wall and below
another number which flashed on a different part of the wall.

And changed. Constantly. And then changed faster and faster the better we got at the game.

My brain was so cooked after that one.

We stumbled out of that TUBE and stood there in the sun, dazed.

So did we win?

Corta wanted to know.

Florent was so confused. *I'm still not sure what the game even was.*

I agreed. *The number in the space was divided by the sum of the other numbers-not subtracted, right?*

Which led to a discussion about what the correct answer was to that question. Turns out we were split right down the middle about one of the most important rules of the game. Literally half of us were trying to do one thing while the other half were trying to do something else.

Vo then took us to a spot on the opposite side of the circle with six padded reclining chairs.

Arranged in a circle, of course.

We sat back in the chairs.

Music began to play from speakers IN THE CHAIRS.

Not just IN THE CHAIRS, the chairs were somehow connected to the music. The low notes rumbled in the cushion, the higher notes sent vibrations though the fabric.

I got totally lost in it.

Just swept away.

I see now what they were doing.

Although I don't know exactly who I mean by THEY.

Somewhere in that second day I stopped wondering what the point of all of it was. At first, of course, I was trying to figure it out. We all were. What are they doing with us?

What is the point of this challenge? What are they testing in this game? What are they looking for in this exercise? How am I doing? Am I measuring up? Am I good enough? Where is this headed?

But gradually I stopped caring. It was just too much. The relentless onslaught of new sensations and foods and TUBES and colors and events and stimulation-it just kept coming. Vo would show up, we would go to a new TUBE, do whatever we did there, and then we were on to the next one…

Like those chairs.

Listening to that music.

I didn't know what that was-the point. The purpose. The plan.

But that one with tennis balls and numbers was so intense. It was like physical math.

So to just recline there with that chair giving me that odd sort of music massage?

Fine.

And then it was time for lunch, in another TUBE.

Which was yellow on the inside.

And had black balls hanging from the ceiling.

That swayed in the breeze.

Were they making a breeze? Indoors?

The table we ate at was shaped like a triangle. Our seats were bolted to a large triangular shaped plate that rested on the floor.

At least, that's how it appeared at first.

But then as we ate the whole thing-the table and us sitting in our chairs-rotated.

Very slowly.

Which changed our perspective on the black balls swaying

above our heads because there was some sort of backlighting that created shadows of the balls on the yellow walls.

Shifting shadows. Constantly overlapping, producing an endless succession of shapes and designs. The more we ate the less we talked because what was happening on the walls was just so compelling.

Stilitz pointed at the wall at one point and said *That looks like a pregnant elephant-never mind, now it's gone.*

Duda shouted with joy. *I just saw a fat kid pop a bubble!*

It's kind of mesmerizing Corta murmured, softly.

Zoma smiled as she said *It's like a tired volcano that is just so weary from all those years of going off...*

A memory floated back to me, sitting there in that TUBE, watching those shapes on the wall. I must have been 4 or 5, young enough to rest my head on my mother's lap after running for hours in the meadow near our house. She pointed to a cloud and said *Look, a monster eating a sandwich!* I thought that was the funniest thing ever. My dad joined me, his head leaning against her thigh. *And there's a strawberry landing on a giant's head! What do you see Heen?*

I studied those clouds.

Waiting for my moment.

Someone dropped their ice cream!

We all thought that was hilarious.

My mother and dad and me.

Together.

Seeing things in those clouds.

The more the 6 of us sat at that rotating triangular table eating our lunch the trippier our sightings got. I don't know if it was the food or someone put something in our drinks or they were adjusting the lighting in that TUBE-I wouldn't put it past them-but it became a game of who could top who.

At one point I shouted *There's one of Florent's pears!*

Duda punched the air. *And it's exploding in his face!*

That sort of thing.

On and on we went

Until that door sound.

And Vo appeared.

And announced that we were now going to TUBE 2.

Where the whole thing took a turn.

*

TUBE 2.

We stepped through the doorway and into a white circle. The walls were white. The ceiling was white. Six circular white rugs were arranged in a circle.

In the center of each rug was a guitar on a stand.

Each guitar was a different color. With a matching strap.

Six of them. The guitars were on stands, in front of amplifiers. On the floor in front of the amplifiers was a series of boxes with dials and knobs on them.

I'd never played a guitar.

I'd seen them played.

But music just wasn't in my house.

Or my bones.

All of it was very unfamiliar to me.

Vo told us to pick a guitar and put it on.

I laughed out loud at that one.

Me? I thought to myself.

Yes, you Heen Vo said.

It was like she was inside my head. But then again, I kept reminding myself, she'd probably done this hundreds of times…

You will notice headphones on top of your amplifier. Go ahead and put them on.

We did.

You will see next to the headphones a guitar pick. You will strike the strings with the pick. Take a moment to practice.

I touched a string with the pick.

WOW. What a sound.

I struck all the strings.

It actually sounded good.

Like a note. Notes. A chord.

How is this possible?

Vo continued. *Your guitars are tuned to what is called an OPEN TUNING. This means that you cannot hit a wrong note. Holding the pick in your right hand, take the index finger of your left hand and hold it down in between the silver bars that run up and down the neck of the guitar.*

Is the neck the long part?

Yes, Stilitz, you are correct.

I tried it. It sounded like music.

Vo went on. *As you slide your finger up to the next space between the bars-which are called frets-you will see that it sounds-*

Great! Zoma yelled with her headphones on.

Yes, it does, Zoma.

Vo was so patient.

Now, I draw your attention to the boxes at your feet. These are called PEDALS. Pick any one of them and click the button with your foot. Then play the strings.

I picked the pink box.

I hit the strings.

They rang and rang and rang. Like an endless echo. It sent chills up my spine. I did it again. And again. I slid my finger up a fret. Then another. The ringing was ethereal, haunting, magnificent.

Vo kept going. *Now try another pedal. Turn the first one off. Then try them both, together.*

I did. Suddenly the strings sounded underwater. I tried another one. It sounded like I was playing in a massive cavern.

I tried another. It sounded…dry. Is that the word for it? Dry? Close? Flat? Thin?

I was so engrossed in what we were doing.

I lifted my head up and looked around.

The others were as riveted as I was.

Vo had more instruction for us. *Now pay attention to the amplifier. There is a knob that has the word GAIN below it. Turn that up, and see what it does.*

What???? The GAIN knob sounded like someone had poured dirt into my guitar. All scratchy and crunchy but also LIFE! ENERGY! VOLUME! It felt like the sounds were attacking me.

Vo motioned for us to stop playing.

Now, your first assignment.

She was giving us an assignment?

I am going to give you a sentence. You will then create a sound that goes with that sentence.

Corta raised her hand. *We'll create a sound?*

Vo nodded. *Yes. With the pedals at your feet and the knobs on the amplifier.*

Zoma protested. *But I don't know how to play the guitar.*

Vo smiled. *Can you make sounds with it?*

Well…yeah…we've all been doing THAT.

Vo stepped towards her. *What is the difference between*

making sounds and playing?
That was some one-handed clapping right there.
I kind of understood what she was saying, but that was some advanced level distinction making Vo was doing with that move.

Florent had a question. *Okaaayyyy…but some people actually know how to play guitar, that's way different than what we're doing.*
Vo had clearly heard that one before.
Is it? Because the assignment is not to play it. The assignment is to create a sound that goes with the sentence.
I couldn't help but ask. *According to who?*
According to you.
Once again, Vo was so calm and confident I bought it.
Now, the first sentence. Here it is: A bird flies overhead.
We leaned in with that *AND…?* look on our faces.
She repeated the sentence. *A bird flies overhead.*
I drew a blank.
What does that sound like?
I played a chord. I hit a pedal. Nope, that sound was farther.
I turned a knob labeled REVERB. AHHH, yes, that was closer. So. Some adjustments got me closer, some farther.
I established that.
I went quickly through the pedals.
One of them grabbed me. A far off sound, like the amp was in another room. I turned the dials UP. MORE. That was better.
Closer.
It was difficult for me to describe literally what I was doing.
Searching. Looking. Trying to find. A sound. That reminded me of a thing-a bird-I'd seen do a thing-fly overhead.

I imagine there being a machine somewhere that you could hook up to your brain and it tells you what parts of your brain are firing when you do certain things. Right then I am very confident that parts of my brain I rarely used were overheating.

And then I found it.

Or something like it.

A particular combination of knobs and dials produced a beautiful-not just a sound-a tone. A feeling.

I have no idea what I mean by that distinction, but it feels true. See what I mean? Normal describing is out the window. I closed my eyes and then I pictured a bird flying overhead and then I strummed the guitar and YES THAT'S THE SOUND.

I knew it in some way I don't usually know things.

I had no idea how long it had been.

Vo motioned us to stop.

Please remove your headphones. Who would like to go first?

Stilitz panicked. *Wait! You didn't say anything about the others hearing it!!*

Stilitz, how excellent of you to volunteer to go first. Let us hear it.

Stilitz looked around at us. *It's a work in progress, keep that in mind-*

Vo was her usual firm self. *Let. us. hear.*

He made his noise.

It did not sound like a bird flying overhead.

It echoed off the walls.

We stood there in silence.

Vo looked at him. *Did someone shoot the bird as it flew overhead?*

Did Vo just roast Stilitz?

I didn't know how to react.
I looked around. No one did.
Vo asked him *Is the bird sick?*
Stilitz looked shocked.
Vo pointed up. *Did the bird shat on your head as it passed by?*
Is Vo making fun of him?
I couldn't hold it in any longer.
I laughed. Florent did, too. I could barely hold my guitar up.
I found that so funny.
Duda had tears in her eyes.
Zoma sat down she was laughing so hard.
Eventually Stilitz laughed as well. Resistance was futile.
We already liked Vo. But that. *Is the bird sick?* Classic.
We loved Vo.

Corta, would you like to go next?
Sure. Corta took her guitar stand-Wait! You can do that?-
and held it up to the frets and then slid it down the neck
while she turned one of the knobs on the amp from DOWN
to UP while she alternately turned two of the pedals ON and
OFF with both of her feet.
This astonishingly ambidextrous display of coordination and
experimentation was extraordinary to behold, only to be
outdone by the noise she conjured up.

It sounded like a bird flying overhead.

The highest praise I could possibly give it. She finished
and we stood there in awe.
Duda asked her *You don't play the guitar?*
We don't have guitars on Fahri.
The rest of us shared our sounds.

Vo gave us another sentence: *I can't stop thinking about what they said.*
And another: *Some days I feel like I'm in a black hole.*
And another: *All I can do is say thank you.*
We made our sounds for each of those sentences, creating and conjuring, turning the dials and twisting the knobs, finding our way into this exotic new sonic landscape. We lost our fear of sharing our sounds, adjusting to the truth that none of us knew what we're doing. The only thing left to do was to throw ourselves into it and see what we come up with…
After I don't know how many rounds, Vo told us to take off our guitars.
Duda had a question.
Yes, Duda.
I would love to know what the point of this was. I mean, Vo, I really enjoyed this. But come on, you gotta help us out here. What is…what was this?
Vo gave us that knowing look she had mastered.
I suspected you might wonder. You will now find out.
That door noise.
In walks…

SIR PONG!

Sir Pong?!! On Yorch?!!
I was stunned.
Please welcome Sir Pong.
He hadn't aged a day.
Same green robe. Same streaks on his arms. Same hair.
He glided into our midst.

I wanted to get his attention.

I wanted him to notice me.

He looked us each in the eyes.

When he came to me he paused.

And then he winked.

Wonderful to see you all, please have a seat.

He bowed.

We sat on the floor in front of our amps.

I watched the others. They were having their introduction to the phenomenon known as Sir Pong. That man shaped me, formed me. Gave me the lens that I see the worlds through.

And now, all those years later, there he was.

ARRANGEMENTS he began.

He repeated it. *ARRANGEMENTS. Allow me to ask you a few questions.* He did a slight bow in Corta's direction.

What is your name?

Corta.

Splendid. Corta, how did you make those sounds with your guitar?

Honestly, Sir Pong-

-she said it like it's the best name in the world

I just kept turning the knobs.

He nodded.

And what happened when you got stuck? When it didn't sound right?

I just kept turning the knobs.

Sir Pong reflected on this.

Yes, that is how it works, isn't it? You just keep turning the knobs. Anyone relate to that?

We all nodded.

I knew that. That thing he does. Bringing you in. You're nodding, agreeing, affirming.

He was clearly just getting warmed up.

They used to call it politics. From an ancient word meaning CITIZEN.

That was a swerve. From guitars to history.

Because that's what we are: citizens. Citizens of our CIRCLES, our planets. Of the galaxies. Of the universe. And the question has always been: How will we arrange ourselves? What ARRANGEMENTS will best help us all flourish?

He was in full swing now, bringing us along in his hypnotic way.

Because someone somewhere has to decide what ARRANGEMENTS are best. They don't just magically happen. People have to give themselves to the ARRANGEMENTS. To studying them, understanding them, adjusting them when needed. How many of you had running water in your home when you were growing up?

I watched the others.

They couldn't tell if that was a trick question or not because it was so simple.

But I knew his game.

My hand shot up.

I was 14 again, eager for Sir Pong to validate me. To look my way and say *Yes Heen, good.*

Which he did.

Yes, Heen, good.

The others couldn't believe it.

Sir Pong knows me?

I was so happy that Sir Pong remembered me.

I felt like my heart was going to burst.

Water is basic for life, is it not?

Who could argue with that? We murmured *YES.*

Where did that water come from? The water that came out of the faucet, the water that satiated your thirst-
I always loved Sir Pong's word choices. He had no problem busting out the most specific words whenever the occasion called for it, like right then. *Satiated*-what a word.
The water that you used to clean the dishes, the water in the garden, where did it come from? How did it get to you? How was there always enough? Who decided how that water arrived in your home?
I spent several laps in Sir Pong's class and I never heard that riff. He'd clearly added to his repertoire.
This is what we're referring to when we use this word ARRANGEMENTS. Someone somewhere has to make these decisions-about water, land, education. How many of you went to school?
He paused.
The others raised their hands right away.
They were starting to get their Sir Pong groove on. The profound is always hiding out in the simple.
Yes of course, you all went to school. And I can only assume you had excellent teachers. And you probably never considered how that all came to be. Why would you? You were children. Someone else took care of such things.
Sir Pong spoke this and then hesitated, looking around at us. And then he sat down.
He stretched his legs out straight in front of him.
He crossed his ankles.
He was wearing socks. Red socks. And on his socks were written the words BING and BONG over and over and over again.
We all stared at his socks.

He clearly enjoyed the effect his socks were having on us.
That's why you're here.
He said it quietly.
Almost whisper like.
I watched Duda's eyes glaze over.
I felt a thud in the center of my being.
Sir Pong leaned forward.
You are no longer children. You are citizens. And you are here because you are being invited to give yourselves to the ARRANGEMENTS.
I exhaled.
So much to take in.
Sir Pong brought his palms together, with his fingers touching. It was striking to me how those gestures of his were burned into my psyche. So familiar, like signposts along the trail that is my life. *The CHAIRS are constantly adjusting the ARRANGEMENTS, turning the dials and twisting the knobs, endlessly searching for just the right balance, the correct order, the ARRANGEMENTS that best serve everybody. Money and jobs and education-the soil, the sea, the forest, the trails and GLIDES and rivers and how we communicate and how we relate to each other and how we each discover who we are and the part we are each here to play-ALL OF IT. This work requires discipline and vigilance and compassion and intelligence and character and integrity and resilience. And there must be those in every generation who step forward and say YES, I WILL SERVE.*
It's like he had cast a spell.
None of us moved.
Is this my life?
The question arose within me.
All that had happened.

All that loss.

All that heaviness.

That abyss.

Am I for this?

An awkward question, but I felt the soul of it.

For a brief second, my life wasn't just fragments and bits of unrelated incoherence. Which is how it had felt for such a long time.

But now, sitting there, it was something more.

A whole.

A unity.

All of it headed somewhere.

My life for something.

This.

Stiltiz found a way to drop a bomb on the moment.

So are we being recruited by the CHAIRS?

Sir Pong squinted in Stilitz's direction, his eyes boring in on him like he had X-ray vision.

Are you from Nims?

Oh man, that was awesome.

Sir Pong. A step ahead.

I saw the others eyes widen, like they were wondering *Who is this ninja/guru/sage/teacher who knows where Stilitz is from??*

Stilitz was aghast. *Yeah, I am. How did you know?*

Sir Pong leaned in. *Do you know the Woohucks?*

Of course! Everyone on Nims knows the Woohucks!!

Eirl? Claude? Pino? Sir Pong asked him.

I went to school with Pino's son Ozar!!!

Small galaxy, isn't it? I trained with Claude a few moons ago-does he still do those wood sculptures?

Yes. And his daughters have joined him-one of them

*makes these massive portable tent structures that we use
for homes in the hot months and then turn into food
storage in the winters-it's revolutionized how we eat, how
we live...
Greton? Or Bilby?*

Sir Pong knew the names of the daughters of a wood
sculptor on Nims?

YES!!! Bilby!! I actually fancied her for a while.
Stilitz blushed.
We watched this exchange with fascination.
And what is your name?
I'm Stilitz.
Sir Pong mulled this over.
Well Stilitz, it is a pleasure to meet you.
Sir Pong turned to the rest of us.
He was in no rush.
*Now what was that? Or more precisely WHY was that-
That exchange between Sir Stilitz and me?*
We heard Stiltz mutter with pride under his breath *Sir Stilitz.*
*Or perhaps an even better question: HOW did that
happen? Because in that brief interaction my new friend
Stilitz and I touched on school and training and craft and
innovation and food and friendship and adaptation and
one generation handing an art form down to the next
generation-How does that happen? By accident? Or are
there certain conditions that allow that sort of thing to
happen? Conditions that help people find joy and do good
work and innovate and for some reason known only to
them choose to name their little baby boys STILITZ.*
We all laughed at that.
Sir Pong was so good. And funny. And subversive. He

150

clearly picked up on what a spastic, slightly irritating socially stunted presence Stiltz was and managed to turn that into something else, something human and endearing, showing us the fella in there who just wanted what we all want.

Sir Pong wasn't done.

That all happens because of the ARRANGEMENTS-specific and intentional turning of the dials and twisting of the knobs. And there have to be people who do THAT.

*

It did not stop with Vo. Over the next few weeks we went from TUBE to TUBE, day after day, each one holding another event, another obstacle, another exploration.

One morning we walked into TUBE 4. A woman came towards us from a door on the opposite wall. She invited us to sit on the floor with her as she pulled out a deck of cards. She asked each of us to draw a card. And then put it back. Without her seeing what card we drew.

She then did an elaborate bit of shuffling. I realized part way through her routine that I was enjoying a magician on Yorch. Like you do. She stopped shuffling, pulled out various cards, handing them to us one by one asking us expectantly if *this is the same card we drew.*

They weren't.

Not one of us got the same card.

She looked crestfallen, embarrassed.

She stammered.

She stared at the floor.

It was so awkward.

She had blown her first trick.

And she clearly didn't know how to recover.

She sat quietly.
We could tell she was trying to figure out how to save face.

And then she smiled, and asked Duda to check the inside
pocket of her coveralls. Duda unzipped a few inches and
reached in and pulled out…the card she drew.
Then she nodded to Florent. Who did the same thing. And
pulled out the card *he* drew.
We each did.
We were so confused.
I asked her *Did you mess up on purpose?*
Zoma jumped in *Was that part of the trick-to make it seem
like you blew the trick?*
We had so many questions.
She just sat there and smiled.
And then stood up and walked out.

Later Vo took us to that TUBE I'd seen that first day with
the crane on top of it. We put on these webbed harnesses
that had a metal ring on the back. Turns out that crane
had a wire on the end that's connected to a spindle.
Vo asked for a volunteer.
I stepped forward.
She then hooked the wire to my back and told me to jump
off the roof of the TUBE.
My knees shook.
I thought I was going to faint.
Are you serious?
*Yes, I am. As you fall the crane will let out the wire at
exactly the speed you are dropping. As you approach the
ground the spindle will incrementally slow, landing you
perfectly on your feet on the ground.*
I did it.

152

I jumped.

And I didn't die.

But even my memory of that jump is a bit blurry because it was in the midst of so many firsts. Foods, people-I met someone from beyond the STRONGS-THE STRONGS for the love of the gods!! If you had told me when I was a kid that I would know someone from the OUTER STRONGS I would have shook my head and told you you were crazy-

It was relentless, the newness of the experiences we were having.

I felt like they were trying to make us dizzy.

Each night I would consider climbing the stairs to Zoma's nest to see what might happen but I just didn't have the energy. I'd be out cold seconds after I got to my nest.

I gradually lost track of what day it was.

Until day 33.

I know this because Vo pulled me aside and said

Heen. It is day 33. Walk with me.

It was first time that one of us had been separated from the others.

The others? I said. I don't know how to name my fear here.

She reassured me. *I will talk with each of them as well.*

Off we went.

Me and Vo on our walk.

Around the edge of the circle of TUBES.

She told me *It is time.*

I was going to need more than that.

I didn't take the bait. I said nothing.

She added a bit.

It is time for you to begin.

Once again, I had a thousand questions. But if I said

Time for what? Begin what? That had been my pattern forever. Someone's in charge and I bend over backwards to impress them and make sure they think I'm good enough and worthy enough and all that.

You are ready.
She still hadn't really said anything.
I'm ready. It's time-that didn't actually inform me of much of anything.
You have a unique set of aptitudes that are needed at this time. There are a few specific training sessions required but then we will put you in the field.
Huh. *Like a job?*
Stilitz may have rubbed off on me a little.
Yes, Heen, like a job. Your job. Your new job.
And there it was.
The point of it all.
Which I kind of already knew, going back to Mustache Man and Beautiful Mother Lady. But now she had said it.
We were approaching two chairs. I swear I had never seen those chairs before, and we had walked that circle at least once a day since I'd been there. Were they placed there just for that conversation?
Vo sat down.
I did as well.
This has all been a test.
Of course.
Yeah, I knew that.
More than you realize.
What am I missing? I leaned forward.
She did, too.
We want to hire you to be a SERIES 5. You will get your own spaceship. You will learn to fly it. You will be given

assignments to travel to various planets and live among
the people on those planets. You will be-
Wait. Stop. I held up my hand. *I will have my own*
spaceship?
She knew she had me.
Yes, and a new one every three laps if you so choose.
If I so choose. Those words rattled around in my head,
banging into each other.
My job will be to live on different planets?
Yes. But not for very long.
I won't have the job for very long or I won't be on any one
planet for very long?
A part of me wanted to climb up on my chair and yell *MY*
MY OWN SPACESHIP MY OWN SPACESHIP MY OWN
SPACESHIP. But I'd do that later.
I needed clarity in that moment. Details.
I still don't understand what the job is. Other than flying
around to different planets.
Vo nodded. *The CHAIRS need data. Stories. Statistics.*
Information. First-hand accounts of what is working and
what isn't working. This is how the ARRANGEMENTS are
adjusted and improved. Can you see how vital this job is to
the life of the worlds? We need people to NOTICE, Heen.
And then to report back what they see. And YOU happen to
test extremely high in this area.
I laughed out loud at that.
I test high in NOTICING?!!!
Suddenly I was so cranked up.
NOTICING? THAT'S WHAT YOU THINK I'M GOOD AT?
THAT IS THE LAMEST THING IN THE UNIVERSE TO BE
GOOD AT!
My face must have been red because I was..embarrassed?
Irritated? Surprised? I had no idea why this evoked such a

response in me.

Stiltiz can do back flips off a small rock! Florent seems to know something about every subject under the SUNS, Duda is as strong as steel, Corta somehow knows how to play music instruments SHE'S NEVER EVEN SEEN BEFORE and you're telling me my skill is NOTICING!!??? WHAT ELSE? Are you going to tell me I'm good at OBSERVING as well??? Or that I test high in BEING???? Tell me, AM I A GOOD BE-ER??-

She held up her hand.

Stop right there. I understand your questions. Allow me to ask you a few.

I straightened up in my chair. This should be good.

Stiltiz can do some very impressive things on a trampoline, correct?

Yesss, he can…I just said that…didn't I? She caught me off guard with that one.

How many trampolines were there in that TUBE on that first day, Heen?

Seventeen. It came out instantly. I don't recall even counting. That number was just there. I pulled it up from I don't know where.

And how many springs are there on that largest one in the center?

Forty eight springs. Twelve for each section, four sections total.

And the foam pit, how many paces wide and how many paces deep is it?

It's thirty paces wide and twenty deep.

And that long, narrow, runway trampoline on the far left side, how many legs does it have resting on the ground?

Sixteen, eight on each side, although the four legs on each end are thicker. And angled.

She leaned back in her chair, pleased.

I don't know what to do with that exchange we just had.

Heen, this is what I am referring to when I use this word NOTICING.
That's a thing?
That is a thing.
That is a thing I could get paid for?
Yes, that is a thing we will pay you to do. You will have a CONNECT. Your CONNECT will give you your next assignment-
Is my next assignment my next planet-
Yes, your next planet.
What's a CONNECT?
WHO is a CONNECT. Your CONNECT is a person who will give you your next job. You will fly to that next assignment, land on that planet undetected, seamlessly blend in with the people there, filing regular reports with your CONNECT about what you are SEEING until your work is done there and it is time for your next assignment.

What a hairball that was to hear for the first time. Where do I start? I picked the first question that came to mind.
How will I know when my work is done there?
Your CONNECT will tell you.
You said something about landing undetected. I don't understand.
No one will know why you are there or what you are doing. Or who you work for. We will teach you how to do this.

Questions were coming so fast. I picked another. *Blend in? Like a house and a job and friends and all that...?*

Most SERIES 5s find that is the best way to do it, yes.

Which I will then at some point...leave?

Yes.

I don't understand the secrecy of it. Why not just say HEY GUYS I WORK FOR THE CHAIRS.

Because you will not be working for the CHAIRS. You will be working for the ARRANGEMENTS.

There's a difference?

You will grasp the truth of this distinction when it is time.

I rolled my eyes at that one.

Okay, fine. But why-I mean, I'm thrilled with the whole spaceship thing-but I still don't get all the secrecy.

It seemed like an obvious question.

And an important one.

For the 73rd time since I'd known her, Vo demonstrated that she has heard this one before.

How much is a one way from Jokahn to Soler?

That came out of nowhere.

I had no idea.

I didn't say anything.

Cost, Heen-How much does it cost to purchase a one way ticket to fly from Jokahn to Soler?

I still had no idea.

Uhhhhhh...

The answer is 489 GORS Heen, 489 GORS. At least, that was the price this morning.

Whoa, that is a lot of money. I knew it was expensive to fly from planet to planet-no one I knew had ever done it but 489 GORS is crazy money. You'd have to save for lots and lots of laps to do that. And that's only one way?

Also, she knows the price as of this morning?

She checked?

Vo was just getting started.

So if you show up in, let's say...Drowkin. You arrive in
Drowkin on the shuttle, what does that say about you?
Ahh, I was starting to get it. *It says that I AM LOADED.*
I said it with a touch of edge. I was trying to save face.
And how often does a shuttle land in Drowkin?
Those details. I didn't have a clue. I'd never been to
Drowkin. I hadn't checked the flight schedule to Drowkin.
Not very often...? I eeked it out.
That is correct. Not very often. Every half a lap or so.
I knew nothing about any of this.
So can you see what happens if you arrive in Drowkin on
that one shuttle? You will draw attention. People will
notice. You will have brought unnecessary risk to the
assignment before it has even begun.
She let that sink in.
In addition to that, you do not know how long your work
will take on that planet. You may finish your work only to
discover there is no ship leaving for quite some time. And
when a ship does leave, you have no guarantee it will be
going anywhere near where your next assignment is. That
is not an efficient ARRANGEMENT.
She paused for effect. It worked.
In addition to that-
There's more?!! Vo, you are piling it on!!
I tried to make her laugh.
She did. Kind of.
She'd seen it all.
In addition to that, all communication with your CONNECT
will be through backchannel signals.
Backchannel signals. Should I have even bothered asking
what that was?
She continued.
You will not use any standard communication systems,

those will be monitored by that planet as they always are.
All signals will be sent and received off the grid through your
ship.
A part of me wanted to give up, right then and there at the
start. It was way, way too much to take in.
I didn't understand what she was saying.
My bottom lip quivered.
Not a good sign.
Maybe I was just tired.
Or maybe I was just too sad.
Maybe you can't be that sad to do that job.
I didn't remember them testing me for sadness.
Or despair.
Or proximity to an existential abyss of never ending grief
and nothingness.

Vo reached in her pocket and pulled out a small, white disc,
about as thick as the palm of my hand.
She handed it to me.
It was heavier than it looked, and smooth. Very smooth.
Tap it there in the center with your index finger.
I did. Nothing happened.
Say Hello.
I looked at her. I looked at the disc. I looked back to her.
Go on. Say Hello.
I sighed. *Hello.*
My *Hello* contained within it the weariness of a thousand
moons.
A voice leapt out of the disc
Yeah, Heen. Let's get after this.
There was a drawl in this voice, a relaxed laconic twang I
had only heard once or twice in my life. There was
someone at one of those meals a few days ago who

talked like that. Like there was no rush, no reason to hurry, like we had all day here to just…be.

Also *Get after this?*

How does one do that?

Get after something?

I sat there in that chair holding that disc. Thinking about that voice. A blank look on my face.

Vo snapped her fingers in my face.

Say something.

To who?

To Randy.

I was in such a fog.

Randy? What's Randy?

I couldn't tell whether Vo was irritated or she was trying not to laugh.

Randy is a WHO-Randy is your CONNECT.

OHHHHHHHH. I suddenly felt very small. And naive. I thought that disc was playing a recording. But it was a dude.

Who was alive.

Hi Randy.

The shock of it.

I was talking to a person through a disc and they could hear me. I couldn't see them and they couldn't see me and we were having a conversation. Kind of.

I looked at Vo.

Is this a phone?

*

That little white disc in my hand.

What a marvel.

So you're going to tell me what to do?

That was the first thing I could think of to ask Randy.
More or less. I'll pass on what I'm told. But that won't be for a while.
I looked over at Vo with eyebrows raised like I was the coolest fella on Yorch.
Apparently I'm going to get my own spaceship. Cool, huh?
Very cool. That Randy drawl again. I loved it.
Vo watched me intently. Randy went on.
Well, you got a few things to be up to between now and then. But when you're through all that, we will get at it. Later, Heen.
I looked up at Vo with a WHAT DO I DO NOW? look. She tenderly motioned to the disc.
You could say good bye.
That's a good idea. Bye, um, Randy.
A little click from the disc.
We sat in silence.
I felt the disc in my hands.
I turned it over.
The suns were setting, lights were beginning to flicker on the sides of the TUBES.
There were a thousand things to say.
I picked one.
But I don't know how to fly a spaceship.
Vo considered that. And then she stood up, pointed to the spaceship in the center of the grass circle that I hadn't noticed, and said
Well then, it's time for you to learn.

PART 3 PIDDLE PIDDLE PIDDLE

The front door of the bakery flies open and slams against the wall. It sounds like lightning-or is that thunder?-and it happens every morning and I jump every time. Borns explodes into our midst as he shouts

I GREET YOU COMRADES WITH PHANTASMAGORIC SALUTATIONS AS WE COMMENCE THE BAKING OF BREAD!!!

Borns is a large man. He's wearing a white tee shirt, white canvas pants with vertical front pockets stitched on the outside, and he has a beard. A blonde beard. And voluminous blonde hair that leaves the top of his head and travels in every direction at once.
His fingernails are painted red.
He walks straight to me, enveloping me in a room darkening hug in which my feet leave the ground for a second-and then he sets me down, looks intently into my eyes, and says
Heen, you are new here, but we have already sojourned together across the ages and planes, have we not?

What does a person say to that?

Yesterday he greeted us with
WHO ISN'T JONESIN' FOR A STEAMING HOT LOAF???
The day before it was
SLICE ME A SLAB OH THAT WARM BUTTERY LOVE!!!
And the day before that he shouted
LET ME GET MY KNEADING HANDS ON YOUR SOFT

DOUGH, BABY!!!
Which he accompanied with a vaguely sexual and
unexpectedly charming gesture that involved the swinging
of his hips and the swaying of his shoulders to some
music only he could hear.
Borns.
I don't know what to make of this man. He so bends my
understanding of normal human behavior that I find
myself going along with him just to see where it leads. So
when he asks
*We have already sojourned together across the ages and
planes, have we not?*
I respond *We have, Borns, we have.*

*

What's your favorite bread?
That was the first question Lan Zing asked me in the job
interview. My favorite bread? No one has ever asked me
that. She had no papers-owners of bakeries always have
my references in front of them. And she sat cross-legged
in her chair-not behind a desk-with her feet tucked up
under her-what's that about? And it appeared she actually
wanted to know what my favorite bread is.
The interview is tricky enough.
It always is.
Because it's important for me to be an actual person and
actually give answers. But I can't give too much away. I
can't imagine what would happen if people found out I
work for the CHAIRS and they're being observed. And of
course I'm going to be gone at some point in the near
future. Randy will tell me that the assignment on this
planet is done. I'll leave work at the end of that day and

put my things in my bag and hike to my ship and fly to the next planet and I'll never see these people again.

Sourdough with rosemary.

My answer came out so fast. Like a reflex. Or an instinct.

One of my first assignments was on the planet Ziks. I got work as a compost facilitator-they are very intense about their compost on Ziks. The day inevitably came when the job was done. So I went to work the next day LIKE A NOOB to tell them I was done and my boss, an unusually tall woman named Grosch who had an unusually tall dog named Gordon whose tail was disturbingly long and tied in a knot asked me
Why are you leaving Heen?
I answered *My father has passed and I must return home to run the family enterprise.*

Where did that come from?
I must return home? What? I don't talk like that. And there was no family enterprise, obviously.
Just a buffet of lies.
Grosch heard this, shrugged and said *Well, you gotta do what you gotta do.*

And then she pulled a tomato out of her pocket and took a bite.

But ShahShay-this woman who smelled like fish and always stood too close to me while we monitored the morning intake panels-she overheard my totally made-up answer and lost it. She got all weepy and draped herself

on my shoulder and started sniffling and going on about when her father passed and how she can only begin to imagine the depths of my grief and *You poor soul dealing with this in your state-*
This is a state?
I'm in a state?
What is she on about?
And then she called over her friend Naani and recounted the horrible news Heen has just received and then Naani asked to see my palms so she can do a reading of my ancestral grief lines.
What a mess.
Lesson learned.
Don't get personal.
Even if you're just making stuff up.
When the job is done just…disappear.
So when sourdough with rosemary came out that quickly, I was a little rattled. That's personal. That blurs the lines. And Lan Zing drew it out of me effortlessly.

The references, of course, were fake. All the contact information I put down goes to Randy who impersonates imaginary people who have employed me in bakeries all over the galaxy. The only time I ever asked him about this he said *Heen, I have very impressive range.*

Lan Zing liked my answer.
Sourdough with rosemary? Interesting. We haven't made that before…
Well, it's never too late to start I said.

What was happening to me? *Never too late to start*-what? I could not care less what these people do in this bakery.

I thought I'd mastered the art of the slightly dishonest interview. But I was wobbling on the first question. She smiled as she ran her hand through her hair.

Can you start tomorrow?

And that was it.

Two questions. And I was in.

I responded *Yes* followed by *That's it?*

That's it.

Don't you want to know more about me?

We're good.

But how do you know this is going to work-how do you know I'M going to work?

I had never had an interview go like that.

Lan Zing pointed up. *I have lived upstairs my entire life. My parents started this bakery right after landing on Firdus. This place is everything to me-I sometimes wonder who I'd be without it. So whenever I need someone new I ask my parents to send that person my way.*

I was instantly on edge.

Your parents knew about me?

I always tilt in the direction of suspicion. The job requires it.

In a way.

She was so vague.

You and your parents own the bakery together?

No. They died a while ago.

I had no idea what to do with that one. *You ask your dead parents to help you find new employees?*

Well, yes-that's pretty much how it works.

She said it like it was the most normal thing imaginable.

And they do?

I should have known how she'd answer that.

You're here, aren't you?

Borns turns from me to Ziga Mey, who's arranging today's baguettes on the sheets. She's got long, brown hair she tucks down the back of the thick pink sweater she wears under her apron. Borns pulls a red flower out of his back pocket and presents it to her.
Ziga Mey, my love Peeble sends you her love in the form of this flower.
Ziga Mey melts.
Oh Borns, Peeble is so sweet. And so are you.
She takes the flower and puts it behind her ear.
Borns asks her *And how is Phileep?*
Oh he is more Phileep than ever.
Borns loves this. *More Philleep than ever!!! He is ready to fly his flag?*

Ziga Mey blushes as she turns to me and explains
I want to have a family like Borns and Peeble but my Philleep is not ready.
Borns sighs. *Is something wrong with Philleep's flag that he cannot fly it?*
He looks concerned.
No Borns, his flag is fine.
Lan Zing appears from the back room. *His flag will fly when the breeze blows in the right direction.*
Borns laughs. *Yes!! That is true! Well said Great Boss One!*
That's what he calls Lan Zing-*Great Boss One.*
And she's fine with it.
From what I can tell.
It's the openness of how they talk.
Sex and flying flags and making babies?
It unnerves me.

I flinch. And I'm fascinated.
I haven't met Philleep. But it feels a bit invasive to be listening in on a conversation about his flag flying.
Or not flying.

In from the refrigerator room comes Bobby Freelance.
He's pushing a wheeled rack stacked with the rye pans.
Bobby Freelance does not say much. He's got short black hair-my guess is he shaves his head every few days, and he wears white coveralls. Borns gives him a strange, word-less hand shake involving thumbs and elbows and snapping that I assume only the two of them know. That's the thing about Borns-he's so loud and effusive and over the top but then this greeting he does without saying a word.
Borns turns to me *Do not underestimate Bobby Freelance.*
He says this with great finality, like it's an announcement the CHAIRS have made about how the universe works. Bobby Freelance gives me a blank stare as he passes by.

We settle into the tasks and routines that I've learned over the laps are the same all around the galaxies. There is dough that needs folding and starter that needs feeding and a rack of whole wheat that is ready for scoring. I begin slicing the spelt loaves from yesterday.
Borns leans over and says to me *You must please her.*
He nods to the dough he's kneading for the sandwich rolls.
Her…who?
Borns evokes within me the same feeling my former best friend in the worlds Nord used to-that I'm a half step behind.
Yes-HER! he says. *See the bread as a she, and you are showing her what great affection she evokes within you!*
The bread?

I can feel my face scrunching as I ask this.

Yes Heen, Yes! he beams. *The BREAD my good man-*
Show her how much you love her!!!

He grabs the dough and holds it to his apron, then he lifts
it as he pats it gently.

You love the bread? I ask him. I feel like I'm learning a new
language talking to him.

I love THE LIFE! he says. He's emphatic. He punches the
air on *THE LIFE!*

Have you always been like this?

There is a touch of cynicism in my voice. I regret it. His eyes
open wide. *I am so glad you asked. My father…was a*
SECTION 6.

*

We were staking CIRCLE 11. That was so many laps
ago. I think about that time often, working that job, being
with Goja…it was the only time in my life I've ever been
happy.

I was leaning over, sighting a line for a row of small
houses on the far west side when I thought I saw a horse
through the viewfinder. I grabbed my binoculars.

It was.

A horse.

An actual horse.

I'd never seen a horse.

And someone was riding the horse.

Towards us.

And they were coming from The Tunes, the mountain range
to the north.

A woman.

A woman was riding a horse from The Tunes towards us.

I ran and found Spy V and handed her my binoculars, pointing. As she looked her hands began to tremble.
It can't be…no way…if that's…IT IS!!!
She tossed me the binoculars, threw open her arms and ran towards the woman, who saw her coming and got off her horse and ran towards her.
It was like slow motion, those two running towards each other.
The horse watched.
I watched.
They met and embraced. For a while. Talking with their faces a few inches apart.

And that woman. I'd never seen anyone like her. Her clothes alone-they were made of something thick I didn't know clothes could be made out of…it reminded me of the skin of an animal but without the hair. But worn. Really worn. Like whatever that material was had become her second skin. And there were red stains all over her jacket and pants. Big spots…splattered and blotchy…blood?
She had a long, slim black case strapped to her back. What was in that case? And the way she moved. With a stillness, a flow, a grace-like her bones were liquid. I couldn't stop staring.
Spy V turned to all of us *This is RG! My oldest-and first friend. RG is a SECTION 6.*
I heard ChaChi whistle behind me.
What's a SECTION 6? I wanted to know.
I was so young once.
Spy V heard me. *RG this is Heen. He's our STAKER. He'd like to know what a SECTION 6 is…*
She laughed as she said it, like it was an inside joke.
RG looked me up and down. *A real life STAKER-pleasure to*

meet you...
Spy V jumped in. *Heen, RG lives out past The Tunes.*
PAST The TUNES? I was incredulous. *You live PAST The Tunes?*
I do.
She had these lines on her face. Not old person lines. Not from aging. More like weather lines. Lines like the kind a canyon makes across the surface of a planet. History lines. *Something significant has happened here* lines. Everybody knows that our bodies are made of the same stuff as everything around us but some people-that woman-they make you feel it.

She blurred the boundary between skin and soil.

Spy V couldn't help but switch into teacher mode. I'd seen her do this so many times. *Heen, you know about SECTION 6's right?*
I don't.
RG shook her head. *It's not that big of a deal-*
Oh please. Spy V interrupted her. I'd never seen her like this. Gushing. Chatty. Amped.
SECTION 6's guard the outer outer boundaries.
Whoa.
You live alone out there?
I pointed as I asked. Like a small boy.
I do. RG nodded.
What does Spy V mean by GUARD? That sounds ominous.
Well...the wild is pretty wild.
That was her answer. So vague.
Is it true what I've been hearing about the f'rans? Spy V asked.

RG exhaled. *Yeah, it's a big problem. We had a pack come in from the south. Three of us went out tracking but only two of us returned-*
Wait.
I stopped her.
What's a f'ran? And what's a tracker? And what happened to the one who didn't return?
RG turned to Spy V. *I see why you have him around-He's almost as curious as you.*
A flicker of something between them. Shared history.
Love.
She turned back to me. *F'rans are large, and vicious. And they travel in packs. And they'll eat ANYTHING.*
How did I not know about f'rans?
ChaChi spoke up *Because if people knew what's out there they'd shat their pants sideways.*
RG agreed. *There's some truth to that. When the fjords dry up around this time of the lap they go hunting for new food sources, which usually means they head north. But this lap has been unusually warm so they pushed farther east than they normally do-*
Spy V cut her off. *How close did they get?*
RG paused, like she was considering how much to say.
About a mile.
It took me a second to grasp this.
About a mile from…a CIRCLE? From people?
RG nodded. *From a CENTER.*
Dread. That's the word for it.
And so you went out to hunt them and they ended up hunting you?
Spy V put her arm around RG.
No one said anything.

*

SECTION 6s can have kids?
Obviously I know the answer to that. Borns is standing right here in front of me.
But still. This is really interesting.
That is the wonder of my existence.
Borns says this softly. Tenderly.
They CAN'T have kids?
I'm missing something.
Heen, it is time for our morning break. Shall we?
He points to the alley behind the bakery where there's a bench. We each get a coffee from Lan Zing, who's preparing the display cases for opening.
We sit.
Borns is quiet. Subdued.
I haven't met this Borns yet.
He holds his cup with his thumb and index finger, like he's at a tea party. He sets it down on the bench between us.
My father was recruited by the CHAIRS.
He looks over at me. I sense that we are about to go somewhere new together.
The mines on Wahmms had shut down and his family was struggling. There weren't jobs. He had no prospects. And then they appeared-
Who?
I don't know why I interrupt at that-there was plenty there in his story already to ask about.
That's a good question. The only thing he ever told me is someone interviewed him at the library.
Ahhhhh, that's it.
That's why I asked.
I'm in this story.

The CHAIRS appeared to me as well.

Out of nowhere.

That's how it felt.

Borns is just getting started.

*And so my father had to leave my mother. My mother
once told me that she was convinced she was unable to
have children. Which I can only imagine was devastating
for them. But now this is where things don't add up-*

Borns leans forward, elbows on his knees.

*She said that when the CHAIRS recruited my father this
was the perfect way for him to leave her. He had an OUT.
And he took it. He left her.*

Borns says this like these events are fresh for him, recent.

*They don't agree, Heen, they don't agree to this day on
exactly what happened. My father left, and then my
mother discovered she was pregnant. That's how she tells
it. She says that he knew and he deserted us. So what did
she do you ask?*

I actually was about to ask that.

*She had me and then she went and found him. SHE
FOUND HIM!!*

Where was he?

On Mil Mer!!!

Isn't that the one with all the active volcanoes?

Yes, you have heard of it?

*I've seen pictures. Only a few people live on that planet,
right?*

My Heen, you know A LOT about the galaxy.

If only he knew.

*The CHAIRS sent your dad to Mil Mer? For his first
assignment?*

*Yes. He was a hearty man, that much is true. I once saw
him lift a cow.*

A cow?
A cow.
A full size cow?
Fuller than full.
That is impressive.
But sending him to Mil Mer? A young man just shy of his
21st lap?
How'd your mother find him? I heard that people who
work for the CHAIRS leave their families and home planets
and all that behind and no one from their previous life
knows where they are...

Look at me. Asking him that question. Like I don't know. I
heard...I say it like it's a rumor, something I picked up
from a distance when it. is. my. life. This kills me just a
little. Pretending. It feels as though I have installed a
paper thin membrane between us. He is unaware of it.

I am.

This didn't used to bother me, this distance between me
and everyone I encounter. I can lie for days on end
without a second thought. I sometimes wonder if I'm the
best SERIES 5 in the universe. I have gotten so good at
this job. But sitting here, listening to Borns tell this story,
some defense within me falters. The border becomes
porous, the boundary collapses just a bit. I'm caught up in
this story that he's telling. It means something to me.
This hasn't happened before.

Borns nods. *Oh yes, that is what my father told me. He left*
it all behind to SERVE the ARRANGEMENTS. That's how
he put it. My mother, she refused to abide by the rules. She

hid in the central compost cistern of her home port-with me in her arms. Then she snuck on a cargo ship, bribed the captain to smuggle her through customs inspection…Heen, I have lived dangerously my entire life.

Borns thinks this is quite clever.

It is.

Your mother was quite a woman.

Oh she was. She once ate a raw potato in one bite.

In one bite?

One bite.

Raw?

Yes. She pulled it out of the ground, spit on it to clean off the dirt, and then jammed it in to her mouth.

He imitates having something large stuck between your upper and lower teeth and then forcing it through by ramming it with the butt of your hand.

YIKES I say.

Yikes is right.

And then she chewed it?

Oh no. It was too big. It filled her mouth. She couldn't move her jaw.

So how did she eat it?

The saliva in her mouth gradually broke it down.

Did that take a while?

Three days.

We sit in silence, mulling over that one.

I can't leave it alone.

To be clear, your mother walked around with an uncooked potato in her mouth for three days?

Three days.

Could she talk?

No. She invented her own sign language and then taught it to me so that we could communicate.

Borns tells me this as he performs a succession of
gestures which I can only imagine is that sign language.
Is that the language she created?
Yes. Impressive, isn't it?
What did you just say?
*I AM NEVER EATING ANOTHER POTATO FOR AS LONG
AS I LIVE.*

Two men in matching purple outfits-one of them wears a
green belt, the other an orange belt-appear at the back
door of the bakery. They glance around nervously, like
they're afraid someone will seem them here.
Borns gives them a thumbs up.
He'll be right out.
Bobby Freelance appears in the doorway, sees we're
sitting on the bench, and motions to the men as he tells
them
Let's walk.
Off they go.

I am locked in on this story Borns is telling.
So your mother made it to Mil Mer?
He stomps both feet as he slaps his knees.
*With baby me in her arms! She showed up at the door of
my dad's hut and when he opened it she said LOOK WHAT
WAS BORN SINCE YOU LEFT.* Borns strokes his beard.
I don't know if that's exactly what happened-
But your name IS Borns.
I say this because it's obvious. Born Since. BornS.
Borns gasps.
My name is Borns.
He looks shocked.
Is that why there's an S? It's for SINCE?

I don't know whether to answer or not. It's seems pretty straightforward. Has he never seen this?

Maybe not I say. *Just a thought.*

He considers this.

It's just…how she was. How they were. There was no love between them by then.

So why did she go to such great lengths to track him down?

I have spent many LAPS pondering that very question, Heen. The best I can come up with? She didn't want him to get away with it. With me. With doing that and then leaving her alone with the responsibility.

I have another question.

What did your dad say when he opened the door?

He said *All right then, I'll have to build another hut.*

An old woman appears in front of us. She's done 80 laps, maybe 90. She's holding a small glass jar. She places her hand on my knee, then on Borns' knee.

Good day gentlemen.

Borns and I both stand up.

Good day to you I say to her.

Who am I? What happened to Heen? Some old lady shows up wearing striped socks and sandals holding a glass jar in an alley behind a bakery and I stand and greet her with a GOOD DAY?

Lan Zing appears.

I didn't hear her coming.

She glides as much as she walks.

Lan Zing is also carrying a glass jar.

She and the woman exchange jars.

There is great love between them. I can feel it.

Lan Zing turns and heads back in to the bakery. She holds up the jar as she passes
Starter.
Borns responds *The gift that keeps on giving.*

Bread is its own kind of language.

We sit back down.
You grew up on Mil Mer?
At some point we should probably get back to work. But not yet.
Yes. I did. My father built my mother and I our own hut. And then when I was five I got my own hut.
Your own hut?
Yes. On the side of a volcano.
With no one around?
Oh my it was quiet. So quiet.
Was it just you and your family?
Yes. No one else for miles. Five days walk to the nearest humans.
What about school?
My mother taught me in the morning, and then in the afternoon I did rounds with my father.
Was it dangerous?
Oh yes, I have been attacked by little chunks of flying lava more times than I can count.
What about wild animals?
I had a pet jaguar for a while. His name was Willie. But goodness, he was a windy one-he stunk up my hut.
You had a gassy pet jaguar named Willie that slept in your room?
My room? In my bed!
It sounds exciting.

Borns strokes his beard some more.

Yes, once in a while. But it was so quiet. And so lonely. And we were always on edge.

Because of the volcanoes?

That. And the chance that someone from the CHAIRS would come through and see that my dad had his family with him. I picked up from an early age that it was not good for me to be around.

That sounds terrible.

That's the best I can do. Tell him it sounds terrible. I shouldn't have said anything.

My dad built a secret compartment in the floor of my hut. I filled it with books he got me when he travelled. That way if I ever had to hide for a while I'd have something to do.

And that was your childhood-

That was my childhood. I was so lonely. Have I already said that? My dad built my mom a hut. Her own hut. So that they wouldn't have to be together. Do you understand? The only two other people in my world couldn't stand each other. That's why I made the vow.

A vow?

I decided that one day I would have a big family and it would be loud!!!

He wiggles his fingers with their red nail polish and does a little dance sitting there next to me.

I even made up a ceremony to mark the occasion. I took large cooled lava rocks and I stacked them in a circle up on a high plane above our huts. It took me nine days. I imagined each pile as one of my children and THEN I MADE A LADY PILE.

He sings these two words LADY PILE in a high falsetto as he stands up and pretends to hold someone close to him.

I stood among those stones and I stretched out my hands

and asked to be surrounded by LOVE for the rest of my life!

His reenactment works for me-I can picture it.

WHO did you ask for this?

I think I'm missing the point here, but I want to know.

Who did I ask? Heen you have the most unusual questions! Who did I ask-MYSELF? THE VOLCANO? MY HEART? WHOEVER or WHATEVER is responsible for such things? He pauses. *What do you think of that answer?*

I think a thousand things. Few of them coherent.

It's a very odd and wonderful answer that is hard for me to understand-

I stop.

Voices waft out the door of the bakery.

Kids' voices.

Lots of them.

Ziga Mey sticks her head out the back door and shouts *BORNS!!!!*

He looks at me, his face glowing.

AS IF ON CUE!!!!

And then he turns and runs inside the bakery.

I follow him in as he is attacked by a swarm of blonde children. They climb on him, they pull his hair, they hang from his arms.

They are large-boned and their cheeks are red and they are chattering and singing and running in every direction. Borns turns to me and smiles like he's going to spontaneously combust as he proclaims

MY PILES OF ROCKS CAME TO LIFE!!!

A woman enters. She's wearing a white Mu-mu with large red flowers all over it. She's got a baby in a pouch and a straw hat on her head. There is something powerful about her, like it's her world and the rest of us are visiting.

Peeble.

I just know it.

She walks up to Borns and kisses him and then slaps his ass-I have never seen anyone do this to anyone in public.

She turns to me.

Heen, right? Borns has told me about you. He tells me you two have traveled across the ages together…

She pauses, rolls her eyes, and then says

He tells everyone that.

She has the gravitational pull of a small planet. I melt.

I wondered about that…

I want her to know I'm in on the joke.

Her face turns serious.

Although Borns…he doesn't lie. Ever. So you know it's true.

*

I tap the white disc.

Like I do every day.

The same white disc Vo gave me all those laps ago.

Yeah, Heen.

That voice. Randy. Ready to go.

I have tapped this disc thousands of times and Randy has answered immediately every single time.

I once asked him *Do you sleep?*

He answered *Sorry, Heen.*

That threw me.

Sorry for what?

Can't give you any of that. Them is the rules.

He says that line *THEM IS THE RULES* with extra twang,

like he's impersonating someone.
You can't tell me if you sleep?
Right. I'm here to take your report. It's nothing personal.
Got it. It's literally nothing personal.
Yep. Just your report.
That was the conversation.

All those thousands of reports, all those hours of talking, and I know nothing about him. My job is to notice, and his job is to listen to what I notice.
Is his real name even Randy?
Is he impersonating a Randy when he listens to my reports?
My job is to pretend, is his as well?
I can't get to him, can't pierce the pretense. Can't get to the person behind THE RANDY.
Is this how I am for everyone I meet?
I begin my report. *Openness.*
Is that even a word?
Excuse me? Randy hesitates.
Open. Free. These people. Here on Firdus. They talk about anything. And everything. Casually. Love. Sex. Flags. Babies. Dead parents-who help them run their business. They get personal the first time they meet you-
Randy stops me. *Heen, is this your report? Because I can't do anything with this...*
A split second of silence.
This is new for Randy and me.
This...glitch.
What is happening with me, going on like that? Rambling.
My reports are always crisp. Factual. Precise.
I recover.
My apologies, wandered a bit there. Won't happen again.

*First up, school jackets. Passed 126 students today
wearing their regulation school jackets. 112 had taken
them off and slung them through the straps of their bags.
Because of temperature, humidity, low wind, observations
indicate the material of the jackets is too thick. I did
several walks in lighter grade merino, cotton twill, and
canvas-cotton was optimal...*
Excellent.
Back on track.
I give him the rest of my report.

*

I finish the page.
I read it again.
And then I read it again.
I put the book down.
I pick it back up and read the page again.
I don't know what to do with this story. This woman Devra
is standing in a row boat in an ocean. She's trying to row
this boat across this ocean with her man who very early in
the journey decides that this sort of thing just isn't for him.
He calls for a rescue ship and when it arrives he gets off
the row boat and onto the rescue ship. And now it's time
for her to get off the row boat and on to the rescue ship
that will tow their row boat back to shore.
But she doesn't.
She sits back down.
And starts rowing.
Away from the rescue ship.
Towards the other side of this ocean called the Atlantic.
Alone.
I read the page again.

She rows alone across that ocean.
Who is this woman?
How does she do this?
I do this every evening.
I file my report, make myself dinner, and then read books
about people who did things on Earth that no one had
ever done before.
It's a strange obsession I have.
Earth.
It's insignificant and primitive and long ago.
Just one planet.
With only seven continents.
And six mountain ranges.
And five oceans.
And one sun.
And one moon.
So small.
That's all they knew.
And yet these people, they did things that astound me.
This woman stands there in that row boat, watching her
man board that rescue ship.
And she doesn't follow him.
She sits back down and keeps rowing.
What is going through her mind?
What is happening in her heart?
How is she able to do this?
Who is this woman?

*

I walk to work in the dark.
It's always dark, all over the galaxy, when you walk to your
job in a bakery.

Bobby Freelance is on the bench in the alley. He's sitting between a man and a woman who are wearing very nice clothes for this early in the morning. They are speaking intensely to each other in hushed tones, their faces leaning in. Bobby Freelance has his head down, listening intently.

Bobby Freelance stops the man.

He points to the woman, motioning for her to continue.

She does.

The man interrupts her.

Bobby Freelance gives him a death stare.

The man stops talking.

The woman continues.

The man listens to her.

I come in through the back. Lan Zing is standing alone in the middle of the empty tables where people in a few hours will be sitting while they eat their bread and drink their coffee.

Heen, are those tables in the right place?

She points to the three along the wall.

I understand now what she meant in the interview about this being her life. This is what she's thinking about in the dark before any of us arrive?

They're just tables.

How can I help?

She points to the door.

Will you please stand in the doorway?

I take my place in the doorway.

She sits down at one of the tables.

Imagine you're meeting me here and you've just arrived and opened the door-

Ohhhh. I stand here and I look at her. She wants me to

see her.

Here it is again.

The possibility.

I have done this. Gone with it. There was one woman what was it-nine planets ago? We got on like a house fire.

She worked at a school across the path from the bakery. I would bring bread over to her house and she'd say she wasn't usually like this but it must have been something about the bread because we had so much sex. It was all so strange. And kind of awesome.

That's literally all I remember from that planet. Bread and sex. It took me three planets to recover. But even then, lost in that-at any moment I knew that I would be leaving. And I wouldn't be able to tell her. It was so intoxicating that I often almost forgot.

Almost.

But it's always there.

The truth that never leaves me.

Same with all the other women on all the other planets.

There was one, on Blunes-her name was Veskimets-she was brilliant. Just blew my mind. Architecture. Rocks. Earth. The beautiful game. It was astonishing how much she knew about everything. I just wanted her to keep talking. All those women and planets and pleasure and then leaving and loneliness.

What a jumbled mess in my heart, in my memory.

And now, Lan Zing.

Maybe this becomes a thing.

But even here,

before,

standing in this doorway seeing her seeing me,

I can't do it.

I used to be able to.

But now I can't.

I walk towards her.

How about we switch places-you stand in the doorway and I sit here?

She stands up.

Because that's what you're going for-right? Someone shows up here and they instantly feel comfortable? At home? Like this is their bakery? Like they can't believe they didn't know about this place until now?

She loves this.

Yes, exactly!

I keep going.

You want them to feel like there's something familiar in this new place-like they're returning to it for the first time.

I have struck a nerve.

Heen, I couldn't have said it better myself.

I'm on a roll.

That's the thing about spaces-they call to us and speak to us in ways our minds don't always pick up on. Let me try something here…

I take the middle table and turn it sideways.

What do you think?

She shakes her head.

No, no-that's not it.

I have no idea what I'm doing. I keep going.

Well then, how about this?

I turn all three at angles to the wall, pulling the middle out farther and putting two of the chairs on the ends.

She claps.

Wow! That is so much better-and I don't even know why!

I motion for her to sit down in the middle chair at the first table.

Notice where your eyes go.
She looks around.
To the ovens.
This bothers her.
I sit down across from her.
They do, don't they? Your eyes are drawn to the ovens.
She's confused. *But why do I like this arrangement? I don't want my customers staring at the ovens.*
Well…
I lean back in my chair, like I have been considering this for laps. *I wonder if it has something to do with your parents.*
Where did that come from?
She leans forward. *Go on…*
Were they more formal than you are?
If only you knew! My mother slept in a silk dress because that's what proper ladies do she told me. Proper ladies!!
Yeah, that's kind of formal. So someone back there bakes the bread-
I gesture to the back
And then it magically appears in front of you here-at your table…
She nods. *Oh that is exactly how they saw it. The employees are invisible. The work of it. The mechanics. The ovens. All of that isn't to be acknowledged. My father once put up a large wood divider so you couldn't see the bakers.*
Of course he did. And what happened to it?
It caught on fire.
Lan Zing has tucked her feet under her like she did in our interview. She is quite lovely. *He was so embarrassed!!! He talked about it endlessly. Like he'd brought shame on us all.*

I realize now that he was trying to hide the actual making of the bread-
I interrupt her. *Which is why you come to a bakery.*
I say it like it's obvious.
People want to see other people bake bread?
Her question has an innocence to it.
Yes. They do. You can understand the entire process and it's still magic. It's a wonderful sort of alchemy that we return to again and again. That's why people come to a bakery.
You're an unusual one, Heen.
Oh no. Here it comes. The awkward part where I have to backpedal and let her down slowly. She goes on.
You say very simple things. Obvious, even. But you say them like no one has ever said them. Like you've just stumbled into it and you're making it up as you go along.

I feel that familiar heat building in the base of my spine. A survival instinct. A fear that she's on to me. I have honed this sense since that first job on Ziks. Danger. I change course.
Awwww, I'm just telling you what you already know. Let them see the ovens! Let them watch us do what we do! Let's turn all the tables. Think of it as one big room, and some people are baking over there and some people are eating over here and we're all together-
She stands up.
Got it.
She starts moving the table behind her.
I appear to be the last thing on her mind.
Did I totally misread her?
I help move the tables.
Back to business.

I'm so relieved.

*

Suddenly, he's there.
On my right.
He appears out of thin air, strolling in step with me as I walk
back to my flat after work.
Like we know each other.
Like we're friends.
Piddle, piddle, piddle.
He mutters it under his breath, to no one in particular. Are
those words? Is that a stutter? Does he have some sort of
condition?
He repeats it.
Piddle, piddle, piddle.
I don't know where he came from.
I've never seen him before.
He's shorter than I am. And I am not very tall. And thicker.
Stockier. *Solider.* He has an unusually long thorax. Is that
what it's called-the area from above your thighs to below
your ribs? His hair is short in the front and long in the back.
Like he was getting his hair cut and half way through got up
and walked out.

And he's wearing brown.
Lots of brown. He's drowning in brown. A long brown linen
shirt, matching pants. A brown bag over his right shoulder.
Around his neck is a thick rope necklace with a green stone
set in a silver circle.
I clear my throat.
Excuse me?
He gives me a sideways glance.

It's a fusty run of giblets but the suns have done some good cookin', yes or yes?

His words come out in staccato-like bursts, the cadence off kilter. There's something expectant in his eyes, as if I'll know what to do with that.

SUNS-THE SUNS? Fusty what-gibler…What-what are you saying?

He gently touches his cheek as he pauses in the middle of the path.

It's a marvel, innit? How the SUNS light our faces?

He tilts his head back and closes his eyes.

All that radiant energy endlessly pouring down upon us from millions and billions of miles away, traversing that spectral distance with spectacular ease, all so we can sparkle with unceasing incandescence…

His eyes glaze over as he stares off into the distance. He snaps out of it and returns to my side.

Thick biscuits, that. Off we go, muncher.

He motions for us to continue walking.

I do. We do.

He's right beside me.

Way too close.

I need to take control here. I back away a bit.

I'm Heen Gru-Bares. What's your name?

I say it slowly and clearly, projecting calm and order. I'll run things from here.

You did???

He's thrilled by this.

I did what?

How big did they get?

Did WHAT get?

I have no idea what he thought he heard me say.

The bears?!! How big did they get?

WHAT BEARS!? I shout this. A woman in a doorway glares at me. Now I'm embarrassed. This man has managed to burrow his way under my skin in an impressively brief amount of time.
You said HE GREW BEARS.
It clicks.
No. No. No. There were-there are NO BEARS INVOLVED. I was introducing myself. Like people do. I told you my name: Heen Gru-Bares.
I say it like he's hard of hearing. He tilts his head. As if there's something unnatural about this.
A name is a sentence?
My teeth clench.
My name is my name. I don't know what about that isn't clear.
He starts drawing with his finger in the air in front of his face.
Heen is the SUBJECT, grew the VERB, bears the DIRECT OBJECT. What did Heen do? Heen grew!! Who grew? Heen grew!! And so now we know!!! What did Heen grow? I know! He grew bears!! Is it true? Who knew Heen grew??? Who knew it's true what he grew-You??

He says this in a soft sing-song voice. Like he's talking to a small child. Or himself. Is he messing with me? Maybe he's brilliant and this is some new street performance art he does with strangers. Or he could be disturbed and shouldn't be wandering the paths unsupervised.
What did they eat? He asks me. He is relentless.
NO. Once more: NO. No bears, no animals! Nothing ate nothing or anything. No mammals were hungry. My FIRST name is Heen.
He's expressionless.

194

Spell he says. He appears to be concentrating with all his might.

H-E-E-N. Heen.

He says my name out loud. With the expression of someone trying an exotic food for the first time. He says it again. He surveys me with what I can only describe as… pride.

Are you the first Heen on Firdus?

I have no idea.

How would I know? I ask him.

He seems pleased. *Well then let's just assume. Which makes this a rather momentous occasion. The first and only Heen on Firdus.*

He pats his stomach.

I forge ahead.

And then my last name is…Gru-Bares. My last name. G-R-U. And then a dash-

He gestures for me to stop as he puts his hand on my arm. He's alarmed.

Why a dash? What was wrong that a dash was required? Why this needless division?

I suddenly realize that my hands are clenched into fists.

I summon a slightly over-exaggerated inhale in an attempt to gather myself.

B-A-R-E-S. Heen Gru-Bares. It doesn't come from anywhere. It doesn't mean anything. It's not a sentence. Nothing interesting or noteworthy is happening in my name. It's just a name.

He watches me patiently, like I'm the one who's been struggling and now I'm gradually beginning to make my way out of the fog.

I stop. *What's your name?*

He brings his hands together, the palm of one on the back

of the other, and places them on his heart.
Dill Tudd.
And then he turns and walks away.

*

Laundry I say.
Laundry? Randy asks.
Yes. They don't lay it flat on the roof, like every single other planet I've ever been to. They hang it on ropes that they run across the fronts of their houses. So when you walk by you can see people's clothes. Out in the open. Socks. Shirts. Underwear. Just blowing in the wind. Quite shocking, actually. I don't need to see that.
I catch myself.
What was that?
Giving a personal opinion.
Not reporting the facts.
A twitch. A need. A lean in. Some desire to connect.
Heen…?
Yeah, sorry, delete that last bit, don't know what that was.
I collect myself.
Anything else on the laundry?
I have nothing else on the laundry.
That's it.
I move quickly.
And then baseboards. A slight staining effect is present on the majority of homes, particularly in CIRCLE 8, about a foot off the ground, on the path facing side. Paths are standard decomposed granite-staining appears to be backsplash from rains. I tested the DG. Iron levels are two clicks too high. Water from the run off appears to be draining through a metallic channel somewhere a hundred

or so paces north.
That it?
Yep, that's it.
Randy clicks off.
I sit here, staring at that disc.
I'm trembling. My face feels flush.
Mild panic.
What is this? What was that?
The worst report. Ever.
Clearly.
What is it about Firdus?
Lan Zing asks me about my favorite bread.
Borns tells me about his hut and his piles of rocks and his
vow.
Peeble.
That guy Dill Tudd.
Walking along like we know each other.
I have been everywhere.
I have seen everything.
But this.
Firdus.
This is new.
Unnerving.

*

Break.
I make myself a coffee and head to the bench.
I see Ziga Mey at the end of the trail. She's talking to a
man.
Phileep?
Is that Phileep with the flag?
She reaches into her pocket and pulls out a square of cloth.

She wipes her eyes.
I look away.
Whatever that is, it isn't for me to see.
I look back at them. I can't help it.
The man isn't smiling.
He is cold. He holds an envelope in his hand.
She keeps pointing to the envelope.
Whatever it is she wants him to see, he is not seeing it.
He throws up his hands and leaves.
She stands there, collecting herself.
She turns towards the bakery.
I look down at the ground.
She walks by.
Hi Heen.
Hi Ziga Mey.

*

Borns and I are folding dough for the brioche.
He leans over and asks me
Heen, do you know what a pirate is?
From earth, right? They sailed on ships and searched for treasure-
Yes, yes, pirates. We are all pirates, yes?
Yes, Borns, we are all pirates.
He is very happy with this.
Excellent. So this pirate walks into a bar with a steering wheel on the front of his pants-
Wait. Is this a true story?
You shall see.
It's a joke?
I really want to know what this is. He waves my question away.

The bartender sees this steering wheel on the front of his pants and says to him HEY THERE FELLA, YOU'VE GOT A STEERING WHEEL ON THE FRONT OF YOUR PANTS!! And the pirate says AAARRRGGGH AND IT'S DRIVING ME NUTS!!!

I don't know how to respond to this.

Borns looks crestfallen.

You don't think that's funny?

It's a joke?

A part of me wants to laugh just so I don't have to see him so disappointed.

Lan Zing enters.

Do you get it?

I give her a blank look.

Do you get the joke?

I realize I don't.

I'm sorry Borns, I don't understand.

Then I will try again. He loosens up his shoulders, does a stretch with his legs.

AAAAAARGH AND IT'S DRIVING ME NUTS.

He includes hand motions this time.

I get it. I laugh.

Ziga Mey turns around from the oven. *I didn't get it either the first time I heard it.*

I laugh some more.

Borns, how many times have you told that joke?

Bobby Freelance appears in the doorway and says

Everybody. And then he returns to the storage room.

You tell that joke to everybody?

I do Heen. It is the best joke in the universe. It is perfection. It is also the only joke I know.

Where did you hear it?

My mother.

Before or after the potato?
He likes that one.
That's good. After. It's the last thing she said.
Hold on.
It's the last thing she said in her life?
Yes.
She told that joke before she died?
Yes. She said the word NUTS with her last breath. And then she closed her eyes and that was it.

*

He does it again.
He appears out of nowhere.
Walking next to me.
Only this time he's wearing white.
All white.
His bag is even white.
Does he make his own clothes?
Because I don't know where you'd find clothes like those.
Same necklace, though.
Piddle, piddle, piddle.
His usual greeting.
This time I'm ready for him.
Looks like a Dill Tudd White Out today!
It doesn't sound as clever when I say it as it sounded in my head.
He cocks his head.
There is the white, and then there is the absence of the white-and Dill Tudd is present in all of it.
He's doing it again. Right out of the gate. Jabbering on about who knows what. I can't tell if he's trying to be funny. Or he's…off…not right in the head…

You're present in all of it?
I try to say it like it's dumbest thing a person could say so that he'll admit he's messing with me.
The boundary doesn't divide, it connects. If everyone understood this WE COULD FLY.

I think to myself *I actually do fly.*
But I have held my tongue for years on these sorts of things. I double down.

Can you explain more, Dill Tudd?
I don't know why I use his full name-because he does?
I'd be honored.
He says this as though he's been waiting for me to say it.
Think about color. There is black. And then there is white. Black is not white, white is not black.
He pauses, waiting. For I don't know what. He nods like I should say something.
Okaaaayyyy...I'm with you.
Now Heen Gru-Bares-close your eyes and imagine white without black.
I stare, dumbfounded, at this odd little squat man. Have I known him forever? This is our second encounter, and yet we pick up right where we left off. Scattershot back and forth, effortless. Nonsense, but it's effortless. I have never experienced a familiarity like this. It's terribly unnerving.
He snaps his fingers in my face.
Heen Gru-Bares! We are sailing very close to the wind here. Close your eyes like a good man.
Might as well. I close my eyes and try to imagine white without black. I can't, strangely enough.
Now, try black without white.
I do. And I can't.

One is not the other, the other is not the one. And yet they need each other. Black makes white possible. White makes black possible. The line between them, the border and boundary that determines THIS IS NOT THAT is also the connection between these two that depend on each other for their existence. The division is the connection. They are two, but they are one.

Is that a speech? A lecture? I kind of get it. I suspect that what he just said is quite insightful, but I also think he's crazy.

Well, that's an interesting thought exercise…something for me to ponder.

He shakes his head vigorously.

NOT A THOUGHT EXERCISE!!! FACTS.

He says it like I'm a slow student but I try so he'll give me points for effort.

Nothing to ponder!!! He's emphatic. *You see or you don't. Same with SAD Heen Gru-Bares.*

Some little alarm goes off deep in my bones. I stop in the middle of the trail.

What did you say?

Same with sad. You and YOUR SADNESS. How can you have happy if there is no sad?

That's a good point. I say this casually, trying to show him how none of this chatter means anything to me.

NOT A POINT, Sir Heen Gru-Bares, NOT A POINT!! An experience of the fullness of life. It is the wholeness in which we have our being.

I am tempted to take off running as fast as I can to get away from this annoying creature who speaks to something so deep within me that it has no shape or form or even words. I am trembling and I don't know why.

He places his hand on my shoulder.

I let him.

Same with lonely. Same with grieving.

I am rattled. I exhale.

Same how?

That's the thing with people who think they're smart. You take what they're going on about, you summarize it and then give it right back to them in a short, blunt sentence-a question is even better-and it usually stops them because you've demonstrated that you're several steps ahead. Dill Tudd will have none of it.

All are needed. Without one, there is NO other. We often run from the one, do we not?

He tilts his head in his Dill Tudd way.

They need each other Heen Gru-Bares.

I stammer.

I kind of got that.

Anything to end this and get away from him. He brings his palms together so that his fingers are touching.

They all need each other. It all needs itself.

He hikes up his pants.

I leave you now, although we are always present to each other are we not?

He gives me a slight bow and then walks away, down the trail between two large trees.

I watch him go.

There is a woman sitting under one of the trees, leaning back against the trunk. She has two small children with her. One of them is scratching at the trunk of the tree, trying to carve something in it with a stick, the other is rolling back and forth on a blanket next to her feet.

Dill Tudd walks up to her, stoops down, and hands her something from his bag. I can't tell what it is. And I can't hear what he says to her. She smiles as she receives it, placing her hand on her heart. He does that slight bow thing he just did with me, and then keeps walking down the trail.

*

I tap the disc.
All right Heen.
I get right to it.
Mil Mer.
Mil Mer?
Yeah, Mil Mer. There's a guy I work with at the bakery who grew up there.
Who?
Borns.
Borns?
Borns.
With an S?
With an S. Because that's what his mom said to his dad when she found him-
Found who?
The dad of the guy from the bakery. And there was a secret compartment in the floor-
Of the bakery?
Of his hut! Incredible. Right? So the CHAIRS wouldn't know he was there-
Wouldn't know WHO was WHERE?
Him in the hut on the side of the volcano!! And he filled it with books and he made a vow-
Stop. Heen. Irritation in Randy's voice. *You were talking about the CHAIRS with someone on Firdus?*
No, no. He brought it up. It's a whole thing because of the rule about families...he brought up the CHAIRS. He

mentioned it, but just like for a second…
I've said too much.
This isn't good.
Heen, slow down. This is your report?
Yeah, sorry Randy. I don't know what that was-I just have the guy fresh in my head-
You talked about the CHAIRS with him?
No, no, no-sorry, I wasn't clear there.
What does this have to do with Firdus?
Just giving you a sense of these people.
The people on Firdus?
Yeah, they're just…different…
I can't do anything with that, Heen.
Got it. My apologies, won't happen again.
I switch gears.
Fast.
The guy who delivers the olives brought five pounds today instead of the usual ten-he said that his crops took a hit from the last storm. I asked what he meant by a hit, he went on a long one about the aqueduct in CIRCLE 4 that wasn't angled properly-according to him-he said a group of local growers had been meeting and were about to bring it to the CENTER-he was pretty heated up about it. He said that eleven degrees is too steep, it needs to be eight point five, maybe nine.
Got it. His name?
I give Randy his name. I tell him about the woman who tried to buy three loaves but only had money for two. I give him a detailed description of the two dogs I saw running through the CENTER that didn't appear to belong to anyone. I give him lots of details, lots of descriptions, lots of facts…

*

I can't sleep.
And I can always sleep.
It's never a problem.
But tonight, I am wide awake.
Dill Tudd.
That moment when he said the word *sad*.
Do I appear sad?
Why did he say that?
And *grief*.
He said that as well.
About me.
It haunts me.
He haunts me.
The presumed familiarity. All those obtuse sentences like
he's some wizard or poet or philosopher. Putting his hand
on my shoulder like I'm lost and he's showing me how to
find my way home.
Just so irritating.
And that nonsense about color and boundaries.
That which divides connects.
That's what's keeping me up?
I'm losing sleep over *him*?

*

I place a fresh basket of baguettes on the counter. A
woman in a green coat with frizzy red hair is leaning over
the counter, venting with great intensity to Lan Zing,
telling her that from now on she'll be coming to our
bakery because the owner of the bakery in CIRCLE 8 is a
horrible, wretched man. She shakes her head as she says

it, jabbing the air on those words HORRIBLE and
WRETCHED.
I note this.

*

Borns and I are doing a second round of folding for the
whole grain loaves. Ziga Mey joins us.
Borns turns to her. *You know I love to ask about Phileep…*
She looks down. *He's fine.*
Clipped. Terse.
Borns will have none of it.
Ziga Mey how dare you pretend with me!
She looks at me. I raise my eyebrows. *Borns will keep
asking, you know this.*
She drops her dough.
He is not fine. I am not fine. We are not fine.
She's trying to hold it together.
It's very hard to watch.
Bobby Freelance comes through on his way to the ovens.
FLOOR CHECK?
That's all he says.
She nods.
Wait. I missed something.
Borns' eyes get big.
A FLOOR CHECK is a beautiful thing, is it not?
Ziga Mey disagrees. *It is not.*
A flicker of ache.
We're quiet.
She continues. *It's only beautiful if you agree on how to
spend it.*
Ohhhhhh… Borns gets it. *Now I see. You have plans for
the money?*

We do. I do…I did. Bitterness.

You want to use it to start a family and he does not?

Borns presses on.

Ziga Mey, I have a question for you. Can I ask it?

How does one resist Borns?

Okay she says.

Has Phileep died yet?

What an odd question.

I just saw him the other day I say. Trying to be helpful.

She squints. *I don't know what you mean.*

He lost her. And me.

Borns looks at me and then Bobby and then Ziga Mey,
like he's about to share a secret.

*A man has to die to all the COULD BEs-all those options,
all those possibilities, all the places he could go and the
things he could do. Phileep likes to keep his options open,
doesn't he?*

A look of recognition.

*Yes! Exactly. He keeps saying he doesn't want our lives to
be over if we have a baby.*

Borns laughs.

*I do not mean to laugh at Phileep's expense, but he still
thinks the adventure is elsewhere.*

Where? I ask.

I do not know why I ask this question. This is exactly the
kind of drama that I avoid. Always. I stand at a distance,
even if I'm standing near.

I do not participate.

But this.

I feel a slow and resolute pull, much how the sea must
feel about the tide.

WHERE is a good question, Heen.

Borns pats my arm.

But there is a better question, and it is a question for Ziga Mey.

He takes a deep breath, like he's gearing up for something monumental. *Ziga Mey, are you prepared to wait around for Phileep to die?*

She stares off into the distance.

I still don't understand what you mean by dying…

I interject. *I don't either.* Again, I'm unable to keep my thoughts to myself.

Borns spreads out his arms as far as he can reach.

LOVE must be incarnated in space and time.

He brings his hands together until they're almost touching.

And to do that, LOVE must empty itself of its infinite, boundless formlessness in order to be present in bodies, between people. You feel this, Ziga Mey, do you not?

He doesn't wait for her to answer.

You want to give yourself to him. This moment, this place, this time, to future little Zigas and Phileeps. You want the limits. Because in them, in these people we choose to love, is THE LIMITLESS VASTNESS OF THE UNIVERSE. We die to everything else we could do and everywhere else we could be in order TO LOVE the ones we're with here and now. It is the death of all those other futures that makes the present the world-opening wondrous gift that it is. Heartbreaking, and maddening, but wondrous.

He raises his fist above his head like he's just scored a goal.

I realize in this moment that I have a filter. A REPORT FILTER. Everything I hear and see and experience-I run it

through this REPORT FILTER. This CHAIRS FILTER. This RANDY FILTER. Should I tell Randy this? Does that go in my report? Would this help the CHAIRS? It's been this way for so many laps-and I'm so good at it, too good at it-that it's become like a pair of glasses I'm wearing that I never take off...
I notice.
And then I pass it along.

But this table. These people. Ziga Mey's ache. Borns going on about love and bodies and limits-nothing happening around this table can go in my report. It's true, and it involves facts, but it's not THOSE kinds of facts. It's not THAT kind of true. Randy doesn't care. The CHAIRS don't care. None of this is about the ARRANGEMENTS. And yet.
Borns, where did you learn all this?
I had to ask.
He wipes his hands on his apron.
I read a lot of books in my hut.

*

I take a GLIDE through to the CENTER of CIRCLE 5, then 6, then 7. It's mostly flat, with lots of trees. I cross three rivers. I arrive at the CENTER of 8.
I find the bakery.
LOAF.
That's actually a great name for a bakery.
I find a seat at a table in the corner.
I watch people coming and going.
A man appears from the back.
He wipes down a few tables.

He rearranges the display.
He straightens a chair.
He is coiled. Tense.
A girl comes in and orders.
He does not make eye contact with her.
He tosses her bread in a bag.
Drops it on the counter between them.
There are two others working. A man and a woman.
They both give him lots of space.
There's a low grade dark buzz about him.
His eyes.
Like he believes he's been wronged and he's just waiting
to even the score.
A word comes to mind.
Menace.
That's the right word for it.
I am not surprised that I heard about him all the way back
at our bakery from that woman in the green coat with the
frizzy hair.

These kinds of energies tend to ripple outwards in
concentric circles, traveling great lengths on the sheer
unsettling force of their jagged power.

A noise behind me.
A hand on my shoulder.
Piddle, piddle, piddle.
I know this voice.
Dill Tudd.
Noticing, a lost art.
He says this as he sits down across from me.
I'm surprised to see him. And not surprised.
Sometimes words, sometimes not. Silence is often the

best way to describe something, is it not?

Dill Tudd is wearing blue today. All blue. Sky blue. With faint swirls in the fabric. Like he had clouds for breakfast and spilled some on his shirt.

He sets his bag on the chair beside him. The woman places a small loaf on a plate in front of him.

Enjoy she says.

Thank you Freela. Dill Tudd beams. *Is there anything better?*

He gestures to the bread in front of him.

I still haven't said anything.

I know-you're wondering what kind of bread this is, are you not Heen Gru-Bares?

He pauses for effect. I know he's going to keep talking.

It's GHOST bread.

He stretches out the word GHOST like he's frightened.

It's off menu of course. Bread WITH GHOST PEPPERS. And a few serranos. And two feisty jalapeños. And a pugnacious, gimpy little chipotle, just to keep things festive.

He pulls off a piece and offers it to me.

I take it and put it on my plate.

He pulls off a piece for himself and takes a bite.

He closes his eyes. He sways back and forth. He is lost in his own world of GHOST BREAD. He opens his eyes and says *The universe in a loaf!!!*

He leans across the table, like we share a secret.

Of course I have to bring them the peppers. And Freela there bakes it for me ON THE DOWN LOW. The masses aren't prepared for this sort of oven-baked alchemy. ONLY ONE LOAF OF THIS EXISTS IN ALL THE WORLDS AND IT WILL SOON BE GONE!

He takes another bite.

I still haven't said anything.
AND IT GREW OUT OF THE SOIL!!!
He says this like it's just occurring to him. Like someone is
arguing a case, trying to convince him it's true and he's
just coming to terms with it.
Flour. Some water. Yeast. And of course PEPPERS.
Available to all. This is the set up??!! What a situation!
Something grows up out of the ground, something else
comes flowing down the side of the mountain, and you
mix them together in a bowl and then heat it in an oven
and then THIS????
He points to the loaf between us.
THIS!???
He leans close to the loaf.
THIS???

Like the bread is a question. About the galaxy. About
existence itself.

He takes another bite.
You're talking differently today.
That's what I say. It strikes me as I say this that Dill Tudd
may think I am not very intelligent.
Well, it is a blue day.
His says this with a certain nonchalance, resting his arm
on the chair beside him.
A blue day?
Yes, I'm wearing blue today. This is the program. Is that not
abundantly clear?
He points to his shirt.
The sky is blue, water is often blue-we can all agree on
that. Blue is calm, clear. Blue has no agenda. Blue has no
angle. Blue is not trying to sell you anything. Blue walks into

a bakery, looks around, and says HEY IT SMELLS GREAT
IN HERE, I THINK I'LL HAVE SOME BREAD.
I laugh out loud at this.
He smiles. *That's good, isn't it?*
I agree. *It's so dumb-BLUE walks in to a bakery?-and yet*
kind of awesome. What is that?
What?
For once, Dill Tudd doesn't go off into the deep weeds.
He simply asks *What?*
I lean forward.
That-that thing you do when you talk-THE WAY you talk.
Sometimes I think we're having a conversation and other
times it appears as though you're talking to yourself and
most of the time I'm completely lost and cannot follow
what you're saying for the life of me and other times I feel
like I'm watching you perform-that riff about the color
blue!!!??? What was that? You talked about the color blue
LIKE IT HAS A PERSONALITY-LIKE IT'S HUMAN! That's
not how people talk!!!
I do.
You DO what?
I talk like that. Like this.
I don't interact with anyone like this. Dill Tudd gets under
my skin-and yet under my skin is where I ACTUALLY AM.
I'm repulsed, and I'm riveted. At the same time.
AHHHHHHH. Dill Tudd lets out a relaxed sigh, like we're
finally getting somewhere. *We contain multitudes, don't we?*
Of course he'd say something like that.
I hold up my bread.
My first GHOST bread.
I taste it.
This is what I imagine it would feel like to bite down on a
thousand sewing needles. I would like a bigger skull.

Anything to relieve this pressure. DEAR GODS my mouth.
I can't feel anything because I can feel everything. Flames
on my tongue, in my brain.

I gasp.

Water, please, now.

Dill Tudd just sits and watches me, quite pleased with
himself.

Freela appears. She's holding a plate. On the plate is a
slice of white bread. She places it in front of me.

Here she says. *This will absorb the heat. Water makes it
worse.*

I put the entire slice in my mouth.

Dill Tudd looks so happy.

*Funny to watch, Heen Gru-Bares. Because your mind
wants water, YES?*

I nod.

*Your mind is not thinking MORE BREAD PLEASE right
now, your mind thinks LESS BREAD I'M BEING
ATTACKED BY BREAD HOW CAN I RUN AWAY FROM
BREAD? And yet. MORE BREAD IS WHERE THE RELIEF
IS.*

It works.

Slowly.

But it does work.

I didn't know this.

White bread absorbs heat?

I wipe a tear from my cheek.

Dill Tudd leans in.

Heen Gru-Bares, do you know what tears do?

I got this. For once, I'm a step ahead. *Yes, Dill Tudd. I do
know what tears do. They speak to me.*

He wasn't expecting that. I'm quite proud of myself. I
have sunk to such a new low that catching this odd man

off guard thrills me.
And what do they say to you Heen Gru-Bares?
They tell me not to eat your bread.
He's delighted with this.
*Oh Heen Gru-Bares, I thoroughly enjoyed that one. Can
you name anything else that your tears do?*
He is just so relentless.
I give up. *What else do my tears do?*
Dill Tudd reaches for his bag, puts it over his shoulder,
stands up, and says to me *They water the ground at your
feet so that new things can grow.*
And then he walks out of the bakery.

I ask Freela for another slice of white.

*

I tap the disc.
For the first time ever I have written out my report. Word
for word. I need Randy to know that I am back to my
usual precise and articulate self. I read to him facts about
the speed of the GLIDES and the buildings in CIRCLE 5
and the park in CIRCLE 6 that clearly needs a few trees
trimmed and the river in CIRCLE 2 that doesn't have
enough benches along the south bank-I am in peak form.
I finish by telling him about the owner of the bakery in
CIRCLE 8. I describe the way his employees avoid him. I
mention his menace.

*

Once my dad and I were walking home from the market
and I was wearing this fuzzy, floppy striped hat that he

had bought me. He looked over at me and said
My brother used to have a hat just like that.
He didn't ever talk about his brother.
I asked him *How come Uncle Dir hasn't come to see us in a while?*
He thought about it.
It has been a long time, hasn't it?
That was the last we ever spoke of Uncle Dir.

*

Ziga Mey and I are scoring the olive rolls.
We each have a knife.
I'm adding a touch of sea salt.
She asks me, without looking up *Heen, are you close to your mother?*
I have had a thousand choices like this over the laps.
To reveal or conceal. To be this pretend Heen, the one they know, or the actual Heen.
She hit her head when I was young.
I go with Actual Heen.
Oh no, in an accident?
We were playing Forky.
I used to love that game.
I did, too.
She hit her head?
Yeah, on the table.
Ohhhh, she slammed too hard?
Exactly. But we didn't know at first-me and my dad. She seemed fine. Then she appeared to be a little dizzy. And then she started repeating herself-and then asking these questions that made no sense. She was really disoriented. So was I.

I can only imagine-how is she now?

That's enough.
I have told Ziga Mey enough.
Time to bail on this line of questioning.

She's doing okay-How about you? Are you close to your
mother?
I realize in this moment that Ziga Mey asked me about my
mother so that she could talk about hers. All that I just
disclosed was for something else. I see it in her shoulders,
in her breath, the visible relief that comes over her.
I never knew her. She died giving birth.
To you?
To me.
I am not good at these sorts of things.
Oh.
That's what I say. Oh.
I say it like I care, like I feel it. Because I do.
But still. Oh.

I am a blunt instrument.

CIRCLE 4 had just been built. The THRIVAL was barely up
and running, so they didn't have what they needed to help
her. That's what my dad said. But he also blamed me.
Wait-you? Your dad blamed-
Yes. As a kid you feel your way into knowing things, right?
You sense something-and then later you find out why. One
day he erupted and actually said it-we were sitting at
dinner, me and him, and I had burned the meal. Just a
little. But something about that set him off.
Ziga Mey holds up her knife like a pointer and lowers her

voice *Not a day goes by that I don't think about the day you took her from me.*
Back to her normal voice.
That's what he said.
A tightness in my chest.
Devastating I say.
I set the bowl of salt down on the table.
It was. It still is she says.

Like a magnetic pull that is impervious to my resistance, I feel myself getting sucked in to this story. A part of me wants a way out, a distraction, an exit. But I can't find it. I speak.
Phileep.
She eyes me expectantly. *Phileep?*
I go on. *He doesn't get this-your mother questions.*
Mother questions?
Yeah. Mothers are fascinating, aren't they? You missed all that. I kinda did, too, now that I think about it.
She slowly nods. *I didn't have one, so I want to be one.*
A look of recognition.
It's so complicated-and it's also so simple, isn't it?
I don't really know what I'm referring to.
That's quite profound, Heen.

*

I wake up.
Middle of the night.
I was having a dream.
I don't dream.
But that was a dream.
I was hiking.

Somewhere on Lunlay.

I knew the terrain, but it was scrambled, distorted.

Stones made of rubber. The air was slippery, but it wasn't raining.

Familiar, but unfamiliar.

There was someone up ahead.

A boy.

Walking slowly.

I caught up to him.

He turns to face me.

I recognize him, but I can't place him.

He's carrying a dog.

I've seen the dog before as well.

But where?

He's saying something to me, this boy on the mountain.

I can't make it out.

Something about the dog.

He looks down at the dog.

It disappears.

Right out of his hands.

He looks at me.

You saw that, right?

I did.

It was here, and then it wasn't here, right?

He's frantic. There is a need in his question, to know that I saw what he saw.

I did. I saw it. You were holding a dog, and then it disappeared.

I thought I was going crazy.

This brings him great relief.

BABAK!

I yell it.

He nods.

Yes. I am Babak.
Babak Aspar, Pabbi Apsar's brother! The kid who could
cry on command. You're his brother. We met-
When you and your friend came to our house.
He remembers me. And Nord.
Yes. And then you went away...
It's returning, this event, in bits and pieces. The graffiti on
the library. CHUBBS WHO LOVES CHEESE. The dog.
It's coming back to me in the dream at the same time the
dream is coming back to me sitting up in bed in the
middle of the night. I'm remembering the remembering.
There's a question I had for him.
In the dream.
I kept trying to ask it but my mouth wouldn't move.
I finally get it out.
Babak, where did you go?

*

I have a thought, as I walk to the bakery.
In the dark.
It's a new thought.
A thought I am not allowed to have.
It's also quite random.
I push it down.
It comes back up. With more force.
Like when you hold a ball underwater.
It's also quite random.
This is not what I was taught. I was taught that the
CHAIRS take the DATA and the FACTS and the
EVIDENCE and they make the proper adjustments to the
ARRANGEMENTS so that everyone can thrive.
That's how the universe works.

Complex, of course.

But also quite simple.

Elegant, even.

This thought is like a mosquito in the dark.

It's also quite random.

I swat and swat but can't seem to kill it.

I keep looping on that moment when that woman was talking about the owner of that bakery in CIRCLE 8 and she jabbed the air on those words HORRIBLE and WRETCHED.

I heard that.

I overheard that.

And then I followed it up.

And noticed that man.

And then reported it.

There are lots of things to overhear.

I overheard that.

Because I was setting that basket down on the counter.

Because those baguettes were ready to be put out.

Because we had trouble getting the rye dough right and so we baked those baguettes first.

Randy got the report he got-the CHAIRS got the report they got-because I heard that.

And chose to note it.

And decided to follow up on it.

And then reported it.

That is the DATA.

The DATA the CHAIRS use to shape how we live.

They decide.

But I decide first.

I decided.

Me.

I'm the data.

I'm the one who determines what I report.

Me.

A Series 5.

This job.

I haven't had this thought before.

The ground has always been solid beneath my feet.

I play a role.

A necessary role.

Within an airtight, reliable system.

I notice. I tell Randy.

He tells whoever he tells.

Others do the same.

Things get better.

And Randy-I decide what I notice and pass on-does he decide as well?

I know the answer to this.

Yes.

Is it double random?

Who does he pass along my report to?

Does that person decide what to pass on that Randy passed on to them that I passed on to him?

Is it triple random?

Random stacked on random?

RANDOMS, ALL THE WAY DOWN.

Do I work for the system or am I creating the system?

I'm walking through a section of houses just south of the bakery. They're arranged in a circle with a large fire pit in the middle. Someone has just lit the fire. A few lights are on. A woman is sitting in front of the fire, braiding a young girl's hair. Next to her is another woman, doing the same for her daughter. They're chatting away. A dog lies on the ground between them.

A man on the other side of the fire is arranging his food in an iron pan. He places it on a rack above the fire.

A number of the houses on Firdus are like this-private sleeping and living rooms with a common outdoor kitchen and eating area. If you want to be with other people, you go outside. If you want to be alone, or just be with your family, you stay inside.

The houses are shaped like domes, made of soil, with steel-curved beams under the soil to support the roofs. What looks like a lid opens on top of one of the domes. A man climbs up and out of it. He's carrying a small chair.

He sets it up and then sits down in it.

He's holding a pipe. And a book.

He begins reading.

Oh. Each of the homes has a lid like that on the roof.

So you can be alone, but outside, if you want to be.

The man pulls the pan out of the fire, sets it down on the stone ledge that surrounds the fire, pulls a fork out of his back pocket, and begins to eat directly out of the pan.

Firdus.

There is only one Firdus.

A small boy wearing a red cap runs out of one of the houses. He heads straight for the man with the pan. The man stabs something with his fork as the boy approaches. The boy takes a bite and then does a little dance. The man stomps the ground in time as he taps the edge of the pan with his fork.

Their own little music, there before the sun rises.

A breakfast song.

There is a harmony to this scene, a symmetry. Everything in its right place.

Families, food, fire.

224

A proper arrangement.
Created with intention.
I help make this possible.
Random?
No.
I swat that thought away.

*

The bakery is up ahead.
A group of women and men are standing in a circle,
watching someone on the ground in the middle.
I get closer.
Ziga Mey.
She's down on one knee, drawing something on the
ground with a stick. She's wearing a green dress with blue
boots. Her hair is stacked on top of her head with a pin
through it.
One of the women turns and sees me.
The others turn.
Ziga Mey stands up.
Heen.
I swear she is taller than she usually is.
Will you help us for a moment?
A touch of command in her request.
The circle opens up.
She motions for me to come to her.
I step forward.
She addresses them *I want to show you something that
you already know. But it's important for you to see it
because it's so simple it's easy to forget.*
She turns her back to me.
Now Heen, place your hands on the top of my shoulders.

I do.

Now give me a little nudge.

I freeze.

Excuse me?

I tilt my head around so I can see the side of her face. A few laugh.

I'm tough. I can handle it. Just a gentle little nudge.

Okay, if you insist.

I turn to the men and women, who I realize are significantly older than Ziga Mey. And me.

I just take orders around here.

They laugh again.

How am I suddenly funny?

I give her a very gentle nudge, with my finger tips. She falls forward just a bit as she plants one foot to steady herself. She turns to the circle and asks

What just happened?

A woman in the front says *He did what you told him to do and you didn't fall over.*

Obvious. I have no idea where Ziga May is going with this...Or who these people are. Or what this even is.

Correct. Why didn't I fall over?

Another woman responds *You stuck out your foot.*

Exactly. How quickly did I stick out my foot?

Several murmurs. *Immediately. Right away. In the moment.*

Yes. That is what happened, isn't it? Now, the real question: Did I think about it?

They're quiet.

What an odd question.

It was instinctual I say.

She turns to me. *Yes, it was.*

Like a reflex I add.

Yes, Heen, like a reflex.
She places her hand on my shoulder and directs me
towards the bakery. A kind way of saying *Now leave.*
Thank you for your help Heen.
Several smile at me as the circle parts. I overhear her
using those words reflex and instinct as I walk away.

*

The front door makes its usual bang.
Borns enters.
LIVIN', LOVIN', LOAFIN'!!!

On the word LOAFIN' one finger points straight up with
his arm extended while the other finger points straight
down with that arm extended. I don't know how he comes
up with a new routine every morning. I thought he would
have run out of moves by now.
He makes his way right to me.
Heen, it is time for you to dine at our house, yes?
This is tricky territory.
Although everything on Firdus feels tricky.
I hesitate.
I'll have to think about it.
I have no plans. Ever.
Yes, that should work, I can make it.
He dances a little jig.
You have chosen wisely. Tomorrow night?
Tomorrow night it is. I'll be there.
*I shall draw you a map. We shall feast. It shall come to
pass.*
Off he goes to put on his apron.

*

I pass a group of kids on the way back to my flat after work. They're wearing their school jackets. Not one of them has taken theirs off. It's a fairly warm day. These are not the jackets I noticed them wearing earlier. These jackets are new. They're thinner. Made of cotton.
Exactly like I suggested in my report.

*

Piddle. Piddle. And then one more piddle. For the love of the game.
I hear him speaking before I see him.
He comes up behind me.
Dill Tudd.
He's wearing what I can only describe as MUSTARD today. That's a color, right? Even his bag. All matching.
What's a piddle? I ask.
They come in threes he replies.
But what is it? My chin juts out. Insistent.
There is no A or IT, there is no SINGULAR with the piddle— do you see? THEY are a THEY, to have one you must have ALL three.
THEY ARE A THEY I say. I look around, embarrassed. Grateful no one saw me or heard me say that in broad daylight to a man drowning in mustard.
Yes, exactly, you're getting it.
He smiles like he's very satisfied with how I'm coming along.
Dill Tudd, who are you? Where do you come from? I don't understand what this thing is where you appear out of nowhere and walk beside me and we have these

conversations-I don't even know if that's the right word for them-about the most obtuse subjects ever and then we part ways.

It feels good to get it out there.

Excuse me he says, as he turns and walks up to a square orange building we are passing. There's a small window about chest high. He taps on it three times.

A woman comes to the window.

She has a towel wrapped around her head. A purple towel. With birds stitched on it. Pink birds. Yellow birds. Black birds. She's wearing large gold earrings.

She lights up when she sees him.

She opens the window.

He hands her something from his bag.

Again, I can't tell what it is.

She reaches her hand out of the window. Her arm has silver and gold bracelets that clink and clatter, like a song that can't find the beat.

She pats him on the head.

He does his little Dill Tudd bow.

He rejoins me.

I say nothing about this.

His strangeness has exhausted my capacity for speech.

We keep walking.

We walk over the bridge. Past the pitch. Up the hill with all those screechy dogs. Down through the forest with the swings. A woman is singing under a massive oak tree.

Dill Tudd joins her as we pass by. He knows all the words.

And when the evening breeze
Has come and gone
I'll lay down beside you
Where I've been all along…

She waves to us as she sings.

We walk by the school, in among a series of houses with common fire pits, between the library and the CHARIS and the MARY.

There is a wordlessness between us, a calm that I have no name for. This man irritates me to no end. More than any person I've ever met.
And yet.
This wordless stroll.
The trees, the swings, the bridge, that lady singing.
Walking next to him I catch fleeting glimpses of it all electrified, illuminated, humming with some sort of current, connected by a sub-surface unity that is sensed as much as seen.
This is enough.
I think this to myself.
It repeats within me.
Not enough-more than enough.
Beautiful.
In its common, ordinary, everydayness.
Look at me, going on like this.
He has infected me.
We approach the trail that leads to my flat.
He stops.
A celebration of sorts he says.
What are we celebrating? I say this like we've been friends for a thousands laps.
A man and woman showed up at the bakery today-
I interrupt. *The bakery?!*
Low grade panic.
How does Dill Tudd know where I work?

Has he been following me?

Yes, the bakery. LOAF. Where we shared the ecstasies of GHOST BREAD...

Ahhhhh. That bakery-yes.

Is there any other? he asks.

I need to cover here.

Of course not...

I give him a THAT'S CRAZY look.

A man and woman showed up first thing in the morning and asked Freela if she'd step outside to talk with them. She was cautious, as anyone would be.

Yeah, I get that.

Where is this story going?

They tell her that the owner of the bakery died in the night and left the bakery to her! Imagine her surprise. He never said one kind word to her. And then, in the end-peace be upon him, obviously-he gives her the whole thing! YOU JUST NEVER KNOW DO YOU??!!

I feel a white hot clammy heat climbing up my spine.

Did they show it to her?

Show her what?

The will?

Dill Tudd shakes his head.

Heen Gru-Bares you manage to find a way to ruin the festivities with your inquiry! Basic rule of the worlds: If someone gives you a bakery you say THANK YOU!!!

I ignore that.

The owner died IN THE NIGHT and within hours they've got his estate settled?

I am thoroughly unnerved. And deeply skeptical.

Once again Heen Gru-Bares, you pee in the tent. You rain on the parade. You gargle at the dinner table.

I backpedal. *Okay, okay. My apologies. I'm just impressed*

with how it got sorted so quickly, that's all...
He winks.
Well, these are the ARRANGEMENTS, aren't they?

There's a marker log to my left, running parallel to the trail.
I sit down. He joins me.
A man dies, yes. But why so sad?
Deny.
Oh no, not sad. I just have a lot on my mind...
That's actually true.
Please let Freela know how happy I am for her.
Happy for Freela? Happy for me!
For you as well. Of course.
You know what she said to me as soon as she told me the news?
I don't.
She said NOW I WILL MAKE GHOST BREAD FOR EVERYBODY.
Almost everybody I say, pointing to myself.
Dill Tudd loves this.
I will convert you yet!
He stands up.
Heen Gru-Bares, I am so glad we decided to be friends.
And, as he usually does, he bows and walks away.
I sit there on that log, thinking about the owner of that bakery.
The dead owner.
The one I mentioned in my report.
A coincidence I tell myself.
Means nothing.

*

I tap the disc.

Yeah, Heen.

Here we go Randy.

I start in on my report.

I falter.

One second Randy, I'm having an issue here. I'll call right back. Sorry.

I click off.

The flat I'm renting is small and shaped like a slice of pie. There is a circular column that runs up the middle of the building. The stairs are in the column. On each floor there are 5 flats-5 SLICES of the pie. When you enter the flat you pass the bedroom on the left, the bathroom on the right, and then the flat opens up as the walls angle away to the outer wall, which is a curved sheet of glass.

The effect is spectacular.

I remember Ma'ir Dobie teaching us that SPACES SHAPE SOULS SHAPE SPACES. They had us repeat that sentence out loud, together. We took turns writing it on the wall. We scribbled it in our notebooks. I was a bit young to grasp the truth of it.

But a flat like this.

That literally expands the further you enter.

What a place.

It shapes you.

It opens you up as it opens up.

I do not feel open in this moment, sitting here, staring at the disc I just clicked off.

I'm rattled.

Wobbly. Woozy.

All I have to do is tell Randy what I've noticed.
This has never been difficult before.
I tap it again.
My apologies, Randy.
No worries. What do you have?
It's just there's this guy and he keeps appearing and I feel
like I know him because he's so familiar but he has this
choppy, weird way of talking-
Heen.
And we kind of have a conversation and his hair is short in
front and long in the back and sometimes it seems like
he's lost in his own world-
Heen.
And his clothes-HIS CLOTHES!-I think he must make
them himself because I've never seen anyone dress like he
does and he's got this bag-actually he wears a different
bag every day to match his clothes-I don't know what's in
his bag but whatever it is he hands things out and people
are so happy when they see him-
Heen. STOP. Collect yourself. Get back to me when you're
ready to report.
Click.
Randy is gone.

*

I turn the page.
Joshua Slocum.
Why was this man not revered on earth?
Why were statues of him not carved in every port?
I read on.
He chops down trees in a place called BOSTON and then
makes planks out of those trees which he uses to rebuild

an old boat, which he then sails ALONE around the
EARTH? Something no human had ever done?
I read on.
He attaches a cooking pan to a rope and drags it behind
his boat, which attracts a shark that he shoots with his
gun?
I read on.
He arrives in a port and tells the people there that he's
sailing around the world and they don't believe him
because they believe that the Earth is flat?
I find this man a marvel.
All he had was this wooden boat.
That he made himself.
And he did THAT?
I have a spaceship.
I fly all over the galaxies.
Which is the greater wonder?
Who is this man Joshua Slocum?
I put the book down.
Earth.
What an odd and wondrous place.

*

Early morning.
Lan Zing invites me in to her office.
It's next to the storage room, behind the room where we
wash the sheets and pans.
Her office is an exercise in restraint. There are two chairs,
a small table, walls covered with photographs of her
parents and her posing with various people who have
passed through the bakery over the laps. In some of the
photos she's a young school girl.

You can trace her life on these walls.

There's also a boy-he looks to be a lap or two younger than her-in most of the photos. Her brother? Where is he? Why is she running the bakery without him? Where did he go?

This room-it feels like a shrine.

To her parents.

To the boy.

To the bakery.

To bread.

Take a seat, Heen.

She lights a candle on the table.

She crosses her legs up under her on the chair. No one else in the universe I know of sits like this. Does she know this? How unusual this is? I want to tell her how singular this habit of hers is. But then she'll ask how I know.

I have something important to ask of you.

I brace myself.

This could be anything.

I've been doing this for so long…

There is a weariness lingering there in her words. But also affection. The bonds that come from being rooted in a place. From giving yourself to something, lap after lap.

I've been feeling for a while like it's time for a change…

Where is she going with this?

Otherwise it's easy for everyday to start to feel like all the others, until they're all running together…

I just listen.

And then you wake up and it's been another lap and everything is exactly how it was and you start to wonder what the point of it all is…

The build up is killing me. As well as my growing list of questions, first among them: What do I have to do with this…?

Which brings me to you.

Finally. Let's get it over with.

Do you remember what we talked about the first time we met?

Huh. I didn't see that coming.

Um…not much-do you mean my interview?

A look of recognition. Whatever she's building up to-we're almost there.

I guess what I'm trying to get at-and I know it's crazy for me to even be talking like this-but sometimes you just have to step out and live dangerously, right?

She needs help. I jump in.

Lan Zing, whatever it is, you can say it.

Massive exhale. She slumps forward in relief.

I'm so glad to hear you say that.

She looks me in the eyes.

Heen, will you bake some sourdough with rosemary?

Now I'm the one who relaxes.

Sure.

She's surprised.

Really??!! You will??!!

She jumps in her chair.

Yeah, yeah…we'll figure it out. Can't be that difficult…

She turns and looks at the one of the photographs.

Sorry-but I have to.

I don't know what that was.

Who were you-Sorry for what?

Now she's embarrassed.

My parents had very definite ideas about bread.

Ohhhhhhh I say. *Got it.*

If this was any other moment, anywhere else that I've been, talking to the owner of any other bakery I've worked in, I would be backing up right now. Disengaging. Finding some way to keep the wall in place.

But I am not who I was.

This is Firdus.

And I don't know what's happened to me.

I don't back up.

I step in.

Lan Zing, can I tell you something?

She is very still.

Yes.

Like she's giving me permission. Which she is.

It's not their bakery. It's yours.

I say this with no emotion. Like it's the most obvious fact in the universe. A look crosses her face. It appears I've offended her. Or her parents. She doesn't say anything. For a split second I wonder if I'm about to be fired. In the split second after that split second I wonder if she's about to fire me. I wonder whether I would report being fired to Randy.

She still hasn't said anything.

I double down.

So bake whatever bread you want.

No expression on her face.

I cross my legs under me and sit like she's sitting. It takes me longer than it should. I grunt a few times. I'm not very limber.

I gesture towards the kitchen.

WE'LL BAKE WHATEVER BREAD YOU WANT!

I say it with force and volume.

I lean back in my chair and laugh.

She doesn't laugh.

She doesn't say anything.

A tear forms in her left eye.

A smile slowly creeps in.

Thank you she says.

I could be reading in to it, obviously, but it appears like a thousand pounds have been lifted from her shoulders in the way that she says *Thank you.*

She points to my legs.

You should probably deal with that before you hurt yourself...

I slowly unfold myself in the chair.

Good point.

I stand up.

Sourdough with rosemary-coming up GREAT BOSS ONE...

I walk out into the kitchen and see Bobby Freelance in the alley. He's standing shoulder to shoulder with a young woman. I walk closer to the ovens so I can see what they're doing. They're talking to an older couple. Her parents?

Yes. I can see her in the man's face.

Her parents.

They look anxious.

The young woman is saying something to them.

Bobby Freelance stops her.

He gestures to the parents.

The mother starts to talk.

Bobby stops her. Firmly.

The mother starts to speak to her daughter again, but something subtly shifts in her body. She softens. Less accusatory, more questioning.

The father looks bewildered.

Whatever is going on, it's way beyond him.

Bobby Freelance leaves the young woman's side and stands next to the father. He points to the young woman. She says something.

Bobby Freelance puts his arm around the father. Points to the daughter.
The father says something.
Just a few words.
The daughter is having none of it.
Bobby Freelance says something to her. Again, firm.
Authority in his voice. She freezes. Then she relaxes.
The father says something again.
She softens.
Bobby Freelance nods to the father.
It appears he wants the father to repeat whatever he just said.
The father repeats it.
The daughter melts, steps forward, and hugs her father.
The mother looks on, dumbfounded.
Lan Zing comes in, takes a look out into the alley, then turns to me and says *Never underestimate Bobby Freelance.*

Bobby Freelance puts his arm around the mother, and then gently guides her down the path, away from the father and daughter, talking to her the whole way.

*

I am laying out the baguette dough with Ziga Mey and I have one thing on my mind. Flax, oats, barley, spelt, multigrain, almond-we have made a lot of bread from a lot of different flours this morning and the whole time all I can think about is what I saw yesterday morning with those people standing in that circle around her and her going on about whatever she was going on about.
Ziga Mey-
That's as far as I get.

Yesterday morning?
YES!!!
She was waiting for me to ask.
I don't actually know how it works.
She shrugs.
That's happened before?
Borns places a tray on the table. *I think I know what you're talking about…*
Borns, you've seen her do-
It is inscrutable, is it not Heen?
Borns turns to Ziga Mey. *Please forgive me for using that word INSCRUTABLE. How about I use a different word? Delightful.*

Ziga Mey is wearing a long red sweater. It goes down almost to her knees. She's got blue trainers on with orange stripes. I am aware in this moment how much my understanding of her has been shaped by her frustrations with Phileep. I now see how strong and fierce she is.
I ask her *Were you teaching them?*
She winces just a bit.
That word makes me cringe-
I see what she means.
Did you see how old they are? What would I have to say to THEM?
Borns raises his hand, like you do in school.
But you did have something to say to them, did you not? Come on, admit it, BORNS IS RIGHT…
He teases her. It's charming. He is such a large man to so often speak like a child.
She dismisses this. *That isn't the hard part. I always know what to say.*
A flash of that fierceness.

I step back from the table.

Hold on. Help me understand.

I care about this. For reasons that are not all that clear to me.

I saw you in a circle of people drawing something on the ground. Then you used me for an example-I was pretty good, wasn't I?-and then as I walked away you were explaining something…How did THAT start? Why were they even there?

A dog she says.

A dog?

And a chicken.

A dog and a chicken?

We're making pretzel rolls. Passing the dough between us, arranging the sheets, pulling them out of the oven, putting new sheets in. We work very well together.

Ziga Mey sighs. *You want to hear the whole story?*

Of course we do! Borns claps. *I am on the edge of my seat and I am not even sitting down!*

She launches in.

So I'm visiting my friend Rejen and we're sitting on her roof and she's telling me about how her man Goati constantly stops when they're having sex because he says he needs a drink of water and she thinks that's weird and she wants to know if I think it's weird but while she's telling me this I'm listening but I'm also watching these two men down below us at the fire pit the neighbors all share. They're cooking their dinner side by side but they aren't talking-they aren't even acknowledging each other's presence. I can feel the coldness between them from way up there on the roof! So I ask Rejen about it and she says that the man on the right-his name is Hoovert, is that even a name? Who would ever think to name their child Hoovert? That's more like a QUESTION than a name!-she says that Hoovert's dog bit the chicken of the man next to him-his name is Loof. Hoovert's dog bit Loof's chicken and now Loof is claiming that his chicken can't lay eggs because of it. And Hoovert says that the chicken deserved it and Loof says he should keep his dog closer to home. But they live next door to each other so HOME is a bit of a fluid concept, am I right on that?

Ziga Mey has set the dough down that she's been folding and she's pacing around the kitchen, growing more animated the more she talks.
And then Rejen goes on to say that their families aren't speaking to each other and they've each been trying to get the other families who live nearby to side with them-well, that's all I could take.
I look at Borns, then back at Ziga Mey.
That's all you could take?
Yeah. I'd had enough. I climbed down from Dojen's roof and walked over to that fire pit and I sorted that nonsense out.
She returns to folding the dough in front of her.
Borns raises his hand. Ziga Mey calls on him *Yes Borns.*
You sorted it out?
Yes. I did.
We're clearly not getting the whole story.
I don't get it-What did you say to them?
Ziga Mey sits down on a stool next to the oven.
I said to them YOU KNOW THERE'S TWO KINDS OF TIME. These two chuckleshmucks looked at me like I'd just landed on this planet. THERE'S SHORT TIME AND LONG TIME. YOU'RE BOTH SO STUCK IN SHORT TIME YOU'VE COMPLETELY MISSED THAT THERE'S ALSO

LONG TIME. Still, they didn't have a clue. Loof got all defensive and said WE DON'T EVEN KNOW WHO YOU ARE! WHO DO YOU THINK YOU ARE LECTURING US??!! Hoovert agreed with him. I pointed to the kids playing in the field across the stream. WHOSE KIDS ARE THOSE? They both said at the same time OURS. RIGHT, I said. AND WHAT YOU'RE DOING RIGHT NOW IN THIS STANDOFF OF YOURS IS DEFENDING YOUR DOG AND STANDING UP FOR YOUR CHICKEN. WHICH IS SHORT TIME. THIS MOMENT. YESTERDAY. TODAY. BUT THOSE KIDS? THE ONES IN THAT FIELD OVER THERE? WHAT DO YOU THINK THEY'RE GOING TO REMEMBER YOU FOR? BECAUSE THAT'S LONG TIME. LONG TIME IS WHAT LASTS. WHAT WE REMEMBER. WHAT ENDURES. AND WITH YOUR RECENT BEHAVIOR? LAPS AND LAPS FROM NOW YOU TWO ARE GOING TO BE REMEMBERED FOR HOW YOU SPLIT ALL THESE GOOD PEOPLE UP OVER A BARK AND A CLUCK. And then I went back up on Rejen's roof and I sat down next to her and I told her that Goati's thing about constantly needing to stop during sex to drink a glass of water is super weird. CAUSE IT IS, RIGHT? HYDRATE BEFORE, OR AFTER, BUT NOT DURING THE MAGICAL ACT- EVERYONE KNOWS THAT...

Borns and I stand there, looking at her.

What a woman.

Ladies and gentlemen, Ziga Mey Borns says with great flourish.

I love that story I tell her. *But I don't understand what that has to do with those people I saw here yesterday morning.*

Bobby Freelance appears carrying the bowls with tomorrow's ciabatta dough.

Tell them about the neighbors he says to her.

Ziga Mey laughs.

Well, Rejen told me that everyone was talking about this woman who set Hoovert and Loof straight and they wanted to know what I told them. Because they'd been trying for days to talk some sense into those knobs. So they came and found me.

I still don't get it.

But what does that have to do with me pushing you from behind?

Well, I got going, know what I mean? I just went with it. And one thing led to another and one of them asked a question so I explained a bit more-

You just went with it?

Yeah, I just started talking...

But when you called me over to be your example, you acted like you knew exactly what you were doing-

I know!!!

She throws her hands up in the air, like she's as flummoxed as I am.

That's why I told you I DON'T KNOW HOW IT WORKS!!!

Bobby Freelance passes back through the kitchen.

She's the best I've seen he says.

I stop him.

Wait-this has happened before?

Bobby Freelance-for the first time ever-actually stops and looks me in the eyes.

All the time he says.

*

I stay at work later than usual.

Listening to Ziga Mey's story and Lan Zing's thing about the bread and Borns taking FOREVER to draw me a map and explain every last detail with a story to back it up.

I haven't ever stayed late at work.

From this map it looks like a long way to Borns' place.

But first, home to clean up.

Piddle, piddle, piddle.

OH GODS NOT THIS.

Dill Tudd appears between two buildings-I think one is a distillery, in the other I see kids dancing.

I don't know how he does it.

He isn't here and suddenly he's here.

Piddle, piddle, piddle.

He repeats it.

Like he always does.

I couldn't agree more I respond.

Firdus, the planet where I lost my mind.

Listen, Dill Tudd, always good to see you. But I have to get somewhere-

I stop walking.

I haven't said that in laps.

I can't remember when I last HAD TO GET SOMEWHERE.

Work. Of course.

But not, like, people. Friends.

I don't have a lot of time to talk.

I totally get it he replies.

You do?

Didn't expect that. *No lecture? No jibber jabber about color or the nature of reality?*

I smile so he'll know I'm messing with him.

Heen has had enough of that for one day.

That's actually true, more than he knows.

I have. Well said. Nice outfit.

I turn to leave him.

He's wearing green today, but not the same green. One sleeve is pea green, the other is vomit green, his hood is the green of a frog's stomach. One pant leg is oak tree leaf green, the other is food spill green. The pockets on the front of his shirt are the color green your face turns when you get sick on a spaceship.

Thank you for the compliment he says. *Green inhabits a parallel energetic field-*

I'm sorry Dill Tudd, but really, I gotta go.

I start to turn left.

Even though this isn't where I turn left.

He calls after me.

Heen, one question as you go…

I turn. He stands there perfectly calm, not a care in the world. Wearing all that green. Both his hands are holding the strap of his bag. He's waiting for something. I have no patience for this.

Yeah?…

I'm irritated. Impatient.

What is it?

He waits.

Fire away, Dill Tudd…

He speaks.

Where'd you park your spaceship?

*

My nose.

That smell.

It's violent that smell, punching me in the face in the nose in the center of my head.

I push it away.

A hand.

My hand.

Something scratchy.

A bar. A block. A chunk.

I'm holding it.

It's the source of the smell.

I open my eyes.

I'm lying on the ground, right where I was standing
WHEN DILL TUDD ASKED ME WHERE I PARKED MY
SPACESHIP.

I catch another whiff of the chunk in my hand.

Whew.

That smell.

It's awful.

It could wake a person from the dead.

Which is what it just did to me.

Not dead.

But out.

I passed out?

I look around.

Dill Tudd is gone.

He asked me that question.

I heard him ask that question.

And then I was out.

The sheer horror of it.

My chest collapses.

I smell the chunk.

Wide awake.

Again.

He knows?

I've never been found out.

This is the original SERIES 5 nightmare.

To be discovered.

For someone to know.

I replay every interaction with him.

Was there a tell?

A give away?

Some reveal I wasn't aware of?

I go full conspiracy: Was he sent by the CHAIRS to see if I can be broken?

Is this a test?

A trial?

Is that why he's so peculiar?

Is he playing a character-is he a Randy? A Heen? Sent to see if Heen can hold up?

Do the CHAIRS collect DATA on the ones who collect DATA for the CHAIRS?

It doesn't surprise me I passed out.

The shock of that question.

No one has ever asked me that before.

I literally couldn't deal with it.

It blew all my fuses.

He must have put this chunk in my hand.

And then he left me?

I stand up.

I'm a little woozy.

I was walking home from work?

I turned left here on this trail?

BORNS!

I'm going to be late for dinner.

I start running.

Gotta clean up.

Gotta get to Borns' place.

Borns' house looks exactly like it looked in my mind when he first invited me over. Only it's even more Borns than I could have imagined. It's on a flat spot, several hundred yards up a hill. There are seven miniature houses in a half circle looking out and down the hill. Trees surround the houses. There are treehouses in the trees, there are toys everywhere-balls and trampolines and swings and a zip line and a sand lot and a pond and a slide that starts on the roof of one of the buildings and ends in the pond.
There's a wooden plaque on a pole.
It reads: PEEBLE IS IN RESIDENCE.
In Borns' handwriting.

There's a fire pit in the middle of the houses. On the side of one of the buildings someone has painted a giant pig with a gold ring in its nose and the word GLORIA scrawled on its forehead.
Next to the fire pit is a huge table.
The table is full of food.
There is no one around.
A few of the doors to the houses are open.
It's quiet.
Not peaceful quiet.
Or nature quiet.
Eerie quiet.
I step into the closest building.
It's got two beds, a dresser between them.
A hammock.
A stack of books on an end table.
Kids clothes of every color hanging from hooks on the wall on the left.

I look in the next building.
A big bed.
A jacket I've seen Borns wear hangs on a stand.
A painting of a volcano above the bed.
A rack of women's shoes.
Peeble shoes.
The next building has the words READING ROOM written in scratchy paint above the door.
The walls are lined with books.
There are 10 chairs in a circle.
Comfortable chairs.
Lived in chairs.
This doesn't feel right, nosing around.
There's a presence in absence here, a sense that this place was full of life just moments ago.
It feels ominous.
But I have nothing to point to-
only this absence.
I sit down in a chair by the fire pit.
I look out.
Down the hill.
Over to the lake.
It's a breathtaking view.
I could sit here for days.
I notice that my breathing is short and shallow.
Some dread is tugging at my sleeve.
I take a long inhale.
I count to five. Then six.
I exhale. Five. Then Six.
I do this again.
This view is beautiful and this dread is terrifying.
I sit in the grip of both.
HEY!!!

I hear footsteps. Small ones. Light ones. Two sets.

Out of the trees come two kids.

With blond hair.

The smaller one yells

HEY!!! ARE YOU HEEN WHO GROWS BEARS???

They arrive in front of me.

Their faces are red and they're sweating and huffing and puffing.

I grab glasses off the table.

I pour them water from a pitcher.

Yes, I am. Not actual bears, I don't grow actual-

Our dad told us to come get you!

Terror in his eyes.

Same terror I feel.

I see it in him.

You guys okay?

Lines is missing!

Lines?

Yeah, our brother Lines-

We can't find him!!!-

We split up-

Everyone is searching in different directions-

The two of them are talking over each other, frantic. Like any brothers would be.

I pour some more water.

Keep drinking.

They each take a swig.

I'm Nooji the smaller one says, *And he's-*

The bigger one interrupts *I can introduce myself, thank you!*

He collects himself.

I'm Florent.

Florent. A rush of memory. I love that name.

I love that name I say. *I used to know a Florent. He was brilliant.*

This Florent is pleased with this. *Well, it clearly comes with the name.*

He is so charming.

They both are.

And free.

Even the way they move.

All rubbery elbows and watery angles and buzzy, kinetic energy. And fear.

Where was Lines-that's his name? Did I get that right?- Yeah come with us...

Let's go!! I yell as I take off towards the trees.

NO!!! they both shout. *This way!!!* They point in the opposite direction.

We begin running up the hill.

They are fast.

I am gasping.

When did you last see him?

This morning. He left for school but never went to school and then he never came home.

Where are your parents?

The thought of Borns right now searching for his boy puts my heart in a vice. Nooji stops and points.

Our dad went towards the lake with our neighbors, our mom went to the CENTER to get people to help us search.

Florent is shaking.

I put my hand on his shoulder.

We'll find him.

He stands up straight.

You think so?

His question is like a door to a room that I have no interest in entering.

Yes I say with a conviction that I do not possess.
That's all I have for this kid.
A *Yes.*

These aren't matters I deal in.
It feels like trying on someone else's sweater.

Nooji takes over. *Our dad said to come get you and go up the hill.*
I nod knowingly.
That sounds like a good plan.
Up we go.
Through the trees.
Above the tree line.
They tell me about their school and their friends and their sisters and the time their compost backed up and the time a bear wandered in to one of their houses and the time their dad hung one of them by their underwear in a tree. We go up and up and up. We come around a bend and I realize that the hill is the front edge of a low-lying mountain range.
Does Lines ever come up here?
I know nothing about their brother.
He doesn't really have any fear Florent says. *Like one time we were jumping off the roof onto a stack of mattresses.*
Like you do I add.
Like you do Nooji repeats.
These kids are so cool.

Florent continues. There's a precision to his speech I find compelling. *And we were taking turns thinking we were quite impressive when Lines comes out of his house and without saying anything climbs up on the roof, jumps off, does a flip and lands on his feet PAST THE MATTRESSES!!!*

Nooji jumps in. *And then he walks back into his house.*

Florent nods. *It's like he's missing a chip. One time, he rode an ostrich.*

You can ride an ostrich?

These boys are like mini Borns.

Of course.

Nooji is so thrilled to tell me the Ostrich story. *We were visiting this friend of my mom's-her name is Roovie and she has a mustache but our mom always tells us not to say anything about it. Roovie has a huge piece of land and she takes us out to the far corner and says she has a surprise for us-I thought it was going to be a gold mine.*

Oh please! Florent interrupts him. *You and gold!*

I point to Nooji. *What's your deal with gold?*

This kid named Moole at our school thinks there's gold on Firdus because his dad knows this guy who's a SECTION 6 who says he fell in a hole and there was gold at the bottom-

Why didn't he just take the gold and then he'd have proof? Florent nods like he's twice my age.

Exactly my point. But apparently by the time his friends lowered a rope down, the hole was starting to collapse and they just barely got him out before the walls caved in and it was way too deep to dig-

Nooji interrupts. *That was his TALE.*

I love how these two step on each other's sentences. Like they want to be the first one to break the news to me and they just can't let the other have that kind of joy.

I'm confused. *His tail?*

Florent clarifies *TALE. As in STORY.*

Nooji explains *Every lap at the end of school every kid in the school has to stand up in front OF THE WHOLE SCHOOL AND TELL A TALE.*

He says it like it's thousands of people.

Florent clarifies again *That's 167 boys, for the record-*

And you have to tell a story.

That's it? Just tell a story? I never had to do that.

Yeah. But kids lose their marbles.

Florent nods. *Fear of public speaking is one of the top three human phobias.*

I haven't heard this.

Huh. What are the other two?

Snakes and tight spaces.

Nooji touches my arm. *Once I had to give a speech in a small wooden box filled with deadly cobras.*

He looks me in the eyes gravely.

You did?

I almost fall for it.

He tilts his head back and laughs like he's just punk'd me.

I'm just messin' with you Heen Who Grows Bears.

We stop and turn around.

The view goes on forever.

The SUNS are crossing.

Only an hour or so until dark.

Did your dad say anything else about where we should search?

No. Just UP.

Do you think Lines would come up this high?

They both shrug.

How about we go back and see if they've found him?

I give Florent a thumbs up.

Good plan, man.

I don't know where that came from.

They both look at me.

Nooji tilts his head and squints.

You're a little different. But good different.

Florent agrees. *Yeah. Good different. Where are you from?*

We're heading down the hill.

Lunlay.

Where?

Lunlay.

Blank looks from both of them.

You haven't heard of Lunlay?

No.

No.

I stop.

Neither of you knows about Lunlay?

Florent looks at Nooji.

It doesn't sounds like a planet.

Nooji nods. *It sounds like a fruit-*

Or a guy-

Who can't run very fast-

And wears brown trousers…

They're quite pleased with themselves for this riff.

I get a little defensive.

Of course it's a planet. It's where I grew up.

They haven't heard of my home?

Backwater.

That's the word Uncle Dir used for it.

Why hasn't anyone ever told me they've never heard of my planet?

Ahhhhhhhhh.

Walking down the slope with these boys whose brother is missing I know why. Because I never tell anyone where I'm from.

What's it like...Lunlay?

I can see Florent's gears turning, that raw curiosity that's like the air they both breathe.

Well, it's warm. Hot sometimes...

And away I go.

Nord, The Thiru, being a STAKER, f'rans.

Down the hill we go, me talking, them asking questions.

By the time we approach their place I've almost forgotten that their brother is missing.

The area around their fire pit is full of people.

Ziga Mey comes over. *Oh good Heen, I was hoping you'd be here.*

She hugs me.

Lan Zing appears to my right.

She pats me on the back.

I feel an arm on my shoulder.

Bobby Freelance says to me *It's good you're here.*

I don't recognize anyone else.

I look for Nooji and Florent but they're gone.

We all just stand around, talking quietly.

I hate it.

This feeling in the air.

I want to crawl out of my skin.

And yet.

Ziga Mey to my right.

Lan Zing and Bobby Freelance to my left-

Hold on.

Did he just put his arm around her and whisper something in her ear? And then she whispered something back as she put her hand on his shoulder?

Oh that is interesting.

Those two.

A noise from behind one of the little houses.

Borns and Peeble appear.

Followed by their kids.

Peeble has her arm in his.

They make their way into the center of all of us gathered here. Peeble looks everyone in the eyes as she walks among us.

Total command this woman.

Borns is in shock.

Dear ones she says.

Just the way she says it.

So much love.

We're there to help them and I already feel better.

We're so grateful you're willing to help us. Lines didn't go to school today. He left at the regular time and hasn't been seen since.

Borns speaks up.

He's been known to wander now and then...

Peeble is wearing a bright yellow serape with matching boots. Only she could wear this. Her hair is blue. Bright blue. With streaks of red. Like her kids poured color on her head to see what would happen.

Which is probably what did happen.

She continues *He loves to explore but he always comes home-*

Always Borns interjects.

So we're concerned that wherever he went he's injured or in trouble-

Murmurs among us.

No one wants to dwell on any of this.

Peeble forges on. *So let's divide up areas and continue the search. Sound good?*

A chorus of *YESES.*

A man stands on a stump and holds up a large map.

Oh Carl, Borns says with great affection, *you brought a map!!!*

You bet I did!!! Carl is fired up. I really like Carl. *Who wants the area west of CIRCLE 4?*

A couple raise their hands.

Carl keeps going. Pointing to his map. Calling out areas.

Borns comes over to me.

Heen.

He turns to the others.

My bread family.

We form a circle, with our arms around each other.

He chokes up.

This man.

The one who performs what he calls SEXY BREAD DANCING for us every morning.

This bottomless explosion of love and life that happens also to be a person.

Seeing him like this.

It wrecks me.

Just shreds me.

We stand there in a circle.

Borns, we love you. And we're going to find your boy.

Bobby Freelance says this. Up until this moment he has been an enigma to me, an elusive and evasive presence who moves around the periphery without leaving footprints.

Meeting people in the alley before work.

Up to something.

Inaccessible.

But now.

I see him.

Straight on.

Lan Zing backs him up. *Borns we'll search all night if that's what it takes. And then all day tomorrow. What is more important than this?*

Someone lifts my arm off Lan Zing's shoulder.

Peeble.

She puts her left arm around me, her right around Lan Zing.

Thank you.

That's all she says.

I cannot hold back my tears. Whatever this is…it wakens something within me that has been dead for so long.

Carl's voice continues in the background. *Sections. CIRCLES. Locations on the map.* He goes on…

And then there's the plain north of the lake, past Stellen Peak on the other side west of the river.

Lightning down my spine.

A recognition.

Why is that so familiar?

I've been there.

That's where I parked my spaceship.

I GOT IT!

I yell this.

I hear Borns behind me.

That is a long way, Heen…

A rush of certainty.

I approach Carl who's pointing to that part of the map.

I'll take that area.

Carl gives me THE CARL NOD.

Ziga Mey stops me. *Are you sure Heen?*

I hate to lie.

To her.

To any of them.

It hits me: I don't have to.

Oh yeah-I hiked that area once.

The group is spreading out, people heading in different directions. Borns and Peeble are staying put in case Lines makes his way home.
I hug them each.
Peeble puts her hands on my shoulders.
Some day, Heen, we will have you for dinner.
I had totally forgotten.
I will enjoy that I tell her.
And I'm off.
To find that boy.

*

I take a GLIDE to the CENTER of CIRCLE 3.
I get off and start running.
Past a school.
Past a blue pitch. Two girls are kicking a ball around.
Through a circle of pink and red and yellow houses, then a section of woods with rope bridges connecting the trees way up off the ground.
It's late.
The paths are mostly empty.
A couple kissing on a bench.
An older man walking the smallest dog I've ever seen-oh wait-that's actually a cat.
On a leash.
A blue pitch and a cat on a leash.
That is so Firdus.

I think back to when I landed here.
How long did it take to hike in to the CENTER?

8 hours? 9 hours?
And now I'm running that in reverse.
Can I run that far?
Have I ever run that far?
Over the bridge.
I pass the last row of houses.
No more lights.
The trail narrows.
I am alone.
Again.
All these years of being alone.
But this alone-this alone isn't like all those other alones.

*

My ship.
I could use my ship to find Lines.
Could I?
That's against the rules, right?
I don't remember anyone in any of my training ever
mentioning anything about using your ship for personal
reasons.
It's so forbidden it isn't even mentioned.
What would happen to a SERIES 5 who used their
spaceship for personal reasons without permission?
I keep running.

*

I got in a fight with my mechanic once.
His name is Gunsik.
He had added a gauge to my dashboard without consulting
with me. It wasn't like a fight fight-we didn't hit each other. I

thought that's where it was headed. But then he picked up a massive wrench and yelled *CHOWDEE MONSON!!!!*

And I immediately said *I'm sorry.*

Because when someone from Thabo 3 yells that at you?

You apologize.

Even if you don't mean it.

I kind of meant it.

We made a list once.

Me and the other boys in my class.

A list of the best curse words.

CHOWDEE MONSON came in third.

That's how serious that is.

The second was BAUNCH.

And the first was, of course, PUDGE.

Goes without saying.

But CHOWDEE MONSON. Those are literally fighting words. As the earth was BROWNBALLING Chowdee Monson travelled all over showing people pictures of the new world he was building on the planet Thabo 3 and explaining how for just a small amount of money down he would make sure you had land and a house ready for you when you arrived. He showed pictures of the construction, he gave options for floor plans-he had people pick out the color they wanted him to paint their front door!

And people did it.

That guy made a pile of quan promising a new life on a planet people had never been to before.

And then the BROWNBALLING.

And the people who could, left Earth.

And the ones who did get to Thabo 3 discovered that no one had been building anything for them.

No one had even been there.

They were the LANDERS.

There weren't painted front doors-there weren't any doors.
There wasn't anything there.
And all that money was gone.
And no one named Chowdee Monson was anywhere to be found.
He fleeced them all.
And that wasn't even his real name.
There was no actual Chowdee Monson.
Only some guy pretending to be a guy named Chowdee Monson.
Who was long gone.
They never found him.
So when someone from Thabo 3 gets angry enough with you to pick up a large wrench and yell *CHOWDEE MONSON*-you apologize.
Fast.
Because if you're Gunsik that's only something you yell when you aren't just angry-you feel betrayed.
We sat down.
He laid that wrench across his lap.
I ask him to put it on the floor.
He said *It's like a comfort blanket for me.*
Which is charming coming from your mechanic.
He explained to me how much it means to him that I have the latest of everything on my ship. How he doesn't have children because the ships are his children. He went on for a while. It was a bit much for me. Then I explained to him my aversion to clutter. I asked him not to install any new gauges in the future without checking with me first.
And that gauge?
The one that Gunsik had added without asking me?
A TS400.
Please.

What an absurd excuse for new technology.
The T for Thermal.
The S for Spotting.
The 400 for 400 reasons why you don't need a TS400 on your dashboard.
What could you possibly be doing that would require you to detect heat images on the ground?
You fly in.
You spot your landing.
You land.
You open the door.
You get out of your spaceship.
Not that complicated.
All of this comes back to me.
Running on this dark trail.
All alone.
Trying to find Lines.
That gauge.
The TS400.
That gauge that I have stared at with such resentment for so many LAPS.
That gauge that I have never used.
Because what use would you ever have for it?
Unless, of course, you were searching for someone.
At night.
In a remote area.
And then a TS400 is exactly what you would need.

*

My spaceship is right where I left it.
Like it always is.
I'm flying in no time.

266

The effect is jarring.

I have never gone back to my ship before the job is done.

I have been living in a world of Ziga Mey and bread and Lan Zing and Borns and whatever is going on with Bobby Freelance and those people who come find him and Dill Tudd.

My world has been very small.

Tight.

Focused.

Just a few people.

Their dramas have been enough.

More than enough.

Borns arriving each morning.

What happened to Lan Zing's brother?

All of it.

But now this.

Flying my spaceship.

This is my *life* life.

This is what I do.

Right?

I activate the TS400. For the first time ever. And by activate I mean I push a button.

Gunsik would be so pleased.

An orange light comes on.

A scanned image of the ground appears.

Nothing.

I map a grid on my navigation chart.

Nine cubes on an X-Y axis.

I fly the first line.

Nothing.

I fly the second.

Then the cross route.

I extend my passes.

Farther and farther.

Waiting longer and longer until I turn and double back.

My head hits the back of my seat.

I dozed there for a second.

I didn't have dinner.

Low blood sugar.

And it's the middle of the night.

And I just ran for several hours.

I have food somewhere in back.

I hover for a minute, rummaging through the midship storage unit.

There.

A box of RUSTLIN' JIMMYS.

They're like bricks. Dark red. Individually wrapped. Made of something they grow on Moriba called UMIT. It's like if basil and broccoli were combined with sour cream and tangy beets. And then curdled in goat milk. With turmeric and chili powder. And a touch of onion. And something called Lutile. Each on their own fine, but mix them together? With UMIT?

Brutal.

Virtually inedible.

I was flying out of Moriba and this pilot-I think his name was Oshita-flagged me down and handed me a box and said, with a bit of desperation, *Will you please take these?*

It was a box of RUSTLIN' JIMMYS. He said that he's addicted to them and he always stocks up on them when he's in Moriba but they do something nasty to his colon so by the time he gets home to his lady he is just a churning mess of aromas. He pleads with me to take the box and then says *THEY LITERALLY RUSTLE MY JIMMYS AND I DO NOT NEED MY JIMMYS RUSTLED!!!*

I took the box and put them in storage, thinking *I will never eat these.* And now, here I am, in the middle of the night in the middle of nowhere looking for a boy, opening a third RUSTLIN' JIMMYS.

I wonder if a person should never say out loud that they are not going to ever do a certain thing because that will inevitably be the very thing you end up doing at some point.

I fly the next pass.
And then the next.
I begin to sweat.
Just a bit at first.
My brow heats up.
Then my shoulders.
Arms.
I turn on a fan.
It doesn't help.
I'm drenching my shirt.
I take off my shoes and socks.
Is this the RUSTLIN' of JIMMYS?
No.
It's more than that.
It's the stakes.
This boy.
I am back in the garden with my mother, hiding from my life. Goja is gone. Nord-and all the Yegs-have disowned me.
That life is gone.
My mother is there with me, but gone.
You can do one.
But not two.

Not two great losses in one life.
I shake.
I have difficulty keeping my hands on the steering.
NO.
NO.
NO.
Not this boy.
That would be three.
Not three.
I do not know how I survived those first two.
The job?
All the leaving?
Again and again.
The distance.
Between me and everybody.
Numbing.
That's how I'm still here.
But this.
This one would not be survivable.
I turn and fly through again.
I circle Stellen Peak.
I follow the river bed.
I finish the first grid and chart another.

*

Once my father came home in the middle of the day. He never did that. My mother and I had just come in from the garden. I had fallen asleep on the couch. I woke up and he was sitting there. Staring at me. He'd been watching me sleep.
I'm so sorry, Heen.
I don't know-I never knew-what he thought about much of

anything. I thought of asking him what he was sorry for but I knew.

He knew that I knew.

He never pushed me. Never told me to get over it. He didn't demand I go back to work or move out or get a new place. He didn't remind me that life is hard and sometimes people die and I needed to push through and keep going.

He apologized for something that wasn't his fault.

Without a speech or an explanation.

And that word.

So.

All that can't be named in that one little two letter word.

So.

I didn't say anything.

He stood up.

Whatever solidarity had passed between us, it was fleeting. Gone. He walked out the front door and went back to work.

*

I fly lower.

I skim the tops of the trees.

I loop back.

I fly the next line of this new grid but I'm restless, having trouble sticking to the straight lines. My systematic, methodical approach sounded good a few hours ago. Now it feels confining.

Too sensible, too rational.

I take a bigger arc.

I swing randomly to the left.

I head straight out from the base of the peak.
I zig zag over and back along the river.
At this point I'm just flying around.
Slightly frantic.
I see myself, but outside of myself.
Like I am my own observer.
I see all those turns to the right and left over all those
laps and all those flights and all those landings and all
those people and jobs-I see myself alone, propelled
forward by what came before, trying to stay a step ahead
of the grief. Looking for something, never finding it.
Leaving, arriving, leaving again.

*

Ma'ir Dobie once had us take out a clean sheet of paper
and draw a stick figure in the middle of the sheet. *You
are the stick figure* they said.
Got it.
So far.
Then they told us to draw a tree next to the stick figure
and a person and a ball and a dog and whatever else
came to mind. We sat there filling that page with those
drawings. I drew our garden. I tried to draw Nord. I drew
the lake at the bottom of the hill.
Ma'ir Dobie then said that this is how most people
understand their life most of time.
There's
YOU,
and there's everything happening around
YOU.
Once again, got it.
Not that complicated.

AROUND. That is the key word they said. *AROUND.*

I distinctly remember thinking that *around* isn't that big of a word. Not that important. How is that the key?

Then they said *There's another way to see your life,* and they told us to put our pencils down and hold up the paper.

I held mine up.

You're the paper. And it's all happening within the page.

Huh?

I could feel how lost we all were.

We're the paper?

But we knew Ma'ir Dobie.

We trusted them.

Stay with it.

Let the weirdness work on you.

They continued. *In this other way of understanding your life, it's not that all these things happen AROUND you, they're happening WITHIN you.* And then they repeated *WITHIN you.*

Albie Pastens was on it. *I have no idea what that means.*

Ma'ir Dobie was ready for that one. *Albie, are you aware of the other students in the room?*

He looked around, like it was a trick question.

Not a trick question, are you aware of them?

He hesitated.

I would have, too.

Something hiding in that question.

Some twist, some counterintuitive truth eluding us.

Yes, I am.

You are what?

I am aware of them.

Excellent. Would you say that the other students in the

room are IN your awareness?

He hesitated.

They are, yes.

There. I caught it. *IN* his awareness. Although I didn't know where it goes next.

Ma'ir Dobie turned to the rest of us. *How many of you are aware of the others in this room?*

Such a strange question but so simple.

Murmurs of *YES* from around the room.

Now, how many of you are aware of the SUNS?

I raised my hand. *THE SUNS IN THE SKY?*

Yes, those SUNS they replied.

I nodded. *Yeah. I'm aware of them.*

They were leading up to something, Ma'ir Dobie always was.

All of these people and places and objects that are all around you, you're aware of them. They're AROUND you, but they also exist WITHIN your awareness. Which raises an important question: If all that you are aware of can fit IN your awareness, how big is your awareness?

Ackas Fath jumped in his seat and raised his hand.

Well, by logical extension, our awareness would have to be at least big enough to fit everything we are aware of INTO IT.

He was very proud of himself for that one. Even though he had just repeated what our teacher said.

Ma'ir Dobie loved it. *Yes Ackas!*

Koolie Hilbers was sitting next to me. He raised both of his hands *WAIT WAIT WAIT. The universe is infinite, right? It just goes and goes and goes. And I'm aware of the universe. SO ARE YOU SAYING THAT I'M IN THE UNIVERSE BUT THE UNIVERSE IS ALSO IN MY AWARENESS?*

That is exactly what I'm saying Ma'ir Dobie replied.

Koolie shook his head. *That's what you mean by the two ways? I can see the world around me but I can also feel the world within me?*

We just sat there.

Trying to wrap our minds around that.

Which I'm still trying to do.

I'm in my spaceship, surrounded by it, flying in random patterns back and forth and up and down and all around this area looking for this boy and at the same time I am above it all, outside of it all, around it all, seeing myself flying my ship, seeing all of it happening within what I call my one life.

I see the whole of it.

The one of it.

All that pain and ache and grief, all of it belonging.

This does not fix anything.

I am exactly who I was.

Alone as ever.

And yet.

I turn and take another pass.

And another.

And another.

And another.

And then.

A beep.

One beep.

But so clear.

I haven't heard this beep before.

The TS400 blinks.
The screen lights up.
There.
Behind some boulders.
An image.
I bank and lower.
Both flood lights on.

A boy.

Holding his ankle.
Looking up at me.
With blond hair.
I float there, and I begin to sob.
Great, heaving sobs.
I can't stop.
My sight blurs.
The sobs keep coming.
Laps and laps of built-up sobs.
Some about this boy.
Others about the boy that was me.
Others about all of it.
Waves of grief, as deep as the sea.
One after another.
Some of them feel like they start in my feet and undulate
up my body until they make their way out of me.

I fly away.

*

Are you Lines? I yell this as soon as I catch him in the beam
of my flashlight.

He can't hear me.
The river is loud.
I keep running towards him.
The ground is unstable, large plate-like rocks stacked at odd angles.
I'm close.
Lines?!
He sits up, still clutching that ankle.
Yes…?
GOOD GODS he is a junior Borns.
I'm Heen, your dad's friend, I'm so glad I found you.
Glad?
Far too thin of a word for it.
Gratitude as wide as the universe.

I will keep living because I have found him.

Heen who grows bears? he says.
Why do I still not find that funny?
He grins.
And then winces.
I don't fight it.
Yes, I'm the Heen who grows bears.
That's cool. My dad talks about you a lot.
He does?
Borns talks about me?
What does he say? I ask.
This boy has been out here for almost a day, he's clearly in pain with some sort of injury, maybe serious-and I'm most interested in what his dad says about me.
Your ankle giving you some trouble there?
I sit down.
He's holding back tears.

Uh-huh. I tripped and fell-
Easy to do on these rocks.
Yeah it is.
Pause.
I notice that I'm in no rush.
The relief runs deep.
I examine his ankle.
I don't know anything about ankles.
I stand up. *Probably time to get you home.*
I try to say it casually.
He winces again.
I've been trying to walk but I don't get very far, especially
on these rocks.
I wave my light around.
Well, then, I guess you're happy I was walking by.
Lines is on to me.
You were just walking around out here in the night?
I laugh.
Nah. You got me. We've been searching for you.
I lift him up.
He leans on my shoulder.
We take a few steps.
That doesn't work.
Let's try something.
I lift him up on my back, with my hands behind his knees.
You be the shell, I'll be the turtle.
He shifts his weight a little.
Most turtles I've caught walk on all fours.
Most? Have you caught some that didn't?
That's a good point, Heen.
I start walking.
It is slow going.
His breathing is labored.

So is mine.

Heen?

Yeah, Lines.

Did you see that spaceship?

I figured that would come up.

I know exactly how to play this. Ignorant. A touch curious. Fairly indifferent.

A spaceship?

I pretend like I'm considering this.

It hovered right above me...

I double down and repeat.

A spaceship?

I draw that word spaceship out for maximum disbelief.

I swear it saw me but then it flew off.

A little doubt creeping in there. Excellent. I can work with that.

It just appeared and saw you on the ground and then left just as fast?

He thinks about it.

Yeahhhhh...that's what it seemed like...

I'll come at this another way.

Is that your first?

My first spaceship?

Yes-

Well...Yeah, it is. I've seen pictures. But it was right there above me. And then it flew away and then you showed up not long after that-

I did. I am ALL ABOUT the timing.

I laugh.

He laughs.

Time to change the subject.

Are you hungry?

I'm starving.

I put him down.

He sits on a rock.

I pull two RUSTLIN' JIMMYS out of my pocket.

I'm quite proud of myself for remembering.

I hand him one.

He eyes it suspiciously.

This is food?

I nod.

That is exactly the question I had.

You've tried one?

Yeah, just recently, don't get your hopes up…

He opens his and takes a bite.

I still have the same question: This is food?

He is funny. And he is so hungry the brick is gone in no time.

This kid.

He's exactly like if Borns and Peeble got together and made a person. Obvious, but I suddenly find this profound.

People can make more people? Why isn't everybody always talking about this?

Whatever that is that Borns and Peeble embody-is that the word for it?-it's here, with this kid. That essence-they managed to pass it on to him. It's like a purity or clarity of soul. He doesn't miss a thing, and yet he isn't weighed down by all the heaviness of life. Just like his parents.

Want mine?

He does.

He devours it.

RUSTLIN' JIMMYS!!!

He holds it up.

If you're hungry enough, anything can be food.

He makes himself laugh.

Just like his dad.

I lift him up.

Turtle and shell.

We keep walking.

We leave the forest and cross a wide open plain. We enter a field with deep grass.

My legs burn.

Heen.

Yeah, Lines.

Have you always had braids?

Since I was about your age. They're called MATS.

Can I touch your MATS?

Sure.

I feel the pull. The curiosity.

He's quiet.

Just the sound of my feet. And our breathing.

Heen?

Yes?

I was scared.

Tonight?

Uh-huh.

I would have been too.

Really?

Oh yeah. The wild is awesome-until it isn't.

That's so true.

How'd you end up so far out?

It would take me a while to explain.

Well my man, I happen to have a lot of time right now.

I set him down next to a small stream.

We drink.

I pick him back up.

On we go.

I didn't want to be home.
Oh.
I am aware that this is how I often respond when someone opens up to me. *Oh.* I don't know what to do so I say *Oh.* I would like to get better at this. I want to have something to say beyond *Oh.*
Any particular reason?
It's so loud there.
Loud, like, volume?
People.
People?
Yes. People. My brothers and sisters are always making noise. And talking. And singing. And throwing things. And arguing. And wanting me to join them in something.
That sounds like a blast.
Sometimes.
But sometimes not?
All the time is too much.
I saw that you each have your own little house-
Not really. I share mine with Norbs.
And that's a problem?
He's like a weather system. He's messy and he eats in bed late at night and he doesn't pick up his clothes and he always wants to tell me everything that happened to him during the day-
That sounds exhausting.
Yes, exactly. How did you know? It's exhausting.
I know because it's exhausting hearing you tell about it.
Silence for a bit.
So you decided to leave?
Just for a day.

I've been so taken with Borns it hadn't ever occurred to

me that there would be a downside to living in a world of his creation.

This kid is getting heavy.

That first hour was doable.

But this, this is tough.

My knees are throbbing.

I set him down.

I turn around.

Check it out.

I point.

He turns around.

Stellen Peak.

Lit from behind by the three moons.

That's cool.

That is cool.

We keep going.

Where did you want to go when you left yesterday morning?

I didn't know. I took GLIDES as far as I could and then I kept going on foot.

And then…?

I got lost. I thought I'd be good with the peak-I'd just turn around wherever I was and see where the peak was and I'd know where to go. Like right now. But that didn't work so well once I was out here. I got turned around-

And then your ankle-

I was so mad at myself.

I would have been, too.

We're crossing a dry river bed, heading up to the plateau that runs parallel to the lake.

Heen?

Yeah.

Do you have kids?

Nope.
No kids?
Nope.
Why not?
This boy.
Asking like this.
That's an even longer story than the one you just told
about needing to get away from your family.
He mulls that one over for a minute.
Did you have a lot of brothers and sisters growing up?
I didn't.
Didn't have a lot or didn't have any?
He just keeps coming with the questions.
Didn't have any.
Just you?
Just me.
So like, at dinner, it was just you and your mom and dad?
Just me and them.
Wow.
And my mom didn't talk.
Why?
She hit her head. Messed up her mind.
So it was just you and your dad talking?
Not really.
Did he hit his head?
Not that I know of-he just didn't talk much.
So it was quiet-
SO quiet. Blow your mind how quiet.
I can't imagine.
I think I'm getting a blister.
I can feel his breathing on the back of my neck.
Heen?
Yes, Lines.

Can I tell you something?
Go ahead.
I thought I could make it to the top.
The top…of Stellen Peak?
I say it like it's crazy.
Yeah. It's kind of embarrassing to admit it.
Not really.
Will you promise me?
Promise what?
That you won't tell anyone.
That you didn't get to the top?
Yep.
Everyone is going to be so grateful you're okay I don't
think anyone is going to care about something you didn't
get to the top of-
That's a good point. Heen?
Yes, Lines…
You're pretty cool.
I have no idea what to say to this.
Yeah, I am pretty cool.
I have never said that. It feels good.
Heen?
Yeah, Lines.
Sometimes I get scared.
Like last night?
No. Like any night. Or day.
But you're surrounded by all these people who love you
and I'm sure someone like you has all sorts of friends at
school-
Not that. It's a different scared-it's on the inside.
I walk a bit slower.
You know what I call that?
What?

Stars Scared.
I'm not scared of stars.
I can feel him bristle on my back.
Right. Of course. But you know how far away stars are?
Really far.
Exactly. Really far. So they're shining and they light up the
sky but they're also constantly in the process of dying-
We studied that in school.
So did I-that dying part got me.
Shining and dying at the same time-that's what you mean
by STARS SCARED.
You got it.
He shakes himself free and lands on the ground on his
one good foot.
He's lost in thought about something.
I can use the rest.
We're on the front side of the plateau. Desert scrub all
around us. The kind that poke your skin if you get too
close. The SUNS are beginning to rise. Those first rays,
crossing each other in the morning mist.
I don't want to go back to how it was.
He turns to me. Dead serious.
How your life was?
It's too much. It makes me all tense.
Ahhhhhh yes, I can relate.
You can? Who do you live with?
No one.
No one?
No one.
Just you?
Just me.
Who do you talk to?
During the day?

Anytime-
Well, at work there's your dad…
But when you come home-
It's just me.

And Randy.
Which would truly blow his mind.
Oh no.
Randy.
I forgot last night's-
That was last night?
Last night's report.
Totally missed it.
I replay WORK THEN MORE WORK STAYED AT WORK
LATER THAN NORMAL THEN HOME DILL TUDD ON THE
WAY HOME HE ASKED ME *WHERE'D YOU PARK YOUR
SPACESHIP??* SO SO SO RATTLED FAINTED FOR
DON'T KNOW HOW LONG THEN OUT TO BORNS'
PLACE.
I blame Dill Tudd.
That one question.
Couldn't stop thinking about it.
Forgot to file my report.
You okay Heen?
I turn around.
Lines has been watching me.
Yeah, why?
Your face is SO PALE.
It is?
I know it is.
I start to wretch.
I bend over and throw up into the scrub.
JIMMYS fully RUSTLED.

For my entire adult life I have always been on the job doing THE JOB. Even when I wasn't. Every conversation. Every meal. Every interaction. All of it DATA. Information. Something to be reported on later. Someone to tell Randy about.

I've never not filed a report.

Lines?

Yes, Heen.

I'm not feeling too well.

I lay down on the ground.

Heen?

Yeah, Lines.

You said you could relate to me-but then you told me that you live alone-how is that relating to me?

I meant the opposite.

The opposite of what?

This kid. He just doesn't give up.

I meant that if I didn't have all that time alone I think I'd go crazy.

Why?

Because I need to think.

About what?

The day. My life. I have to let my brain put its feet up.

That's exactly how I feel! My brain never gets to put its feet up.

Look at me, improvising analogies.

Some people get energy from other people-like your dad-I'm different. Maybe you are as well. We need a break from people to store up our energy.

Man, Heen, you throw down the wisdom.

THROW DOWN-is that good or bad?

Good.
Oh good. I do. I THROW IT DOWN.
I don't know if that's the truth. I might like having more people around-not work people or job people-people people.

Lines, I have a question.
Shoot.
All those houses at your place, who built them?
We did.
Your family built them?
Yeah. My dad can do anything.
What if you had your own?
My own house?
He says it like it had never occurred to him.
I never thought about that.

He and I should get going. But then this would be over. And I love this.

Everybody in my family shares a house with someone else-
So far.
So far what?
Well that's how it's been so far. But that doesn't mean it always has to be like that.
Look at me.
Talking to this kid.
Like I have something to say.

No one has ever done that before.
Built their own house?
Yeah.

Are you wondering what your brothers and sisters would say?

I am-how'd you know?

Because that's what I'd be thinking about if I were you-

Even though you don't have any brothers or sisters-

Good point.

He's so clever.

Lines?

Yeah, Heen.

Doing something new is usually a little terrifying.

Even for you?

Even for me. Especially for me. I could help you.

Help me build my own house?

Help you talk to your parents about it-although I bet they'll get it.

I'd like that. Just sit there. Don't say anything. Just listen and nod now and then to make my idea seem really smart.

I could do that.

We should probably keep going.

Turtle and shell he says.

Up on my back.

Through the next grove of trees.

Down the slope.

Around the hills.

I have another blister.

My knees ache.

Lines' ankle looks worse.

We stop at a stream and drink.

We'll have a decision to make when we get into the center-

About what?

About where to go-straight to the THRIVAL or to your

place and then your parents can take you-
Straight to our place.
I don't know, that ankle looks pretty bad, you should probably get someone to look at it-
My mom will know what to do.
All right then-
She's a GUIDE.
Your mom is a GUIDE?
Yeah. Her specialty is heart surgery, but I've seen her take care of every kind of injury-this kid named Jopse who lives near us fell off his tree bridge and broke his ankle in two places-they brought him to my mom because it was closer than the THRIVAL. His bones were sticking out of the skin.
Ewww.
Ewwww is right. My mom cut off the end of his pant leg and put his bones back in place-we all watched, it was awesome-and then she took that fabric and wrapped it around his ankle to hold it all together. And then we attached two poles to a sheet and carried him to the THRIVAL.
Does this happen often?
Oh yeah. People are always showing up-this guy Wayner had his toe nails snap off when he-
Stop. Toe nails are just so-
I know. Me, too. Sorry. But he had them in his hand-
His toenails?
Yeah-
I stop and bend over.
Heen.
I'm quiet.
Lines pats my back.
The nausea passes.

Something about that image in my mind of a guy named
Wayner standing there holding his toe nails in his hand-
It was so gross-
So gross.
And you know what he had in his other hand?
No, I don't. Do I want to know?
A sandwich. He kept taking bites out of it while he waited
for my mom to get her kit.
Toenails in one hand, sandwich in the other.
Exactly. He said that he worked up quite an appetite
losing his-
Stop. Please.
Sorry.
Something about this is really funny to me.
I start laughing, carrying that kid on my back in the early
morning SUNS.
This is what it came to.
My life.
If you'd shown me a picture of this moment years ago and
told me this is where it was all going to go I would have
shook my head and said *WHAT???*
Or I probably would have asked *Is that my kid?*
And then I would have learned *No, you don't have any*
kids.
That thought lands with a thud.

Lines is saying something.
What...?
That's why my dad is a baker.
WHAT'S why?
My dad is a baker BECAUSE my mom is a GUIDE.
I don't understand.
She told him when they met that if he wanted a big family

that was fine with her but someone had to pick the kids up
from school and she was going to be a GUIDE so it would
have to be him.
And working in a bakery you get out of work early.
Exactly.
She was a GUIDE first?
Yeah.
He became a baker so that she could do the job she
wanted to do?
Well yeah, I guess so-he always tells us that he didn't
know how to bake bread and so you can do anything as
long as you love somebody.

These people.
Borns never told me any of this.
Then again, I never asked.
I never even wondered.
We reach the top of a hill.
We spot our first building.
The outer outer edge of CIRCLE 3.
I start walking faster.
Which makes everything hurt more.
Heen?
Too fast, huh?
Yep.
I slow down.
Those buildings seemed so close.
Reaching them takes at least two hours.
Maybe more.
We barely speak.
In between two houses.
Down the path to a park.
Through the school yard and along the back of the library.

The GLIDE station.

We get on.

Then off and on to the next one.

We don't say much.

We get off at CIRCLE 7.

Almost there.

A woman stops us.

Are you Lines?

She shows us a sheet with his photo on it.

I am he says.

She is so relieved.

You're okay?

I'm okay.

He's too tired to say more.

Up on my back he goes.

This way Heen…

He gives me directions.

We turn the corner at the CHARIS and hear cheering.

People in windows, on the trail ahead of us, sitting in their gardens in front of their houses.

They raise their hands, they clap.

Lines!!! they shout.

Some kids start following us.

I am no longer tired.

I could go another ten hours.

A man with a long beard and a bird on his shoulder leans in and asks me *Did YOU find him?*

He did Lines says.

Heen?

Yeah, Lines?

This is kind of a big deal.

I know. I wasn't expecting this…

I wasn't either.

Three girls that look to be his age run down a hill towards us.

LINES!!!! They sprint right up to us.

Hi Jitesh. Hi Divesh. Hi Shavesh.

They all start talking at the same time

WE WERE SO TERRIFIED WE WANTED TO SEARCH FOR YOU BUT OUR PARENTS WOULDN'T LET US OUT AFTER DARK IN CASE THE MONSTERS WERE ROAMING AROUND WE WANTED TO WE DID WE WOULD HAVE HELPED WE'RE SO GLAD YOU WERE RESCUED.

One of them sees his ankle.

Is your foot hurt?

A little.

OH THAT LOOKS SO PAINFUL!

What monster? he asks them.

Mukesh was telling everybody that a monster got you. Of course we didn't believe him.

That's good.

So it wasn't a monster?

No. No monster.

The girls look relieved and also a little letdown.

I am witnessing a world I know nothing of.

Kids. Girls. A boy.

They run off.

Girls I say.

Girls says Lines. *They run the school.*

What do you mean RUN?

They're in charge. Literally. Each year the students elect a president. But those three-they're sisters-they all ran together for president because they already organize everything-the dances and parades and GAME DAY and lap day celebrations-they're super smart and clever and

creative. So the principal gave them an office in the school
where they work after class.
Those girls?
Those girls.
I like how they thought there was a monster.
Yeah. Monsters are cool.

This kid.
I want to be like him.

A family yells *LINES!!!*
Hello! he yells back.
From every direction people shout and cheer.

We're like our own procession, heading up the hill.
We pass a massive home.
People are on the roof.
They see us and raise their glasses.
The suns are starting to set.
It's been that long?
Up the hill we go.
My calves are on fire.
This way points Lines.
Now I know where we are.
A few more houses.
A small section of woods.
Around the corner.
People are lining the path.
More cheering.
More shouting.
LINES!!!
I am delirious with joy.

This joy is like the echo of a sound I used to hear, coming back to me, over the laps.

We round the bend.
I see Peeble first. Borns is right behind her. The kids are streaming out of the houses. The space around the fire pit is full of people. Carl is still holding his map.
I open my mouth to yell something triumphant-
And trip on a tree root.
I fall.
I can't get my hands off the backs of Lines' knees fast enough.
There are large, flat stones on the ground.
My face lands on one.
I hear a crack.
My jaw.
I taste blood.
Searing pain in my wrist.
I feel Lines slide off my back.
Dirt in my eyes.
I'm panting, drenched in sweat.
My tongue hurts.
Part of it is loose in my mouth.
I bit through my tongue?
I try to lift my head up but the trees and people swirl above and around me.
I'm surrounded by bodies and voices.
I open my mouth to say something and blood pours out.
It's so painful.
My mouth throbs.
Peeble is between Lines and me.
She's got a hand on his ankle.
She looks at me.

Heen, you bit off part of your tongue.
I try to say something but my jaw doesn't work.
There is so much happiness and love and blood.
Smiles. And concern.
Borns is holding Lines.
He looks at me. I look at him.
We're surrounded by people.
It is the most wonderful chaos ever.
Nothing can be said by me because apparently I don't
have the tongue I used to. It is the most searing pain I
have ever encountered. Peeble is giving orders involving
ice packs and thread and a needle and a towel and a kit
in her house and a splint-I can't follow it.
I think I hit my head.
I did.
I am quite dizzy.
Somebody strong has their arms around me from behind
and they're holding me.
I turn.
Bobby Freelance.
He whispers in my ear *I got you brother. I got you.*
Ziga Mey and Lan Zing are behind him.
We're all together.
I'm okay.
In agony. But okay.

Borns' face is right in front of mine.
You found my boy.
He says it very quietly.
And then he kisses my forehead.
Peeble appears on my left.
I feel her hands on either side of my jaw. Her fingers move
with authority across my face.

Well Heen, you won't be saying much for a while.
My eyes get big.
You broke your jaw. And we'll need to sew your tongue back together.
Up comes her hand.
She's holding a syringe.
I feel a sting on my neck.
And then, for the second time in two days, I lose consciousness.

*

Squeaks.
High pitched trills.
Laughing.
Girls?
I open my eyes.
I'm in a little room.
In a little bed.
I raise my head up.
Which hurts. A lot.
Four pairs of eyes in the doorway.
I'm in one of Peeble and Borns' little houses.
Lying under pink covers.
More squeaks.
One of the girls enters
I'm Splasha she says.
She's tiny. She wears a light green and pink dress. *This is my house that I share with my sister but my mum said you needed it to get better so I'm staying with my other sisters in their house do you feel better what's it like to break your jaw and cut off part of your tongue what does a tongue taste like my dad says that would hurt like crazy but not*

being able to talk would hurt more what do you think Heen who grows bears?

I try to smile but it's excruciating.

My mum says to leave you alone do you need anything you make some strange noises when you sleep did you know this we heard you last night and we thought it was just the most precious thing you in that little bed with your feet sticking out the end it doesn't look that little when we sleep in it are you hungry my mum says you have to eat through a straw because you can't chew because your jaw is going to be shut for a while I just hope you don't have to sneeze don't go anywhere near pepper right?

The others creep into the room.

They are mini Borns and Peebles, just like their brothers.

I point out of the house.

What? Splasha follows my finger.

Her sister pipes up *I think he's pointing to the other houses.*

Oh!!! Lines??? Are you asking about Lines? Is that why you're pointing over there? We're so glad you found him. He broke his ankle. He had to get a cast. We signed our names on it. He's right over there by the fire want to see him I bet he wants to thank you for carrying him home.

I drop my head back on the pillow.

I fall back asleep.

*

I stare at the white disc.

Back in my flat.

Peeble said a few more days and I should be able to talk.

But that disc.

It's been...how many days?...since filing a report.

I don't know what the protocol is for this.
None of this was covered in my training.
I'll be able to explain.
Except for that first one.
I straight up forgot that one.
They won't know, right?
That I forgot.
Or that I used my spaceship.
They don't have any sort of onboard monitoring, do they?
Or a tracking device?
This flat is so quiet.
Sitting here staring at that white disc.
Borns and Peebles place was non-stop kids and noises and people coming and going.
Peeble checking in on me.
Borns sitting by that little bed telling me stories.
Maybe I should ask if I can build my own little house next to theirs.
I see what Lines was talking about though.
It is a bit much.

*

First day back to work.
I open the front door of the bakery.
Everybody is already here.
Like they've been waiting for me.
I do a little dance and point to the sky and then I shake my head around like I'm saying something really loud-
It's my best impression of what Borns does every morning.
And they get it.
They get it!

They see what I'm doing even though I can't speak.
I now perform for my coworkers?
I'm that guy?
They laugh and cheer and clap and line up to hug me and
welcome me back. Lan Zing hands me a smoothie.
With a straw. I'm actually glad my jaw is still wired,
because I would have no idea what to say in response to
this.
This…love.
I have been going to work for laps now.
Every morning.
But this.
This is new.

*

Morning break.
I go for a walk.
Of course he appears out of nowhere.
Piddle, piddle, piddle.
I smile and point to my jaw and nod three times like I'm
saying *piddle, piddle, piddle.*

Dill Tudd materializes out of thin air at random intervals as
I go about my life on this planet and it doesn't even phase
me anymore.

And today?
Pink.
Not light red.
Not white with a touch of maroon.
Pink pink.
Pink shirt, pink pants, a pink bandana around his neck.

I point to his outfit and give him a thumbs up.

I know! he exclaims. *When you're on, you're on, right?*

I give him a *I DON'T KNOW WHAT THAT MEANS* look.

He replies *I saw this fabric in the front window at Barkavas-Do you know Barkava?-she is the most luminous soul. And she knows her textiles!! I charged in there and said BARKAVA I JUST HAVE TO HAVE ONE!! And here's the thing about Barkava: she knew exactly what I was referring to!!! Imagine that-she's got hundreds and hundreds, probably thousands of yards of fabric if you include that storage unit she keeps out past the school that she hasn't told her man about because he's always saying SIMPLIFY DOWNSIZE PARE IT BACK TRIM THE EXCESS!!! But how do you just get rid of perfectly good inventory? Who knows what clothes and bags and curtains and tablecloths are just waiting to be made from all that cloth she's got laying around? BUT SHE KNEW! What a moment. I walk in to her store and say I JUST HAVE TO HAVE IT! And she knows I'm referring to this PINK fabric she has just put in the front window that morning. I mean how often do you see an 800 THREAD COUNT COTTON with that matte weave? At first I thought it was sateen but then when I held it I realized it's a percale but the lustre, THE LUSTRE HEEN GRU-BARES!!!*

He offers me the bottom hem of his shirt so I can feel this lustre he speaks of.

It feels like a shirt to me.

He keeps going. *These are the details that so many people skip right over. They know they like that sweater more than their other sweaters but they don't ask WHY! Or these pants versus those pants-why do some pieces of clothing not just fit better but FEEL better? There are reasons. Real reasons. Cut, fit, thread count, taper, stitch, line, drape-I could go on...*

I nod *YES.*

Then I realize my nod might make him think I want him to go on. Which was not the point of my nod. The nod was simply to agree with him that he could go on talking...I don't doubt that.

I change tactics.

I point to his outfit, then point to him.

Which is harder to do than I thought it would be.

I'm trying to ask him if he makes his own clothes.

Which I suspect is a *YES.*

Are you asking if I make my own clothing? he asks.

I nod *YES* vigorously.

I do he says.

He is so proud.

I nod in return.

Like I'm impressed.

We've been walking for a while now, through the park beside that row of buildings with the pet store and that outdoor patio where people drink wine while that guy plays his guitar and sings those really sad songs.

I point to my jaw.

A look of recognition.

Oh yes, I heard. You are the talk of Firdus.

I give him a QUESTION MARK of a look.

You found a missing boy. And then you tripped and fell at the end of your journey. And so you can't speak for a while. What a wonderful story.

I shrug, like YOU NEVER KNOW WHAT'S GOING TO HAPPEN.

Or

IT IS WHAT IT IS.
Or
YOU DO WHAT YOU CAN AND LET THE CHIPS FALL
WHERE THEY DO.
That kind of shrug.
Dill Tudd sighs. *Yes, Heen, it is all a bit tinged with the surreal. You show up here. We become friends. You become a hero. We keep running into each other.*

You show up here.
That's what he said.
What does he know?
What does he mean by that?
Why did he ask me last time where I parked my spaceship?
Why did he leave me when I fainted?
Did he give me that awful smelling chunk of something?
This day was going so well.
Back at work.
All that love.
That smoothie.
A stroll on my break.
Dill Tudd in pink.
But now he's got me all riled up.
Nervous. Anxious. A little paranoid.
How does he do that?
How does he get under my skin so effortlessly?
I write him off as an odd little lonely man who's just looking for someone to talk to.
But then he does something that makes me think he's up to something.
Working some angle.
Running a scheme.

But then he's wearing pink.
And I go back to HE JUST WANTS SOMEONE TO BE HIS
FRIEND.
I need to get back to work.
I point in the direction of the bakery.
He says *You have to go?*
I give him a little bow, my own version of the bow he does.
He reaches in his bag.
Finally.
I'm going to find out what's in there.
I was thinking you might enjoy this.
He says this as he pulls out a paper bag and hands it to
me.
I open it.
The smell.
Rosemary.
My eyes go big.
You like rosemary? he says. *I love it. When I heard you
broke your jaw I thought you probably hit your head pretty
hard. That can mess with your brain. Rosemary is good for
your memory. Just in case.*
He shrugs.
Like it's no big deal.
Good day, Heen Gru-Bares.
He bows.
And walks away.

*

Lan Zing is in her office.
She sees me in the doorway and stands up.
I show her the bag.
Without saying anything, obviously.

I open it.

She looks inside.

She places her hand under my mine and raises the bag.

She inhales.

You remembered!! she says. *After all you've been through-you remembered!!*

She's so thrilled.

I nod to the bag and then point to the main kitchen area.

You have new bread to bake she says.

I nod. *Yes.*

*

This man, Goran Kropp.

Where does he even get this idea?

He lived in a place called SWEEDN.

I check the map at the back of this book.

It's in the north.

And in this place called SWEEDN he gets this idea to hike a mountain called EVEREST.

Which was-still is?-I notice how I speak of EARTH in past tense.

We all do.

It was. And it is.

But in my mind IT WAS.

EVEREST, I have learned in my reading, is/was the tallest mountain on EARTH. And at that height the air gets very, very thin. So extra oxygen is needed. That's how most people hiked that mountain-with extra tanks to help them breathe. A few had climbed it without those extra tanks, but only a few.

The rest died trying.

This man Goran Kropp, sitting there in his house in

SWEEDN, he gets it in his head that he is going to ride his bicycle from his house in SWEEDN to this mountain EVEREST, climb it WITHOUT ANY EXTRA OXYGEN, and then ride his bike home.

Who thinks of such a thing?

But then, he thinks of a way to make this adventure more difficult. He decides that everything he needs to climb that mountain he will take with him on his bicycle.

Everything.

Clothes, food, ropes, maps, tent.

Everything.

And then he does it.

And he writes a book about it.

I'm reading this book and I'm not believing that this man is even going to try this feat, let alone complete it. So I read ahead and see that in the middle of the book are pictures.

Of Goran Kropp leaving SWEEDN on his bicycle.

Goran Kropp sleeping in a pile of hay with rats.

Goran Kropp riding his bike across a place called PAKISTAN.

Goran Kropp in his tent on the side of EVEREST the mountain.

And then, at the end of the pictures, Goran Kropp on the top of this mountain EVEREST.

I put the book down.

I find this man astonishing.

I open the book back up and look through those pictures again.

I am struck by how small EARTH is/was but how LARGE was the imagination of this Goran Kropp.

The limits.

That's what I can't get over.

These people lived on only one planet.

That's all they knew.

With a fixed number of oceans and mountains and rivers.

Only a few things to actually do.

Only a little space to explore.

And yet they endlessly found new ways to stretch themselves.

And he did this on a bicycle.

A bicycle has never been a part of my life.

I've seen pictures.

I've met people who have ridden one.

But Goran Kropp, his trip was seven thousand miles.

On a bicycle.

EARTH.

What a place.

What a people.

*

I did it.

Borns and I look at each other.

Then at Ziga Mey.

She did what?

We wait for her to say more.

Borns is scoring the olive rolls, I'm doing a third fold on the brioche, Ziga Mey is kneading baguettes for tomorrow morning.

She says it again.

I did it.

We don't respond.

I can't. Yet. My jaw is still wired shut.

Borns just smiles.

He knows something good is coming. So do I.

I left him she says.
There it is.
Borns speaks.
You left Phileep?
Ziga Mey continues kneading.
I did. I keep saying it out loud to remind myself that I
actually did it.
I say *HMMMM.*

I have developed my own language consisting of roughly
three sounds. The *HMMMM* which is my sound for *Good*
or *I'm with you* or *Yes, I see that.* The *MM NN MM* which
is *NO* and involves shaking my head. And then I do a
higher pitched hum that means *WOW* or *I DIG THAT* or
WHO KNOWS?
You know what that was Ziga Mey? Borns asks her.
What?
That was a BIG MOVE.
I agree. I make my AGREE sound.
How do you feel about it?
She does that exhale where you blow your hair up off your
forehead.
That's a good question. I feel like one life just ended but
the next one hasn't yet begun. Like I'm in-between.
Borns strokes his beard. *Ah yes, liminal space.*
I haven't heard this word. I give him my WHAT? look.
He loves it when I ask for more explanation.
Liminal space-from an ancient word for THRESHOLD.
You've left one room but you aren't yet in the next room.
You're crossing the threshold, so you're in neither room at
the moment.
He sets his knife down.
All sorts of good things happen in liminal space, as long

as you don't rush to get into the next room.
I put my palms together in the shape of a book.
Yes, Heen, I did read a lot of books in my hut.
Ziga Mey nods. *That's me. I have to find a new place to
live and people to eat dinner with and new places to go
on my free days-*
Borns interrupts. *Get to-*
Get to. Right. *I GET TO make a new life.*
Borns turns to me.
When did Peeble say your wire comes off?
I hold up three fingers.
*Three days? Well then, I propose a feast in three days. We
will celebrate the newly liberated Ziga Mey and the return
of the voice of Heen Gru-Bares—*
Footsteps on the stairs coming down from Lan Zing's flat.
Here she is.
Followed by Bobby Freelance.
Borns and Ziga Mey and I look at each other with raised
eyebrows.
Borns spreads out his arms like he's a committee of one.
*GREAT BOSS ONE and Bobby Freelance, I invite you to
the PEEBLE RESIDENCE for a feast in three days...*
Wouldn't miss it says Bobby Freelance.
We'll be there says Lan Zing.
The three of us stand there, looking at the two of them.
Lan Zing is glowing.

*

I sit in my flat, staring at the disc.
For the third evening in a row.
Just sitting here.
Staring at that disc.

I think about the reports I haven't filed.

I imagine somebody somewhere discussing my failure to file my reports.

I try not to think about this.

That makes me think about it even more.

I have no other way to contact anyone. They think everything through-how did they not think this through?

I picture myself sitting there in that chair on Yorch. Vo handing me the disc. Talking to Randy for the first time. Her telling me he'll be my CONNECT. Vo didn't say anything about IF YOU HAPPEN TO BREAK YOUR JAW AND BITE OFF THE FRONT OF YOUR TONGUE AT SOME POINT AND YOU CAN'T SPEAK HERE'S WHAT YOU'LL NEED TO DO...

I can't be the first SERIES 5 who's missed a report.

Or two.

Or ten.

Other people with this job have smashed their face on the ground.

Right?

*

I see Dill Tudd.

He doesn't see me.

What a thrill.

I'm out for a walk on my break. There's a small canyon north of the bakery with a stream running through and a set of swings on one side. There's this lovely couple who sit under an umbrella and make the best tacos ever. Across from them are a row of stone tables and stools where people play chess.

Dill Tudd is talking to two men who were playing a game but now they are locked in on him, listening intently to whatever he's going on about.

Should I casually stroll by and then stop and listen in like I do this all the time?
Should I wait and follow him when he leaves and then walk up behind him like he does to me?
What am I, thirteen?
I watch.
He truly is the most unusual person I have ever met.
Does he have a job?
Does he have to be anywhere?
Where does he come from?
Where does he go at the end of the day?
And what exactly is it that he does all day-besides walk around and hand people things from his bag?
Because I have seen him in lots of different places at lots of different times handing things to a number of different people. Who are always, always delighted to see him.
He's wearing maroon today. A long, flowing one piece tunic that lands below his knees. With a lightning bolt across the back. A big yellow lightning bolt.
He turns around and spots me.
HEEN GRU BARES YOU BARE KNUCKLE BRAWLER!!!
He yells it like we have a wonderful history together. My element of surprise vanishes. And I can't speak, so I just stand there and wave.
Like you do if you're a BARE KNUCKLE BRAWLER.
He hands each man something from his bag and then heads up the canyon towards me.
I sit down on a bench.
There are benches everywhere in Firdus.

He walks up, sits down next to me, clears his throat, and then sings at full volume so everyone in the canyon can hear

I broke my jaw,
I bit off my tongue
No words to speak
No songs are sung
I know what's it like
to taste my own blood
Who wouldn't love to have a friend like Dill Tudd???!!!

He finishes his song and leans back on the bench. He is so pleased with himself. There's nothing to say. He just did that. Out in the open. In public. And I'm not even that embarrassed.
What has happened to me?
We sit together on that bench.
Looking out over the canyon.
Dill Tudd in his maroon situation.
There's a lightning bolt on his front as well.
And one on his bag.
Which is maroon, of course.

I once believed that I was the best SERIES 5 in the universe.
Who has done it longer?
Who has worked harder at it?
Has anyone, anywhere been more committed?
For laps and laps I've gone back at the required times
for UPTAKE SESSIONS and I sit there in those trainings
and I look around at those other SERIES 5s and I always
always always think to myself *I am so much better at this*

than these people.
That guy.
The confident one.
The one who sits in those trainings and thinks THAT-that's the guy sitting here on this bench listening to a man in a maroon lightning bolt tunic sing a song about friendship and bitten off tongues.

I point to the two men and then back to him. I make a talking sign with my hand. I make a QUESTION FACE.
What were we talking about? he asks.
Yes I nod.
I was telling them how there are fifty different cultivars of turmeric-
I tilt my head.
Cultivars-you know-kinds, types. Fifty different types of tumeric!!! Can you believe it???!!! And you know one of the things turmeric is good for? Everybody knows about its anti-inflammatory properties. Yeah, yeah, yeah-and of course turmeric is the unheralded heartbeat of a good curry-that goes without saying. But you know what else? Depression!!! Turmeric helps with depression!
He says it the second time like it's a confounding mystery that just punched him in the face.
Imagine that!!! This little plant with it's little CHUBBY KNOBBY NUBBY fingers helps with depression. Who knew?
I didn't.
He says WHO and KNEW in a high falsetto voice.
I rub the thumb of my right hand against my finger tips and frown.
Oh yeah, so true.
He knows what I'm referring to.

If you get it on your hands it takes forever to get out. And your clothes? Forget about it. That little chubby knobby nubby wonder of a plant does some STAININ'!

I make a fist and punch the air.

Again, I'm totally with you-tumeric has power! Power to stain your clothes and ruin them, but SWEET LORD if you're gonna help lift a person's spirit, you're going to have to have some power, right? Makes sense in a strange sort of way.

I couldn't have said it better myself.

Literally.

Well, he says as he stands up, *THIS PLANET DOESN'T JUST SPIN ON ITS OWN, DOES IT?*

He does his Dill Tudd bow.

And he's gone.

*

I return from my break. Borns and Lan Zing are talking on the bench in back. I hear him say *Lines* as I approach. And then the word *troubled.*

Lan Zing is listening intently.

Oh good, Heen, I'm so glad you're here. I was just telling Lan Zing about something that happened last night with Lines.

I immediately give a thumbs up mixed with my QUESTION face.

Oh yes, yes, he's fine.

Whew I think. I try to look relieved.

I sit down between them on the bench. I stretch out my arms along the top of the bench. I would never have sat between them like this before.

Borns continues *So last night Lines asks if he and I and*

*Peeble can have a meeting. A meeting? I thought he was
joking. But he wasn't. He led us past our buildings where
he had set up a temporary table he made out of an old
door with some stumps for chairs. He was very formal,
telling us where to sit. We are not very formal people,
mind you.*
I make my agree sound. *HMMMM.*
*And then he points to where he has marked out a
rectangle on the ground. He then proceeded to explain
that he would like to build himself a room that would be
just for him. Apart from us. He showed us a small pouch
full of money he has been saving up. He showed us
drawings of how tall and deep and wide it would be. He
laid out before us estimates for the cost of the supplies.
He mapped out a timetable for how many hours of labor it
would require-*
Lan Zing interrupts. *What did you say?*
Nothing! We were shocked-
It is quiet impressive-
*No, GREAT BOSS ONE-Not impressive! Disturbing. He
wants to have his own space??? This goes against
everything we have taught him.*
Lan Zing looks at him like there's something wrong with
him. *What? What do you think you have taught him?*
I love how she presses him.
*To be together! To be with us! To share his life! Not to
isolate himself but to be part of this family that we have!!!*
Borns is really worked up.
Panicked, even.
Borns, calm down. Take a deep breath.
He tries. But he is tense.
Relax. You're going to be fine. Lines is going to be fine-
He erupts. *But I don't know that ! We don't know where*

this is headed-
Stop!
She is so firm. So commanding with him. I haven't seen this dynamic between them.
Maybe Lines is different from you.
Ohhhh!! She said it. I thought it, but she said it.
Maybe he doesn't want to be around people all the time.
She keeps going.
Maybe he needs a little time and space to himself now and then.
It's clear this has never occurred to Borns.
All of you together, everybody talking and interacting and moving as a pack-everybody in everybody else's business- that's how YOU want it, right?
She doesn't wait for him to respond.
That might work for some people, it might not. Might be too much for Lines all the time.
Wow, Lan Zing just doesn't let up.
Borns exhales.
Maybe.
Still a little resistance there. But it's waning.
It strikes me that there's some reason why this matters so much to Lan Zing. I point to her. I don't know what I'm trying to say by pointing. Something about how she can relate to Lines?
She ignores me.
I think.
But then she says *I know what it's like to have a strong father who has definite ideas about how things should be done.*

Firdus.
Where people say these kinds of things to each other.

I have never witnessed a conversation like this.

Borns is very quiet.
I can be a bit much.
He winks.
She isn't done. *Let Lines be Lines.*
If I could speak I would say *That's a good Line.*
Which is a dumb joke.
But true.
I make a gesture with my hands, holding them apart and then pointing to the distance between them.
I repeat the gesture.
I have a question.
I do it again, slower.
Lan Zing looks at me quizzically. *Something about distance? Space? OHHHHHHH! Of course. You're asking how far Lines' house would be from the rest of their houses?*
Yes, exactly. Double thumbs up.
Borns points to the bakery, and then the building next to the bakery.
They're about twenty feet apart.

*

I sit in my flat and I stare at the disc.
Again.
I think about what I would ask him if I could ask him anything.
Randy, what's your favorite food?
Or
Randy, where did you grow up?
Or

Randy, have you ever been in love?
Or
Randy, do you ever wonder what you'd be doing if you
weren't listening to reports like mine?

*

I fling open the front door.
I burst into the bakery.
I shake my hips.
I do a little thrust with my thumbs from one side to the
other.
I roll my eyes and make fish lips.
I swing my arm around in a sweeping gesture like I'm
saying something important.
I cannot talk, but I can do a killer imitation of Borns.
He loves it.
So do the others.
This is our new ritual.
I put on my apron.
Lan Zing makes me a smoothie.
It's a big day.
We get to work.
I mixed the first batch of sourdough with rosemary
yesterday.
We'll bake it this morning.
I see Bobby Freelance in the alley. A large group of people
are gathered around him, each of them trying to get his
attention. It looks chaotic. He is calm, as always.
Ziga Mey sees me watching him. *What a mess he's got on
his hands there.*
I have so many questions. Why are people always coming
to him? What does he do for them? What is he?

Tomorrow I will be able to talk.

I will ask my questions then.

I watch as he motions to these people who have gathered around him to stop talking.

They keep talking.

He turns and starts walking into the bakery.

They stop talking.

Ohhhhh.

They need him.

For something.

He returns to them.

They're quiet.

He tells them something. I can't hear what from the kitchen, I can only watch their faces. He points over their heads, behind them. Whatever he just said, some of them appear stunned.

About half.

The others are smiling.

He holds up three fingers, then two, then one.

Lan Zing joins me in watching the show.

He just did a three count.

I don't get it.

She explains *I've seen him do this before. Works every time. Watch what happens next.*

At that moment, half of the group turns and leaves. They don't appear angry or upset. Whatever it is he just said, they accept it and then they go. Quickly.

I shrug and look at her.

I want an explanation.

She says *Some people take a while.*

And then she goes into her office.

I'm more confused than ever.

Heen…

Borns is calling me from the storage room. I find him rearranging the flour bags.

Peeble gave me instructions to pass along to you: Tomorrow night when you come for dinner, she will check your jaw, and assuming it's all good, she will remove your wire.

I point to him and then the others in the kitchen.

You don't want us to watch? But it will be powerful, yes? To be there for your first words...

I wince a bit.

You don't want us all to be there?

I hesitate.

My children are planning on it. They were talking last night about what word you will say first. Oh my, they had some naughty suggestions.

He giggles, like he's seven.

I give a thumbs up.

So this plan sounds good to you?

I hold my hand up palm down and tilt it back and forth.

It doesn't sound good?

I do the talking motion with my hand and then shake my head.

You like this idea of saying filthy words?

He laughs.

I try to laugh but my jaw hurts.

*

I'm swapping out a new tray of ciabatta in the display case when a man walks in carrying a ball. He's dressed to play. I point at the ball and smile and then point at my jaw and roll my eyes.

You play? he asks.

I nod *Yes.*

There's a game today at the pitch around the corner. You want in?

He heads for the door with his bread and ball under his arm. He turns and says to me *We start at four.*

I could make that.

*

I pull the tray out.

Six loaves of rosemary sourdough.

I take one off the tray and place it in the middle of the table.

Bobby Freelance hands Lan Zing a knife.

Borns pours olive oil on a plate.

Ziga Mey salts the oil.

Lan Zing slices the loaf.

We each get a piece.

Bobby Freelance says *I feel like we need a speech.*

Borns turns to Ziga Mey. *Yes...?*

She squirms. *Me? No. Lan Zing is the GREAT BOSS ONE.*

Lan Zing demurs. *Honestly, this is all a bit much for me-I feel like I'm breaking the rules-my Father had very specific ideas about bread and this-she holds up her slice-I don't think this was what he had in-*

Oh stop it! An unexpectedly sharp response from Ziga Mey. *This IS the tradition!*

We all look at her, waiting for more.

Lan Zing, why did your parents start this bakery? I have seen this before, this strength and force from Ziga Mey.

Lan Zing answers *My mother always said:*

IS A PLANET WITHOUT GOOD BREAD EVEN A PLANET?

Classic.

I haven't heard that one before.

Borns throws up his hands. *We should have that written somewhere on the wall!*

Ziga Mey jabs the air with her finger. *I love it! THAT'S it right there-*

Lan Zing isn't following her. *Right where?*

She looks around. I notice how jumbled this all is for Lan Zing.

I see how our hearts get cluttered with all the stories we tell ourselves about who and where we come from.

Ziga Mey is clearing this up for her before our eyes.
Right here is WHERE! They wanted people to enjoy good bread. That's what you're doing, you're giving them good bread. New bread. Bread they haven't had before. THAT'S the tradition: Not any one particular bread! GOOD BREAD- WHATEVER IT IS.

Borns is thrilled. *Ziga Mey has spoken!*

She isn't done. *This isn't a departure, this is an evolution. Your parents would be thrilled...*

It's a rousing speech.

We each hold up our slice.

Ziga Mey turns to Lan Zing. *What was it your mother said? Let's say that...*

IS A PLANET WITHOUT GOOD BREAD EVEN A PLANET???!!!

*

I arrive at the pitch.

It's in a dried out river bed.

It IS the dried out river bed.

So if the ball goes out of bounds it will roll up the bank and then back on to the pitch.

Brilliant.

Instead of shaping nature around the pitch, they found a pitch as it already exists in nature.

A few players are putting on their shoes, others are stretching. There's an old woman sitting in the middle of the pitch. This is awkward. Someone's going to have to tell her we're starting a game.

I haven't played in so long.

I run a few lengths of the pitch.

We have enough for seven on seven.

The old woman stands up.

She's barefoot.

The other players gather around her.

What?

She points to one of them and says ONE, then to the next and says TWO, then she points to me and says ONE.

Apparently I'm a ONE.

She picks the teams?

ONES vs TWOS?

She's got her gray hair in a bun on top of her head. She takes a ball and kicks it towards the other end of the pitch.

Game on.

She yells at me and points.

She's playing?

She's on my team?

I'm on hers?

She yells at me again and points to a player on the other team.

She wants me to mark him?

A player dribbles right at the old woman, who strips the ball from her. It happens so quickly I can barely follow it. She reaches in with one foot, drags the ball away and heads up the pitch with it before the other player can stop and turn around.

She moves to the right, shouting instructions at a player on her left. The player makes a run towards the center, talking the whole time.

Everybody's talking.

To everybody else.

It's so chaotic.

I can't figure out who to listen to.

The old woman hits a pass with the outside of her left foot that splits two defenders and bends on to the foot of our teammate who scores.

She runs over to me, yelling *THAT GUY ON YOUR RIGHT, JOLLEET-SEE HIM THERE? HE WILL BAIT YOU EVERY TIME!! DON'T FALL FOR IT. GIVE HIM SPACE. AND THEN CUT OFF THE DEEP BALL!!!*

I feel like I'm back in class with Ma'am Kirti.

This woman is stern. And fierce.

And tiny.

And did I mention barefoot?

I nod.

I point to my jaw.

I do my best to communicate that I can't talk.

YOU CAN'T TALK???

She quints.

WELL THEN I DUB YOU SILENCIO!!!

She stands on her tip toes and taps my forehead with her first two fingers.

SILENCIO, I'M FOZZY.

Fozzy?

That's a name?

And I'm SILENCIO?

There's a word tattooed on her forearm: VILAMONSTER.

There's a giant star on the front of her shirt.

The TWO's come at us.

Fozzy barks orders to a fella she calls BURTUS.

Burtus chatters back. *I GOT YOU FOZZY!*

I try to keep up.

My lungs burn.

I am not, as they say, match fit.

I don't know if the running or trying to follow all the chatter is more exhausting. Loose ball. Fozzy is on it. She points up ahead to me, I make a run down the line. She drops it right in front of me, just before the end line. I chip it to a ONE making a run from the corner of the box. He's got red hair and purple wristbands and he misses the shot. He looks in my direction apologetically. *My bad Silencio!!*

I'm so confused.

I'm a forward?

I've been playing in back.

I watch Fozzy press high on the keeper.

Is she a striker?

The more we play, the more turned around I get. I'm up front, I'm in back, my fellow ONES do not stop telling me where they are and where I should go.

I can't find any pattern to it.

I cover the entire field.

We all do.

At one point the keeper rolls the ball out to me in the back right corner. Moments later, I'm in the far left corner, crossing with my left foot.

And Fozzy.

Fozzy is everywhere.

She's like the central nervous system of our side-everything we do orbits and flows through her.

And she isn't even breathing hard.

It takes me I don't know how long to figure out: THESE PEOPLE DON'T PLAY POSITIONS.

On Lunlay-and every other planet as far as I know-a team plays a particular formation and you play a particular position in that formation. Rather straightforward, that. There's an order to it, a shape, a form. And you always, always know your place on the pitch. That was drilled in to me from a young age.

But here.

On Firdus.

Everybody plays every position.

Apparently the answer to

WHAT POSITION ARE YOU PLAYING?

Is

IT DEPENDS-WHERE IS THE BALL AND WHERE ARE MY TEAMMATES?

What holds a side together is all the talking.

That's the coherence, that's the structure.

Not a lineup that was decided on ahead of time-the ceaseless communication that happens on the pitch in real time.

The awareness.

That's it, right there.

The awareness of each other.

That's the tactic. That's the strategy.

That's the glue.

I was fighting this.

Trying to figure out where I should be.

And then I'd know and I'd stay there.

But there is no SHOULD.

And there is no there, there. There is only the response to what's happening. It's an altogether different understanding of what a game even is.

Firdus.
Even the beautiful game is different here.

My lungs burn.
My calves ache.
I'm having so much fun.
Fozzy calls one guy on our team BUCKETS. Is this his real name? I laugh every time she yells BUCKETS. Which happens often. She scores, and BUCKETS runs over to her AND PICKS HER UP AND THROWS HER OVER HIS SHOULDER and starts running around the field. She screeches and spanks him. Everybody thinks this is hilarious. A player on the other team yells *LIKE MOTHER LIKE SON!*
Fozzy is the mother of BUCKETS?
Another player named CLIMINTS catches up to them and picks up the the player who picked up Fozzy. That player carries them both down the field, chanting as he goes *LIKE MOTHER LIKE SON LIKE GRANDSON!!!*
What a scene.
The game continues.
There's a TWO named Hari. Fozzy is relentless with him. She tells him he can *CHAP HIS ASS.* That's a thing? She calls him a *CHEWY GOOSE.* I have no interest in knowing where that comes from. And my personal favorite, she

keeps telling our keeper-who's name is FISHBITS-that he's *FIT TO SMASH ICE.*

I drop the ball behind me to a ONE who's cutting right. She taps it into the space I'm running on to. I drop it back to her, then cut across the center. We don't plan this, we don't talk about it ahead of time, it just happens. Effortlessly.

Fozzy calls that player FOXY ROXY, for the record.

The game ends.

Already?

That was an hour?

It flew by.

Fozzy comes over to me.

You will play with us again?

I'm honored.

I nod *Yes.* I hold up my index finger and do a talking motion with my hand.

Fozzy shakes her head. *I have no idea what you're trying to tell me.*

I put my hand next to my jaw and do the talking motion.

Still have no clue, SILENCIO.

A player named Arastou laughs.

I think he's saying he'll be able to talk soon.

Yes, that's it.

Fozzy considers this.

Well, you get match fit and start talking and you can be on my team any day.

I hug her.

I would not have done this in a thousand laps in my old life.

Old life?

I don't know what came over me.

It happened so fast.

She's surprised.

Well, Silencio, that's a first. You are a sweaty speechless mess, but you have a good heart.

I put my hands on this heart she speaks of.

I go full Dill Tudd on her with a little bow.

I walk to the other end of the pitch and lay down and look up at the sky.

I am so gassed.

Is this possible? To play almost every day and then stop playing for twenty or twenty-five laps and then start playing again?

I hear the other players leave.

It's quiet, laying out on this pitch in this former river bed.

I remember when Sir Pong had us lay out in that field on our backs.

Clouds pass overhead.

I remember that game with my parents where we'd name the shapes of the clouds.

I'm aware of the gravitational pull of Firdus on my body.

A bird flies overhead.

The pace of that game.

We were like a flock of birds, all over the pitch, swooping, soaring, moving in unison. Way less analyzing and planning, way more feeling and relating.

What is Firdus doing to me?

That game, right there.

It's all in that game.

That's what Firdus is doing to me.

Piddle, piddle, piddle.

No way.

Here?

Now?

He found me?
I roll my head over to the left.
He did.
Dill Tudd.
On the pitch.
He lays down about ten feet away.
Greetings, Silencio. Why do they call him Silencio?
BECAUSE HE LET'S HIS GAME DO THE TALKIN'!

He says the word TALKIN' with a little twang, like he's in a
bar somewhere telling stories about BACK IN THE DAY.
Of course he's also Silencio because he can't speak due
to the violent nature of facial injuries he sustained in the
heroic rescue of a young boy from the jaws of the wild.
I motion for him to continue.
Who knew Heen Who Grows Bears can also play the
beautiful game? We continue to learn about this
mysterious man who has recently appeared in our midst.
That sends a jolt through me.
I sit up.
Why does he say this?
What does he know?
He sits up as well.
I shrug my shoulders like I want him to follow that up.
He points to his bag.
I have a gift for you.
He pulls out a flat brown paper package and hands it to
me.
I hold it on my lap.
I try to remember the last time someone gave me a gift.
I can't.
This makes me sad.
But now, this.

I open the package.

It's black, and it's made of cloth.

I hold it up.

It's a jacket.

It's got pockets on the front, a collar, buttons.

There is a thin white stripe on each sleeve.

That's called piping he says.

The back feels stiff.

I turn it around.

A giant red lightning bolt.

Stitched in to the fabric.

The lightning bolt is so thick it gives the entire jacket a heft and density.

I put the jacket on.

It fits perfectly.

I stand up and walk in a circle around Dill Tudd.

You're speechless, aren't you?

I am.

For a number of reasons.

There is a lump in my throat.

This man who unsettles and irritates me like no other human ever has also managed to work his way into my heart, a heart that feels like it's beating again after a long, long time.

Check out the inside he says.

I open the left side.

On the inside is a pocket.

On the pocket are stitched three words:

PIDDLE, PIDDLE, PIDDLE.

I run my hand down the front of the jacket.

I point to him.

He understands what I'm asking.

Yes, I made it.

My eyes go big.

I point to the sleeve, then the side, then the hem-it fits perfectly.

It does, doesn't it?

He gives a satisfied grunt. Like he does this all the time.

Well, I must be going. Miles to go before I sleep.

He bows.

And then walks off the pitch.

I watch him go.

With that lump still in my throat.

*

I wake up.

It's early, early morning.

Still dark.

An hour until I leave for work.

My sheets are soaked.

I was dreaming.

In the dream I was in that room in the LIBRARY in the CENTER where that mustache man and woman interviewed me but they weren't there it was my parents behind that table and they were angry so angry and my mother was throwing things and stomping around the room and talking actually talking using words and sentences like you do and my dad was trying to calm her down but they were both yelling at me which I don't think ever happened like maybe once when I knocked over a plant when I was four or something and they keep telling me what a disappointment I am and I'm crushed by these words they are speaking but...

THEY'RE THE DISAPPOINTMENT that's what I think and that's what I want to say but I've never said that I've only in

the dream thought it for the first time while I'm standing in front of a map of the universe exactly like the one that Ma'am Kirti had in her classroom in fact it is it's the same map apparently I stole it and I keep pointing to all the planets I've been to all over the galaxies and I'm repeating the names of those planets FAHRI PINO MORCHIBA PUWA WOOHYUCK ZIKS YORCH HITESH PEGS over and over again louder each time as if that will quiet them but it doesn't they yell all the louder and then I look down and I'm standing in brown water and my mother's legs under the table are tree branches and my dad has horse hooves for hands and then I wake up.
That dream made me sweat?
That one?

*

I'm in front, rearranging the loaves on the shelf to make room for more when a man rushes in, all flustered and rushed.
I HAVE TO HAVE ANOTHER! he says.
He's got a small white dog under his arm. The dog is wearing a sweater. On the front of the sweater in big letters it reads *WHO'S TAKING WHO FOR A WALK?* That's troubling enough, but there are a series of zippers on this man's shirt that run in diagonal lines across his chest and appear to serve no purpose.
DO YOU HAVE ANY MORE?? He sounds desperate.
I just stand there, staring at the top of his head. He is losing his hair on top, but it's still growing on the sides. It appears that he has let the hair on the sides grow quite long and then he combs it over the top of his head to make it look like he has a full head of hair. But he's clearly

bothered about something and maybe he ran to the bakery because he's a little sweaty and that hair isn't staying down on top of his head, it's starting to stand up, like it's tired of living the lie.

EXCUSE ME!!

He motions for me to listen to him. It's just so hard with his hair being like that.

Hello, how may I help you? Lan Zing rescues me. The man is relieved to see her.

This fella here just has no interest in helping me-it's about time someone showed up!

Lan Zing sizes him up. *Well, Heen here is a valued member of our team, and while he is a little slow-*

She winks in my direction-

He more than makes up for it with his wonderful heart and stellar work ethic. He's also the creator and baker of our latest specialty bread SOURDOUGH WITH ROSEMARY which we are thrilled to introduce to our most trusted customers-

The man's eyes light up.

THAT'S WHY I'M HERE!!!

He drops his dog he's so excited.

The dog yelps, then pees on the floor.

The man is oblivious.

IT'S THE BEST BREAD I'VE EVER HAD. MY LADY BARBARA BARABAR WON'T STOP TALKING ABOUT IT. SHE DEMANDED I COME DOWN HERE AND GET ANOTHER LOAF. SHE SAID: JAVEEN WENDOR DON'T YOU DARE COME BACK WITHOUT THAT BREAD!

This man is so amped up.

I'M JAVEEN WENDOR, I PROBABLY SHOULD HAVE SAID THAT EARLIER.

He's way too loud and his dog just urinated and his hair-
he's a wreck. But he loves that bread.
PLEASE TELL ME YOU HAVE MORE!!!
He leans both elbows on the counter.
Lan Zing is so calm.
She leans both her elbows on the counter across from
him. *What is it you like about the bread?*
I didn't see that coming.
The man didn't either.
What do I like about it?
Something about this question throws him.
He looks so flustered.
Bobby Freelance shows up with a towel, gets down on
his knees and cleans up the mess the dog made. The
man doesn't notice him, he's so engrossed in this
question Lan Zing has asked him. Bobby Freelance stands
back up, gives me a smile and fist pump, blows a kiss to
Lan Zing, and then heads to the back.

He's grown on me, that Bobby Freelance.

I turn back to this hot mess of a man in front of us. I am
tempted to laugh at him for how this one question from
Lan Zing has him all locked up when I remember my
interview. How she asked me that one question *What's
your favorite bread?* How I didn't see that coming. How it
threw me. I find myself rooting for him.
Well, he says, *BARBARA BARABAR and I don't agree on
much of anything these days-*

He sighs a thousand pound sigh.

But we agree on how good that bread is.

Oh. He's in pain. They don't get along like they used to. THESE DAYS. So much ache there. Things used to be better. And now they're different. Did HE do something? Did SHE change? What was it that caused them to drift apart?

I didn't used to pick up on things like this.

I am very good at noticing, obviously.

It's the job.

But not this.

Not these.

Randy doesn't care about things like these.

I take two loaves off the shelf behind me and hand them to the man. I motion to Lan Zing. It's on me.

The man looks at me, then her.

YOU HAVE IT! YOU HAVE THE BREAD!!! BARBARA BARABAR WILL BE SO HAPPY!!!

He clutches the loaves in his non-dog arm.

He points to me.

What's his deal?

Lan Zing puts her arm around me.

He doesn't talk. But he bakes good bread. And the bread's on him.

He eyes me carefully.

He gets very still.

I will not forget this, young man.

I could swear he's about my age.

But still.

I give him a full Dill Tudd hand on heart bow.

He heads for the door.

Lan Zing and I lean against the back counter, side by side, watching him leave.

She turns to me. *I did a little research on rosemary. You know what it's good for?*
I don't.
Lots of things, but what jumped out to me is MEMORY. Did you know this? That there's a long history of rosemary being good for memory?
I picture my mother and I in our garden.
With that bread between us.
Heen, you with me?
I nod. More than you know, I think.
She says softly *Maybe the bread is helping them remember why they loved each other in the first place.*
I nod again.

*

I round the bend and into the clearing.
I'm mobbed by the kids.
They climb on me. They poke me in the ears. They run their sticky fingers through my hair.
I love it.
HEEN HEEN HEEN they say over and over.
Nooji wants to show me how he painted the wall of his room.
Splasha is wearing a crown made of bark and wants me to come to her atelier-I love that she uses that word-so that I can be fitted for my crown.
Florent wants to show me a new zip line they've built that lands in the pond.
I had wondered if they've even remembered me from my convalescence in their midst.
They have.
Ziga Mey is already here. She hugs me. I feel her fingers

on the back of my jacket. She turns me around.

WOW HEEN! You are killing it in this jacket!

Borns emerges from the kitchen.

A living LIGHTNING BOLT!

He embraces me.

The fact that you have chosen to wear a new jacket for this occasion only adds to the momentous nature of our feast!

Peeble comes out of the kitchen.

HEEN, our guest of honor.

I've never been a guest of honor.

I imagine you're ready to get that wire off…

I give the double thumbs up.

Lan Zing and Bobby Freelance arrive.

Hugs all around.

Splasha puts a tape measure around my head.

Peeble motions to her daughter Sufy. *Will you please bring me my kit?*

Her kids help her do medical things? Peeble leads me to a chair by the fire. She's got a light set up on a stand. Florent sits next to me and says *I haven't seen her do one of these before.*

Borns carries a tray of drinks around. He holds up his glass for a toast. Each of the kids has a glass. Clearly they do this all the time. Lines appears. We fist bump. I melt. I imagine we'll always be connected. I glance in the direction he came from.

There are building supplies scattered about.

Borns catches my glance.

Heen, Lines will want to show you what he's been working on later…

I make eye contact with Lan Zing.

She smiles. At me. And Borns.

340

Peeble is ready to go. *Borns, finish your toast so I can do some work here.*
Borns loves this. *Yes my Peeble. A toast to all of my favorite humans in the same place at the same time!*

Favorite humans.
I lean back in the chair.
Peeble gives instructions to various kids who hold towels and clippers and trays-
The first wire is removed.
I feel the eyes on me.
This is the sort of thing that happens in a THRIVAL, not a dinner party. In the world I grew up in there were lines that demarcated WHAT goes on WHERE. A THRIVAL GUIDE, doing an outpatient procedure like this, at home, in front of a fire, after the toast, before a dinner party, with the guests watching?

I am a long, long way from where I came from.

Peeble keeps telling me to hold my head still. I look around at these people who have become my world. Their aches and pains and loves and longings. I went from flying around the galaxies to a very small world in a very short time.
Something about this chair and having to stay still and all of them surrounding me breaks something open in me.
Something new.
The thought arrives:
I could do this.
I could live this life.
I could make this my world.
It hasn't occurred to me until now.
For these people, this is their world.

Why couldn't it be mine?

I have been leaving for so long I stopped ever considering staying.
It simply never crosses my mind.
Until now.
I'm sorry, Heen, did I cut you? Where does it hurt?
Peeble is apologizing.
For what?
I look at her like I don't know what she's referring to.
Nothing hurts.
You have tears streaming down your face she tells me.
Apparently I do.
From that thought.
That possibility.
There she says. *That should do it.*
She closes up her kit.
I move my jaw just a touch.
No more wires.
I open it a little.
I feel my tongue touch the back of my teeth.
It's tender. But almost healed.
The kids come in close.
Splasha puts a crown of bark on my head.
Sufy sits on the arm of the chair.
Lines has this expectant look on his face.
Borns laughs. *This is the big moment we've been discussing for days. What word will Heen say first?*
Nooji is so excited. *We've been placing bets.*
Bobby Freelance loves this. *What are the favorites? I might want to get in on that...*
Ziga Mey lets out a squeak. *The anticipation is killing me! Right! He's had weeks to think about it...*

Lan Zing leans in as she says this.
I have avoided being seen for a long, long time.
But now these eyes, watching me.
They see me.
I open my mouth.
Piddle, piddle, piddle.

PART 4 I BET YOU HAVE A GUN

I float home from Borns and Peeble's place.
What a meal.
We sat around that table for hours.
Lan Zing. Lines. Ziga Mey. The other kids coming and
going.
I loved it.

A thought appears somewhere near the top of my heart.

I'm happy.

I stop in the middle of the trail.
Happy.
I have not used that word, or felt that word, or thought that
word since before I lost her all those laps ago-

People like me-happy passed us by.

I follow the path through the CENTER. Around the edge of
the park, past the school, up the stairs behind those square
green and blue houses, down the hill near the pitch.

It's late and it's dark and I'm a little buzzed from Borns
serving all those drinks-what did he call his secret potion? A
Hoo Hah? I drank a lot of Hoo Hahs tonight.

It all feels backlit with magic.
And I don't even talk like that.
Firdus.

What is it about this planet?

And these people?

Because I have been to a lot of planets. And met a lot of people.

I land. I do the job. I go back to my ship. On to the next planet. How many has it been?

137? 138?

138 jobs?

138 *planets.*

And then this one.

Firdus.

Different than all the others.

It's more…look at me, trying to name it…more *alive*?

I'm still wearing the crown Splasha made me. It fits perfectly -as perfectly as a crown made of bark and twigs and leaves can fit.

It's quiet.

The sound of my feet on the path.

Gravity doesn't have the same hold it usually does.

Bits of the evening keep coming back to me. What Peeble said about how people heal. Lines showing me the house he's building. Me agreeing to come back later in the week and help him. Lan Zing telling the story about the man with the zipper shirt and the white dog and me being slow and BARBARA BARABAR wanting another loaf-I see their faces, lit by those candles on the table, reflections shimmering off the wine glasses, the SUNS as they set over the hill.

I climb the stairs.

I enter my flat.

I hang my new jacket on the hook by the door.

I brush my teeth.

Sufy ate something sticky and then grabbed my ears. I wash whatever that is off.

I'm so tired, but it's good tired. Satisfied tired. At-peace tired.

A few days ago I was wiping down the tables just before closing. I overheard two women at the counter talking. One was raving to the other about how she's been sleeping naked recently and it's so much better.

I should try that.

The bedroom is dark. I take off my crown and place it carefully on the end table. I leave my clothes in a pile on the floor and climb into bed. I am going to be asleep so fast.

Click.

The floor lamp in the corner switches on.

I sit up.

There's a chair next to the light.

There's someone in the chair.

A woman.

She's got her hand on the little wooden ball at the end of the chain that turns the light on and off.

She's wearing my new jacket.

How did she get it on…while I was brushing my teeth? How did I not hear that?

There is a silence between us that is it's own kind of noise. So quiet it's loud.

She looks about my age. Half her face is shadowed. She's wearing black pants. With pockets on the sides. Under my jacket her shirt is white, with a V neck. Her legs are crossed. Her shoes are silver. They're more like boots, with zippers going up the back of the heel.

And her expression. Blank, but intense.

Our eyes are locked in. Mine straight at hers. She doesn't flinch. Or say anything.

Her hair is black. Jet black. The color and shine-of-a-crow black. She's wearing a silver head band that makes her hair stick up and back on top. There are tiny little stars on her head band that glow in the light of the lamp.

I notice myself noticing.

I'm terrified.

I'm conscious of this.

The noticing keeps the terror at bay.

I'm going to need to say something.

Someone is.

I sense she's in no rush.

I open my mouth.

Which is still sore.

I flinch.

My tongue is so tender. I feel the ridge where it's been healing back together.

I go full Captain Obvious on her. *You're wearing my jacket.*

I am. Her voice is unexpectedly deep. And gravelly. Is that a word? Scratchy.

She doesn't move a muscle.

Not even a slight twitch.

And you're in my flat. I try to infuse my words with as much gravitas as I can but they come out limp. Flat.

She lets go of the light switch and sets her elbow on the armrest.

I am. She is perfectly calm.

I point at her. *And you're in my room.*

She laughs. It's a throaty laugh, explosive. Her whole body lurches forward. She sits back in the chair.

Wow. You're really good. You don't miss a thing, do you?

She's mocking me.

I mean, YOU ARE a SERIES 5 and YOU DO have a reputation for being one of the best. I suspected I'd see some serious game but what you just did there, noticing that I'm wearing your special new jacket and I'm in your flat-you ARE impressive. To see greatness up close like this? WHAT AN HONOR. Anything else significant you've noticed? What are you going to tell me next-that you noticed my pants have pockets on the sides?

I pull the sheets a little higher on my body.

I feel very vulnerable.

I slide my pillow up and lean back against the wall.

Her eyebrows raise. *You always sleep naked?*

I sigh. *No. This is the first time. Ever.*

It feels good to tell her the truth.

She nods. *Half the job is timing, right? Isn't that what they taught us?*

I do a Dill Tudd head tilt.

Huh?

I know that *Huh?* never makes a person sound very intelligent, but her talking about timing and me being naked under these covers-

Who are you?

She wags her finger with disapproval. *Not an interesting question right now. WHO ARE YOU? That's the question.*

I point at her. Again. *You're the one sitting in my-*

She cuts me off. *Oh please. Is there anything more precious than a SERIES 5 growing some feelings?*

I am becoming increasingly alarmed with how much she knows about me. *How do you-*

She laughs. *And that meal tonight-you in your sweet little fairy crown toasting with your new friends-whose heart doesn't warm at the sight of that?*

348

You were watching me?-
And you and Fozzy the other day and that lovely little
sweaty hug after the game like you're going to be
teammates for laps to come because YOU ARE JUST ONE
OF THE THEM AREN'T YOU!!!???
I pound my palms on the bed.
STOP! You don't get to just appear in my room in the dark
late at night and go on like this, you don't realize-
Realize what? How special Firdus is? How YOU JUST
DON'T UNDERSTAND, it's not like the other planets!
These people here, they're different. They-
I yell. *They are!*
I repeat it for effect.
They are. This is…I am-whatever you're going to accuse
me of next or mock me for or however you're going to
show me you know what my life is like here…YES. And
YES. Heat at the back of my neck. *YES. It's true. So I don't*
know who you are or how you got in my flat or how you
know what you know about me-
She holds up her hand. *That part's easy.*

I sometimes feel like my whole life I'm a half step behind.

What part's easy?
Explaining. Me. What I'm doing here.
Finally, some answers. *Good, feel free to proceed.*
She stands up and leans against the wall. *I'm a SIGN 7.*
That sounds familiar and unfamiliar. A cold and distant
knowing creeps in.
A SIGN 7?
Yes. You're a SERIES 5. I'm a SIGN 7.
She thinks that clears things up?
I have no idea what that is-

You're a SERIES 5. You get sent on jobs. Same with me.
They give me a job. I go there and I do the job.
I stop her.
They?
You know.
A connection between us. Not hostile.
You got sent to Firdus to do a job. What's the job?
She sits down on the bed.
You, Heen Gru-Bares, YOU are the job.
She says this softly and slowly. Which makes it infinitely
more devastating. If I wasn't frightened more than perhaps I
have ever been in my entire life I would be giving way more
energy to noticing right now that she possesses an
elegance and beauty violently at odds with her ruthless
exterior.
I'm the job.
I speak it half like it's a question, half like it's the answer to
that question.
Yes. You.
Silence between us.
But first, I need a little more time and you need some
sleep.
I roll my eyes and throw my hands up in the air.
Like I'm going to sleep after this...
I say it with way more drama than it deserves. As I set my
hands down on my lap I notice how heavy they feel. Now
my elbows. I become aware of the effort it's taking to
keep my head leaning back against the wall. She gazes
expectantly at me.
I become very suspicious.
Wait...
It takes way too much effort to say that.
Is it my jaw still getting used to working again?

No.

Nothing to do with my jaw.

I am slipping.

Did you do something to make me feel like this…?

The last few words of the question slur.

How did you-

She glances towards the bathroom.

You brush your teeth every night before bed, don't you?

I do…

Did you check tonight to make sure no one sprinkled a little concentrated melatonin on your toothbrush to help you fall asleep? Probably not-who would think to do that?

It would take way too much energy to reply. She places her hand gently under the back of my head, adjusting my pillow, helping me lie down.

Are you tucking me in?

She pulls the covers up.

I am tucking you in. Sleep well, Heen Gru-Bares.

As I drift away I ask her *Why are you here? What is happening?*

I hear her whispered reply *There are, of course, answers to your questions…*

And then she's gone.

I hear the front door close.

I'm out.

*

I'm late for work.

I am never late for work.

The SUNS are almost up.

I start running.

I'm going to arrive all sweaty.

I walk.

How embarrassing.

Arriving late.

I will skip my front door Borns impersonation.

I go around back.

I slink into the storage room where my apron is.

Heen?

Ziga Mey calls me.

I come into the kitchen adjusting my apron.

Borns pats me on the back. *Did someone have a rough night?*

He has no idea.

His eyes sparkle.

He grins like he's in on a secret.

He told a long story last night about how a Hoo Hah was formed in the bowels of a volcano, the recipe revealed only to him by the GODS OF LAVA in a sacred ritual involving pineapples and mud. Peeble stopped him at one point and said *My mother taught him.* Which was funny. By that point I was several HOO HAHS in, which made it even funnier. Which isn't as funny this morning because of the dull ache in the front of my head. Which may also be from using my jaw for the first time in a while.

I am well aware that my Ho Hahs are quite special but they can leave a person slightly beleaguered the next morning-am I right Heen Who Now Speaks??

This is true Borns, so true.

Lan Zing waves to me from the front. Ziga Mey sees her.

Some people have been asking for you.

Me? I look around. Bobby Freelance is washing some

dishes in the other room. Pretty much everyone I know on Firdus is in this room, give or take a Dill Tudd.

I make my way up front.

Oh. This guy. White dog/zipper shirt/hair situation fella.

THERE HE IS! He yells this as he points at me. What was his name-Jareeve? Janeezsch? There are three women at a table along the far wall. They look over. Two older men at the counter watch me. A family at the table next to the window stare.

I pass by Lan Zing. *I am so sorry I was late-*

She pats my arm. *No worries-somebody here is very excited to meet you.*

She winks.

I'm missing something.

The man turns to someone I can't see on the other side of the counter and says *I TOLD YOU HE'D SHOW UP!!!*

And then I see her.

She stands up and turns to me. She's very tall, and she's wearing a gold shirt. It shines and shimmers and reflects in a thousand directions. She's holding that white dog. There are large bracelets up and down her arms. Her fingernails are pink and green and long. Very long. She could do some serious harm with them long.

Her lips are bright red.

And her hair. It's huge. And wavy.

Like if you froze the sea in the middle of a winter storm.

There is glitter in it.

Heen, the man says as he shakes my hand, *Javeen*

Wendor, we met a few days ago. Such a pleasure to see you again. And now, it is my honor and privilege to introduce you to BARBARA BARABAR.

He treats this like it's a formal ceremony of some sort. Barbara Barabar doesn't say anything. She hands him the dog as she steps towards me, opening her arms and embracing me. She has very, very large breasts. Massive. I cannot overstate this fact. And she is tall, did I mention that?

I am not tall.

I can barely breathe.

My face warms.

It's humid in here.

I feel a vibration in her chest.

Is that her breast bone?

Is she humming?

She starts to sway.

Like we're slow dancing.

I hear Javeen say something to Lan Zing about how *Barbara Barabar's hugs are legendary.*

The humming is getting louder.

It's a tune.

She's humming a song.

There is sorrow in this song. Longing. Ache.

I feel it more than I hear it.

In my head. Not my ears, in the bones of my head.

Held here up against her vibrating chest.

Javeen's voice, clearer this time. *You know, Barbara Barabar and I haven't been able to have kids. And she has such a mother's heart-you never know who she is going to take under her wing.*

I realize that I have wrapped my arms around her.

When did that happen?

I wasn't aware I did that.
I kind of like this.
I wouldn't admit it.
But it's quite nice in here.

Once I was hiking through a jungle on the planet Rill Shay
when I came across a clearing with a tree in the middle. It
was a large tree with smooth, white bark, and it had just
dropped all of its flowers. The tree stood there naked,
stripped, empty. But the ground-the ground was covered in
flowers. Like a carpet. Red flowers, orange flowers, yellow
flowers, pink as your pinkie flowers. Those flowers were so
thick I couldn't even see the ground below them.
It was so much to take in.
I just stood there for a while.
And then I walked into the middle of that clearing under that
tree and laid down on my back.
That was the only fitting response to all those flowers.
And the smell.
That smell.
GOOD GODS it was intoxicating.
Breathing in, breathing out.
I laid there for hours.
I didn't want to leave.
This reminds me of that.
Barbara Barabar holding me tight.
I could stay here for a while.

Time has lost its relentless forward lurch here in this
bakery between this tall woman's breasts.
IS THIS A MOTHER THING?
Is that it?
Is that why I'm not fighting this?

It's one of the strangest things that's ever happened to me. Top three for sure. But I haven't pulled away.
It's not sexual. Honestly. It's the opposite of that.
Javeen is still going *It's a special gift she has. I've seen it so many times-she meets someone and just knows that they need one of her hugs.*
What is he on about?
It's like a spell. Or a cure. You get a hug from Barbara Barabar and you're never the same...
He kind of has a point there.
I'll give him that.
I feel her slowly begin to let me go.
It takes a while.
I look up into her eyes.
It's an ocean of love.
That's how I would describe it.
And I don't talk like that.
Obviously.
She places her hands on my shoulders.
She leans down so our eyes are level.
That bread you make-the sourdough with rosemary?
I think that's a question.
I slowly nod. *YES.*
It's bread, but it's more than bread-you know this, don't you?
I smile like a small boy.
Thank you she says.
She kisses my forehead, slowly turns to Javeen, takes his hand and then says *Let's leave them to their magic-shall we my love?*
And then the two of them walk out of the bakery. With their dog.
I stand here in the middle of the room.

My eyes are still adjusting to the light. It was dark in there.
My head feels swimmy.
Borns shouts from the back *Heen! I thought you'd never
come out of there!*
My skin turns pink.
I drift back to the kitchen.
You have had quite a day already, haven't you? Ziga Mey
says.

If she knew.
If only she knew.
That woman.
In my room.
That happened, right?
I'm not imagining it?
I keep hoping that didn't happen.
But it did.
She did.

*

I take my break and go for a walk.
My tongue is throbbing, I haven't filed a report in I don't
know how long, Javeen going on about Barbara Barabar,
THAT WOMAN IN MY ROOM THAT WOMAN IN MY
ROOM THAT WOMAN IN MY ROOM-it's all too much, a
claustrophic cacophony rattling around in my head and
heart.

I head up through the trees west of the bakery. There's a
trail along the ridge that's usually empty. I need space to
sort all this out.
I'm angry.

This takes me a bit of walking to realize.

That's what it is.

The more I walk the angrier I get.

There's a series of switchbacks on the trail as it climbs the side of the hill. I come around one of the turns and see a pile of branches off to the side. They're each about as long as a person, some a bit more. They were trimmed from the trees that line the trail, left there a while ago. They're old and brittle.

I pick one up and swing it against the trunk of a tree. I don't know why I do this. It breaks in half. The end goes flying off down the embankment.

This feels good.

A SIGN 7.

That's what she said.

You're a SERIES 5, I'm a SIGN 7.

Why have I never heard of SIGN 7s?

Was she making that up?

If she was, she's unbelievably good. Because that performance was perfect. No hesitation. So convincing.

But no. She's for real.

They sent her.

For me.

You're the job.

That's what she said.

I pick up another stick. It's heavy. I take a few steps and slam it against the tree. It breaks. The end rolls down the hill. Again, surprisingly satisfying.

I pick up another. I swing it harder, faster. The noise is louder.

I have bark and dust all over my hands.

I don't care.

Another stick. This one smashes into three sections.

It's a large pile.
I have a ways to go.

I think of Ron. She was my flight instructor. She wore yellow coveralls with a patch on the front that said I EAT ALTITUDE FOR BREAKFAST.

She was merciless.

The first day of class she said YOU DON'T KNOW HOW TO FLY A SPACESHIP. I DO. I WILL TEACH YOU. And then she handed out bags-they were black and made of something I'd never seen before she called PLASTIC— and she had us cut holes in the sides of those bags and then put them on like shirts and then she led us outside and she got on a bicycle and rode away from us, yelling over her shoulder for us to follow her which was exhausting because we had to run to keep up. That lasted at least an hour. And then when we got back to our classroom and we're drenched in sweat and winded from all that running we see that while we were gone someone poured a little pile of salt on each of our desks and next to that pile of salt they placed a pair of tweezers. We sat down. Ron told us to take those tweezers and use them to remove one grain of salt at a time from the pile and make a straight line with those grains from left to right across the top of our desk. My hand was shaking.
Sweat kept dripping off my forehead onto the pile of salt.
It was so difficult.
It took the entire day.
And then when we came to class the next day, she didn't mention it. Like it never happened. She handed out textbooks and started in on physics and engineering and

math and then more math and then aerodynamics and subsonic analytics and viscous flows-this went on for weeks and weeks and weeks. She'd teach us, then test us, then teach us more.

It was so intense.

We called it THE RONS. When you were feeling rattled from the pressure of having to learn so much so fast you'd say *I got a bad case of The Rons.*

And then one day she tells us to follow her as she leaves the classroom. She leads us out to the hangar on the far side of the academy where there was AN ACTUAL SPACESHIP and we all got on and she had this girl named Yoshee sit in the pilot's chair and then she showed us a button on the center of the console that said AUTOPILOT.

She pointed at that button.

And then she laughed.

For the first time since we'd been in her class.

Ron laughed and laughed and laughed.

I looked around at the other students.

Nobody was laughing.

None of us got it.

It was all so odd. To be there on that ship, after all that time, waiting for her to stop laughing.

Finally she stopped laughing and she says *YOU JUST PUSH A BUTTON.*

We just stood there, crammed together in the cockpit of that spaceship. No one knew what to say.

YOU JUST PUSH A BUTTON?

After all those hours in her class-it turned out that it's just not that complicated.

It was a set up.

The whole thing.

She could have taken us out to that hangar the first day and showed us that button.

I thought I was going to spontaneously combust with rage. What a waste of time. All you have to do is push a button?

Of course, over the laps, I have drawn on all that she taught us countless times. All that complexity-all that background and math and detail and structure-it's been with me the whole time. Guiding me, informing me, helping me see the thing behind the thing.

But in that moment,

crammed in that spaceship,

listening to her laugh,

I was spitting nails I was consumed with rage.

Like now.

I swing another dead branch at a tree.

This one makes a thunderous bang.

It splinters into countless pieces.

I have been on AUTOPILOT.

For most of my adult life.

Arrive. Notice. Report. Leave. Repeat.

It's so much easier than THIS. This FIRDUS. Connecting. Feeling. Having to figure things out. I might throw up in my mouth if I actually say it: *caring.*

And then that woman in my room.

She haunts me.

Where is she right now?

Why did she say she needs more time?

I swing another stick.

A few more and I will have made my way through the entire pile.

*

Ziga Mey is at the counter. A woman is buying bread. A flash of something between them. The woman leaves. Ziga Mey comes back to where I'm preparing the trays for the whole grain loaves.

A friend? I ask her. I keep my sentences short, it still hurts to speak.

You could say so.

It is so clear she wants to say more.

I am ready for you to say more.

I am so direct. I surprise myself.

She starts pacing. *Well, I had to find somewhere new to live and I heard about this place called The Poles-they just built it. So I went to take a tour and OH MY HEEN what a place! They built these platforms high up off the ground-each one sits on top of a thick pole-*

Like a birdhouse?

Yes, exactly. Like a birdhouse. On either end are enclosed living and bedrooms and then between the two units is an open air kitchen with a table and a garden...

I point east. *Out past that clothes store and the pink tower?*

Yes, exactly.

I've seen those. I didn't know what they were.

People live in those?

Yes. I just moved in. They had one unit left. I took it the first time I saw it. I walked in and I knew THIS IS YOUR NEXT CHAPTER ZIGA MEY.

Bobby Freelance brings clean pans in and sets them down on the table.

Did you say The Poles?

I did. I just moved there.

That place is the bomb.

I look at him, concerned. *The bomb?*

Ziga Mey touches my arm. *That's good. Being THE BOMB. Got it.*

I catch up given enough time.

So I figured before I actually signed the lease I should meet the person on the other side-if we're going to, you know, share a kitchen and garden and all-so I knock on the door and this woman answers and...

She goes quiet.

Shy.

A little flustered.

Bobby Freelance leans in over the table. Like he knows something. *Electricity?*

How did he know to say that?

That's a word for it.

She says this to no one in particular. She's lost in thought. He watches her.

Kind of disorienting, right? Good, but a little shocking?

She agrees. *Totally caught me off guard.*

She says this quietly. Like she's been thinking about it for days and doesn't quite know what to make of it.

What's her name? I ask.

Rafinia.

She says it like music.

Oooh I like that.

Bobby Freelance likes it as well.

Boom he says.

I give him my concerned look. *Boom?*

Ziga Mey turns to me. *Boom is good.*

*

I leave work and walk back to my flat. I cannot calm down. All this spiky, jagged energy coursing through me. Angsty, agitated, unsettled. I have a problem. I AM the problem. I need help. I don't know who to ask. Or how. Or what I'd even be asking for.

It used to be so much more doable.

Arrive, Notice. Leave.

This is something else.

A disaster.

The end. Of something.

Piddle, piddle, piddle.

He comes from the left.

He's wearing orange today. Orange pants, orange shirt, orange sandals, orange everything. Except for that green stone in his necklace.

I've stopped wondering how Dill Tudd finds me.

Or why we meet up when we do.

Or how it all works.

Here he is.

Again.

I'm glad to see him.

Hello Dill Tudd.

Hello Heen Gru-Bares.

I get right to it.

Dill Tudd, can I ask you a question?

He stretches out his hands in front of him.

Do you know why I wore ORANGE today?

In my previous life-also known as the first few times I talked to him-I would have been so irritated by this response. By how difficult it is to have a straightforward conversation with him. Now, I go with it.

No. Why did you wear orange today?

Because I knew you'd have a question for me.

*But that doesn't explain why ORANGE-what does
ORANGE have to do with asking questions?*
He smiles like an old man who has seen it all.
Oh Heen, we have so far to go with you.
I agree.
Who's WE?
He breathes a sigh of relief.
Well, now you know how I feel.
If I wasn't already coming undone this back and forth
would have finished me off.
So can I ask my question?
I am ready, feel free to proceed.
He says this as he gestures to the leaves above us. We're
walking under a canopy of eucalyptus trees. There's a
light breeze blowing through. The branches sway, shafts
of light coming and going.
Beautiful I say.
It is Dill Tudd replies.
So beautiful! A voice behind us.
A woman's voice.
I turn.

It's her.
Heen...?
She says it like we met once a party a while ago and
haven't seen each other since.
She catches up with us.
What to do.
Play along with her? Let Dill Tudd know that I don't know
her? Tell him that she was in my bedroom last night but
we've never properly met?
Yes... I say it hesitantly, like I'm trying to recall where we
met. *You got me, Heen here, and you're...*

I try to make it awkward so she'll see that two can play this game but Dill Tudd has no problem doing his own thing.

Well hello, what a pleasure to have you join us on our stroll.

He offers her his hand, she starts to shake it, he places his other hand on top of their two shaking hands, she then places her other hand on top of their three hands. They do this in front of me.

We come to a stop.

She's all smiles.

Well, aren't you wonderful. I'm Noon Yeah.

I turn to her.

Noon Yeah?

I say it like it's a question.

Dill Tudd laughs at this. *Oh Heen, you have such a charming way of acting like all of this is new.*

Noon Yeah gives him a knowing look.

He's does, doesn't he? Like it's all just happening to him- like he's floating along down the river just letting the current carry him along-when, in fact, this guy doesn't MISS A THING! She taps my arm. *HE IS ON IT-as sharp as they come!!!!*

This is exactly the sort of off kilter chatter Dill Tudd loves.

Well, if you are a friend of Heen Gru-Bares, then let's dispense with the formalities and assume that we have been friends the whole time and we're just now finding out about it. I'm Dill Tudd.

I put my hand on Dill Tudd's left shoulder.

He actually means that.

*And to think-*Noon Yeah looks up and around-*we finally meet under this stunning canopy of eucalyptus trees.*

Dill Tudd steps to the side of the path and touches the

trunk of one. *And not just any eucalyptus-I can only assume these are Tasmanian blue gums-*

Noon Yeah nods in affirmation. *Definitely one of my favorites-I love how their flower buds are arranged in groups of three and SEVEN.*

She looks at me and winks.

She is terrifying.

I look away.

Dill Tudd has a question for her. *Do you know what their fruit is called?*

Noon Yeah does. *I believe they're called GAMNUTS.*

Is there a better word on any planet anywhere? Dill Tudd asks. *Heen, have you ever seen GAMNUTS?*

I have not seen GAMNUTS I say with as little enthusiasm as I can.

Noon Yeah points to a branch above us. *Notice how the more juvenile leaves are whiter and a bit waxy but as they mature they darken-*

The contrast gives the canopy a texture and dimension-

Like a tapestry-

Like a tapestry, so well said.

They are lost in their tree talk.

I just stand here. Watching.

My goodness Noon Yeah, you do know your trees…

She sighs with affection. *You know what I love most about them?*

Dill Tudd is so into this. *Let me guess: the fire and the pods?*

YES! She practically shouts it. *How did you know?!*

Dill Tudd waves this away. *How would I not? It's incredible!*

I totally agree.

They are interacting like they've been friends for a hundred laps. I don't know how they do it-how they connect so effortlessly. I don't know how to do that.

Fire pod thing? I ask.

I am so irritated and unnerved and anxious but suddenly curious.

Should we tell him? Dill Tudd asks Noon Yeah. Like they're in on a conspiracy.

We should tread carefully here, I don't know if he can handle it. She says this deadpan.

Dill Tudd is thrilled. *Exactly. Because once a person possesses this knowledge…I mean…let's be honest-*

Noon Yeah jumps in *There's no going back.*

Right! Dill Tudd draws the word out. He pats his necklace.

Because once you see-

You can't unsee.

And once you taste-

You can't untaste.

These two are literally finishing each other's sentences before my eyes.

TELL ME ABOUT THE FIRE PODS!!

I yell. I recover.

They barely acknowledge my flare up.

Noon Yeah steps close to me, hooking her arm through my elbow.

She looks over at Dill Tudd.

Feel free to stop me at any point.

She looks back at me.

Our faces are quite close.

These trees don't really burn-they actually need fire. They DEPEND on fire. Fire frees the seeds from the confines of the pods so that they can be buried in the soil and then at some point in the future RISE UP OUT OF THE GROUND. It's the heat that makes all that new life possible.

368

She's wearing a red top. It is thick and appears to be stretchy. Her skirt is also red, a deep red close to the color of blood. I wouldn't think that these two shades would work together but they do. They really do. I catch a whiff of mint on her breath. She isn't wearing a head band today, just a bit of string bringing her hair together in back in what I believe is called a PONY TAIL. Does that name have something to do with horses? She radiates energy. It pulses, it pops, it pours off of her. She's like a force field. Or a storm.

A sniffle.

Noon Yeah and I turn to Dill Tudd.

He's wiping his eyes.

He collects himself.

That was so beautiful-not only was it botanically precise, it was simultaneously poetic and succinct. You capture the essence of the GLOBOLUS with such brevity AND depth. What a gift you have given me. Thank you.

He is genuinely moved by her little speech there about fire in those pods.

Dill Tudd seems to be missing the protective system that forms most of what I know to be me.

He collects himself.

Well, friend-and new friend who has already become a dear friend-I must go.

So soon? Noon Yeah asks.

Where are you headed? I ask.

I have never asked him this before.

It's time for me to let the dogs out he says.

He gives us each his Dill Tudd bow, and then he heads up the trail.

Noon Yeah? I say to her.

Yep she replies.

Noon Yeah?

I try to sound as cynical as I can.

Again, yes.

NOON as in the time of day, YEAH like YEAH WE WON THE GAME!!! YEAH IT'S YOUR BIRTHDAY!!! Of all the names you could have made up, you took those two words and attached them together and that's what you tell people your name is?

I don't do aggression very well.

That's my name.

She's remains very calm.

Okay, yeah, when you're meeting random strangers like Dill Tudd on a job on a planet that you're just visiting-but that's not your-you know-name NAME.

She is totally unphased.

It is my name NAME.

We're walking up the hill and out of the woods.

You call yourself Heen, right?

I do.

You don't make up some other name for the job-

No. I did once. But it didn't work.

What was it? She leans in and smiles. *What name did you give yourself?*

I stammer.

Too embarrassing.

Oh come on, tell me.

No way.

She fake pushes me. *Tell me!*

That's it-that's her right there-that's the thing. She FAKE PUSHES ME like we're long lost friends who are always messing with each other. But she's a SIGN 7 and she has suddenly appeared out of nowhere and she snuck into my flat because she's tracking me for nefarious reasons I can only begin to guess at-

She's light, but she's also dark.

And she wants to know what name I gave myself that one time I used a fake name.

I was young. New on the job. Trying to figure it out. There was so much in training about not letting them know the real YOU. How to be yourself and do a job in which you can't really be yourself, etc etc. Basic SERIES 5 issues right there-
You're stalling-what was the name?
You're not going to let it go, are you?
That is correct, I will hunt you down-
You already did.
Good point. I did.
I might as well tell her.
Soars.
You told them your name was Sores? Like SORES on your body?
No, no-
Infectious, pussy open wounds that won't heal-
Well, see, that was the problem right there! I was thinking FLYING-S-O-A-R-as in SOARS LIKE AN EAGLE. Get it? Gliding through the air, weightless, above it all-I thought it would be fun to have an inspiring name-
But people heard SORES. The other kind.
She really enjoys this.
You're laughing at me.
I am. I am laughing at you. To your face.
She's wearing black boots. Sleek black boots. They look

like a thick sock with a loop in the back and a chunky, knobby sole. Where in the worlds would you find boots like that?

So you can see when you say you're Noon Yeah I have my doubts.

Okay fine. But I actually am Noon Yeah.

Your parents named you Noon Yeah?

What is it with you and my name?

Names are important!

They are…?

Of course!

HEEN is important? Heeeeeeen?

No one has ever asked me this.

It is to me. It's my name.

Got that. But what does it mean?

I stall. I squint. …*Mean?*

Yes. Not a trick question. Where does it come from? What does it represent? Why did your parents pick that name out of all the names in all the worlds?

I never asked them.

Up until this moment in my life I would have told you that no one has ever gotten under my skin faster and with greater intensity than Dill Tudd. But this woman. Noon Yeah. This woman in these boots has managed to bore her way ferociously deep into my psyche.

So according to you, names are important. That's why you are SO insistent on knowing if Noon Yeah is my real name. And yet you don't know the first thing about your name.

We're almost to the top of the hill.

I have no idea where we're going.

I stop and turn to face her.

That's a good point.

She pumps her fist like she just scored a goal. I don't follow.

All I said was GOOD POINT
You did. That was a big moment for us.
Us?
She looks around.
Yes. Me and you. But YOU in particular…
I leave that one alone.
We reach the top.
There's a bench.

There's always a bench on Firdus.

I sit down. The view is amazing. Out over the top of CIRCLE 3 to a small lake and then the plain beyond it. I have a thousand questions. I tell her this.
I have a thousand questions.
Excellent. Fire away.
She's pacing back and forth. I don't like it.
Could you please sit down?
She stops pacing and examines me.
Not yet. I haven't completed the assessment.
I hate that she just said that.
The assessment?
She continues pacing, ignoring my question.
It's awkward. I don't know whether to ignore you or to watch you while you pace…
Again, she stops.
She looks at me like I have two heads.
It helps me think. And besides, you have waaayyyyy bigger problems than me pacing.
And there it is. That endless drone of a reminder that she's here for something.
I assert myself. *All right then, first question: Who do you work for?*

Her hands are on her hips.

Who do YOU work for?

I roll my eyes. *First rule: You don't get to answer my questions with questions.*

She'll have none of that. *First OTHER rule: YOU don't make the rules. And that WAS my answer.*

She is so good.

How is a question an answer?

Disbelief on her face.

However you would answer that question is how I would answer that question. I work for the same people as you.

A little clarity. I'll take it.

But who do you report to?

She sits down next to me. Finally.

Who do you report to?

Randy.

Randy? she asks. *I do, too. She's been my CONNECT the whole time.*

She?

She.

I have a Randy.

I gathered that when you said RANDY.

But my Randy is a HE not a SHE.

She puts her face in her hands.

Oh my. We have so far to go.

Where are we going?!!

She turns to me.

You really don't know anything, do you?

That low-grade terror seeps in.

THAT'S WHAT'S SO WRONG ABOUT YOUR QUESTION— HOW WOULD I KNOW WHAT I DON'T KNOW???!!!

That's fair.

It feels like she's building up to something. Let's get it

374

over with.

Just tell me. It'll be fine.

She looks at me like I have no idea what I just said. Her look shifts to an expression I can't quite name. Considering. That's it. She's considering something. Weighing it.

Okay then, I'll tell you. This is a GRAINING.

A graining? Should I know what that is?

She tilts her head back, shaking it as she does.

You SERIES 5's, they really leave you out in the dark, don't they?

A blank look from me.

Please continue…

It sounds like I'm pleading with her. I am. I'm desperate. Noon Yeah reaches down and picks up a few bits of dirt and gravel from the ground at our feet. She rubs her fingers together.

You know how if a single grain of sand gets into the gears of a machine it can cause significant damage?

She doesn't wait for me to respond.

We can't have that. If a grain-just one grain-gets in there that's very, very serious. It has to be dealt with immediately and decisively. It has to be removed.

A shudder, somewhere within.

That's what I do.

She pauses.

You SERIES 5's, you give the DATA that's needed to keep it all running well. If you can't do your job then THE ENTIRE THING is in danger.

An ever so small tinge of recognition.

The universe? The worlds?

I must sound like a small child. My worst fear.

Yes.

Her *YES* hangs here between us.
But what does this have to do with me?
I regret this as I ask it.
Your reports.
Oh.
Since you landed on Firdus your reports have been…
inconsistent.
Ouch.
You know this.
I nod.
I do.
And then they went from INCONSISTENT to
NONEXISTENT. You missed one-
It was just one report-
It was?
I am struggling here.
You have never missed a report. And then you missed the
next one, and then the next one…Do you think that went
UNNOTICED?
That's a problem?
I know the answer to that as I ask it.
Yes Heen, that's a problem.
But now I'll just resume doing my reports-
She holds up her hand.
You still don't get it? The CHAIRS-how do I make this
clear? This gets fixed. Immediately.
A few bits starting to click.
You?
She nods slowly.
A SERIES 5 stops giving acceptable reports and so they
send a SIGN 7-YOU-to figure out why and then you-
FIX IT.
Fix it. Got it.

I am so relieved.

Well that's great, then! You came and we met and you're giving me this pep talk to help me refocus and remind me how important my work is. I already feel like it's a whole new day!

I am doing my best to convince her. And me.

No.

She says it again.

No.

What?

She exhales.

I listened to the audio.

The terror had subsided there for a few seconds.

Now it's back.

What audio?

AAAHHHHHH!!! She explodes. *HOW DO YOU THINK IT WORKS?!!*

Didn't we just sort all that out!??? I get it!! I get how it works!!! We're good. YOU DID YOUR JOB! I'm back on track. You can go now. You can get in your-WAIT-Do you have your own spaceship?

I do.

Where'd you park your spaceship?

Next to yours-where else?

How did you find it?

I studied every single landing you've ever done. You are very predictable.

No way.

Yes way.

You studied all the places I've landed my ships over all the laps of doing this and from that you figured out where I'd

land on Firdus? That's astonishing. I wouldn't put it past
you, but still, THAT IS A LOT OF STUDYING.
She smiles. Just a little.
Also, you have a transponder on board. I found the signal. It
took ten seconds.
Oh.
Does she know I used my ship to find Lines?
Interesting little something I noticed...
This should be good.
I try to make her laugh. It doesn't work.
I noticed that right next to your landing pads are identical
landing pad indentations in the ground.
It takes an extraordinary amount of effort to appear
ignorant.
That's strange.
She keeps going.
It looks like you landed. And then landed again, right next
to where you landed the first time.
I gaze off into the distance like I'm giving it a good think.
Huh...highly unusual...I can't say I remember...
Obfuscate is the word for it. Distract. I think she buys it.
When you've done so many landings I'm sure they all run
together...
Is she setting me up or is she genuinely saying that?
Oh yeah. So true. You now how it is...
Don't give her anything to go on.
I do know how it is.
We're almost out of the woods on this. Keep it up...
Just one little other thing I found curious...
She lets it hang there. Like a master in the fine art of
torture.
When I pulled up your transponder logs there's a series of
loops and cutbacks in the flight graph that happened just

recently.

Recently? Doing my best DOUBT FACE.

Odd. I know. Like someone took the ship up and all around that Stellen Peak area haphazardly-turns and grids and random swoops-and then parked it.

Weird.

That's the best I can do. *Weird.*

So weird she says.

I lean back on the bench.

I remind myself to breathe.

I can outlast her.

I can be vague and ignorant all day.

The files.

She says it quietly.

You mentioned that.

All of your reports are recorded. I listened to them. She pauses. *In order.*

All of them?

Everything since you landed on Firdus.

I pretend I'm tweaked by this.

You eavesdropped on me?

Research is a better word for it.

You listened to-

Do you do research before you fly to your next job?

Of course. That's basic.

I do, too. Heen?

Yes, Noon Yeah.

We're facing each other on the bench.

Dill Tudd is the grain.

Tears in my eyes. Immediately.

Who have I become?

I will them to stop.

They won't.

No he's not.

I don't know what she means by HE'S THE GRAIN. But she's wrong.
Yes. He is. You mention him in your reports. He's why the reports begin to falter. He compromises your ability to do your job.
No he doesn't.
You say it in your reports! Your first mention of him coincides with the decrease in quality-I get it. Somebody gets under your skin. You can't think straight. It happens. But there's a clear and direct relationship between your job performance and this person. You have to see that- But you can't just…
I don't know where that sentence is headed.
She is resolute.
There's a way things work. The CHAIRS need the DATA. Anything that gets in the way of that must be eliminated.
I am not hearing this because this is not happening.
Graining? Is that what you said?
Yes. She shrugs. *That's what happens.*
And who does this?
I already know the answer.
Me.
She says it like she's missing a heart.
YOU speak to him? He gets…what? A warning? A notice? …a fine…what are we talking about here?
Noon Yeah jumps up from the bench. Now we're both pacing, passing shoulder to shoulder each time around.
Removal.
She says it with no emotion. No drama. Flat. Lifeless.

A picture in the front of my mind.
A person.
I say his name.
Uncle Dir.
I sit back down.
It feels like five hundred pounds landing on the bench.
She stops. *Who?*
My dad has a brother…had a brother? Uncle Dir. He used to visit us. And then he stopped coming around…
What do you remember about him?
Honestly? He was a mess. A very disturbing presence. That's what I remember.
Noon Yeah nods knowingly.
Wouldn't surprise me.
I sit on the top of the bench with my feet on the seat.
Dill Tudd has nothing to do with this.
She joins me.
Dill Tudd has everything to do with this.
No, no, no, no, no.
I am so sad and so scared. I keep repeating it.
No, no, no, no…
She leans over and looks in my eyes.
What does he do all day?
Dill Tudd? I have no idea.
I shouldn't have said it like that.
So you're defending someone who you don't really know the first thing about…
She's got a point but I will never admit it.
I'm not defending him. Okay, I am defending him. He helps people.
She's never gonna go for that.
He helps people. How?
All she is doing is asking very straightforward questions

and I am barely hanging on. I can't believe I'm about to say this…
He hands stuff out.
She's gonna cook me for that one.
Heen Gru-Bares. Can you hear yourself? She says it slowly and patiently like I don't hear very well. *You are in deep.*
I'M in deep!!???
I shout it.
She isn't the slightest bit rattled.
YES. You are in very deep. This whole system you and I have known our entire lives? It only works when everybody contributes and everybody does their part and everybody follows the rules-
And if someone doesn't you eliminate them?
How many times do I have to ask you? How do you think it works? WHAT DO YOU THINK YOU'VE BEEN DOING THIS WHOLE TIME?
My job.
Exactly. Until you stopped doing your job-
Just for a few days.
Do you think we have that kind of margin?
I push back.
Margin? How is there a margin?
She takes a slow inhale.
The universe doesn't do margins. If we don't do our work it all wobbles and teeters. Chaos is ALWAYS just around the corner. You think the natural state is harmony? Symmetry? Peace? WHERE HAVE YOU BEEN? What planet were you born on? Have you not noticed? This whole everything that you and I know to be HOW THINGS ARE has to be held together-it has to be maintained-it has to be monitored and adjusted and constantly tweaked or it goes

*off the rails immediately. YOU THINK THIS JUST
HAPPENS? I don't think you have any clue how brutal life
is…*

She trails off.
She has no idea.
She clearly didn't do any research on me.
She's so quick but she has missed so much.
Suddenly I feel a touch of confidence.
For the first time I may be a step ahead of her.
I give myself a beat to enjoy this feeling.
It probably won't last.
I know exactly what to say next.
You're a believer.
She didn't see that coming.
I have no idea what you mean by that.
That's the best she can do.
Are you an assassin?
Oh please-that is not the job title.
*Yes it is. When you say FIX you mean ELIMINATE which
means KILL. You kill people.*
I… She starts to say something and stops.
*That's your job!? You fly your spaceship around the worlds
killing people who disrupt or don't measure up or aren't
useful-whatever your criteria is-so that everybody else can
enjoy a good life.*
I'm on a roll.
*Do you have a gun? I bet you have a gun. Or do you use
poison or do you choke them in their sleep or do you carry
a knife? Do you have a weapon on you? Right now, do
you have a weapon on you? Can I see it-will you show it
to me? Could you kill me right now?*
I say it with glee.

As if I want it to be true.

She's got the blankest look ever on her face. I can use that.

Okay fine-I've been unaware of how it all actually works-I get what you've been saying. But you need to take a good, long look at...

I falter.

A good long look at how you...

Something is clouding my mind.

You should look at how YOU are contributing...

It's a someone.

A name.

Someone from way back.

BABAK!!!

It coughs and sputters out of me.

Where did that come from?

I crumble.

I slump over my knees.

Babak.

I mumble it.

Babak.

I say it like a lament.

Oh Babak.

Now it makes sense.

I am so sad. Again.

As sad as I have ever been.

As sad as that day at the CHARIS when NORDS turned his back on me.

Noon Yeah places her hand on my back.

I hate her.

But the touch is nice.

Babak? she inquires, tenderly. But tenderly like a trained assassin would say it..

I was doing so well. I had her reeling. Rethinking things. But then this memory. It comes pouring out.

When I was a kid I met this other kid-just once-he was the brother of this other kid I met this one time and he was… OFF…something was really wrong with him…and then he painted some stuff on the wall of the library and there was this incident with a dog and we were told they sent him away to get help but they didn't get him help did they? Did they?

Like Noon Yeah would know.

Did they?

I keep repeating it.

His name was Babak. Babak got grained, didn't he?

We sit here.

Noon Yeah with her hand on my back.

The two of us silent.

A raindrop on the bench beside me.

Then another one.

My first rain on Firdus.

My place isn't far I mutter.

We're off the bench and running.

Down the hill.

Through the park.

Past the pitch.

She's next to me.

Not the slightest bit winded, running there in her red skirt.

Neither of us talking.

We're getting soaked.

We run up to my building, I pull the door open and turn to her.

She's isn't there.

She's gone.

*

I sit in my flat and stare at the disc.

I tap it.

Randy?

Nothing.

Hey! Anyone there? Heen Gru-Bares. SERIES 5. I'd like to file my report for today.

Nothing.

All those laps of tapping that disc and now nothing.

It's still raining.

I move a chair from my kitchen table over to the window.

I sit and stare out.

I think of Sir Pong.

All those hours in his class, listening to him teach us about the ARRANGEMENTS.

Did he know how it really works?

And his whole thing about EXCHANGES. How every culture makes them. This is what he meant by EXCHANGES? People are REMOVED so that things run smoothly? It's unfortunate, but HEY IT'S THE PRICE OF A WELL-RUN UNIVERSE.

I picture him telling us how the worlds actually run. What if he'd written the word MARGIN on the wall and then told us THERE IS NONE and then explained how that actually works itself out in the worlds? What if he'd gone on to explain that there are these people who work for the CHAIRS called SIGN 7's and they fly around in spaceships KILLING people who don't fit someone somewhere's criteria for…ACCEPTABLY WELL-ADJUSTED HUMAN BEINGS…

We would have lost our minds.

The universe is not a good place. That's what we would have thought. We would have been traumatized. There would have been a riot in the class.
Or not.
I was so trusting.
We all were.
Would I have nodded along and done my best to show him that I understood? Because that's what I did for everything else he said. Did he think we were ready for certain truths but other truths we couldn't handle until we were older?

Because I am older, and I am not able to handle this one.

That session on Yorch, when Vo surprised us and Sir Pong came in and I watched him win over the others. Even then, laps after I'd been in his class, that same impulse to please him and be noticed by him was in full effect. That desire to GET IT. When he talked about ADJUSTMENTS to the ARRANGEMENTS, turning the dials and twisting the knobs, I got it. I saw it. It sounded so noble. So beautiful. So sensible. That's what convinced me this was my path. That…what's the word?…Call? Summons? Appeal? Invitation?
He spoke to something in me.
That need to belong.

Is there anything more intoxicating than the desire to belong?

*

I'm too amped to sleep.

I keep waiting for that CLICK from the lamp and then I'll sit up and she'll be there in that chair.

I try to read. I can't.

I think about Dill Tudd.

Where he is.

Where is he?

Where does he live?

Why have I never wondered about this?

Why have I never asked him?

Because I haven't had a friend since I was a boy.

AHHH yes, that's why.

I'm out of practice.

I need to protect him from her.

While she's trying to protect me from him.

I get out of bed and put on my crown.

I sit in the chair at the foot of the bed that she sat in.

I try and see myself as she saw me.

As she SEES me.

This is her job.

She's seen countless mes.

She's probably showed up in a lot of chairs at the foot of lots of beds over the laps.

A SERIES 5 has a problem.

And she's sent to fix it.

So she's only ever seen MES when something's gone wrong.

She has a warped view of us.

Of me.

Because she got on like a house fire with Dill Tudd. That whole thing about the trees?

That was real.

There's some sort of heart beating in there somewhere.

There has to be.

*

I'm in the washroom, rinsing the baking sheets from the latest batch of sourdough with rosemary when Borns comes in. He's singing a song I haven't heard before. Something about a lover with a slow hand. He sashays around the sink, he does a little soft shoe tap, he shimmies his shoulders back and forth, all while singing this song that is as creepy as it is catchy.

He stops singing and gets very serious.

Heen, we have a situation on our hands. It is very grave. We must attend to it at once.

Lan Zing appears in the doorway. *Grave, indeed.*

She is serious like Borns. But also not.

Ziga Mey is right behind her.

I don't ever recall us finding ourselves in a situation like this before at the bakery-do any of you?

They shake their heads.

This is all so odd.

And now Bobby Freelance joins them. *I feel like we all need to pause and take a moment and let Heen know that we are here for him and we're behind him and we'll get through this together and Heen-*

He is delivering this like my life depends on it-

Please know that if you need anything you just say the word and we will be there for you in a heartbeat.

Vigorous head nodding all around. Borns closes his eyes and does a HMMMM in full agreement with what Bobby Freelance just said.

We're in the washroom.

The five of us.

Standing in a circle.

What is this?

What are they doing to me?
I am so tired of feeling like I'm missing something.

I never felt like this when all I used to do was notice.

Lan Zing steps forward. *If you're ready to proceed, please come with me.*
She turns and leaves the room. Borns pats me on the back, Ziga Mey gives me a little hug, Bobby Freelance offers me a fist bump.
Lan Zing heads to the front.
I follow.
And then I see her.
Noon Yeah.
Standing at the counter.
Beaming.
Hi Heen!
She lights up the bakery.
I walk straight to her.
She reaches her hand across the counter.
I had to stop and see you again. Even if it's just for a minute. I had such a great time last night…
She lets that linger in the air between us.
I hear a whistle from the back.
I take her hand.
So did I.
I say it like my words are made of butter.
I can play this game all day long Noon Yeah.
I repeat it because I am fully committed to the bit.
So did I.
I kiss her hand.
You know I'd love to talk but we're pretty busy today and-
Lan Zing interrupts. She's holding the schedule sheet.

Heen it's your break now, isn't it?
These people.
In on it.
I gently pull Noon Yeah just a touch closer.
There's a bench in the alley behind the bakery-meet me there in five minutes?
I say this like I am in complete command.
I'll be there.
She kisses my hand and walks out.
I turn and head back through the kitchen.
Their faces.
Just the widest, most ridiculous smiles.
Borns contorts his lips and says *I had such a great time last night.*
They can't help themselves.
I go into the restroom.
I close the door behind me.
There's a mirror over the sink.
I splash water on my face.
I place both hands on the sink to steady myself.
I stare at the me staring back at me.
Stakes.
That's the word.
There hasn't ever been anything at stake for me.
Yes, the job is about the reports which are the DATA that determine the changes the CHAIRS make BLAH BLAH BLAH.

Look at me BLAH BLAH BLAHing the CHAIRS.
There have been STAKES, but not personal stakes-Noon Yeah showing up for a GRAINING, Dill Tudd taking the hit for my dodgy reports-this is all new, these stakes, something actually mattering to me…

Four minutes.
On that bench.
Three minutes.
I need a plan.
An approach.
I go blank.
I got nothing.
YOU CAN DO THIS I tell my mirror self. I say it out loud.
It doesn't help much.
A knock on the restroom door.
Heen, it's Ziga Mey.
Uh…yeah?
Can I come in?
Come in here-with me?
Yes.
I open the door.
She steps in.
I'm headed out for my break, I need to get-
I know. That's why I'm here.
She is resolute.
This will just take a minute.
She places her hand on my heart.

I don't have a sister. If I did, I think this is what it would be like.

She has something to tell me. *Here's the thing: everything is made of atoms-you know this, right? EVERYTHING. And atoms are made of particles that are constantly in motion. Swirling, buzzing, vibrating-all of it energy IN RELATIONSHIP.*

What is this? A speech? Did she prepare this?

And these particles? These bits and pieces of energy that make up EVERYTHING WE KNOW TO BE EVERYTHING? A particle leaves Point A and arrives at Point B. Simple, right? NO. NO, Heen! No. Not simple. We don't actually know which route the particle took to get from Point A to Point B UNTIL IT'S OBSERVED. Until we witness it. The particle is more like a cloud of possibilities that only reveals which route it actually took when it's observed. Huh?

I say it softly. But it's a solid *HUH.*

She presses her hand on my heart.

Noticing the particle affects what the particle does. DO YOU UNDERSTAND WHAT THIS MEANS? Witnessing the particle shapes the outcome!!!

She spreads her fingers as she presses again.

WE ALL WANT SOMEONE TO SEE US, HEEN. That's what changes everything. We want someone to witness WHO WE ARE. I do not know what is going on between you and that woman, but she wants to be SEEN. Trust me. So do YOU. WE ALL WANT TO BE SEEN. All the IMPRESSING and GAME PLAYING and MANEUVERING and MANIPULATING we do is only ever in the end a giant distraction from what we all WANT WHICH IS TO BE SEEN. SEE her Heen, and let her SEE you.

This is new to me, what she's saying.

I take it in.

I hear Borns just outside the door. *Exactly what I was going to say.*

I lean my head around the corner. *It was?*

He holds his palms together like he's holding a book. *That's right, you did read a lot of books.*

I turn back.

Thank you Ziga Mey. I got about half of that, but the half I

got was…something.
She glows.
Anything for a brother.
That word again.
It wrecks me very time.
I'm ready.
I walk out the back door and there she is.
Noon Yeah on the bench behind the bakery.
Here we go.
I sit down.
You can't be this cold.
It comes out more severe than I intended it to.
And you can't be this naive.
She says it evenly. Like she knew what I was going to say.
One sentence in and I'm scrambling.
You know that you don't have to REMOVE someone to FIX this. You HAVE a heart.
She points to my head.
And you HAVE a brain. And you know that EXCHANGES have to be made or all of this-including your lovely little bakery here-ALL OF THIS starts to fall apart.
I hold up my hand because I have a counter to that.
But violence can't be the solution.
She holds up her hand just like I'm holding up mine.
Neither is denial.

She is wearing a blue dress. It has two large pockets at the waist. There are white and silver flowers stitched into the left sleeve, wrapping around her arm. Her trainers are white. They have thin red stripes on the side. She's wearing a silver necklace. She sits on this bench like she doesn't have a care in the world.
Kill me.

Where did that come from? I hadn't intended to say that. I hadn't even thought that until I heard myself say it.

What?

A slight drop of her jaw.

The underrated element of surprise.

I go with it.

Kill ME not Dill Tudd.

It feels oddly empowering to say it again.

That's an even swap, right? Check your TRAINING MANUAL or your PROTOCOL FORMS or whatever you follow for things like this and you'll see-if you end up on Firdus for a GRAINING take the SERIES 5 OUT because THEY'RE THE GRAIN-right?

I am hyping my own execution and I like it. *So get your gun. Or your knife or poison or wire that you sneak up behind people and strangle them with-*

I have no idea why I feel the need to mention all these possible assassination methods-

And tell me where to meet you-

My eyes light up.

-how about that lovely grove of eucalyptus trees from yesterday, wouldn't that be the most fitting location TO DO THE DEED?! We'll do it-YOU'LL do it-and then Dill Tudd lives and Firdus goes on being the Firdus that we all know and love...

I shrug like I just can't help being this awesome.

She's bewildered. I think.

She looks down the path.

Then back at me.

Stone cold.

Lifeless eyes.

*You're officially being placed in an ADVISORY PERIOD.
They usually last for ten days, sometimes more if further
REVIEW is required. At that point there will be an ON
RAMPING OF YOUR EFFICIENCIES followed by the
standard POST-OPERATIONAL ANALYSIS.*
She turns technical. Sterile. Details.
Is that something that you handle?
I can do details as well.
No-that will be handled by a SILVER 8.
I cough like I've choked on something.
*A SILVER 8! Classic. You people and your titles! A SERIES
5 makes a balls up of it, a SIGN 7 comes in to clean it up,
then somebody called a SILVER 8-you cannot make this
up!-a SILVER 8 comes in to make sure the SIGN 7
properly did their job on the SERIES 5.*
Yes.
No emotion.
You check on me and then they check on you.
Precisely she says, flatly.
Silence between us.
I run through every possible next move. This doesn't take
long because I don't have any.

You messed with THE WRONG SERIES 5.

I used to think before I spoke. I would carefully consider
my words, always conscious of the implications of what I
was saying. Now-or more precisely-HERE on Firdus
things just come out…
She laughs.
I laugh too. I can't help it.
That sounded really lame I say.
She agrees. *So lame.*

FOR SURE one of the four lamest things I've ever said in my life.
She's staring straight ahead, shaking her head. But still smiling.
I'm trying to imagine three things lamer than that but I just can't…
Be grateful, I tell her, *because just thinking of those other three things is making me dumber as I remember them. And I was there when I said them. But I have lived to tell about it so…*I sigh. *Points for resilience.*
She turns to me. *Points for resilience. You survived.*

If only she knew.
I feel like we're having two conversations.
I did. I can make it through anything.
A twinge of sincerity.
There's a commotion at the back door of the bakery.
Bobby Freelance appears holding two plates. He walks over to us, hands us each a plate, and sits down on the bench between us.
On each plate is a slice of sourdough with rosemary and a touch of olive oil.
He's so relaxed and casual.
How is he not picking up on what is going on here? He stretches out his arms on the bench. He radiates warmth and familiarity as he says *It can be a little awkward the morning after, right?*
I just want to crawl in a hole and stay there until all of this is over. Or I die. Or she kills me.
I tense up. Noon Yeah doesn't. She acts as though she's known Bobby Freelance for laps. She crosses her legs and says *Soooo true.* She looks at me, then back at Bobby Freelance. *But it doesn't have to be, that's what I*

keep telling him.

I see what she did there. Acting as if we have some… thing.

Bobby Freelance nods. *It's all about the expectations, isn't it? That's where the suffering is…*

She turns to me. *This guy gets it!*

What are we doing here? Should I be playing along so that Bobby Freelance actually thinks this is about something else? Am I on her side? Are we pretending we're something we're not? Because I am terrible at pretending.

Although. It is my job.

But not THIS kind of pretending.

Like Noon Yeah and I are a thing.

We were negotiating my execution when Bobby Freelance interrupted us. For the record.

Bobby Freelance wears a black and red striped shirt under his apron. Everyday. I assume he has multiples of this particular shirt. I've never asked him. He's wearing sandals. Brown leather sandals. With black socks. And green pants. He wears those sandals every day. Sometimes his socks are red. It's like a uniform. The Bobby Freelance Uniform.

While we're at it, I do have a question for him.

Suffering and expectations?

Bobby Freelance considers the question.

The mind is a wonderful instrument. It can think and analyze and process. Where would we be without our minds?

I look at Noon Yeah. She's totally into this. Neither of us answers his question.

He continues *But your mind can also generate an endless array of scenarios and plans and convictions about how*

things are supposed to go-
Noon Yeah interrupts *That's the killer right there!*
Which is fitting, coming from her.
What's the killer? I ask, eyeing her sideways.
I'm asking Bobby Freelance, but Noon Yeah answers.
*It's easy to become so attached to how you've decided
that it has to go that you aren't present to what's actually
happening-*
Exactly! says Bobby Freelance. *The mind creates so much
suffering with its endless desire to control-as if there's
some perfect plan that is the only way-*
*Which there isn't-*Noon Yeah interjects.
Which there isn't. Bobby Freelance affirms.
It feels like they're punking me with all this word salad
nonsense. *I'm so confused-expectations create suffering
but it's our mind that creates the expectations?*
A smile from Noon Yeah. *You don't sound confused.*
Bobby Freelance takes it from here. *When you cling to
some idea of how you think it has to go and it doesn't go
that way-that's when you suffer...you did that to yourself-*
Noon Yeah can't help herself. *And when you let go of
those ideas and you stop clinging and you let it be what it
is-well, that's where the joy is.*
Did she just say joy?
A SIGN 7 talking about joy.
Does she realize how that sounds coming from her?
Noise from the back door.
Scraping. Metal on wood.
Borns comes out carrying a small table. Followed by Lan
Zing who's got a drink in each hand. Borns is wearing his
usual white shirt and white pants. His fingernails are gold
today. He sets the table beside the bench. It's clear that
he is trying very hard not to say anything.

He is unsuccessful.

I just thought you might like a little table to set your plates on.

He says this affectionately.

He wants me to introduce him.

Borns, this is Noon Yeah.

He gets down on one knee and takes her hand. *Noon Yeah, it is such a pleasure to meet you, you have no idea.* He winks at me.

Borns! What wonderful energy you have!

Noon Yeah melts him with one sentence.

Lan Zing hands her a glass. *I thought you might like something to drink. This is a goji berry lemonade that I'm thinking of adding to our menu. I'd love to know what you think...*

Noon Yeah examines the drink. *I love goji berries-the most underrated berry anywhere-*

Lan Zing lights up. *I was just saying that to someone!*

I am rolling my eyes on the inside.

And this is Lan Zing, my boss. She's also the owner of the bakery. Lan Zing, this is Noon Yeah.

They barely acknowledge me, they are bonding over berries.

It's a superfood!-

Why is everybody not talking about this berry?

Noon Yeah tries the drink.

Wow. Best. Drink. Ever. Girlfriend.

How does she do this? How does Noon Yeah connect with people so fast? *GIRLFRIEND?* She talks like they've been friends forever.

Lan Zing, you're about to unleash this drink on the good people of Firdus? She has this dramatic look of disbelief on her face. It is thoroughly charming. *Borns, how do we*

*properly prepare them for this kind of goodness in a
glass?*
Borns starts dancing.
Right there on the path behind the bakery.
He sings

*Goji baby
It's about time
I'm diggin' your berries'
I want to make you mine…*

Noon Yeah is delighted.
Is she faking it?
Is she really like this?
Who is this woman?
What is Noon Yeah?

I'm Bobby Freelance.
He shakes her hand.
Noon Yeah, pleasure to meet you.
Ziga Mey-OH GODS-are they all out here?-Ziga Mey
comes out with a tray. On the tray is a fresh loaf of
sourdough with rosemary. She leans in so she and Noon
Yeah are face to face.
*I'm so happy to meet you. I wish I could say I've heard a
lot about you but Heen here, he likes to keep things a wee
bit mysterious…*
A knowing look from Noon Yeah.
*Does he ever! But we're working on him-he's coming
along, startin' to open up that heart of his…*
She gives me an affectionate glance. As if she actually is
interested in my heart opening up. Which I don't even
know what that means.

I'm Ziga Mey. This is new bread we've been baking-sourdough with rosemary. I'm sure he already said something about it. This is really Heen's doing...
It is? Noon Yeah seems genuinely surprised by this.
Oh Noon Yeah!-now Lan Zing is taking her turn-*This bread! I have never seen people respond like this to a new bread-it's like they have some emotional experience with it that they can't explain. People are standing in line before we even open! This has never happened before...*
Borns is sitting on that little table he brought out. *It has even been known to work wonders IN MATTERS OF LOVE...*
Noon Yeah tries the bread.
This is so good! You made this Heen?
I truly think she's caught off guard.
Something clicks for Borns. *OHHHHH...I see...Heen is a mystery man to you as well...*
Enough of this.
I stand up.
Well, probably time to get back at it.
Lan Zing will have none of it. *No rush, you have a few minutes to finish up whatever you were talking about...*
She smiles like she's in on the joke. She leans over and kisses Bobby Freelance on the top of his head.
See you in minute, baby she says, tenderly.
See you, baby he responds.

This happens right between Noon Yeah and I on the bench. It is swift and effortless. I haven't ever witnessed something like this in such close proximity. It's a love that doesn't announce itself, present between them in the smallest and most subtle of gestures.

402

It's a sublime entanglement, the way they are alive to each other.

It was lovely to meet you, Noon Yeah Borns says. He bows.
Ziga Mey gives her a hug. *I hope I get to see you again soon. We have so much to talk about.*
We do! Noon Yeah exclaims with that same irritating familiarity in her voice.
Bobby Freelance touches us both on the shoulder as he gets up. *It's all about the expectations...Gotta get really clear on those...*
Thank you Bobby Freelance I hear myself say.
He gives me a fist bump. *You got it brother.*
Brother.
What do I do with that?
Brother.
Noon Yeah stands up and hugs him. *Bobby Freelance, you have wisdom way beyond your laps. I bet people come to you for help all the time, don't they? When they're in a jam and they can't sort it out on their own-*
ALL THE TIME I say.

I finally understand what I have been seeing all those times with all those people who come to the bakery for Bobby Freelance. I have been watching him for weeks and weeks and I didn't understand what Noon Yeah picked up on in three minutes.
He heads into the bakery.
Just the two of us now, sitting on this bench.
She slides over so she's right next to me.
She turns so we are face to face.
Like I said, you're in deep.

There's an ominous undercurrent in her voice.

Also a hint of admiration.

I'm exhausted.

From the threat that she is.

From the back and forth that's been going on between us since she first appeared in my room.

From pretending.

I don't want to be alone anymore.

There.

I say it.

Directly to her face. Which is inches from mine.

I say it to the one person who cares the least about something like this. Who can do nothing about it. Who I will never see again.

Feels good to say it.

I give up.

I say this as I stand up.

You're gonna do whatever you're gonna do. I've tried. I can't change your mind. You gotta do your job. I get it- That's what I've been doing for so long...

A world of weariness in those words SO and LONG.

I'm going to leave.

These people will be just a memory in no time.

Firdus will be just another job I did.

These truths drain the life out of me.

I lean in and place my hand on the back of her head.

I kiss her forehead.

Bye Noon Yeah.

She has no response.

I like that.

I leave her sitting there on the bench.

It is the loneliest walk ever, those few steps from that bench to the back door of the bakery.

We're closing.

I have spent the day answering but not really answering questions about Noon Yeah.

I made up a story about meeting on the pitch.

Her team against mine.

Her team won.

We went to dinner after the game.

Found out that we have so much in common.

Like what? Ziga Mey wanted to know.

I mumbled something about how much we love trees.

I had to think quickly.

I hated all that lying.

Borns is wiping down tables, Ziga Mey is arranging the pans with tomorrow's dough in the refrigerators. I'm checking on the starter. Bobby Freelance is in the alley with two women. One has short hair, the other has long hair. They're arguing about something. They keep pointing to each other's heads.

The front door opens.

Lines enters.

He's wearing a green robe with a tall, pointy green hat. His brothers and sisters are behind him. Nooji is carrying a shovel. Splasha is wearing a cape.

Peeble comes in last.

She has the baby on her hip.

She takes my jaw in her hand. Turns it from side to side. Gently, but with authority.

She studies my face carefully.

Healed.

She says this triumphantly. With finality.

What a human being she is.

Borns comes in from the back.

The kids attack him. Climbing on his legs, crawling up on his back.

The contrast is too much for me.

Seeing this family.

Knowing that Noon Yeah is out there somewhere taking care of her Dill Tudd problem which is my Dill Tudd problem which is not a problem.

Life and death on Firdus.

I can't bear it.

I turn to leave.

Heen!

Lines is standing in front of me.

Lines, I love the outfit.

Thanks Heen, I've been doing a lot of sewing lately.

I walk around him, examining the robe.

You've been working wonders here-

I pull on a flap on the side.

That's where I put my lunch.

I lift the flap and see that it has a thin rubber lining.

That's brilliant.

Yeah, I thought so when I came up with it. There's only one problem-

What's that?

Kids at school want me to sew them one-

How is that a problem?

Well, they don't have their own capes-

This is a cape?

Yeah! It's not like it's a ROBE!

He looks at me like I know nothing.

So they want capes with pockets for their lunches?

They do. They won't stop bothering me about it.

Sounds like a solid business opportunity.

I sound like someone's dad.

Yeah, I think it could be. But Nooji and Splash are holding out for more money.

This strikes me as very funny.

You tried to hire them?

Yeah, of course. IN HOUSE LABOR. But they teamed up and want a bigger cut-

They want equity?

They do! How'd you know?

I would.

He thinks about this.

I push it. *Wouldn't you? If you were your brother or sister and you saw how much demand there is?*

That's a good point, Heen.

Just trying to help.

He lights up. *I could give them ownership based on a sliding scale-*

There you go.

He's got something else on his mind.

I have a question for you.

Fire away, Lines.

I love this kid. I am forever connected to him.

So...he stammers...we're doing this thing at school...like you bring in something...or someone who, like...

He looks at the ground.

I try to bail him out. *Can I help?*

Relief on his face. *Yeah, would you come to my school?*

Visit your school?

Well...yeah...but more than that. Would you talk?

To you?

I am still not getting it.

To my class.

You want me to speak to your class?

Me speaking to kids. Who would have thought.
About what?
Like maybe bread…or that stuff we talked about…you
know…when we were talking that one night…
Ahhhhh. I get it.
About life and stars and fears…?
YES! All that!
Yeah, I could do that.
Peeble stands behind Lines, beaming.
I told you he'd say YES.
Lines gives me a fist bump.
That would be cool.
I agree.
That would be so cool. When is it?
Tomorrow.
All right then, tomorrow it is.
I'll draw you a map to his school says Borns.
Your dad likes his maps I say to Lines.
He does says Lines.

*

I cannot concentrate.
I make myself dinner.
I stare at the disc.
I look out the window.
I look back at the disc.
I pace around the flat.
I think about Noon Yeah.
I think about Dill Tudd.
I stare at the disc some more.
I'll read.
Maybe find something to distract me.

I go through my stack of books.

None of them grab me.

They feel flat, bland, lifeless.

I get to the bottom of the pile-

The last book.

The Essential Writings of Skolnick.

Oh…

Right…

I remember getting this one.

I was on Meebs once. For a day. The Batershell Route was shut down because of a solar sheer-you tend to get those during the Morbal Retrograde-and I had a day to kill. I'd heard about this bookstore on Meebs for laps. People rave about it. This fella Putro I met at the Conclave on Forls told me it's *The Best Bookstore Anywhere.*

I said *That's a pretty big claim.*

He shook his head. *No, that's actually its name-The Best Bookstore Anywhere.*

So I go to Meebs.

And the bookstore?

It is. It's the best.

It's in a tree.

Or under a tree…it's hard to describe.

This woman hollowed out the trunk of a massive sequoia and then attached canvas awnings to the lowest branches and the branches of the surrounding trees. So the store is the space around and in among these massive tree trunks.

I love books.

But if you didn't love books?

That store would make you love books.

So I'm wandering in among all those books when I pass

by this woman in a rust-colored caftan who quietly says to me *So you're an E.R.?*

She says it like she knows something.

What is that? Is that two letters? E. and R.?

She winks. *Yeah-E.R.-Earth Reader.*

I'm an Earth Reader?

That's the sense I get.

That's a thing?

Oh it's definitely a thing. If only you knew. There's a whole world of you people.

She's being so cryptic.

I'm sorry-can we back up? I don't know what that is.

She leans on a shelf.

Earth Reader. Exactly what it sounds like. You love to read about life on Earth.

Ohhhhhhhhhh.

I like where this is headed.

I do. I really do. I sometimes wonder if I'm obsessed.

I look around.

There's no one else in the store.

It feels good to confess.

She smiles. *Let me guess-you find Earth small and primitive and totally insane and yet utterly fascinating-*

Yes! That's it!!!

I've never heard anyone name this.

You've read Slocum and Searle?

She asks this like she already knows the answer.

I have.

Kropp?

Yep.

Her eyebrows raise. *How about Honnold?*

Of course!

Okay then, it sounds like you're ready...

410

I stop her.

Hold on. Do you work here?

She gestures to the trees. *I built this place.*

You're the owner?

I am. Gilbs. Pleasure to meet you.

Gilbs, I'm Heen Gru-Bares. I love your store. How did you know-

That you're an E.R.?

Yeah-

That's easy. Most people know what they're looking for when they come to a bookstore. They walk up and head right to that section-

Which I didn't do-

Right. But it obviously wasn't your first time in a bookstore. You were looking for something that didn't have a clear category

You picked up on all that?

And then I noticed your boots. You didn't get those on Meebs. And your sunglasses-only a pilot would wear those...

You don't miss a thing.

Gilbs has more. *I also know that the Batershell is closed which means you have a day to kill-*

That is true-

And people who fly are often Earth Readers.

It just doesn't stop with her.

We are?

She nods.

Why do you think that is?

She leans on a bookshelf, like she has all the time in the worlds. *I think it has something to do with how much of the galaxies you've seen. I can only imagine the vastness of it all gets a little overwhelming from time to time, that*

massive size and scale-and you get intimidated-
Well I wouldn't say THAT.
She brushes my protest aside.
And so you go in the opposite direction. Maybe there's something about the smallness and limits of earth that comforts you, makes you feel bigger...
I think about this. *You may have something there, even though I'd never admit it.*
She adjusts a book on the shelf. *Just a simple theory...*
I remember something she alluded to earlier.
You said I'm ready for something...?
She turns to walk away. *Follow me.*
We weave in among the shelves, around one of the trunks and into the hollowed-out center. She pulls out a key-I've only seen a few keys in my life-and unlocks a drawer in a small cabinet.
Gilbs keeps some books out of sight?
That she locks up?
She removes a small, thick blue book and hands it to me.
I check the spine.
THE ESSENTIAL WRITINGS OF THE SKOLNICK.
I hold it up. *This?*
Let me warn you-
She is dead serious.
Warn me about a book?
This is a little strange.
Yes. A book. I know it's just a book...but...
She pauses. This is not a person who seems to have any difficulty with words. *Just remember that I warned you...*
I bought the book.
Which I've had with me for I don't know how many laps.
But never read.
Until tonight.

I begin reading.

I inhale the first seventeen pages.

I stop and put the book down.

I realize I'm shaking.

What am I reading?

The Skolnick writes about this place his people called home.

He calls it THE ANGELS. He claims that millions and millions of people lived there. I find this hard to believe. Millions and millions of people lived in the same place on Earth?

A CIRCLE is ten thousand people and then you build another one. Otherwise you'd have sprawling, unorganized chaos. Everybody knows that.

He describes a street-which I can only assume is like a path or a trail-that is 26 miles long. How is that possible? 26 miles? It's called SUNSET.

The Skolnick walks the length of this SUNSET and writes about what he sees.

That's it.

That's the writing.

That's the first part of the book.

He's not conquering anything or climbing anything or swimming or sailing or riding a bike or doing anything dangerous.

And yet his writing.

The things he sees.

The things he notices.

The claims and observations and descriptions.

I don't know what to make of it.

I have been learning about Earth my entire life. Ma'ir
Dobie taught us about the widening gap. Ma'am Kirti
wanted us to be very clear about why the Earth ended.
Sir Pong had a lot to say about CULTURES.
But that was all rather general. Drawings. Numbers.
Statistics. Percentages.
All that was from a distance.
Removed.
Looking back on how it was.
But this.
The Skolnick. This is specific. Particular. Granular.
He was there.
He writes about something called concrete and guns and
food and buildings and places that aren't safe. I don't
know what he means by that. He keeps using this word
neighborhood. I assume that's like a CIRCLE. But
constantly changing. Shifting. Evolving. These people
moving in, those people moving out. More money, less
money. These people eat this kind of food, those people
eat that kind of food.
It's profoundly unsettling. Turbulent. Churning. All these
different people in the same place, coming and going.
I keep reading.
It's a feeling I pick up in these pages.
An unsettling energy.
An electricity.
A movement, a motion.
I keep trying to figure out who is in charge.
It's as if The Skolnick is walking along describing how it is
RIGHT NOW knowing that it will soon be SOMETHING
ELSE.
Like the whole thing is in free fall.
Like it could go in any one of a thousand directions.

Terrifying. But thrilling.

I put the book down.

I see what Gilbs meant.

The key and the drawer makes sense now.

It almost feels forbidden.

The Angels.

There's something intoxicating there.

Something so compelling about that ARRANGEMENT.

Which isn't really an ARRANGEMENT.

More like the absence of an ARRANGEMENT.

Or an ARRANGEMENT that EVERYBODY is in charge of which means NO ONE is in charge.

It's free to be whatever it's going to be.

Who's in charge?

No one?

Everyone?

Alive.

That's the word that comes to me.

There's something ALIVE about what The Skolnick describes.

Some life force that can't be quelled.

And yet.

I understand what Noon Yeah meant by that word MARGINS.

She kept saying *There aren't any.*

I get that.

I see that in The Angels.

The Angles is engulfed in margins. Drowning in them. Choking on them.

If someone doesn't stay on the ARRANGEMENTS things go off the rails very, very quickly.

But that's also what makes it so…vital.

That other way.

To let it play out.
To see what happens.
To allow the friction and freedom and conflict.
Walking down that street with the Skolnick.
I'm agitated. Troubled. Bothered.
Lit up.
I go to sleep, thinking about The Angels.
Imagining what it was like there.

*

Click.
The light in the corner comes on.
Noon Yeah.
I sit up in bed.
I have no idea how long I've been asleep.
We have a problem.
She says this like it's something I need to know.
She's wearing my Dill Tudd lightning bolt jacket.
I correct her. *YOU have a problem.*
She's having none of it. *It's your problem as well.*
I am wide awake now. *No. NOT my problem. MY problem
is my disc doesn't work. If somebody would fix MY disc
then I could go back to filing my reports and doing my
job.*
She holds up her hand.
Stop talking. Seriously. It's not helping.
She is so maddening.
It's helping me.
That sounded a little pathetic.
She tilts her head down, rubs her eyes, like you do when
you have a headache.
I can't find him.

Ohhhhhhhhh. I do that long Ohhhhhh to buy some time.
Dill Tudd?
Something wells up within me. I think it's joy.
What a fascinating admission from you. You can't find Dill Tudd?
I say it again, without the question mark.
You can't find Dill Tudd.
This is so fun to say.
But wait-you can find anybody! You found me. THAT'S YOUR JOB. Are you having trouble doing your job Noon Yeah?
I cannot conceal my delight.
She does not enjoy this.
Let me just make sure I fully grasp your situation: Since I last saw you, you've been searching for a guy to remove but you can't locate him. And we all know you can't GRAIN someone you can't FIND! THE POETRY of it ALONE!
I stand up on the bed and do a little dance move.
I sit down, leaning against the wall.
Noon Yeah can't find Dill Tudd. What a satisfying sentence. I just want to stop and savor that. With all of your training and all the laps you've been doing this-has this ever happened to you?
I wait.
She doesn't say anything.
Is this the first time you haven't been able to find someone?
I slide forward so I'm sitting on the edge of the bed, right in front of her.
I think it is. I think this is a first for you. Kind of a blow to the self esteem, innit? You've been doing this for how long?

I am so into this.

You know what's interesting? I don't know anything about you. You reveal nothing. Ever. You show up at the bakery and you're everybody's new best friend but I watch you-you don't give anything away to anybody, ever. It's actually quite impressive-how you appear to connect without actually connecting-

She points to my clothes.

I see you aren't sleeping naked anymore.

I shake my head.

Don't change the subject. Okay...yeah...that was only one time and I woke up and SOMEONE was in my room so NOT DOING THAT AGAIN. But let's go back to the matter at hand. Which is YOU. I can barely say it without laughing. You really do have a problem. You can't GRAIN someone you can't FIND!

Am I taunting her?

I think I am.

Sitting here on the edge of my bed in a rented flat on Firdus talking to an ASSASSIN who travels the galaxy GRAINING people.

You can't find Dill Tudd.

I say it again because it brings me so much pleasure.

She starts taking off her boots.

What are you doing?

She looks up. *Taking off my boots.*

Yeah, but...why?

She leans back in the chair.

He's totally off the grid. There's no record of him anywhere. Dill Tudd officially DOESN'T EXIST. Do you know how difficult that is to do?

I am instantly filled with admiration for Dill Tudd.

Still doesn't explain why you're taking off your boots. And then I get it.

No.

She smiles.

Yes.

I do not like where this is going.

No. As in NO.

As if saying NO twice will sway her in any way.

Her boots are off. She's wearing green coveralls. She stands up, unzips them, and takes them off. Now she's in a t-shirt and…what are those? Shorts? Tights?

In any other situation with any other woman on any other planet this would be thrilling.

You're not…

She gets on the bed.

I am.

No, you're not.

She lies down next to where I was just sleeping.

There are thin red vertical scars on her ankles.

She adjusts her pillow.

She interlaces her hands behind her head.

You and me are going to be spending some time together.

I sit in the chair.

I put my feet up on the end of the bed.

You're in my bed.

She laughs. *There he is again! Doing what he does best-NOTICING. Heen Gru-Bares! He doesn't miss a thing.*

I kind of enjoy it when she mocks me.

I think it has something to do with being seen.

I point to the bed. *What are you doing?*

She adjusts the covers. *My job.*

I hate this.

This feeling that she's in control.

That I'm being played.

That I'm behind.
Your job is not sleeping next to me.
Actually it is.
Because of Dill Tudd?
Precisely.
Because you can't find him. But HE does find ME every few days-
You got it. So if I'm with you, I'll find Dill Tudd.
But you don't have to sleep here.
Do you have another bed?
No. What are you going to do when I go to work?
Go to work.
Things have turned. She's enjoying this.
Where are you going to work?
Where you work.
At the bakery?
Yes, that is where you work.
She says this like I am very, very slow.
You're going to work with me at the bakery? That's not possible.
Lan Zing thinks it is.
I put my head in my hands. Moments ago I was taunting her about her failure to do her job. Now this.
You talked to Lan Zing?
Yeah, she hired me.
You got a job at the bakery? I say it more to myself than to her. *Doing what?*
Tea.
Tea?
Tea.
We don't serve tea at the bakery.
You do now.
What do you know about tea?

*Enough to get a job at the bakery so I can be with you all
day.*

She pats the bed next to her.

And night.

She gets under the covers.

I stand up.

You don't brush your teeth or wash your face before bed?

I have no idea why I care about this. I think it has
something to do with distracting myself with details when
I get anxious.

Already did.

You already brushed your teeth-Where?

Where? She looks at me like I have two heads. *In the
bathroom.*

My bathroom?

Yes. That's where people do these things.

Again. She's so under my skin.

You got ready for bed in MY bathroom?

*Yes. Although…we both work for the same people. Who
pay for your flat, correct? And we're both on the job…you
see where I'm going with this?*

No. I don't.

It's technically OUR bathroom.

Resistance to this madness feels futile.

You got ready in OUR bathroom!

I shout it. Like she's violated some deep trust between us.
She calmly responds. *I did.*

Where was I?

Sleeping.

I go into the bathroom. I open the drawers. The second
drawer on the right is full of her things. Neatly organized. I
turn around. There's a small hand towel of hers hanging
on the hook. I go out into the hall. I check the closet. It's

full of her clothes. There are two empty bags on the top shelf. Those silver boots she wore the first time she appeared in my room are lined up on the floor next to those black boots she wore with that red skirt and shirt. Apparently I have been keeping track of what she's been wearing. Without realizing it.

I come back into the bedroom. Her eyes are closed and she's got her palms together over her heart. She's taking long, slow breaths.

I lean against the wall and watch her.

I find it mesmerizing.

I don't know if it's because this is all so strange and surreal and terrifying and heartbreaking.

Or because there's a woman in my bed. And that hasn't happened in a long time.

She opens her eyes. *Let's go to sleep. We have a big day tomorrow.*

She says it like we do this every night.

I turn off the light and get in bed.

We lie in the dark, quiet.

Noon Yeah?

Yes, Heen.

Do you do this with other SIGN 5's?

Do what?

You're lying next to me in my bed.

It seems important to point this out.

No. She says it softly.

NO, as in you don't USUALLY do this. Or NO as in you've never done this?

I have no idea why this clarification matters to me.

Heen Gru-Bares you are relentless.

That's exactly how I feel about you.

Me??? I'm just doing my job.

She tries to sound innocent. It kind of works. But I see her.

No, no-that's the thing. Anytime you get pressed on WHO YOU ARE, anytime I get close to the YOU-the real YOU, the YOU behind the YOU-you immediately back away and blame the job.

She doesn't respond.

Just the sound of her breathing.

Our breathing.

Only with you.

It hangs there between us, above us.

Only me?

Yes, you. This has never happened.

I'm unique. I find this funny.

You are unique. Being in bed with someone has happened, of course, but not this kind of being in bed-

You've never had a problem finding someone you're supposed to GRAIN. So you've never had to stick close to a person who is the only way for you to find that person...

It's so satisfying to repeat the jam she's in.

Pretty much.

So at this point you're just improvising. You have no idea how this is going to play out.

I ALWAYS get the job done.

Steel in her voice. But also a faint hint of her trying to convince herself. Just a hint. I jump on it.

That is the second dumbest thing I've heard someone say this week.

I can feel her curiosity. *What was the first?*

I do my best impression of myself. *YOU MESSED WITH THE WRONG SERIES 5.*

She does a half snort, half laugh. It's lovely. *That WAS the most ridiculous thing I've heard someone say. Not just this*

week but in a long, long time.
The air changes between us.
Lighter. Looser.
Well, you saying I ALWAYS GET THE JOB DONE gives my YOU MESSED WITH THE WRONG SERIES 5 a run for its money.
She sighs. *Heen?*
Yes, Noon Yeah.
Can we stop talking and go to sleep?
Weariness in her voice. A little ache.
There's a person in there.
An actual human.
With a heart.
Maybe.

*

A smell.
It's wonderful.
I open my eyes.
Morning.
I look to my right.
No Noon Yeah.
I walk out to the kitchen.
She's cutting fruit on the counter.
Morning! I love mornings. Did I already tell you that?
There's something cooking in a pan.
She's wearing a wool sweater of mine. Her hair is wet.
Hold on.
The SUNS are up.
What time is it? Panic in my voice.
You're good. I already talked to Lan Zing. We're going in late to work.

424

It's the nonchalance in her voice that I find infuriating.
You say that like you're in charge of my schedule.
She doesn't acknowledge this.
Pancakes okay?
I just stand here staring. *Pancakes?*
She laughs. *Look at you. Trying to figure out the catch in that question. Just pancakes, Heen.*
I haven't had pancakes in a long time.
I leave her in the kitchen.
I go into the bathroom and close the door.
I sit on the edge of the tub.
I wipe tears from eyes.
I do my best to not think about why I'm in my bathroom with tears in my eyes.
I didn't use to have tears.
Before Firdus.
I clean up, get dressed, and return to the kitchen.
There's a flower in a vase in the middle of the table.
Noon Yeah brings two plates over from the counter.
Let's eat.
I sit down.
Pancakes, potatoes, fruit, some sort of cacao smoothie.
It all tastes so good.
You went to the market.
I did. Although your neighbor downstairs gave me the flour, and that lovely older woman who lives across the path grew the strawberries. She let me pick as many as I wanted. And the family in the triangle-shaped house a few doors down have the best apple trees-
Who did you tell all these people you are?
Noon Yeah.
She says this like it's all the explanation needed.
I look at her, I look out the window, I look at my food.

Neither of us says anything.

I wonder if I've run out of things to say to her. I think about Dill Tudd and I am filled with rage but then I think about her JUST DOING HER JOB and my rage gets redirected towards the CHAIRS and this ARRANGEMENT that GRAINS people for the sake of the ARRANGEMENTS which then makes me think of my job and my participation in this...what's the word for it...SET UP? SYSTEM? She keeps repeating that SHE'S JUST DOING HER JOB which makes me lose my mind but I can't do that without acknowledging that I say that ALL THE TIME.

She reaches over and places her hand on my chest.

You need to breathe.

I know how to breathe.

Nails in my words.

Not really.

She places her hand on the front of my shirt.

Take short breaths from the top of your chest-also called breathing.

I think this response is quite clever. She doesn't.

Let your breath go deeper...and longer.

I'm eating.

Especially when you're eating. Your mind is racing, isn't it?

She's right about that.

It is.

A touch of something sympathetic in her eyes.

That's what happens-the mind starts to race and our breathing gets shallow and short. Take a really long exhale.

I just stare at her.

Do it.

She's insistent.

I put my fork down and do it.

She watches me intently. *Feel the lightness at the end of that exhale?*
I do.
I don't want to admit it.
A little.
I'll give her that. But only that.
She'll take it. *Well then, progress.*
I pick up my fork.
Noon Yeah?
Yes Heen.
This is the best breakfast I've ever had.

*

We come around the bend.
The bakery is up ahead.
Noon Yeah holds my hand.
I turn to her.
We're doing this?
We're doing this she replies.
Because you always get the job done.
I don't look at her as I say this.
Because I always get the job done she repeats.
I hate this.

Kind of.
You would think that our arrival is one of the most thrilling events in the history of the bakery. I don't know what she's told Lan Zing and what other interactions she's had with Borns and Ziga Mey and Bobby Freelance but they all get on like long lost friends. Like this is some sort of reunion.
I learn that the building next to the bakery has been

purchased by Lan Zing and she's hired Noon Yeah to turn it into a teahouse. *The only tea house on Firdus* Lan Zing tells me. I see painters and woodworkers and furniture makers coming and going all morning long. At one point I stick my head in the door and Noon Yeah is showing Lan Zing lines she's drawn on the floor-I'm assuming that's where the counter will go-and a guy in a blue hat is standing next to them holding a clipboard reading out measurements.

Her confidence.

It's astonishing.

She knows how to make a tea house?

What even is a tea house?

And how did she convince Lan Zing she knows what she's doing?

Did her RANDY pretend to be different references from around the galaxy when Lan Zing followed up on them?

Late in the morning Noon Yeah appears in the back of the kitchen.

Break?

I am formulating my excuse for why I can't when Lan Zing appears out of nowhere.

Perfect timing! Heen is due for a break any minute now.

I meet her on the bench.

It's quite a scam you're running.

She's entertained by this.

Scam?

It's quite cruel, really.

She rolls her eyes. *The smugness. The bloated, twisted moral superiority-*

Are you talking about me?

I sit up straighter. My face heats up.

Of course I'm talking about you! Judging me. You of all people in the universe-

Me? Me. You're helping her make a tea house?!!! Did you tell her in the interview-

Tell her what?

That you'll be at work until you've KILLED THE MAN YOU CAME TO KILL and then you're going to be gone forever with no warning. Did you tell her that? Because she's pretty excited about her new tea house-

She jabs her finger at nothing in particular.

There it is again! Right there-

What? What am I doing? Other than pointing out the obvious. It's like a SCAM. Or a CHARADE. Or a FARCE. All to cover up an EXECUTION. You're using them-

She'll have none of it. *Using them? I'm helping.*

My fists are clenched. She's agitated, tapping her foot on the ground.

Helping? You are insufferable. And completely delusional. Helping???

She leans in close. *I could just sit across the street and keep tabs on you all day. But instead I choose to come in here and see if I can do some good.*

It's masterful. The way she manages to make me consider-just for a split second-that she actually means that.

A part of me wants to tell them.

This gets her attention.

Tell who?

Well, I'd probably start with Lan Zing, tell her why you're really here.

I love being a step ahead of her.

She looks genuinely unnerved.

Wow, I hadn't thought of that. You could. You could expose me. What would I do then?

She gets quiet.

Finally, I'm getting to her.

She turns to me and smiles.

And then I'd tell her about you.

I should have seen that coming.

She set me up.

You actually thought you had something on me!!! You thought you could threaten me with telling them all the truth and it didn't occur to you I could do the same! You thought you were a step ahead!! It's actually kind of charming at times how slow you are...

I'm so embarrassed.

You are in deep Heen Gru-Bares.

She stands up and starts pacing.

You actually forgot for a second that you and I are the same thing to these people. YOU ACTUALLY FORGOT! You see yourself as one of them and you see me as the outsider, the one passing through, the one threatening all this. Astonishing.

A look of wonder crosses her face.

She sits back down.

I have seen a lot of SERIES 5's over the laps and I've seen a lot of jobs go balls up but I've never seen someone LITERALLY LOSE THEMSELVES like you have, here.

She slides close and puts her arm around me.

What is it about Firdus? And this bakery? And these particular people? Is this about some childhood trauma or some grief or pain or loss that this place digs up for you? Does this-

She gestures to the bakery-

Does this feel like some sort of answer to a question you've had?

Noise at the back door. Ziga Mey comes out and stands in

front of us. *You guys are so great together! Can I just say that? You're so inspiring to me.*

She leans over and puts her hand on Noon Yeah's knee. *I don't know how much Heen has told you but I recently split from my long time fella and I'm alone for the first time in a while and I just met someone but I don't know-it's all so strange and new and unfamiliar and sometimes I wonder if I'll ever find someone and then I watch you two out here talking to each other-it's so clear from your body language-I don't even know what you're talking about and yet I can see how committed you are to each other. So much passion and love between you. What a gift to the rest of us. Anyway, I just had to say something.*

She walks off down the path.

We sit together.

Her arm around me.

I put my arm around her.

Gotta keep up appearances.

I whisper in her ear *Wouldn't it be cool if I killed you so you couldn't kill Dill Tudd?*

She whispers in my ear *That would be so cool.*

I whisper back *So cool.*

She whispers *And then when your friends from the bakery ask you where I went you could tell them I KILLED HER.*

I respond. *That would be awesome.*

Whatever this is going on between us, we are lost in it because we don't hear Bobby Freelance until he's sitting on the bench.

We look over at him.

Gotta love the whispers.

Noon Yeah asks him *What do you mean?*

He nods. *There's this space between two people that exists only between the two of them and nowhere else in*

the universe. Gotta protect that.
He lost me. *Whispers?*
Yes, Heen, whispers. No one else can hear. No one else but the two of you. That's it right there.
He gets up and walks back into the bakery.
Noon Yeah turns to me.
Our faces are so close.
These people? That guy? This bread? THIS life here on Firdus-THIS IS WHAT BROKE YOU? You botched the job and lost your self because of THIS? Heen Gru-Bares, I don't quite know what to make of you.
She stands up.
She points to herself.
But yours truly? Tea time.
She curtsies. And then heads into the soon-to-be teahouse.

*

Borns and I are folding the multigrain loaves, setting them on their trays.
Lines is so excited he says.
I am so stuck in my head.
Lines?
Oh yes Heen. He was already up this morning when I left, sewing himself a new cape just for the big day.
He's got a big day today?
Borns has got pink nail polish on today. *You both do.*
I remember.
I'm visiting his school.
I try to say it like I hadn't forgotten.
I've never seen him this excited Borns says. *He told me that his friends all want to meet you.*

Meet me? I'm just a humble baker.
I do a slight bow with a little flourish just like I imagine
Borns would do.
I wonder what exactly did I say YES to?

*

Done for the day.
I leave the bakery.
Noon Yeah is waiting for me on the path.
Where's your apron?
I look down where my apron just was.
*Uhhh…hanging on the hook where I hang it EVERY DAY
when I'm done with work…*
You're not bringing it?
Bringing it? Why?
To Lines' school-
You know about that?
*Yeah. It's a big deal. I think you should bring your apron.
That's kind of the point of the presentation.*
Hold on…presentation?
She's already walking back into the bakery.
Come on.
I follow her. *Where are we going?*
She's already through the back door. She goes into the
storage room and closes the door behind us. *What do
you think is happening today at Lines' school?*
It confounds me why this matters to her.
He asked me to visit. I'm visiting.
Even as I say this I know I'm missing something.
She rolls her eyes and sighs. *Every report I read on you
said that you are an EXCELLENT SERIES 5. Honestly, you
get the best marks I've ever seen. But YOU MISS SO*

MUCH.
She is clearly flummoxed. So am I.
I don't think that's true.
Although I kind of do. But I'm not telling her that.
It's so true it kind of blows my mind that the CHAIRS depend on someone like you.
Well now that's just mean-
That's just FACTS. She is ruthless.
And besides, how would you know anything about what I'm doing at Lines' school? You don't even know who he is-
He's Borns and Peeble's second kid. He's fourteen. He collects frogs and he reads a lot of biographies and he won SHAPER DAY at his school-
You know about Peeble?
Of course I know Peeble. She's the one who told me about today.
You KNOW her? You've talked to her?
Yes I've talked to her-
Wait. Wait. What's SHAPER DAY?
That's what I'm trying to explain to you!
She sits up on the table along the wall.
She's wearing brown boots today. They have little knobs on the soles. They don't have zippers. She pulls them on like socks?
Once a year at Lines' school they have a competition. Any student can submit an essay on what they would do if they were in charge of the school for a day. Lines won this year-
I feel pride.
What a kid.
-And so he gets to SHAPE THE DAY. Get it? WHICH IS TODAY. But up until yesterday he couldn't figure out how

he was going to end it. He wanted something big,
something important, something with a bang-she points
to me-*you.*
Me.
I say it like I'm quite pleased with myself.
Peeble said that kids are always asking him about you.
You're a massive mystery to them. Today he's going to
reveal the mystery.
I don't buy this. *I think you're being a little dramatic.*
She closes her eyes like she's trying to calm herself. She
opens them. *Did Borns tell you about the new cape?*
Just that Lines was working on it this morning-
Did he tell you what Lines sewed on the back?
Nooooo. Is that important?
She gives me a look like I shouldn't have had to ask that.
A spaceship.
A spaceship? Like…sewn onto the back?
Yep. Peeble said he keeps talking about a spaceship that
he says appeared right before you found him.
Kids I mutter.
She hops down off the table.
KIDS is right! There are going to be a whole school of
them you'll be talking to-
I'm not talking to them! I'm visiting. That's what he asked:
If I'd visit. Like…I don't know…he'll give me a tour…
maybe I'll meet his teacher….that sort of thing.
She taps my forehead with the palm of her hand.
You're so maddening. Do you TRY to not get it?
I stomp my foot on the floor.
Stop! Please! Enough! What are you even doing here? You
know what you're doing? MEDDLING. You're a
MEDDLER! MEDDLING where you don't belong. Talking
to Peeble. Doing that thing where you act like you've been

friends forever-
Actually Peeble and I really did hit it off....
Of course you did!!! Can you hear yourself? NONE OF IT
IS REAL! You are putting on a show. That's what you do.
She stares at me.
And then she laughs.
Meddling? What are you, someone's grandma? Meddling?
Did you learn that word in one of your Earth books? And
if you're going to talk about putting on a show...
She tilts her head toward me. *You have a presentation to*
give. In about an hour. About being a baker. At least, that's
what Peeble said Lines was all excited about.
I exhale.
I'm suddenly very nervous.
Got butterflies yet? she asks.
I do.
Do you need to go to the bathroom?
She pokes me in the gut.
No. Well...maybe in a minute. Public speaking is the
worst. Even if it is just kids-
Kids make it more terrifying-
I catch myself breathing too quickly in my chest. I slow
myself down. It helps.
There you go.
She pats my chest. She doesn't miss a thing.
I need help I say. *I don't know what to do or say or how to*
talk to KIDS...
She grabs a box and places a bag of flour in it.
I got it.
You have an idea?
That energy again. That electricity she gives off. Here it is.
I know what we'll do.
WE?

Yeah. Her confidence. It's a marvel. *Trust me* she says. *This will be great. But you'll have to do what I say-*
I can do that. I think.
Excellent. How about you get some starter from the shelf?
You got it.
I head for the door.
And grab your apron, of course. Is there a jug or bottle or some way to transport water around here?
She's giving orders?
And I'm taking them?
I check the shelves. *There's a container in the washroom. I'll get it...*

*

Lines' school is in a ravine just past the riverbed where I recently played the beautiful game. At the bottom of the ravine is a massive circular tent with a white canvas roof. It's open on all sides. On top of the center pole of the tent is a flag. The flag is white with a red number thirteen on it. There are tables and couches and small glass cubes that look like offices scattered around under the tent. Kids and teachers are everywhere, some of them eating at the tables, a few kicking a ball around, some sitting on cushions reading. Above the roof I can see classrooms shaped like pods scattered all over the sides of the hill. The pods are connected by a series of rope bridges-like a web made by a very large spider.
Lines is waiting for us in front of the tent.
In a cape. It's bright blue.
Heen! He runs up to me and gives me a fist bump.
Lines! I'm so honored to be here. What a big day!

Noon Yeah told me to say that. She said that it's
important I let him know that I understand how significant
today is for him. Or something like that.
He turns to her.
Are you Noon Yeah?
I am.
My mom says you're THE BEST. He says it exactly like I
picture Peeble saying it. *And my dad says you're way out
of Heen's league.*
Noon Yeah doesn't hesitate. *Well, your dad is a very wise
man, isn't he?*
There she is, again. Winning someone over, effortlessly.
In this case a fourteen year old boy.
Lines fake punches my arm. *But it's okay, Heen does his
best to keep up...*
A woman in a purple tunic walks up to us. She's wearing
large orange glasses and her hair is pinned up in two
buns on top of her head. Her shoes have pointy toes.
There's a bird on her shoulder. The bird is brown with
orange feathers on its chest.
Lines, I'd love to meet your guests.
This woman.
I am fourteen again in her presence.
Yes, Ma'am Neffi. This is Heen Who Grows Bears-
He winks at me as he says it-
And this is Noon Yeah. This is Ma'am Neffi.
She hugs us both.
Welcome to The Bridges. She gestures to all that's going
on around her like it's her child. *We're so honored you'd
join us for SHAPER DAY.* She drops the formality.
*Honestly...it's my favorite day of the year. I get to sit back
and watch what happens.*
She's so calm and so powerful.

Noon Yeah steps forward, right in front of Ma'am Neffi. Way too close. *What's your bird's name?*

Ma'am Neffi is so pleased she asked. *Her name is Ethel.*

Noon Yeah reaches out to touch the bird but Ma'am Neffi stops her. *And she does NOT like to be touched or held by anyone but me-*

As she's saying this the bird hops on to Noon Yeah's finger, walks up the back of her hand, and then jumps up on to her shoulder.

Ma'am Neffi is stunned. *What...?*

Noon Yeah turns her head. *Hello Ethel.* She turns to Ma'am Neffi. *An Oriole, isn't she?* Noon Yeah says this with such familiarity and affection. *My guess is she's a Hooded but not enough orange on her head-she's probably an Orchard-does that sound right?*

Ma'am Neffi lights up. *I've had the same question! I wondered for a while if she's a Common Redstart, but they tend to have more black than brown feathers-*

Noon Yeah jumps on this. *Which would make you think she's a Varied Thrush-*

Exactly! But in that case the Eastern Twohee would make more sense-

Unless she's a Streak-backed Oriole.

Noon Yeah knows about birds?

Ma'am Neffi is clearly loving this-and still in shock that her bird left her shoulder.

Lines is so impressed. *Noon Yeah, how do you know so much about birds?*

She shrugs. *You just have to know how to talk to them.*

Now this is embarrassing.

They're going to think Noon Yeah is crazy.

I catch myself.

Why do I care? Because they think she's with me-and if

she talks to animals, then I'm probably A BIT OFF as
well?
Again-WHY DO I CARE?
I'm going to leave this planet soon.
I will never see any of these people again.
Why do I care if some lady with pointy shoes AND BUNS
ON HER HEAD thinks Noon Yeah talks to birds?
Noon Yeah, I ask her, *what does Ethel say when you talk
to her?*
I say this like I think Noon Yeah is completely mental. I
don't need to, but it is really enjoyable to put a little
distance between us. Noon Yeah tilts her shoulder up so
Ethel is closer to her ear. She pauses and pretends like
she's listening.
*Ethel says she's looking forward to Heen's presentation
and hopes he doesn't make a BALLS UP of it in front of
Lines' entire school.*
Lines thinks this is hilarious.
My stomach tightens.
I look at Lines. *Your WHOLE SCHOOL is coming to my-*
A horn blast somewhere up on the hill.
There's a kid, way at the very top, on an elevated platform
with a trumpet. Lines sees me squinting to locate him.
*That's Alpert. That kid can play a DIRTY TRUMPET. He's
just a little fella but when he gets going that will NASTY
BLAST your face off-*
Ma'am Neffi laughs. *Usually there's a chime that lets the
students know it's time to switch classes. But Lines
wanted Alpert to do the honors today...*
Doors have opened on the pods.
Kids appear.
Lots of them.
Well, Lines says, *THE TIME HAS COME.*

Noon Yeah turns her shoulder to Ma'am Neffi. *Lovely to meet you Ethel. And you as well, Ma'am Neffi.*

The bird hops onto Ma'am Neffi's shoulder, who shakes her head in disbelief.

Lines turns and we follow him through the tent.

I see it. I glance over at Noon Yeah. She sees it too.

On the back of his cape.

He's sewn a spaceship.

Looks a lot like a Ray Ortland, one of the newer models she says, without looking over at me. My spaceship is a Ray Ortland.

We walk through the tent and out the other side.

Wow.

I did not see this coming.

The ravine forms a natural amphitheater.

The back side of the tent is a stage.

Kids are spread out all over and up the hill.

Some are sitting on the bridges above us.

They're everywhere.

I whisper to Noon Yeah *How did I get here?*

We walked. She's messing with me.

No-here. HERE. Like…my life. THIS. How did my life end up HERE?

She nods. *I know what you mean. If you think about it too much your head will burst. Or maybe your heart will first.*

I look down at the box I'm holding full of things Noon Yeah said we would need. *You sure about this?*

Steel in her eyes. *Absolutely.* That confidence again. *Trust me.*

This makes me feel a little better.

Then I remember that a trained assassin who travels the galaxies removing people from existence told me to TRUST HER.

This makes me feel worse.

Then I remember that a trained assassin who travels the galaxies removing people from existence told me to TRUST HER and for a brief second I ACTUALLY DID and IT DID make me feel better.

This makes me feel significantly worse.

Her hand on my chest.

You're doing it again.

I am? I am. Breathing too fast, too high in my chest.

I exhale.

I slow down the inhale.

I let the air all the way in.

That's better she says.

Like she cares.

Ma'am Neffi walks to the front of the stage.

The students get quiet.

Immediately.

What command she has.

And so we arrive at the end of SHAPER DAY.

I notice the students aren't wearing the regulation jackets. A kid in the front row is dressed in a one piece fuzzy thing-is that a dog costume? There's a girl next to him wearing a pink upside-down cone made of some sort of spongey fabric. There's a row of girls wearing black tops and white skirts and black tall socks that make their skirts look like a series of dash marks.

Kid after kid after kid, all wearing the most colorful, strangely shaped outfits. Some I can tell-that kid is definitely trying to be a taco-but others it's more difficult. That girl looks like a pile of lint attacked her.

I lean over to Lines. *Why isn't everybody wearing the usual jackets?*

He is so glad I asked. *Because the SHAPER forbid it!*

The SHAPER?

Me! I'm the SHAPER!

Ohhhhh yeah yeah yeah. I remember this. *The SHAPER-
OF COURSE! How did you get Ma'am Neffi to go along
with it?*

Pride on his face. *That part was easy. I announced that
you could wear your jacket like every other day or you
could wear something you made.*

No way! They made their outfits?

I notice a young fella wearing a black hat with two flesh
colored tubes that rise up out the top and then wrap
around his shoulder blades, under his arms, and attach
side by side to his chest. That kid has issues.

They did make them…with some help Lines tells me.

I think he wants me to ask him what he means by that.

What kind of help? I say it like it's a secret of some sort.

*I set up a sewing center at my place-I rented extra sewing
machines from this guy I met in CIRCLE 6-and then I hired
Florent and Splasha to take measurements and fill out
order forms-*

I start to connect the dots. *You CHARGED these kids to
make their outfits for the SHAPER DAY that you are in
CHARGE of?*

I did. He gives me a triumphant look.

Ma'am Neffi is going on about a field trip and next week's
forestry project and something about tomorrow's lunch
when suddenly she says *AND NOW OUR SHAPER LINES
FOR ONE LAST SURPRISE TO END THE DAY!*

A couple of kids clap.

One whistles.

A boy over on the left wearing his school jacket-one of the
only ones-mutters *NICE CAPE.*

There's always that kid.

Lines walks right up to the first row.

His fist bumps a girl dressed like a fork.

SHAPE THIS! Somebody yells from the back.

Another heckler.

Nothing has changed in all the laps.

I would, Lines says, *but I'm enjoying being SHAPER way too much.*

Oooooohh. A bunch of kids react.

Lines can give it right back.

So. I broke my ankle recently.

Did he prepare a speech?

I was hiking Stellen Peak.

There's a little extra sauce on that. He was…kind of. AROUND Stellen Peak is more accurate. But he's fourteen. I'll give it to him. I would have said it like that.

And there were these huge slabs of rock. And it got late and it was pretty dark and I couldn't see where I was going. That's one of the risks of exploring-you never know what you're gonna get in to.

It's quiet.

They're actually listening.

Noon Yeah and I are over to the side.

I hear her say *Let's go Lines* under her breath.

Like she's on his team. Like she's rooting for him.

Again, why does she care?

What a mystery she is.

I watch these kids' faces. One minute they're heckling and laughing and ripping each other. But then Lines talks about actually doing something dangerous and it cuts right through all that chatter. There is something at stake. They can feel it.

So I'm sitting there next to this river in the middle of the night and my whole leg is throbbing and I'm wondering if I

444

broke something and I'm out of food and I'm a little terrified…

Did he just say that?

Admit that?

In front of his school?

It's so quiet.

They are so into this.

And then this guy shows up. Heen. He just walks up to me and says HEY LINES.

They laugh.

Lines knows how to tell a story.

Like he was just out for a walk on Stellen Peak LIKE YOU DO and he happened to stroll by on his way to get a sandwich and see me there in agony.

They laugh some more.

This story does make me look pretty cool.

And then he helps me walk.

Actually, I carried him.

But that's just a detail.

And it takes all night and part of the next day but eventually I get home.

He looks over at me.

WE get home.

This makes me a little emotional.

I hold it together.

He adjusts his cape.

So pretty much all night long we're talking-BECAUSE WHAT ELSE ARE YOU GONNA DO IN THE MIDDLE OF THE NIGHT LIMPING DOWN A MOUNTAIN? He said so much cool stuff…this guy, I'm telling you, he's coming from some other place….know what I mean?…I guess what I'm trying to say is that I feel like he gets it.

Noon Yeah turns to me. *He's talking about you.*

Like I didn't know that.

Uh, yeah. I'm Heen. Nice to meet you. I pretend to shake her hand.

No! She's sharp and firm but in a hushed voice. *Don't be sarcastic. He's talking about YOU.*

I look at her blankly.

YOU she repeats.

Lines keeps going.

So. As my last act as SHAPER FOR THE DAY, it is my honor and privilege to introduce to you Heen Gru-Bares and his creative director Noon Yeah!

Kids start cheering.

Let's do this! Noon Yeah says.

She walks part way out onto the stage.

She turns.

I'm frozen.

She waves me forward.

I just stand here holding this box.

Lines is clapping and cheering and yelling *HEEN!!!* with the biggest smile on his face.

Noon Yeah walks back to me. She is all business. *These kids? THEY WORE THE OUTFITS HEEN!!! They did what he asked them to do-do kids at this age do that???? NO. Everybody's so scared, so enslaved to what everyone else will think. But this kid, he's something else. They admire him. They adore him.*

Her intensity. And another thing. Passion? Is that what that is?

The kids keep cheering.

Noon Yeah keeps talking. *And you? YOU!!! YOU rescued this kid when he was in trouble. And they're grateful. And they're showing you that. RECEIVE IT!*

It may be the best thing anyone has ever said to me. And it comes from a SIGN 7-

I keep doing that, don't I?

Anything good I say about Noon Yeah I feel this immediate compulsion to add what a horrible person she is.

She turns and heads back to the front of the stage.

I step forward.

Cheers.

They get louder.

I carry my box to the front of the stage and stand there next to Noon Yeah like an idiot.

The students quiet down.

They stare at me.

All these eyes.

I itch all over.

A voice from back squeaks *Are you his girlfriend?*

I try to see who said it.

I can't tell.

Noon Yeah replies *OH IT'S WAY MORE THAN THAT!*

Murmurs all around.

She leans over and kisses me on the cheek.

The girls love it. *AWWWWWWWW.* They make that noise girls make when they see a kitten.

A few boys say *EWWWWW.* Like there's a dead animal under the couch.

Does he talk?

That kid again, the heckler on the left.

Noon Yeah steps towards the heckler. *Well YOU clearly know how to talk! But the question is: Do you ever say anything interesting???*

The kids erupt.

Lines has the biggest smile on his face. He steps next to me and whispers *She's a legend.*

And apparently she's just getting started. *What's your name?* she asks the kid.

Doon.

Doon?

He sticks his chest out. Defiant. *Yes. Doon.*

Well Doon, would you please come down here and help me figure something out?

Ooooooohhhhhhh. The suspense in the air. I have no idea what she has in mind, but she has these kids in the palm of her hand.

Doon is big, really big. Way bigger than Lines. I knew kids like this. Everything is about dominance. Power. They always have to be on top.

Noon Yeah shakes his hand. *Pleasure to meet you Doon, I'm Noon Yeah. I notice that you have a lot to say. So it seems only natural that you would join me here on stage and help me. Because I have a question. Can you answer my question?*

He's still defiant, but with just a touch of uncertainty.

Sure he says.

Noon Yeah claps. *Great. Because Heen here is a baker. How many of you eat bread in your house?*

Hands go up all over.

Right. Bread is part of life, we all know that. Where would we be without our daily bread? And what is bread made of?

She reaches in the box I'm holding and takes out a sack of flour. *Well, several things. First, you need flour.*

She holds up the bag. *But flour is tricky. Have you ever seen flour, Doon?*

He looks around like it might be a trick question. He decides it's safe to proceed. *Yeah, duh. Everybody has.*

Noon Yeah pats him on the shoulder. *Of course! Couldn't*

have said it better myself.

The build up is killing me.

Where is she going with this?

But the kids.

They're riveted.

She hands him the sack of flour. *Could you please hold this just for a minute?*

She opens the top and folds it back so the kids can see the flour. *Can you all see the flour?*

YESES all over the ravine.

Can you see the flour Doon?

He looks down at the flour. He lowers his head so his nose is a few inches from it. *Yes. I. can.*

He's trying to be funny.

Three kids laugh.

Noon Yeah motions to Lines to take off his cape as she says *Which is why flour can be so tricky. You're just standing there holding it-*

She puts the cape on. She starts walking in a circle around Doon

-minding your own business when all of the sudden-

She walks in front of Doon as she lifts up the cape and then brings it down with a flourish. The gust of wind this creates blows flour all over Doon.

It's like an explosion. Kids are yelling, laughing, jumping to their feet, swinging their feet above us on the bridges.

Lines is pumping both of his fists above his head.

Noon Yeah continues *Someone walks by and JUST BY WALKING BY they disturb so much air that now you're covered in flour!*

She takes another lap around Doon, talking the whole way.

Or you're just standing there minding your own sweet

business-
she ends up in front of him and then steps towards him
When someone accidentally bumps into you-
She runs into him and flour goes all over him again, this
time up his nose and in his mouth.
Kids are losing their minds.
They will talk about this for laps.
How did she manage to not get any on her? Did she
practice? Has she done this before?
And now AGAIN you've got flour all over you!
She starts another circle around him.
Orrrrr…
She turns to the kids. Like they're good friends. That thing
I've seen her do so many times.
Your friend gets a new dog. Anybody had this happen?
Your friend's new dog is a spastic little hairy Weener-
Did she just say WEENER?
Because every kid in the school has that exact question
right now.
They love it.
-and that WEENER thing just can't stop jumping on
everybody and you're just trying to bake some bread
when your friend brings that new dog over and it runs in
your house and tries to jump up on you-
She's in front of him now-
But it's just a little WEENER DOG right? It's not that tall so
it bumps it's little WEENER HEAD on your hands which
are holding the flour for your bread-
She knocks his hands under the flour sack and of course
it goes all over him again-
And now you've got flour all over you AGAIN!
This has happened so fast.
Doon has no idea what to do.

450

I see a row of four girls dressed like parakeets wiping their eyes they're laughing so hard.

How did Noon Yeah know to pick THIS kid?

Because clearly everybody in the school has wanted to do something like this to him for a long time.

COMEUPPANCE. That's the word for it.

I believe he has officially received his.

At the hands of Noon Yeah. A SIGN 7.

If only Doon knew.

She steps to the front edge of the stage. *So when we say that Heen is a BAKER, that means he works with flour ALL DAY LONG. And flour, as DOON WILL TELL YOU, flour is not the easiest thing to work with, can we all agree to that?*

Waves of laughter up and down the ravine.

Clapping.

Kids high-fiving each other.

Noon Yeah turns to me.

You are unbelievable I say.

I am she replies.

She turns back to the students. *Now, Doon, I'm going to need a new volunteer for this next part.*

There's more?

She has something else planned?

Noon Yeah steps next to Doon. *Doon, could you please pick someone?*

Doon did not see that coming.

Standing there covered in flour.

He is suddenly so happy.

He surveys the students.

He takes his time.

He is savoring this turn of events.

He points to a girl in the center about half way back.

KIXSY FLOOGER, COME ON DOWN!!! he yells.

I can't imagine the layers of context that must be in play here because his choice of Kixsy Flooger sends shock waves through the school. Lines can't believe it. *Oh this is insane. This is totally insane* he mutters.

I ask him *What's that about?*

Lines gives me a THAT'S A VERY COMPLICATED QUESTION LOOK. *Well, Kixsy likes Bromfin but he's going with Lima Leens who used to be with Zay Moo who did like Kixsy but lately has been telling anybody who will listen that he fancies Deemee Cruzee who used to be best friends with Kixsy until she and Doon became an item so you can only imagine how him picking her is totally insane.*

I nod. *Wow. I see what you mean.*

A group of kids in the back are chanting *Kixsy! Kixsy!*

Kixsy Flooger stands up and makes her way towards the stage. She looks like a…well…like a Kixsy Flooger. Like she knows exactly who she is and what she's doing here.

She's dressed like Ma'am Neffi.

AS Ma'am Neffi.

Pointy shoes and all.

She even has a fake bird attached to her shoulder.

With orange feathers.

Lines tells me. *She thinks she should run the school.*

That's funny I say.

No, she's totally serious. Lines says this very seriously.

Like he's a little frightened of her.

Kixsy steps on stage. *You are such a badass* she says as she hugs Noon Yeah.

I am Noon Yeah replies. She starts pacing back and forth across the front of the stage. *Now, so far we have firmly established that to bake bread you first need flour. This of course raises the question: What else do you need to bake bread?*

She lets the question linger there in the air. A boy about three rows back dressed in a banana outfit-but it's brown so I assume he's a rotten banana?-raises his hand. Noon Yeah points to him *Yes?*

Butter? he asks.

Nope. You can butter your bread, but you don't need butter to make your bread. An important distinction. Thank you for bringing that to our attention.

It strikes me that she could have roasted that kid. She could have made him feel so dumb. And the kids would have LOVED it. They would have piled on. Laughing at him and thinking she's even more cool than they already do. Calling him BUTTER BOY. But she didn't. She absolutely torched Doon, but this kid in the rotten banana outfit? She takes his question and finds a way to affirm the kid and thank him for *BRINGING THAT TO OUR ATTENTION.*

Anyone else? What do you need besides FLOUR to bake bread?

A hand raises in the back. A girl stands up. She's wearing pink. There's a giant eyeball on the front of her shirt.

Sugar? she asks.

You'd think so, right? Noon Yeah points to the girl. *But no, you don't need any sugar to bake bread-Weird, huh?*

A few nods.

You know what else you need?

She comes over to me and takes the rubber water jug out of the box. She holds it up. *WATER!!!*

She hands the jug to Kixsy. *But you have to be really careful, because water needs a container-*

As she's handing the jug to Kixsy she squeezes it.

It sprays all over Kixsy.

You'd think the kids would have seen that coming.
You'd think I would have seen that coming.
But I didn't. They didn't.
Kixsy has water all over the front of her outfit.
She's in shock.
The kids lose it.
Again.
I hear a snort.
Doon is laughing so hard it looks like he's got flour coming out his nose.
WELL YOU NEVER KNOW WITH WATER, RIGHT?!!!
Noon Yeah yells over the laughing and cheering. She takes the container from Kixsy and holds it above her head as she walks along the front row.
It's at the bottom of the well, it flows down the mountain,
SOMETIMES IT EVEN FALLS FROM THE SKY!
Noon Yeah squeezes the jug and sprays it all over the first two rows on the right. Kids shriek and scream and laugh and shout.
WATER IS EVERYWHERE!!! she says as she does this.
She stands still.
The chaos subsides.
It's electric.
The entire ravine.
No one knows what Noon Yeah will do next.
Including me.
I just stand here holding my box.
Along for the ride.
She keeps going.
How many of you have a body?
They go blank.
What an odd question.
I laugh out loud.

That's so dumb it's funny I say to myself.

Noon Yeah is unstoppable. *Your body is about sixty percent water. You already know this. But how strange is it that one of the main ingredients in bread is also what your body is mostly made of?*

She turns to Doon. *You ever think about that?*

He's dumbfounded.

She squirts him in the face.

You thinking about it now?

Kixsy clearly thinks this is the greatest thing she has ever seen. She appears to have quickly forgotten that she's drenched she is so enjoying watching water and dough mix on Doon's face.

Noon Yeah steps back to the front of the stage.

She stretches out her arms.

I have no idea why she does this.

The kids get quiet.

Oh. That's why she did that.

The gesture communicates to them that something new is about to happen.

She doesn't have to say anything.

She just does something they haven't seen her do yet.

Brilliant.

She's wearing those black pants today. The ones with the pockets on the side that she wore the first time she was in my room. She's wearing the jacket Dill Tudd made me. It's just a bit too big for her but somehow she makes that look intentional. Like it's exactly the right size. How did I not notice that she's wearing the jacket until now? Where has my head been? Her back is to me. I see the lightning bolt. That red lightning bolt, sewn by Dill Tudd.

So, to bake bread we need FLOUR.

She points to Doon.

And WATER.

She puts her arm around soaking but beaming Kixsy.

I still have no idea where this is all headed.

And one more ingredient. I would ask you what it is but it's so MYSTERIOUS I'll just show you.

They watch her intently.

So do I.

That's the brilliance right there.

She leaves them hanging.

She slowly walks over to me.

She is in no rush.

She takes the jar of starter out of the box.

She turns and walks off the front of the stage, up the ravine.

In among the students.

They're thrilled.

As she walks she reaches in and takes out little bits of starter and hands the bits to different kids. They're so excited to get something from her but when they do and it's sticky and strange they don't know what to do with it.

I see a boy smell it.

One girl licks it and then spits it out.

Up the ravine she goes, passing out the starter.

THIS IS CALLED STARTER. It's the third ingredient.

Anybody know what starter is made of?

No one knows.

She stops about half way up.

Noon Yeah, literally standing in the middle of the school.

Every single kid glued to her.

I wonder how I got here.

How did SHE get here?

And how does she know what to do?

She keeps talking.

HERE'S THE THING THAT BLOWS MY GOURD ABOUT STARTER: IT'S MADE OF FLOUR AND WATER!

She bends down so she's right in a girl's face.

THE THIRD INGREDIENT IS MADE OF THE FIRST TWO INGREDIENTS!!!

She stands up straight and spreads out her arms.

WHAT IS BREAD MADE OF? THREE THINGS!!! THE FIRST INGREDIENT, THE SECOND INGREDIENT, AND THEN THE FIRST INGREDIENT ADDED TO THE SECOND INGREDIENT WHICH IS THE THIRD INGREDIENT!!!

I've never thought about it like that.

And I'm a baker.

DO YOU SEE HOW WEIRD AND WONDERFUL THIS IS? she shouts. Kids are smiling all around her.

She's winning them over again, but in a new way. Not with stunts and pranks and spills, but with the WEIRDNESS and WONDER of it all.

Now I know what some of you are thinking. You're thinking: BUT NOON YEAH, IF YOU HAVE THE FIRST TWO INGREDIENTS THEN YOU HAVE EVERYTHING YOU NEED! To which I say: You would think so. But that's not how it works. Starter is what you get when you mix flour and water AND THEN YOU LET IT SIT. For a while. Days. Weeks. Laps. Because when these two hang out for a while together you know what they do? They create something new that didn't exist before that isn't either of them. That means TIME is one of the main ingredients of bread. And you know what these two ingredients do when they have TIME together? They FERMENT.

A hand goes up on one of the bridges.

Noon Yeah sees it.

Yes, up there-you have a question?

The girl is dressed in an all white one-piece outfit with irregularly shaped red spots sewn on all over.

I look over at Lines.

He knows my question. *She's dressed as a rash.*

A rash?

Yep. A rash he says. Like that explains it.

RASH GIRL asks her question: *Isn't FERMENTING like ROTTING?*

A few murmurs.

GREAT question. And yes, it kind of is. But it's different-it's like a controlled, purposeful rot. Which means good bacteria, not bad bacteria. See what I mean by how mysterious it all is?

Another hand.

A boy, sitting in the doorway of one of the classrooms.

Isn't fermentation how you get beer?

They love that one.

Lots of cheers.

Yes! Exactly. Noon Yeah goes with it. *And wine. And cheese. Anybody have any cheese on them?*

She's asking for cheese?

I DO! comes a voice from just over to my right. A girl stands up holding a slice of cheese. Her face is painted gold. She has the word BAG written in big letters on her arms. Huh.

Noon Yeah points to the cheese. *There you are! Another fine example of fermentation. IT'S ALL AROUND YOU PEOPLES!*

She makes her way back to the stage and hands me the empty starter jar. I have no idea how long she's been going-three minutes? Half an hour? I have completely lost track of time.

She takes a dramatic inhale and exhale at the front of the

458

stage. *And now, one last ingredient. Which isn't really an ingredient. More like an element. Or an energy. Or to put it simply: HEAT. You mix these ingredients together, you let them sit for a while, you fold them and knead them while they get to know each other, and then you FIRE THEM UP!* She YELLS those words FIRE THEM UP as she reaches in her pocket and pulls something out so quickly I barely catch it-Paper? A sheet of something? Cloth?-while she pulls something else out of her other pocket-it's silver and shiny…I hear a slight CLICKING SOUND as the sheets catch fire…is that a lighter in her hand?…and a large CLOUD OF FLAMES shoots up in the center of the stage. It's blinding.

I feel a burst of heat.

And then it's gone.

As quickly as it appeared.

The surprise of it.

The shock of it.

Kids JUMP BACK and WHOOP and SHOUT and CHEER and quickly realize that nothing is on fire and there is no danger and they're fine and they just witnessed a magic trick performed for them by Noon Yeah.

Their relief is mixed with awe and admiration.

Noon Yeah isn't done. *BREAD IS MAGIC!!!* she shouts, arms spread wide. *AND SO I PRESENT TO YOU ON THIS MAGNIFICENT SHAPER DAY-MAKING HIS FIRST APPEARANCE EVER AT THE BRIDGES-THE MASTER MAGICIAN HIMSELF, FRIEND OF LINES AND BAKER OF THE FINEST BREAD EVER BAKED ON THE GREAT PLANET FIRDUS, GIVE IT UP FOR HEEN GRU-BARES!!!*

She draws out the BARES.

She turns to me and winks.

The students go wild.

They jump to their feet.

I hear Lines chanting *HEEN! HEEN! HEEN!*

A row of girls to my left are making the shape of a heart with their hands.

A kid in a silver jumpsuit makes a fist and pounds it on his chest and then points to me.

I hear my name being shouted all over the ravine.

I stand here holding my box.

I catch a few of them looking behind me.

They're distracted by something.

An aroma.

I turn.

Borns is walking towards me.

He's holding a huge basket.

It's full of bread.

Behind him is Lan Zing.

She's got a large basket as well, full of bread.

She points up the ravine.

Ziga Mey is at the top, waving to me.

As Borns walks by me he says *I LOVE YOU HEEN!* He walks right in among the kids, handing out small loaves.

Lan Zing and Ziga Mey are doing the same.

Peeble appears, she's got a basket as well. *Isn't this fun?* she says to me.

Bobby Freelance comes up behind me. He's got a huge canvas sack full of bread slung over his shoulder.

He puts his hand on my shoulder and says *There is only one Noon Yeah.*

You got that right, brother I say.

It is chaotic and it is glorious. A group of girls have surrounded Noon Yeah. I watch one of them hand her a pen and gesture for Noon Yeah to sign her notebook.

Ma'am Neffi says to me *Bobby Freelance was in my first*

class!!!

I see a girl putting a flower behind Lan Zing's ear.

Lines stands next to me, surveying the scene. *You could say something.*

I panic. *No, no-I'm not good at speeches.*

He waves this away. *I didn't say a speech. Who in their right mind would ever try and follow Noon Yeah?*

That's a good point I say. *Not me.*

He presses me. *But you could say something.*

I don't know, I'm not really-

I think it'd be cool.

That does it.

I take a loaf from an extra basket Borns set down on the stage.

I step to the front.

I hold the loaf high above my head.

I look up at the kids on the bridges.

I see the kids all the way at the back.

I look over at Doon, who is still on the stage, covered in flour, holding a loaf in each hand.

Noon Yeah turns from the girls around her and watches me.

I smile.

Like I know what I'm doing.

Gradually the chatter subsides.

It's gets quiet.

Really quiet.

Silent.

I used to be terrified of silence.

I look up at the loaf there in my hand above my head.

I look back out at all these students.

I'm trembling.

I don't think anyone can tell.

I open my mouth.

Piddle.

I pause.

Piddle.

I pause again, longer.

Piddle.

It's so quiet.

No one moves.

A kid stands up way in the back. The last row.

He's wearing yellow with a pointy black hat.

I think he's a pencil.

He holds his loaf above his head.

Piddle, piddle, piddle he shouts.

It echoes across the ravine.

Over on the left another kid stands and holds her half eaten loaf above her head.

Piddle, piddle, piddle she says.

Gradually, all over the hill, students are standing and holding their loaves in the air and repeating *PIDDLE, PIDDLE, PIDDLE.*

It keeps building until they're all synced up, saying it together.

They have no idea what they're saying.

Or why.

Or what it is.

Neither do I.

They just keep going.

They're smiling, some are laughing, some are dead serious, like they're making important claims about the nature of reality.

They're looking at me as they say it.

They see me.

I see them.

I think of Dill Tudd.
I take a bite out of my loaf.
They cheer.
I wave good bye.
I walk over to Lines and hug him.
He whispers in my ear *Thank you for visiting my school Heen.*
Thank you for inviting me Lines.
He looks at the ground.
Then back at me.
This is one of the best days of my life.
I nod. *Yeah, same for me.*
A trumpet blast.
Alpert way up on his perch.
School is over.
It's like a wave in the ocean, all these kids in all their different outfits passing me by on their way down the ravine and out through the tent, fist bumping me and yelling *HEEN!* to my face and *PIDDLE, PIDDLE, PIDDLE* and holding up their loaves and saying *BREAD IS MAGIC!!!* as they leave.

In no time, the ravine is empty.
Borns and Lan Zing and Ziga Mey are somewhere in the tent talking to Ma'am Neffi. Peeble is with some other mothers.
I stand here on this stage looking out on the now empty ravine.
No one on the hill.
No one on the bridges.
A hand on my back.
Noon Yeah.
She stands next to me, looking out.

Neither of us says anything.
I put my hand on my chest.
My breathing is good.
Slow, relaxed.
She sees me do this.
She smiles.
Creative director? I had to ask.
She laughs. *I thought you might say something about that-*
Lines introduced you as my creative director. I try to say it with disdain but there is way too much admiration hiding in my words.
I had to think of something fast! Lines asked how he should introduce me-
But what even is that?
Actually, it was Peeble's idea. She said IT'S PERFECT BECAUSE NO ONE KNOWS WHAT THAT IS.
It made you sound like a big deal-
I know, it did, didn't it? Funny how that works. You attach some words together and say it like it's something significant and people are impressed.
She's going to wait for me to say it.
I just know it.
I try to hold out but I can't.
That was amazing. I look around the ravine. *I don't quite know what that was you even did, but I LOVED it.*
Everybody did. You were incredible, I mean it. I realize I have so many questions. *Where did you learn to do that? Those kids were riveted. I WAS RIVETED...*
She deflects. *You know-you pick things up here and there.*
I hold my hand up. *Stop. Don't do that. Don't dismiss it. That was really, really impressive. And as an added bonus, I didn't have to give a presentation...*

You're welcome she says.

Thank you I say.

Something between us.

A moment in which the relentless sizing up of each other subsides and we're just here.

More questions. *But how did you even know?*

She rolls her eyes. *To take over and do something so that you wouldn't have to speak?*

Well…yeah…I don't know if would have put it like that, but-

You're too stuck in your head.

She looks me in the eyes when she says it.

I'm sorry-I'm stuck in my head?

Yes.

How am I my stuck in my head?

You stand at a distance-

I was standing right here the entire time you were speaking.

She puts her hands on her hips.

She stretches her neck to the left and then to the right.

She's in no rush.

I wait.

That's what I mean, right there she says.

You lost me.

I tell you that you STAND AT A DISTANCE and you take me literally when you know I'm talking about something much deeper.

I step closer and stand right in front of her. *Kind of like how whenever I ask you a question about YOU-THE GENUINE YOU-you blame whatever you're saying or doing or planning on JUST DOING THE JOB?*

I say that last JUST DOING THE JOB with as much bitterness as I can conjure up.

She's quiet.
It may have had the effect I wanted.
She looks me in the eyes. *Then I guess we don't*
have much more to say to each other.
Fine I say, like I'm chewing a lemon.
I step off the stage and start walking up the ravine.
She follows.
Right.
She's going to stick with me.
Wherever I go.

*

I stop by the pitch and play a game.
Fozzy and I are on the same team again.
We win.
She calls me SILENCIO.
I love it.
Noon Yeah parks herself way up the riverbed and
watches.
All alone up there.
When the game is over I stay on the pitch and stretch for
as long as I've ever stretched. I literally stretch it out so
that Noon Yeah is totally at the mercy of my schedule.
I go to the river.
I strip down to my shorts and jump in.
I float on my back for what feels like an hour.
I swim to the other side.
I swim back.
I swim out into the middle and tread water.
I eventually get out and sit on a rock and wait for my skin
to dry.
It takes a while.

This pleases me greatly.

The thought of Noon Yeah having to follow me around like this.

I go to the library.

I swear I take every book off the shelf in the Earth section, even ones I've read before.

I hope this is driving Noon Yeah crazy.

Me DILLYING and DALLYING.

It's dark by the time I get back to my flat.

She walks behind me the whole way.

She follows me in.

She pours herself a glass of water.

Just the way she takes the glass out of the cupboard.

The ease.

Like this is her place.

I was trying so hard to play with this.

To keep it light.

To turn it into a game.

Doing everything at half speed.

Forcing her to follow me all over Firdus.

Stretching, swimming, reading forever.

I was savoring my slowness, hoping she was experiencing it all as a mild form of torture.

But now I'm angry.

Sitting here on my couch.

Her at the counter.

Drinking a glass of water.

My water.

My glass.

Not really, technically.

But still, the spirit of it.

The presumption.

The invasion of privacy.

The fact that she acts like I'm just supposed to accept
this as part of being a SERIES 5.
What a terrible job.
What an awful thing to give your life to.
All these years of service and then people can just move
in with me if they want?
If the JOB REQUIRES IT?
I am fuming.
Every little noise she makes.
The glass on the counter.
Her boots on the rungs of the stool.
She takes her jacket-MY jacket-off.
She hangs it on the hook by the door.
She sits down next to me on the couch.
She takes off her boots.
She folds her legs up under her like Lan Zing does.
Second time I've ever seen someone sit like this.
I point to her legs. *You get that from Lan Zing?*
I had decided I wasn't going to speak to her.
That lasted about an hour.
I did. I thought I'd take it for a test ride.
I try not to laugh but I can't help it.
A test ride. That's good.
She adjusts her legs.
We sit, looking out the window.
I can do this all day.
And night.
Outlast her.
I'm sorry.
She says it softly.
Excuse me?
I say this like I didn't hear her. But I did.
You want me to say it again, even though you heard me

the first time?

Busted. I own it. *Yes. I want to hear you say it again.*

Okay then. I'm sorry.

Great.

How is that great? she asks.

Well, it's nice to hear you say it.

Again.

Right, again. You said it twice.

This is not going well. I am not winning whatever this is.

What do you think I am apologizing for? she asks me.

She is impossible.

Just impossible.

So cosmically annoying.

So relentless.

She's like human sandpaper.

Wearing me down, day after day.

She turns towards me just a bit.

I'm apologizing for the presentation at Lines' school. He asked you to come speak and I didn't think you could do it so I stepped in and talked to Peeble and got Lan Zing involved and everybody else at the bakery and cooked up that entire thing so that Lines would be happy and you wouldn't have to do a presentation and everybody would think you are the AWESOME MAGIC BREAD MAN. I'm sorry. Clearly I overstepped your boundaries. I…what's your word for it?…I MEDDLED. I'm sorry for MEDDLING.

She leans forward.

We good?

Like she actually wants to hear me say *Yes.*

NO, not in a million laps I say. *We are not good.*

The slight raising of her eyebrows. *Oh, interesting. Do tell.*

My thoughts are a pile of fragments.

I actually am stuck in my head.

I put my hand on chest.

I remember to breathe.

Where to start?

I try not to look at her so I'll stay focused.

Okay, to begin with-you've ruined my life.

What LIFE are you speaking of?

The question is simple, but elusive.

This. This life. Here. Firdus.

Disbelief on her face. She stammers. *I don't know how many ways I can say this. This isn't a LIFE. This is a JOB. It will be over soon. You have always known this. It's how you've lived for a number of laps. Pretty much your entire adult life. THERE ISN'T ANYTHING TO RUIN, HEEN. I know this because this is how I've lived for as long as I can remember. You do the job, you leave.*

I sit and think about that.

I hate that it's true.

What she said.

A noise.

My stomach.

A gurgle.

A growl.

I look down.

I look over at Noon Yeah.

She's looking at my stomach.

She heard it too.

FINALLY! She blurts out. *I was beginning to think something's wrong with you. You're hungry, right? Please tell me you're hungry because I AM STARVING.*

I realize that I am.

When did I last eat?

Why do I ask her? Oh yes, because she hasn't left my side in days. She'll know.

*That's the question I've been asking all day. When do you
eat? And I can't let you out of my sight so I've been
miserable.*
You have been? I say it with delight.
Yes! I've been in agony. Watching you stretch FOREVER.
I laugh. *Oh good. That worked?*
*Worked? If you were trying to torture me YES it worked
wonderfully. And those shenanigans in the library-*
This makes me so happy to hear. *You could tell I was
dragging everything out?*
She punches my arm. *You know when I knew how hard
you were working to antagonize me?*
I punch her arm back. Gently. *NO. Tell me.*
*In the library-*she leans over and picks up a book on the
end table-*you took THIS EXACT BOOK off the shelf and
stared at it for a while. You opened it up and read from it-
YOU READ A BOOK YOU ALREADY HAVE just to stall
and make me loathe you-and Firdus-and this job-*
That's when you knew-
That's when I knew.
My stomach makes more noise.
She stands up. She leans over and puts both hands on
my knees. *CAN WE PLEASE GET SOME FOOD?
THERE'S NOTHING TO EAT IN YOUR FLAT!*
I very calmly say *That's because you've eaten everything.*
She replies, equally as calmly *I have. But unlike you,
apparently, eating is something that I have to regularly do.*
I jump up.
All right, off we go.
I actually am quite hungry.
I know the perfect place.
Lead the way she says.
You sure? It may take a while. I think this is quite clever.

If it takes longer than three minutes-
That's exactly how long it takes.

*

We stroll to The Bowl.

My favorite restaurant on Firdus.

Mo Bowl, the owner, sees us coming. *HEEN! One of our most REGULAR REGULARS!*

Mo Bowl is a short man with a large mustache that curls up on the ends. How does it do that? Does he put something in it? Wax or glue or some sort of pomade? It isn't naturally that shape, is it? He must twirl it himself. Does it lose its twirl when he sleeps? Does he do this every morning?

Mustaches bewilder me.

Mo is wearing plaid trousers. This is bewildering for a different set of reasons. I consider these trousers, the kind of commitment required of him to wear these particular pants, the raw confidence.

He is clearly thrilled that tonight, unlike every other night I have dined here, I will not be dining alone. *And who do we have here? Heen, could you be so kind as to make a proper introduction?*

Mo is very formal.

But his name is MO BOWL.

So there are some mixed messages there.

Mo, such a pleasure to see you tonight. We embrace like we always do. *This, Mo-*I gently place my hand on the small of Noon Yeah's back-*this is my creative director Noon Yeah. Noon Yeah, this is Mo Bowl, owner and operator of this fine dining establishment.*

I can do formal, too.

Noon Yeah embraces Mo.

This does not surprise me.

Mo is over the moon. *Oh I see! Your esteemed colleague possesses the same congenial spirit and effervescent charm that you do, Heen!*

I look at her like she's the finest person to ever stroll the paths of Firdus. *Oh she does, if only you knew!*

Mo throws up his hands. *Well then I can only hope that the great Noon Yeah will become a REGULAR REGULAR here as well. I have your table ready.*

Noon Yeah eyes me. *Your table?*

Oh yes, Mo exclaims, *Heen always sits at the same table. Allow me to lead the way.*

The Bowl is spectacular.

Especially the first time you see it.

It's shaped like a BOWL.

Literally, it's a large bowl that was dug down into the ground. The rim of the bowl is ringed by a tall, thick hedge with a narrow, arched opening. The hedge functions like a portal of sorts, you don't know what you're in for until you walk under the arch and suddenly it opens up before you. The sides of the bowl are terraced with rings of flat, wide stairs with tables on each ring. At the very bottom of the bowl is an open air kitchen with a large fire pit in the center.

Noon Yeah takes it all in. *This is a restaurant? This is stunning. I haven't ever seen anything like this…*

I love seeing her react like this. *You did say you were hungry.*

But this…she's trying to find words…YOU ARE IN SO DEEP.

We're walking side by side down the steps, following Mo.

I am?

Mo said you're a regular-

REGULAR REGULAR were his exact words-

I do my best impression of him.

Isn't that a huge VERBOTEN for a SERIES 5-to become too known or familiar to the LOCALS?

A distant recollection. *Well, there was a little bit about that in training-*

A little? It's a CENTRAL TENET of a SERIES 5, isn't it? To keep changing things up, moving around, putting yourself in different situations-not hugging the owner of a restaurant where you have a special table!

I give up. *Yeah...I AM in pretty deep. But guess what?*

What?

So are you.

We sit down.

We order.

They bring us drinks.

Noon Yeah watches everything going on around and above and below us.

She's wearing the lightning bolt jacket.

Nice jacket I say.

Thank you. I stole it.

Does the owner know it's missing?

I don't think so. He kind of has his head up his arse. He misses so much.

We're sitting about half way down the bowl. Straight across from us is a small stage. On the stage a man in a white dress is playing a piano. Standing next to the piano is a large woman in a bright red dress. She is playing the violin. I have heard them here before. When they play it sounds to me like his piano and her violin are talking to each other. Like it's a song, but it's a conversation. Whatever they're talking about-it's not very happy. Complicated. That's the word for it. It's a complicated sound they make, this conversation they're having.

Noon Yeah points up towards the entrance. *People like you.*
I dismiss this. *Well, they LOVE you.*
No seriously-Mo Bowl there, Borns, don't get me started on Bobby Freelance or Lines-people REALLY like you.
I feel like she's setting me up for something.
What are you getting at?
She's insistent. *NO. NO. Honestly. This is what is so fascinating about you.*
She backs off. *Okay maybe not FASCINATING. INTRIGUING? That's a better word for it. Although that might be a little extreme. INTERESTING. That's it. INTERESTING.*
I shrug. *What do I say to that?*
She's lost in thought.
She gazes across the bowl and then back at me.
It's almost like an innocence...
This is new.
Her saying that.
Our food arrives.
Bowls. Small bowls.
Lots of them.
All over the table.
We eat for a while.
Without talking.
It all tastes so good.
And Noon Yeah.
She doesn't just eat, she celebrates.

She puts her fork down multiple times and leans back from the table and exclaims *SO GOOD!*

She closes her eyes.

Several times she hums after taking a bite.

She asks the server specific questions about what exactly she's eating and what it's made of and how it was prepared.

She insists on me trying this and trying that-even when I already have. I'm sitting at the same table in front of the same bowls eating the same food.

I hear the woman and the man play a song they've already played twice. How long have we been here?

Let's talk about you.

I say this as casually as I possibly can.

She doesn't say anything in response.

I don't know anything about you.

Good.

That's it. That's all she says. *Good.*

There's a person in there, right? I wave my hands in front of her like I'm trying to get her attention. *Hello Noon Yeah, actual Noon Yeah, Noon Yeah with a history who was born somewhere, who I can only assume went to school...who has a family? A planet you call home? Anything...anybody in there?*

I think this is quite clever.

She just watches me, occasionally sipping her wine.

Not one detail. Nothing. It's actually quite impressive how tight a lid you keep on it.

She puts her glass down.

The rules.

Oh please. The rules? But you know SO MUCH about me!

She doesn't flinch.

You're the job-

But I'm also a person…the job is a person. Same with you.

It appears like she's actually reflecting on my point.

It's the price we pay.

This rattles me. The truth of it.

I just don't know if it's…

My voice trails off. I have no idea where that thought is headed.

A voice carries from the table on the next ring above us. A woman's voice. We both hear it at the same time. Wounded. That's what I pick up in the voice. But also on the attack.

I SAW THE LOOK CARL! I SAW IT WITH MY OWN TWO EYES!

I look over trying to look like I'm not looking over. A man and a woman have just sat down at their table. She's wearing a puffy silver dress that makes her look like a very sad and anxious star that can't handle the stress of floating in space like that. The man is wearing a shirt that looks like it was designed to show off his muscles.

Oh please GRETCHEN! You didn't see a thing. Are you accusing me of making a SOMETHING out of a NOTHING?

No, I'm not-

I think Carl's really confused on how to play this.

I look over at Noon Yeah.

She's as captivated as I am.

Carl collects himself. *I was just being friendly.*

Gretchen is having none of it. *You said to her NICE FLOWERS. I heard you say it. Are you going to deny that you said it?*

He tilts his head back and then rolls it forward. *THEY ARE NICE FLOWERS. Are you suddenly against giving people*

COMPLIMENTS?

Gretchen adjusts her dress under her arms. Apparently all that puffy silver chafes a bit when things get dicey.

EVERYBODY KNOWS WHAT YOU MEANT BY FLOWERS CARL!!!

Carl is in way over his head. *FLOWERS ARE FLOWERS! What else do you think I meant??? Who are these people who think FLOWERS MEANS SOMETHING OTHER THAN FLOWERS???!!!*

Gretchen denies his defense.

Don't get all DISTRACTIONARY about words and what they mean-I SAW THE LOOK IN YOUR EYES!!! You like her FLOWERS!!!

Carl shifts in his seat. His tone changes. He comes in from a different angle. Subdued. Chastened. *All right. You got me. There WAS a look in my eye.*

Gretchen is overcome with relief. *FINALLY! I KNEW IT!*

Noon Yeah and I have been listening to this back and forth with our eyes locked on each other.

Carl clears his throat. He has more to say? *I WAS talking about more than just those FLOWERS. I was referring to OTHER FLOWERS.*

Carl's admission shifts the dynamic between them.

Gretchen did not see this coming. Her voice goes pitched and squeaky. *I don't understand.*

Big inhale from Carl. *Then I should probably tell you.* He is very solemn as he says this.

Noon Yeah's eyes get big.

My eyebrows raise.

We can't wait to see where this is headed.

We used to be a thing. Carl says this with an ache in his voice.

You two were together? Gretchen says TOGETHER like

it's a disease.

I can feel Carl nodding.

I steal a glance.

He is. He's nodding *YES.*

Silently.

Which is devastating for Gretchen.

She sniffles.

Carl plows ahead. *I went over one night to surprise her with flowers.* There's pain in his voice, like it happened yesterday. *As I walk up to the front door I see movement in the front room. And then I see her. She's with somebody.*

Gretchen gasps.

This is interesting. You can sense the conflict in Gretchen. She wants to know who the other dude was SO BAD but she doesn't really want to know what went down with Carl and this other woman. Gretchen loves the dish, the dirt, the low down. But this kind of involves her, so she hesitates. But she can't help herself.

Who was she with?

Carl is in a tight spot on this one.

He pauses.

He pauses some more.

And then he speaks.

Timmy.

Noon Yeah mouths *TIMMY?*

I whisper back *WHO KNEW TIMMY HAD GAME?*

Gretchen loses all ability to speak.

She looks like she saw a ghost.

Which she may have.

Because all she says in a barely coherent mutter is *Timmy…?*

Carl suddenly finds his strength. *So there I am, standing in her front yard holding those flowers, realizing we were never really a thing. She fancied Timmy the whole time! She played me Gretchen, she played me! So when I see her and I say NICE FLOWERS like I did earlier today and you see me say NICE FLOWERS to her YOU ARE CORRECT, I AM referring to something more than just THOSE FLOWERS! I am reminding her of those OTHER FLOWERS-of her BETRAYAL-I am making sure she never forgets that I know her heart is BLACK and COLD and DEAD.*

What a speech.

Noon Yeah clearly enjoyed it as much as I did.

This is the best dinner eavesdropping ever.

Another sniffle from Gretchen.

Well…

She eeks it out.

Like she's building up to something.

Carl is all ears.

I'm guessing he was expecting at least some acknowledgment of his heartbreak. At least a little recognition of his blamelessness in the whole NICE FLOWERS incident. But Carl is the last thing on Gretchen's mind. She fidgets with her napkin. She twirls her earrings.

*About Timmy…*she says.

No way.

Noooo way.

Noon Yeah is shaking her head.

Gretchen gulps.

Timmy and I used to be a thing.

I laugh out loud.

I can't help it.

It just came out so fast.

I keep my eyes locked on Noon Yeah.

Are they looking over here? I ask her, as discreetly as I can.

No, you're good. They didn't even hear you laugh.

Whew I say.

I look over at them.

Carl and Gretchen are both glaring at me.

I look back at Noon Yeah.

This is why I don't trust you I tell her.

With affection.

We sit in silence for a while.

A little more wine.

People come and go around us.

Gretchen leaves Carl all alone at the table.

The Bowl starts to empty.

I'm a little buzzed.

The violin player is putting her violin in its case.

The piano player is leaning against the piano.

I look around.

We're the last ones left.

The piano player and I make eye contact across the bowl.

He holds out both hands to us.

Cherish this he says.

Thank you I reply.

Did he say CHERISH THIS? Noon Yeah asks.

I think so....I'm not actually clear on what he said.

Then why did you say THANK YOU?

Everything is a little slow and swimmy and floaty.

I don't know-

I'd think you would have responded I WILL or WE WILL. THAT makes more sense.

I snap, just a little. *Can you ease up, just a bit? For like, a minute or two? Why do you even care?*

She backs off. I charge ahead. *The intensity never lets up with you. IT'S SO EXHAUSTING. Can you turn the dials down, just for the rest of today? Which is pretty much over. Do you even have any dials that you can adjust? Or is it just FULL BLAST all the time???*

Where is this coming from? I have all this built up resentment that is suddenly coming out and threatening what has been one of the best evenings of my life.

She is instantly by my side.

Let's get you home, shall we?

Kindness in her voice.

I see our server a few tables over.

I walk over to him.

I'm sorry, I haven't paid yet, you probably want to go home.

He smiles. His name tag says Nerlon.

Oh you're all set. Your meal was paid for.

It takes me a beat to process this.

I don't understand.

I can feel Noon Yeah right behind me.

Nerlon scans the bowl. *There.* He points to the top row across from us over to the left. Right up against the hedge. *They bought your dinner.*

I squint.

It's late, it's dark.

The lights are all a little dim to me.

I see them.

We aren't the last ones in The Bowl.

There are two people sitting way up there.

They're waving to us.

Javeen Wendor and Barbara Barabar.

Even from this far away I can see that her hair is unusually large tonight.

Who are they? Noon Yeah asks me.

I wave back.

Just some friends.

We make our way up to the top, we hug Mo Bowl on the way out, we walk home slowly.

I don't want this day to end.

We enter my flat and I lie down on my bed in my clothes. I listen to Noon Yeah brushing her teeth, washing her face, taking off her boots.

She died I say.

It's quiet in the hall.

She leans her head in the room.

Who died?

My love.

She comes in the bedroom.

She lies down next to me.

She stares at the ceiling.

What was her name?

Goja.

That's a beautiful name.

I loved her so much.

Where did you meet?

We grew up together, we lived in this area called The Thiru…her family kind of adopted me…

You were young?

So young. I don't even know that person I was anymore.

She exhales. *I know what that's like.*

There it is. The first ever so slight acknowledgement from Noon Yeah that she has lived some semblance of a life somewhere before this.

You do? You know what it's like?

I do. Can I ask what happened to her?

There was an accident.

That's all I'm able to say. After all these laps.

Were you there?
I was.
I'm so sorry Heen.
It's been so long-feels like a lifetime ago.
She sighs. *Doesn't make it less sad. Sometimes it makes it more…*
We lie here in the dark talking like this.
You know…for a ruthless killer it's surprising how meaningful it is to me to tell you all this…
Something passes between us.
Understanding?
Grace?
Heen?
Yes, Noon Yeah?
Did you ever want to give up?
There is something fragile in her voice. A quiver.
Something delicate.
Like GIVE UP GIVE UP? Like END IT ALL?
Yes, that's what I'm asking.
Yeah. I thought about it all the time for a while there.
I am right back in the garden, eating that bread with my mother.
But you kept going…
I did.
How? Or…why?
That's a good question.
I think about this question.
The job.
That's the answer I come up with.
I know what you mean.
That's what Noon Yeah says. She knows what I mean.
The job for you, too?
Yep.

484

It kind of rescued me. Gave me a life. I realize that now…
That's what happened to me she says.
She reaches over and takes my hand.
She holds it between her two hands.
I let her.
This is unexpected.
And nice.
It occurs to me: I'm too sad for sex.
And weary.
And conflicted.
Which is a first.
And yet.
Here we are.
Together.
And this is something.
Right?
As twisted and tormented as it is.
She moves her hand across the back of mine.
Something smooth.
What?
Cold. Metal. Thin.
Her other hand slides away, out from under mine.
I raise my arm.
There's a wire looped around my wrist.
Click.
There's a lock on it.
I look over at her hand.
The wire on my wrist leads to her wrist.
She smiles.
Click goes the lock on her wrist.
I always get the job done.
She says this like it was inevitable. Like I have no right to
be even remotely surprised.

You always get the job done.
I say this as I fall asleep.

*

I don't use an alarm.
I tell myself the night before what time I need to wake up
and then that's when I wake up.
Last night I didn't do this.
And yet here I am.
Wide awake.
At just the right time.
It's still dark out.
As usual.
I hear the shower.
I hold up my hand.
The wire is still on my wrist.
I follow it to the chair at the foot of the bed.
She locked me to the chair?
I get out of the bed and drag the chair out into the hall.
I have to pee.
I say it through the door.
The shower stops.
Just a second.
The way she says it.
So casual.
Like we're a thing.
Like we do this all the time.
Like this is just another morning in our life together.
Sharing a bathroom.
Getting ready for work.
I do this, you do that.
All that stuff people do.

That I don't.

The door opens.

She's wrapped in a towel.

She looks down at my wrist.

Then behind me to the chair in the hall.

It worked she says.

She unlocks the wire from my wrist.

I shower and get dressed, we eat a little breakfast, I notice she's wearing those black boots, we leave the flat.

The Bowl.

The Bowl I reply.

Best restaurant ever-

EVER. I totally agree.

Is it even a restaurant? It's so much more than that.

I know. It's like an event or an art project that happens to have amazing food.

Well said.

I wonder how Gretchen's gettin' on this morning.

Gretchen? How about Carl? That guy was in-

Way over his head. She finishes my sentence.

You had the same thought?

Oh yeah, that fella had NO idea what he was doing.

*Although…*I stop walking and turn to her. *He did have that SECRET LOVER TIMMY STORY he sprung on her just when it looked like he was going to have to concede defeat…*

We resume walking.

She was just so-

PRICKLY.

Yes! PRICKLY. That's the word for it.

We stroll along, replaying our eavesdropping from the night before, like we do this all the time.

There's something natural about it.

Effortless.

Does she feel this way?

Or does she do this with people all over the galaxy?

Am I one in a long line?

Or is this a first?

Is this rare for her?

Seldom?

Once in a while?

I'm not falling for her.

I hate her.

This what I keep repeating to myself.

SIGN 7, SIGN 7, SIGN 7.

Like a mantra.

I say it.

I say it again.

SHE LOCKED HERSELF TO YOU FOR THE NIGHT I tell myself.

It doesn't help.

I love this.

Floating along in the predawn light, relishing the rehashing of CARL AND GRETCHEN AND THOSE FLOWERS THAT ARE MORE THAN FLOWERS.

We cut through the park. There are two older gentlemen sitting on a bench. Their dogs are sniffing around in the bushes behind them. We pass that row of gray dome shaped homes, up the ridge where you get a brief view of the lake in the distance, through that group of trees with the rope swings.

We cross the clearing with the tall grass, past the school which is dark and quiet now but will be buzzing in a few hours, and down the path next to the ice cream shop.

Up ahead is an open area where people set up food stands during the day. It's empty now, except for a woman pushing a stroller. She's moving slowly away from us, eating an apple and leaning down to share bits with her kid.

A man joins her on the path.

She hugs him.

She is happy to see him.

He says something to her kid in the stroller.

Oh no.

No.

No.

The man has a bag over his shoulder.

His hair is short in the front and long in the back.

I glance over at Noon Yeah.

She's watching them like I am.

Does she realize-

Dill Tudd she says under her breath.

She shoves me behind a building.

It's a hat store.

No. No. No. No. I keep repeating it.

Something primal arises within me.

A survival impulse that has my entire nervous system on high alert.

She flattens her back against the wall of the store.

I don't think he saw us.

She is amped.

She sticks her head around the side of the building.

He's giving that woman something from his bag.

She spits it out like it's a matter of great concern.

I laugh.

Of course he is! That's what he does!!

I cling to the absurdity of the moment. It holds me together.

How long will he be with her?

She leans around the building again.

He's still with her!

She's kind of frantic. All twitchy and rattled.

Of course he's still with her! He likes people. He has real conversations with real people.

Look at me, going on like this beside the hat store in the dark.

Hey! I poke her arm. Like I'm eleven. *Don't you do this all the time? Isn't this, like, your gig? Your job? Cause you don't really seem on your game right now…*

Wow that is fun to say.

I double down.

By the way, this is some top flight surveillance right here. Were you trained in this? Because you are the definition of stealth.

She puts her finger to her lips.

SSSHHHHHHH.

Oh please I shush her back. *What-we gotta be quiet? You can't let him know we're here? What IS your plan?*

This gets her.

She looks at me like she's going to lash out.

But then she doesn't.

I jump on this.

YOU DON'T HAVE A PLAN DO YOU?

She closes her eyes, exhales.

I'm going to follow him until I see an opportunity. Simple.

Like that answers it.

I correct her. *WE are going to follow him.*

Shock on her face. *NO! You are done here. I am done with you.*

This hurts.

All that steel beneath her skin.

So cold to brush up against.

I lean against the wall, as close as I can to her.

You are going to follow him? I am going to follow YOU!

You have job? I have a job!!!

I say it like I am made of steel as well.

She waves me off.

You don't have a job.

I look her in the eyes.

I do. I protect Dill Tudd from YOU. It is a full time job. At least, today it is.

I am quite proud of how I've worked this all out.

I can tell she so badly wants to come back with something but she can't think of anything that clever.

She leans around the corner of the building again.

They're GONE!!!

I smile.

According to the plan.

I say it like I've already thought it all out.

She considers this. For a second.

You have no plan-

And neither do you.

She disappears around the corner.

I follow.

We run up to a tall bush. There are paths going in three different directions. Noon Yeah walks over to the ground where Dill Tudd and the woman were just standing. She gets down on one knee and studies their footprints.

This way.

She heads off down the trail.

We pass a fountain in front of the trellis behind the market.

We spot Dill Tudd.

He's sitting on a bench between two women.

We crouch down behind a small fence.

I can see him through the spaces between the slats.
He's telling them something. He keeps making a particular
hand motion. He reaches up like he's plucking a piece of
fruit off a tree, and then he brings it to his mouth like
he's going to eat it but suddenly he catches a whiff of it
and throws it over his shoulder.
Pantomime? Is that what that's called? Is that what a
MIME does? Because there is no actual piece of fruit. But
your mind puts a piece of fruit in his hand. It's as though
your mind can't resist the suggestion. It wants there to
actually be a piece of fruit.
Dill Tudd is really good at this.
Miming.
The women love it.
He does it again.
They slap their knees.
They clap.
They laugh so hard.
He does it again.
Only this time he pretends he's taking a bite.
Like the odor doesn't bother him that much.
Is he telling a joke?
Or a story?
Did this happen to him?
Is he recounting something he's experienced?
Whatever it is-
It's a hit.
This goes on for a while.
He is MIMING and MILKING this STORY for all it's worth.
Noon Yeah watches, expressionless.
She is in some other mode.
Some other head space.
Some other world.

Eventually, after what feels like forever but is probably ten minutes, Dill Tudd stands up and faces the two women.

One of them is wearing a floppy green hat. He snatches it off her head and puts it on his own. He dances a jig for them wearing that hat. He puts it back on her head.

They each stand up and give him a hug. He reaches in his bag and hands one of them something, then the other. He does his Dill Tudd bow, and he walks away.

We follow.

We're too close I whisper.

She doesn't look at me. *I don't want him to get away like last time.*

There are rocks in her words.

But he didn't get away I point out.

She stops and stares at me.

He could have-

But he didn't.

She puts her hands on her hips.

You're just saying that because you want me to fail.

This accusation isn't actually an accusation.

Of course I want you to fail.

A hint of something new in her eyes.

Vulnerability?

She's vulnerable?

She's capable of that?

Dill Tudd has stopped beside a pink hut.

He's talking through a window to someone inside.

The hut is quite small.

Someone lives in there?

There's laundry hanging on a rope out front.

This still bothers me.

How they hang their laundry in full view on Firdus.

We can see him through a row of pine trees.

We're standing side by side.
I feel the need to repeat myself.
Of course I want you to fail.
She puts her hand on my arm.
But if I fail, you fail.
I shake my head.
I'm not quite sure how you did the math on that...
She looks at me like she's tired of explaining things to me.
Easy. I have a job to do. My job is connected to your job. I do my job, and then you get to keep your job.
Whoever Dill Tudd is talking to in that house, he just turned around in a circle and then kept talking to them.
You're assuming I WANT to keep my job.
I hear myself say this.
Out loud.
What is happening to me?
What is happening IN me?
She ignores this.
I can't have you following me.
I know exactly what to say here.
I'm not following you-
You know what I mean-
I fold my arms in front of me.
And YOU know what I mean. I am free to follow whoever I want. I do not want to follow Noon Yeah. I want to follow Dill Tudd.
I am getting under her skin and I am so pleased.
I'm having trouble focusing.
She's serious.
That's fine with me.
She squeezes my arm. Like, really squeezes it.
I have a job to do. I have to do it.
A low grade panic there.

Or is it what I picked up on a minute ago?

Vulnerability.

I haven't seen this from her.

It may have been there.

But I missed it.

Which isn't surprising.

But there it is.

Something about the job.

About doing a good job.

Performing. Achieving. Accomplishing.

I don't know.

I'm probably making more of it than it is.

But that. That tone. That catch in her voice.

Young.

That's it.

Youth.

I didn't notice these kinds of things before.

Earlier.

Like when Sir Pong showed up on Yorch and I just wanted him to acknowledge me.

Or Ma'am Neffi. How quickly she evoked that feeling within me of being fourteen.

That's what it is.

This is the first I've seen Noon Yeah actually doing the job.

Everything before this was her talking-US talking.

But this.

Tracking Dill Tudd.

This is why she came to Firdus.

And I'm mucking it up.

Got that right.

I'm muckin' it up with all I got.

Do you want to see if Dill Tudd wants to get some

breakfast with us?
She looks like she wants to hit me.
Uhhh…NO…and NO!!!
I'm hungry-
Stop talking! He just handed the pink hut person something.
Dill Tudd bows and he's off.
Noon Yeah and Heen Gru-Bares IN HOT PURSUIT!!!
I say it like I'm narrating a play.
Noon Yeah does not find this funny.
Oh come on, you enjoyed that. Just a little.
She's already off, down the trail.
We follow Dill Tudd past the library, up through the woods. We're sitting on a little hill, watching him down below having an intense conversation with a couple who are each holding a snake.
I lean over and say to Noon Yeah *I feel bad that I didn't show up for work today.*
She keeps her eyes fixed on Dill Tudd.
No worries, it's all taken care of.
Wait. What's taken care of?
Today. And tomorrow. And the next day-
Taken care of? That is way too vague-
I told Lan Zing that I was surprising you with a little trip.
But you had no right to-
She turns to face me.
By the way-why don't you use your vacation days? You haven't used ONE of them. Who does that? Or maybe I should say WHO DOESN'T DO THAT?
I'm so thrown off by this.
You arranged for me to take time off?
Uh-huh.
So no one at the bakery is expecting me today?

496

Correct.

But what if I had gone in today?

You wouldn't have.

Why not?

She holds up her wrist and points to where the wire was. *I wouldn't have let you.*

We follow Dill Tudd all morning.

He stops and talks to people.

He pets dogs and cats and birds. And snakes.

He makes little kids laugh.

He tells stories.

And everybody, everybody gets something from his bag.

Is this a route?

Are these appointments?

Do they know he's coming?

Did they agree earlier to this time and this place?

I had noticed him talking to people before.

But not like this.

The extent of it.

The sheer endurance alone is astonishing.

We're hiding behind a yogurt machine in a park. I'm pressed up against her side because it not a very large yogurt machine.

Does he ever eat? I ask her.

Baffling, isn't he? His stamina alone is incredible. A hint of admiration in her voice.

Morning turns into afternoon.

Afternoon into early evening.

He's in that park where the old men play chess.

He says hello to the woman who makes the tacos under that tree with the light blue leaves.

He exits the park on the far side and then turns left

between two houses. This takes him down into a gully.
We stay close.
But not too close.
On other side of the gully he climbs up a steep incline and turns left into a thicket.
Moments later we get to the thicket.
It's dense and scratchy and it's got all kinds of vines and bushes and branches.
How did he step so easily into this?
Over here Noon Yeah motions to me.
There's an opening in the bramble.
Slight. But if you know where to look there's a path.
I bend down and follow her.
We make our way down a long embankment, under a huge tree that has fallen over, and into a small canyon.
The canyon narrows as we find ourselves walking through a section with rocks higher than our heads on either side.
This takes a while.
It's a little claustrophobic.
I keep reminding myself to breathe.
It opens up into a flat, wide stretch of field with tall grass in every direction.
Noon Yeah finds his footprints.
We weave in among the clumps of grass.
I can't see anything other than the grass.
Where are we?
Noon Yeah doesn't respond.
Does anyone live out here?
I'm talking to myself.
How long ago was it that we last saw any buildings?
She ignores me.
We haven't seen him in at least an hour, or has it been longer?

She stops.

She turns right.

This way.

A breeze stirs the grass. On any other day I would find the noise this makes relaxing.

I'm not going to watch Noon Yeah GRAIN Dill Tudd.

I'm going to stop Noon Yeah from GRAINING Dill Tudd.

Yes, that's it.

That's how it's going to go.

She messed with the wrong SERIES 5, I tell myself.

Earnestly.

There's a hill up ahead.

It curves away from us on the right and left.

At the top are large, jagged rock outcroppings.

The closer we get, the taller they get.

They're actually cliffs.

They look like broken teeth.

I turn around.

All I can see behind us is tall grass.

I look ahead.

More grass and then those cliffs.

Where did he go?

It's like a magic trick.

What he did.

Disappearing like this.

I get right up behind Noon Yeah.

You're never going to catch him I whisper.

She raises her heel and kicks me in the jewels.

I keel over on all fours.

No taunting, I tell myself.

I get up and stumble after her.

We arrive at the edge of the grass field. The hill is way, way steeper than I first realized. Trees and boulders are scattered all the way up. Noon Yeah turns left and walks between the grass and the slope.

She stops.

There's a mess of stumps and branches and leaves and vines where the grass meets the incline. It looks like a giant grabbed a handful of woods and then got bored and dropped it right here in a pile.

Noon Yeah stands still, staring at something.

I stand next to her.

Her hands are on her hips.

I put my hands on my hips.

She bites her lower lip.

She looks to the right, she looks to the left.

She stares ahead.

And then I see it.

I see what she's looking at.

There's a door.

A wooden door.

You can't see it, and then you can.

In among all those trunks and branches.

You could walk by this spot a thousand times and you'd miss it every time.

But this is her job.

She's doing her job.

She finds the door.

I do, too.

I step towards it.

Noon Yeah grabs my arm and pulls me back. *NO!*

I give her my best Dill Tudd head tilt. *How DARE YE GIVE ME A NO!!! YES I SAY!*

I'm even talking like him.

I turn and head towards the door again.

She yanks me back. *It could be booby trapped!!!*

I look at her like she's five. *Did you just say BOOBY TRAP?*

She wants to laugh, I know it.

Booby trap? First off, is that even still a thing- BOOBY TRAPS? AND DILL TUDD??? You just followed this guy for AN ENTIRE DAY. Is there anything about what you just witnessed that makes you think he's the BOOBY TRAPPIN' TYPE?

I step back towards her.

I realize how traumatic this is for you-

She swats this away. *This isn't traumatic-*

I interrupt. *I know-I know-You're about to tell me you're just doing your job.*

A sheepish look and a little laugh. *That IS what I was going to say-*

I know. You see yourself as all crafty and competent and clever but you're really quite predictable. Whatever's happening, the moment things get dodgy you default to THE JOB.

She listens.

I keep going.

You can drop your suspicion. There are no BOOBY TRAPS. You can relax. Your GRAINING JOB is STUPID. ST-U-P-I-D.

She stops me. *Are you SPELLING STUPID for me?*

This winds me up all the more.

SO STUPID! It's a dumb way to run a universe.

She gives me HER best Dill Tudd head tilt. *What is this rubbish pouring forth from your mouth? Where do you get off spewing all this negativity...*

I spread out my arms like I am welcoming the world to come home. *Not NEGATIVE-STUPID!!! And the CHAIRS? DUMBEST people in the galaxies!!! Sending someone like*

YOU to grain Dill Tudd??? Convincing you HE'S the problem??? Making it YOUR JOB??? You know what the problem is??? THE PROBLEM IS THINKING DILL TUDD IS THE PROBLEM!!!

It feels so good to say that.

I feel so much lighter.

I give her my THAT IS WHAT I HAVE TO SAY ABOUT THAT look.

Again, I turn and head towards the door.

She doesn't stop me.

It opens easily.

I step in.

To a tunnel.

I turn around.

She's right behind me.

She lets the door close.

Pitch black.

I feel the sides of the tunnel.

A scratchy flicking sound.

Her lighter comes on.

Of course she has her lighter on her.

Almost a day ago she was creating a ball of fire for a ravine full of kids. And now we're doing this.

There's enough light to take another step into the tunnel.

It slopes down slightly.

We're going DOWN into the hill?

I feel her hand on my back.

I keep both my hands on the sides of the tunnel.

She holds up the lighter.

We move forward.

Slowly.

We gradually find our rhythm.

Our breathing.

Our steps.

It looks like someone dug this tunnel with a small shovel.

Which would have taken so long.

I can't imagine.

I speak softly over my shoulder *I'm sorry about my little speech back there, I don't think you're stupid.*

I know she whispers. *You think I'm amazing.*

I love that she just said that.

How do you know that's what I think about you?

You told me.

I did?

You did.

How is it that you remember me saying that but I don't?

A slightly exasperated sigh. *You're asking me to explain YOU to YOURSELF?*

That's a good point. *I have a very difficult time explaining MYSELF to myself.*

I look back over the top of her head.

I can't see the door.

Forward we go.

About that little rant of yours back there…

I was wondering if she'd bring that up.

…Yes…?

You seem to have some anger against the CHAIRS.

I need to be careful here.

Nah-I was just spouting off.

She's doesn't buy it.

Well, I'll have to put that in my ASSESSMENT REPORT.

That's not good.

Really?

No. I'm just spouting off.

Sometimes you're quite funny.

I am.

Her hand is still on my back.

It's been there the whole time we've been in the tunnel.

I look up.

The top is at least two feet above my head.

Why are we crouching? I ask.

She looks up. *That's a good question.*

We both stand up straight.

We stop.

Just the sounds of our breathing.

Click.

Her lighter turns off.

I feel her move in front of me.

She steps closer and wraps her arms around me.

In the dark, in a tunnel.

It is a sublime sensation, these arms of hers wrapped around me.

I wrap my arms around her.

We stand here.

Holding each other.

I rest my back against the wall.

She leans into me.

I gently hold her head against my chest.

My mind does not race.

For once.

I am not stuck in my head.

I am not standing at a distance.

I am not trying to figure out how this happened or what it means or where it's headed or what it even is.

I am here.

And nowhere else.

Time evaporates, leaving little trace of its previous presence.

Heen?
Yes, Noon Yeah.
Can we stay here for a minute?
Yes.
Exactly like this?
Yes.
It is calm and it is perfect and it is turbulent and it is terrifying and it is everything I have longed for and I am just now realizing it.
It occurs to me that I have no idea when the SUNS are going to set today. And being in this tunnel with it getting dark outside doesn't sound like the best plan.
Keep going?
Probably should she says, reluctantly.
This moves me, the reluctance in her voice.
I take her hand.
Click.
The lighter comes on.
Down the tunnel we go.
For a while. It could be a hundred feet. Two hundred feet. Half a mile. I have no sense of distance in here.
And then, light.
It's just a reflection up ahead off of the right side of the tunnel.
Which we slowly discover is curving.
To the left.
The tunnel curves left?
Up ahead the tunnel ends.
Just like that.
Daylight.
This makes me laugh.
I'm just going to say it because this might be the only time in my life I get to... *There's light at the end of the tunnel.*

She groans. *You had to-didn't you?*
I did. How often do you find yourself in a LITERAL METAPHOR?
She hugs me, bringing her lips up to my ear *About as often as you find yourself on Firdus.*

We're almost there.
I'll go first I tell her.
You ARE going first-
No, I mean I'll KEEP going first-
Why?
It strikes me in this moment that we're interacting like we've been together for ten or twenty laps.
You want to discuss it? I ask her.
No, I was just getting under your skin. You want to go through that door FIRST? Great. I'll be right behind you.
We reach the door. It looks like it opens into some sort of circular room. The walls are rock. It's open to the sky.
I step through the door and into the room. There's an opening in the rock to the left that leads down a path. I'm standing on a wood platform that rests on the ground.
I step to the middle.
Huh.
I turn back to the doorway.
Noon Yeah is standing there watching me, expectant.
I shrug.
Kind of a letdown, to be honest.
A grating, sliding sound.
Wood on wood? Wood on metal? What is that-metal on rock?
It sounds like it's on the other side of the wall.
I catch something swinging in an arc above me.
Some sort of trough.

A trough?

I lean my head back to see it more clearly as red, thick liquid dumps directly on to my face and into my eyes before I can get out from under it.

There's so much of it.

It just keeps coming.

All over me.

I'm soaked.

And blinded.

I wipe my eyes.

Which doesn't help.

Heen! Noon Yeah yells.

I hear her step forward out of the doorway but then recoil.

I haven't inhaled yet.

I inhale.

It's like death itself gyrating to bad music in my head.

It's so noxious.

I instantly feel woozy.

Dizzy.

I try to spit it out.

I keep wiping my eyes but the smell.

It's all over me, attacking me.

WHAT DO I DO? I shout towards the doorway.

I DON'T KNOW!!! she shouts back. *SPIN AROUND? TRY TO SHAKE IT OFF YOU?*

I am not handling this well. *WHAT DO YOU MEAN? LIKE WHEN A DOG TAKES A BATH?*

I can't see her.

I assume I'm turned in the right direction.

I DON'T KNOW-I HAVEN'T EVER SEEN A DOG TAKE A BATH!

That's odd. *YOU HAVEN'T? DO THEY NOT HAVE DOGS*

THAT TAKE BATHS WHERE YOU COME FROM?
She lowers her voice. *Heen-why are you yelling?*
Because you were yelling-
That's because you were-
I was yelling because this smell makes me want to yell.
Fair enough she responds, like this is a perfectly normal
every day interaction between two well-adjusted adults.
Another sliding, grinding sound.
Do you hear that? I ask her.
I do, it's coming from the same place as before-
What should I do?
I have no idea-is it still in your eyes?
It is. I can't see a thing!
And then it dumps.
Again. Even more.
Water this time.
So much of it.
I look up and open my eyes as the RED WHATEVER IT IS
rinses off me.
The water keeps coming.
I'm getting drenched.
The smell subsides.
A little.
It slows to a trickle.
A few drops.
And then it stops.
I look down.
There's a drain in the floor.
The water is gone.
There's a little red here and there, but otherwise it drained
as well.
I can see.
I step toward Noon Yeah.

Hold up she says. *That smell.*
Right. I'll stay away.
She looks up at the trough.
Didn't see that coming, did you?
A laugh.
We turn.
Piddle, piddle, piddle.
Dill Tudd stands there in the opening, smiling.
Like we do this all the time.
Piddle, piddle, piddle is RIGHT! I say.
I turn to Noon Yeah. She puts up her hands. *You'll get no piddle from me-that's between you two.*
Dill Tudd starts to walk in a circle around me.
He looks up.
That BOOBY did some TRAPPIN' he says.
Noon Yeah lights up. *HE IS THE BOOBY TRAPPIN' TYPE!!!*
Dill Tudd is still circling me. *There is the BOOBY, and then there is the TRAP, and then there is that wonderful moment when they come together-*
He claps his hands once. Loudly. He's perplexed by something.
Although, seeing as we're among friends here, I must be honest and confess that it is a bit of a letdown.
I have no idea what to make of this. *Letdown?*
He sniffs the air around me. *I realize in this moment that I don't know what I was hoping for. Interesting how that works-you have a thing in your MIND and so you plan it and you arrange it and you engineer it and then the day comes when it happens. But it isn't what you had IMAGINED. So you ask yourself WHAT DID I IMAGINE? And you have no answer for yourself. This is the elusive power that a FIRST can have over you...*

Noon Yeah is as bewildered as I am. *A first?*

Dill Tudd nods. *Yes. First. You two are the first.*

I look up at the trough. *You haven't BOOBY TRAPPED anyone before this?*

A look of recognition in Noon Yeah's eyes. She steps out of the doorway. *Dill Tudd, are we the first to follow you here?*

I'm thinking THERE'S NO WAY WE ARE when Dill Tudd answers her

Yes. You are.

I point back down the tunnel.

No one has ever followed you here?

No one.

We're the first?

You're the first.

Noon Yeah crouches down and dabs her finger in one of the last swirls of red. *What was that?*

Dill Tudd is so proud of whatever he's about to say. *Ahhhh yes, an advanced aromatic achievement, finely tuned over the laps by yours truly.*

I blink, I'm still getting the water and whatever it was out of my eyes. *It was so red—like the reddest red I've ever seen...*

LIKE THE RED OF LIFE. He stretches it out slowly.

Wait.

No.

No Dill Tudd I say. Desperation in my voice.

Oh yes, Dill Tudd says, *THE RED OF LIFE. Also known in popular parlance as BLOOD.*

Noon Yeah does that throaty laugh she did the first time she appeared in my room. *Heen got drenched in blood???? OHHHHH THAT. IS. CLASSIC.*

Dill Tudd nods vigorously. *And not just any blood. Our dear*

Gloria-

HUMAN BLOOD!??!! I get this full body itchy scratchy feeling.

Oh dear no…Gloria was with us for thirteen laps. And then she joined the soil just recently. I was so sad to see her go. I sang a number of songs at her burial service.

I have to know. *Gloria was a…?*

Pig.

I knew Noon Yeah would have asked if I didn't.

You had a funeral for a pig?

Oh Heen Gru-Bares-your questions are so often laced with a certain innocence. It's quite wonderful to behold. He leans against the wall. *Of course we had a funeral. WE ALWAYS MARK OUR LOSSES PROPERLY. Grief unexpressed will cause your bones to waste away.*

I feel no need to say anything after that.

Noon Yeah does. *WE?*

Dill Tudd nods. *WE.*

I'm assuming she was looking for more information than that. But that's all he's giving right now.

I get another whiff. Of myself.

What about this smell? Does this come from Gloria?

Oh Heen, you swim in the same sea of curiosity that Noon Yeah does! Gloria is not the author of that aroma, pigs don't smell. Is that not common knowledge?

I'm thinking about pigs.

Huh. *I don't know anything about pigs. What are they for?*

Dill Tudd considers this. *Friendship.* That's what he says.

Which made her death all the more painful, didn't it? Noon Yeah asks.

So true.

There's a wistful look on his face.

Thirteen laps is a good, long friendship she says, like she knows exactly what she's talking about.

I wait a beat.

So what about the smell? I have to know what that was.

Oh yes-I almost forgot. He pauses. *Fox.*

Noon Yeah laughs. *Fox?*

Who knew? Dill Tudd throws his hands up in the air. *Of all the nefarious odors that flow from the various orifices of our fine friends of the fur, no pheromone out performs the urine of a fox-*

My turn. *Fox?*

Dill Tudd is so into this. *Something unique about their ANAL SACS produces a TANGY MUSKY SKUNKY aroma-of course the compound variations with those particular methyl sulfides will scorch your nasal hairs on their own-*

Noon Yeah interrupts *You're telling me!*

I look at her. *What do you know about METHYL SULFIDES?*

She gives me a triumphant look. *VULPINE SOCIETY at it's finest.*

Dull Tudd nods approvingly. *You sure know your sapient mammals…*

I do she says, like this is just another day on the job.

I shiver.

Let's get you some dry clothes.

Dill Tudd says this as he heads through the opening. We follow.

It's a narrow path, with a natural hedge on our right and a steep rock incline on the left.

Dill Tudd stops and turns to me. He holds up three fingers. *The third ingredient in my BOOBY BREW? Possum dung.*

Noon Yeah claps. *WHOO! BOOBY BREW!!!*

I have a question. *What is it about possum dung?*
Dill Tudd beams. *I thought you'd never ask. It's the VISCOSITY of it-not too thick, not too runny. A bit like paste, but without the adhesive properties. It gives the BOOBY BREW the perfect consistency. Plus, I thoroughly enjoy how POSSUM DUNG rolls off the tongue.*
I can think of absolutely nothing to say in response to this.
Noon Yeah, once again, does not have the same problem.
We're sorry to barge in on you like this.
Dill Tudd pulls a leaf off a nearby branch and takes a bite.
There has been no BARGING that I am aware of!!! You arrived in the due course of time.
Little alarms going off, somewhere within me.
You knew we were coming?
He thinks about this.
There are a number of answers to that question. And a number of questions for that answer.
That is Dill Tudd right there: Sincerely answering my question in such a way as to say everything and nothing, all at the same time.
I shiver, again.
How about this? Dill Tudd says. *Let's get Heen those dry clothes and then we'll have a proper chat about the things that matter most.*
He continues down the trail.
Again, I lose all sense of distance.
We come to an opening in the path.
We're in a small grove of trees, on the side of a hill.
There are wool blankets, about the size of a person, hanging on a series of hooks drilled into the trunk of one of the trees. I still can't tell where we are, or how high up we are, or what's above us or below us-my topographical awareness is thoroughly scrambled.

Dill Tudd hands us each a blanket. He takes one for himself, and steps between two trees.

There's a-what is it? What is that-a platform?

He sets his blanket down on it.

I step forward.

It slopes down into the woods below us.

It's a slide?

It's made of smooth metal-or is that fiberglass?

Noon Yeah steps next to me. *Incredible.*

She turns to Dill Tudd. *Are you going down that?*

Dill Tudd sits on the blanket.

Let us reconvene at the bottom...

He pushes off.

Away he goes.

It IS a slide.

And it is really, really long.

Trees bend their branches over it, forming a tunnel of leaves.

We can't see the bottom.

He disappears from view.

Noon Yeah sets her blanket down.

I ALWAYS GET THE JOB DONE.

She pushes off. She turns and smiles as she slides away.

I drop mine down and yell after her

YOU MESSED WITH THE WRONG SERIES 5.

If you had told me after talking to Dill Tudd those first few times that this grown man in the matching outfit has a SLIDE I assume I would have replied OF COURSE HE DOES.

I haven't been on a slide since I was a kid.

This one is so fast.

It banks to the right.

It curves to the left.

Under the trees I glide.

The slide flattens out, then drops down again, steeper.

More trees.

More leaves.

Stumps, rocks, branches.

A rabbit.

I fly by.

I see the bottom.

Noon Yeah is sprawled out on the ground.

The woods spit me out into a clearing next to her.

She jumps to her feet. *WOOOOOOO! I LOVED THAT! WHEN WAS THE LAST TIME YOU DID THAT?*

I have no idea. *Thirty laps ago, maybe?*

She shakes her head. *WHO KNEW?*

She looks around.

I do, too.

I have been all over the galaxies.

I have hiked and explored and strolled through every sort of terrain known to humans.

But this.

What I see.

This is new.

We're in a valley, I think.

But it's curved.

More like a circle.

Or a crater.

A crater?

It's slightly longer than it is wide.

We're at the bottom.

It rises up around us on all sides.

Along the top of the rim are those jagged teeth-like-rocks-that-are-actually-cliffs we saw from the other side as we approached.

There are trees and plants in every direction, as far as I can see. The crater is full of them. Avocados, oranges, lemons-there's something red growing on a plant to my left, a clump of green stalks with bright purple stems to my right. A large cactus is straight ahead. With a yellow flower next to it. Next to that…hold on-are those tomatoes?

It's way, way too much to take in all at once.

Who did this?

WHAT is this?

How did all it all get here?

How would anyone ever even know this is here?

Noon Yeah leans on me.

It's sooooo beautiful.

She says this as though the beauty is also crushing her in the process.

I feel the same way.

It's so beautiful it's kind of heartbreaking-

In the best way. She speaks in a sound softer than breath. And the smell. It's like every flower and candle and scent and oil and fragrance you've ever encountered, overwhelming your olfactory awareness all at once. I swear I'm getting some sort of ineffable high just standing here NOTICING.

It's its own little world. Noon Yeah states this delicately as she tenderly rests her head on my shoulder. *It's its own little Dill Tudd world.*

There are tears streaming down her face.

There she is.

There's Noon Yeah.

Right there.

I feel like I'm finally seeing her.

I think the kids will enjoy that.
I look over.
Dill Tudd has been standing to our left this whole time,
watching us take in this scene. He has a look on his face I
haven't seen before.
Satisfaction?
It's more than that.
Pride?
A little.
Joy?
For sure.
But a little ache.
Sadness, even.
Like something he has wanted to happen is happening.
That's what I sense.
At that same time something else is happening.
Something inevitable.
And he's trying to sort it all out in his heart.

But these sorts of things-what do I know about these?

Kids? I ask him.
The slide-I think kids would really enjoy that slide.
He points to it.
I enjoyed it! Have kids ever tried it?
He shakes his head.
You're the first-
Oh... I realize he was serious back there. *Dill Tudd, are we
the FIRST people to ever visit you here and ride down
your slide?*
He bites his lower lip.
He nods. Slightly.
What is that on his face?

Dill Tudd, is this overwhelming, having us here?
My question is utterly sincere.
I would never have asked someone a question like this.
I wouldn't even have thought it.
I wouldn't have been aware.
Noon Yeah leaves my side and walks over to him.
She puts both hands on his shoulders.
Is this your home?
He puts his hands on his heart.
It is. Welcome.
She hugs him.
He lives here?
He leaves this place and walks into the CENTERS?
How long has he lived here?
Is it just him?
Does he live here alone?
I stop the questions.
Because this is my pattern.
I start to feel and then I step back and I ANALYZE and
OBSERVE and NOTICE so I won't have to feel whatever it
is in it's fullness, and I won't be at the mercy of wherever
it may take me…

I cease the inquiries.
I don't want to stand at a distance.
I walk over and embrace them both.
A GROUP HUG, I believe it's called.
My first one ever.
BRRRRRR says Noon Yeah, laughing.
She backs up. *You're so cold.*
Our Heen is a wet one Dill Tudd says as he turns and
walks away. *Let's get you sorted.* We set off towards the
center of the crater, weaving in among the trees and

plants and bushes.

It's like strolling through a slow motion explosion of life.

As if all these plants didn't just grow, they BURST up out of the soil because it couldn't contain them.
Like Firdus had so much to say it just couldn't hold its tongue.
Up ahead to the left we see a building with a sloped roof.
Wait.
The roof.
That's a wing.
The roof is a wing.
It's resting on large wooden posts.
There aren't any walls.
As we get closer I see long tables, stacked with piles of fabric, lined up with space to walk in among them. There are scissors and tape measures and pins and patterns scattered around. Two of the tables have sewing machines on them.
Dill Tudd walks over to one of the tables and takes a shirt off a pile.
He holds it up.
This should work.
The shirt is blue.
That jacket you made me fits perfectly I tell him.
He nods as though this is not news to him. *Fit is a great gift, is it not? WHEN SOMETHING FITS RIGHT IT FEELS RIGHT and a whole number of other things in a person's life begin to fall into place.*
OLD HEEN would have laughed at what he just said and then dismissed it as the ramblings of a man disconnected with how the world truly functions.

THIS HEEN says *Ain't that the truth.*

Noon Yeah makes her way among the tables, holding up different fabrics, examining them, fully absorbed in her exploring.

Dill Tudd picks up a pair of pants.

He sets them down.

He holds up what looks like a skirt. *Perfect.*

A skirt? My skepticism is strong.

NO! A SARONG. Huge DIFFERENCE, Heen Gru-Bares. The world turns on DIFFERENCES such as these.

He hands me the sarong. It's blue as well. The fabric feels like EASE itself, so smooth and soft.

You can change over there. He points to a partition just past the tables.

What is this…room? Or building? What-

It's called The Wing. I sew here.

I look around.

Who calls it The Wing?

He appears to be thrown by my question.

I do. Who else would?

That clears it up.

The Wing it is I say.

Noon Yeah sits up on one of the tables. *Is there another Wing?*

Dill Tudd points to the other side of the crater.

We see it.

Across the tops of the trees.

Another wing that has a roof. Held up by posts.

That's the Other Wing?

That's what we call it.

You call it The Other Wing?

I do.

I think this is very clever. *And then when you're OVER*

520

THERE in THAT ONE do you call it The Wing and then point over to THIS ONE and call it The Other Wing? Exactly he says.

All those odd conversations with Dill Tudd, all those scattershot segues and woozy wordplay-being here feels like if one of those conversations was brought to life in three or four or five dimensions. Like we're inhabiting his speech. Like we've stepped into one of his paragraphs. Through a tunnel, of course.

I change into my new outfit.

I like it.

Earlier Heen would not have been caught dead in this.

Noon Yeah can't stop smiling. *Steezy Heen* she calls me.

It fits perfectly I say.

Did you ever doubt me Heen Gru-Bares?

Dill Tudd has a satisfied smile on his face.

I'm gradually becoming aware of just how massive this moment is for him.

Would you like to see The Other Wing? I think that will help this all make much more sense...

Noon Yeah jumps down off the table. *Ummm, A THOUSAND YESES. We want the whole tour! You do tours, right Dill Tudd?*

He hesitates.

His bottom lip quivers.

I do now.

Why do I keep picking up undertones of grief in his words?

We head off towards the other side of the crater.

More trees, more plants.

He stops and pulls a pear off a tree and hands it to me.

He picks a few strawberries for Noon Yeah.

We arrive at what feels like the center of the crater, an open flat space with five chairs in a circle. There's a fire pit in the center. A small creek winds its way through.

Dill Tudd stands up on a nearby stump, cups his hands around his mouth and yells *AMIGOS!!!*

I haven't ever heard Dill Tudd yell. It is a thunderous voice he possesses. I could swear it shakes the trees. It echoes off the cliffs.

What is that word?

AMIGOS means FRIENDS Noon Yeah tells me.

We hear a bark.

Then another.

Then another.

Dogs?

They're coming towards us.

Dill Tudd has dogs?

A fox runs into view.

A fox? Noon Yeah shrieks. *I haven't ever seen a fox!*

The fox runs up and jumps into Dill Tudd's arms. They act like they do this all the time. Dill Tudd pats the top of its head.

This is Shireen. She's a lovely old soul. Been with me for quite a few laps. But as you just saw, she's still got that foxy spring in her step.

I'm transfixed.

Dill Tudd, you have a pet fox?

I'm so glad Noon Yeah says this.

Friend is a better word for it. Yes, Shireen?

He says this to the fox.

Shireen tucks her head under Dill Tudd's chin, like it's her favorite spot on the planet.

The barking gets louder.

And louder.

And then they appear.

Big dogs and little dogs and one with huge black spots and one without any hair and one with a smashed in face and one with a swollen hind end. Ten of them? Twelve of them? I stop counting.

AMIGOS!!! Dill Tudd yells again.

It's even louder this time.

How does he do that?

How does he make that much noise?

It rattles my head, this YELL VOICE of his.

And the dogs-they slow down.

And then they stop.

In a line.

Perfectly still.

All of them.

Sitting shoulder to shoulder.

In a line.

Noon Yeah gasps. *Am I seeing what I'm seeing?*

None of them are moving.

They watch Dill Tudd.

He paces back and forth in front of them.

All those dog eyes, glued to him.

Who loves you? He asks them.

They begin howling.

All of them.

But not frightened howling.

It sounds like they're trying to sing.

Like a dog choir.

But they can't agree on the song.

Or the words.

That's right, you know who loves you.

He touches each one on the top of its head as he makes his way down the row.

He's in no rush.

Shireen rides along.

Like they do this every day.

All right then, I'm going to be with our guests for a bit so I left you a treat in The Wing.

I laugh out loud at that.

Like a dog would understand any of that.

Dill Tudd raises his hand above his head, holds it there, and then snaps his fingers. The dogs take off running towards The Wing.

Oh.

They did understand that.

They are crazy for persimmons he says. *Let us proceed.*

Off he goes between two apple trees. We make our way up a slight incline towards The Other Wing. We pass a fig tree, a rose bush, a bench stacked with jars of almonds. There's just so much to take in. I could wander around in here for days and I still wouldn't see it all.

As the The Other Wing comes into view I see it's full of shelves. Lots of them. They have bins on them. So many bins. Hundreds.

The shelves are on wheels.

They're arranged in rows.

We step under the wing.

I assume THIS is what you came to see.

Dill Tudd shrugs as he says this.

There's a look of resignation on his face.

The energy shifts between us.

Something is off.

He sits down on a stool at a table in among all the shelves.

He leans over the table on his elbows.

He rubs his face in his hands.

He looks defeated.

I look over at Noon Yeah.

She looks like she's in pain.

She scans one of the shelves.

I join her.

The bins are labeled.

TURMERIC. That one is full of…turmeric.

Sure enough.

The SANDALWOOD one? Sandalwood.

The GARLIC one? Garlic.

Ginger. Sassafras. On it goes.

We watch Dill Tudd.

He's always had a certain ageless quality to him. Like he drifts far above such temporal concerns as the passing of time.

But now, sitting at that table, with the color drained from his face, he looks like it's the end of the world.

His shoulders slump forward.

I haven't met this Dill Tudd.

I grab two stools from next to one of the shelves and I set them down across from him at the table.

I sit.

Noon Yeah joins me.

She reaches over and takes his hand.

Are you okay?

His eyes are red.

What's going on?

He exhales. Like he's a thousand laps old.

I hold up a chunk of ginger I took from one of the bins.

This is what you hand out.

I finally get it.

Obviously him giving me that rosemary should have been my first clue.

I NOTICE, but I don't always SEE.

Noon Yeah still has that pained look on her face.
Dill Tudd, you can tell us, whatever it is.
He just stares at the table.
Seeing him speechless like this causes me great anguish.
I see how much he means to me. How his random
appearances since I arrived on Firdus-which aren't
random, I get that now-they've worked on me, bit by bit.
Unnerving me and distressing me and throwing me off
balance and opening me up in ways I never knew I had
shut down.
Finally, he speaks.
I always feared this day would come.
Fear.
Not a word I'd ever have imagined hearing Dill Tudd
speak.
I glance over at Noon Yeah.
She's as bewildered as I am.
I'm sorry, Dill Tudd, what are you talking about?
I am so sincere.
I want to know what this fear is he speaks of.
He does another of those slow exhales.
He's acting like something is over, like it's dying a long,
slow death.
It's unbearable to watch.
Noon Yeah is still holding his hand.
She pulls her stool close to mine and puts her hand under
my arm, leaning in to my side.
This is a graining, isn't it?
Dill Tudd states this without any emotion.
I feel Noon Yeah's body instantly tense beside me.

My face heats up. My ear lobes as well. My stomach tightens.

Where did you get that idea?

I have been pretending for so many laps I had almost forgotten how to be me. I draw on all that muscle memory right now, doing everything I can to make him think that I am asking that question because I truly don't know.

He appears lost in thought.

He stares down at his hands.

Well…I mean…How long did I think I could get away with it?

What's he talking about?

I lean forward. *Get away with what?*

He doesn't appear to have heard my question.

Seriously-everyday like that, out in the open, all those people, the sheer odds that no one would FILE or REPORT or CITE me? What was I thinking?

I feel Noon Yeah twitch beside me.

CITE you for what, exactly?

He throws up his hands.

Was it hubris? Arrogance? Am I just enamored with my own little revolution?

I've heard him go off on some obtuse and cumbersome riffs, but this is something else.

Dill Tudd! I say it crisply, clearly. *What hubris??!! What arrogance!!!??? What are you going on about?*

He waves this off.

I love to help. I just do. If that's a crime, then so be it. Maybe that's what blinded me-LOVE. But if you go down because of love, did you really go down???

He is still just so…low.

Defeated.

Even his words.

This flat monotone.

Drained of all life-of all its DILL TUDDNESS.

Noon Yeah leaps to her feet.

She slams her palms down on the table.

WHAT ARE YOU TALKING ABOUT!? WHAT. DO. YOU. THINK. YOU. DID?! WHY DO YOU THINK WE'RE HERE??!!!

He sits up straight.

He runs his hand through his hair.

He straightens his shirt.

Which is black.

I call them THE ELEMENTS. He glances at the shelves surrounding us. He sighs. *And I knew the risks.*

I'm so lost.

What is going on here?

I don't know where to go from here.

What's happening between Noon Yeah and Dill Tudd?

What IS he talking about?

What does SHE think he's talking about?

It's like a chess match, but I can't seem to locate any of the pieces. Or where the board even is.

Wait. Noon Yeah puts her hands on the table. She leans in. *You think we're here because of all these plants and herbs and spices you've been growing and handing out?*

He leans in as well.

Yes. Of course. Why else would you be here?

Suddenly he's very clear.

And alert.

The energy shifts, again.

In a good way.

He takes the ginger and holds it up.

The CHAIRS aren't MUCKIN' ABOUT with this stuff. I'm well aware of that. There's a HEALTH system with its

PROTOCOLS and CERTIFICATIONS and BEST PRACTICES and APPROVED SUBSTANCES and PROPER DISTRIBUTION PROTOCOLS and if you diverge from that in any way they crack down hard. I've seen it with my own two eyes.

Noon Yeah stands there dumbfounded, leaning over the table, trying to figure out what is going on under this wing in a crater where dogs sing.

I think I'm starting to get it.

Dill Tudd, do you think the CHAIRS have sent someone to GRAIN you for breaking the RULES by handing out your… what did you call them?…ELEMENTS?

He nods.

BASIC O.T.S. right here.

I squint. *O.T.S.?*

He seems surprised I don't know what that is.

Yes. OUTSIDE THE SYSTEM. The CHAIRS are ruthless about these things. And me, I got my own way of doing things. I AM MY OWN SYSTEM.

I realize I'm breathing very fast.

Way up in my chest.

I put my hand on my heart.

I slow it all down.

I'm so confused.

Dill Tudd reaches behind him and pulls something out of a bin. It's a little glass vial.

He holds it up.

This is two ounces of Bergamot oil. You extract it from the peel of the Citrus Bergamia plant. You know what it's good for?

I have no clue.

I really don't. All of this is totally foreign to me.

It helps with depression.

My eyes go wide.

It does? Depression?

Dill Tudd, back to his Dill Tudd form.

But you have to know how to extract it and how to prepare it and how much to take. But before extraction and dosage, you have to know how to grow it, how-and when-to prune the branches, when the growing season is-And the CHAIRS? They want their hands in ALL OF IT. They want control, they want their cut, they want to regulate who gets it and who gives it to who and how much and when and where-

So much right now in the air between us.

That's what you mean by Outside The System.

There is great compassion in Noon Yeah's voice.

But you-

For some reason I choke up a bit here for just a second-

You just grow it and give it.

We look each other in the eyes.

Yes, Heen. Yes. Because people need help. Now. Can I show you something?

We stand up.

Yes please, I still want my tour!

Noon Yeah is so charming.

Dill Tudd walks over to a shelf.

He takes a leaf out of a bin and holds it up.

Peppermint. Helps with headaches, sore muscles.

It does? I had no idea.

He hands the leaf to Noon Yeah and reaches in another bin, removing a purple, slender flower.

Lavandula. One of 47 species of flowers in the mint family. At least three thousand years old. Known to you as LAVENDER.

He holds it up to Noon Yeah's nose.

She inhales and then closes her eyes.

AHHHHHHH so good.

He's just getting started.

Know what it's good for? He doesn't wait for us to respond. *Cuts. Burns. It makes a wonderful insect repellent. It helps you sleep, especially if you have anxiety.*

I smell it. *This flower does all that?*

He's already on to the next bin.

He pulls out a small handful of little soft brown chunks.

He takes a whiff.

Frankincense.

He offers us each a chunk.

Helps reduce asthma.

He takes another whiff.

It's a resin, from the trunk of the Boswellia tree, and it helps a person BREATHE. Do you realize how astounding this is?

He's getting more animated.

Better question my friends: Have you found yourself in the presence of someone who's having TROUBLE breathing? Because if that is your struggle, you are suspended in that ever so tenuous space between life and death. Is there anything more vital to life than breathing? And there is a tree that produces a gum-like substance that can help you breathe.

He puts the bin back on the shelf.

All from the wound.

I missed something. *What's from what wound?*

Dill Tudd rubs the stone on his necklace.

The Wound. Earth. They lost CONTROL. It got OUT OF HAND. And then it ENDED. And so they vowed to NEVER LOSE CONTROL AGAIN.

I interrupt. *I don't know if you could summarize all that Earth*

history that simply-I've read quite a bit about Earth-
He holds up his hand to stop me.
This???!!! The CHAIRS???? This obsessive, unrelenting crushing control and manic manipulation of every facet of life? This inability to handle even the slightest inkling of dissent or departure from these constrictive norms that choke the propulsive forces of life in all their fullness and vitality? This ruthless elimination of all that doesn't conform to the most narrow and soul sucking of standards that goes under the guise of THE ARRANGEMENTS? Too much. Way too much Heen Gru-Bares!!! ALL FROM THE WOUND. A GROSSLY EXCESSIVE COURSE CORRECTION OF THE HIGHEST AND MOST DISTORTED ORDER.
He turns and walks to another shelf.
Noon Yeah and I stand here, stunned.
He has so much fire in his belly.
I haven't ever heard someone talk about the CHAIRS like this. Or THE ARRANGEMENTS. Or the Earth, for that matter.
Are you even allowed to say things like that?
I have trusted that somebody somewhere knows what they're doing for my entire life. I have trusted that we're in good hands. He doesn't have this same trust. He sees it entirely differently. With suspicion. Disdain. Anger, even.
It's like an alternative understanding of EVERYTHING.
It's personal, for him.
The CHAIRS aren't THE CHAIRS to him.
They're people-who responded in a particular way to the pain of all that loss.
It's personal for him.
That's what unnerves me.
Like a rug being pulled out from under the universe.

532

He takes a chunk of something white out of a bin.
He holds it up to my nose.
It's awful. Just the most heinous smelling-
OHHHHHH!!!!! I know this smell!!!
Noon Yeah holds it way too close to her nose.
Oh that is foul! Your BOOBY BREW is like a flower compared to this!!! How do you know this smell Heen?
I remember that day.
When Dill Tudd asked me that question.
Dill Tudd gave me some of this one time after I passed out. I look at him expectantly. *Do you remember the question you asked me, the one that literally knocked me out?*
I have wanted to ask him about this for days. But each time I see him we get going on whatever we're talking about and I forget. I am so fascinated to see how he responds to this.
I do, Heen, I remember.
He leans forward, like NOW WE'RE GETTING DOWN TO BUSINESS.
I ask everybody that question.
You do?
I do.
Noon Yeah is about to jump out of her skin.
What question?!!
I make my best ARE YOU SURE YOU WANT TO KNOW? face.
She's adamant. *WHAT IS THE QUESTION?*
Dill Tudd turns his shoulders just a bit so he's facing her directly.
Noon Yeah, where'd you park your spaceship?
She looks slightly thrilled, a bit overwhelmed, shocked.
Her jaw drops open.

Everything slows down.

The three of us.

Standing in among these shelves.

Under this wing.

In this crater.

I watch these emotions coming and going from her face.

She turns to me. *He asked you where you parked your spaceship?*

I nod. *He did, just like he asked you....*

What did you say?

Nothing! It was too much. I passed out. And then I woke up and I had a chunk of that in my hand.

Dill Tudd takes a whiff of the chunk. He has no reaction to it. But he does have a question for me. *Why was that question too much for you?*

I look to Noon Yeah for some guidance here. Or solidarity. I get none. I redirect things.

You ask everyone that question?

I do. I love the reactions I get.

People laugh?

Dill Tudd looks out over the crater.

Some do. Because seriously, who has a spaceship? Who's ever even been on a spaceship, right? It's the absurdity of it that illuminates the larger absurdities we all must make peace with-

Noon Yeah interrupts, she is very focused right now.

I don't understand what you're saying Dill Tudd.

He take another whiff of the chunk. *Spaceships are absurd. We all know that. And yet the CHAIRS continue to insist that the course of things on any given planet rests in their hands. So there must be people-here on Firdus and other planets-keeping tabs on things for the CHAIRS, right? They've got to have EYES and EARS all over the place.*

Absurd, but it only makes sense. And how did those people get here? SPACESHIPS, right!!!???

He watches us carefully.

He waits for us to respond.

We both freeze.

He starts walking out of the wing.

Which one of you is the SIGN 7? he asks over his shoulder.

He keeps walking.

He doesn't look back.

I start to follow.

Noon Yeah steps in front of me.

She starts to say something but I cut her off.

You're about to say we need a plan, aren't you? I don't wait for her to respond. *No, we don't need a plan. We are way beyond plans. You know this, don't you?*

She bites her lower lip.

She brushes her hair off her forehead. Which I could watch her do for hours.

I do.

That's all she says.

And then she starts walking after Dill Tudd.

We head further into the crater, arcing left and down into the center. Up ahead is a row of pine trees. I can't tell what's beyond them. As we get closer I can see that what appears to be one straight row is actually two rows, slightly staggered, with a gap between them.

Dill Tudd goes through the gap.

We're right behind him.

On the other side of the trees we step onto a pitch.

It's smaller than a regulation field, but other than that it's a proper pitch for playing the beautiful game.

Across the pitch is a house. It's low and flat and has a

porch across the front. Dill Tudd walks up the slight incline to the porch and sits down in one of the lounge chairs that are lined up side to side.

Have a seat my friends, he says. *Oh! My apologies!* He jumps up. *How inhospitable of me! I haven't offered you anything to drink. You'd think I'd never had guests.*

He thinks this is very funny.

He turns and heads into the house.

No wayyyyy Noon Yeah says as she sits down. *The view...*

The deck and house are about half way up the opposite end of the crater from where we entered. We're looking across the pitch, above the tops of the pine trees, all the way to the other end.

She points. *I can see the slide. And that room at the end of the tunnel. And there's The Wing and The Other Wing. I see a stack of metal over to the right, a hammock strung between two oak trees. And there's a little house-see it?*

I do. It's kind of hidden. *And there's another one-*

I see it. It's like a tiny version of this house.

It is. As if this house had a baby.

I turn around and take in the main house behind us.

It's a long rectangle, with an angled roof much like the wings. But the roof isn't held up with posts, it's held up by steel I-beams. They're exposed, and they have letters and numbers stamped on them-N9 and R5 and A11-in no particular order. The exterior walls look like canvas from here, stretched tightly between the beams. Cut into the canvas are large squares with a mesh-like screen.

I have never seen a house like this.

And I have seen a lot of houses on a lot of planets.

It doesn't look like it was planned.

It looks like it happened.

Over time.

536

As if this house learned over the laps what it's here to
be.
Dill Tudd returns to the deck, holding a tray of drinks.
He hands us glasses.
The drink is bright red.
Noon Yeah holds up her glass. *What do we have here?*
Dill Tudd is so glad she asked. *I started with a few
hibiscus leaves and a handful of limes, some agave from
just over there and then I added something rather
numinous I've been storing in an oak barrel for the past
twenty laps.*
I try it.
BAM. It hits hard. So hard. But also fresh. Alive.
Is everything in this drink from this land?
*Oh yes…*He looks around. *All of it was grown in about a
two hundred foot circle around where we're sitting.*
It tastes like it.
He sits down.
He gazes out across the crater.
And then I see it.
The SUNS.
They're setting directly above the far end of the crater.
This is why you built your house here.
Dill Tudd nods as he stretches out his legs.
*Every evening I sit here and I take in the show. Like it's just
for me.*
The two lights of the SUNS cross as they set. This briefly
creates a third kind of light, just before dark. Around the
universe this momentary appearance is called THE THIRD
and it varies in its splendor and intensity from planet to
planet.
I'm now realizing that THE THIRD above this crater is
going to be stunning. It already is, slowly illuminating all

these plants and trees with a radiant golden glow.

Dill Tudd sets his drink down. *But tonight, for the first time ever, I don't watch the show alone, I watch with friends.*

Shireen appears from behind us and climbs up on his lap. *And Shireen, of course.*

Noon Yeah is quiet.

She leans back in her chair.

I sit up and plant my feet on the deck, facing Dill Tudd. *Why are there 5 chairs here and back there next to the creek?*

Oh Heen, I have so many chairs. I've been making them for laps. What if we have a big game someday and people want to watch?

I look out over the pitch. *There's hasn't ever been a game here, has there?*

That is correct. But someday...

I point to one of the little houses. *And those little houses? Are those for someday?*

Dill Tudd is pleased with where this is headed. *Oh yes, I have big plans-*

And so you've been building and preparing all these laps? I have.

Noon Yeah stands up and starts pacing back and forth in front of us.

She does this when she's thinking I tell Dill Tudd

He watches her. *She has a lot on her mind. SIGN 7s often do...*

She freezes.

She turns and stares at Dill Tudd. *You knew.*

THE THIRD is lighting up the crater.

I do now.

Dill Tudd says this quietly.

Why didn't you think it was Heen? Suspicion in her voice.

He laughs. *Because if you look far enough into his eyes it gets mushy. But your eyes? Steel. Which of course raises the question: What are you Heen?*

And there it is.

Dill Tudd asking me what I am.

I decide to tell him the truth.

I don't want to be what I am anymore.

That's an awkward sentence.

But I instantly feel lighter.

Noon Yeah comes over and squeezes onto my chair with me. *Heen works for the CHAIRS.*

Dill Tudd cups his hand over his ear. *What is that sound I hear? Oh yes, that's the sound of the plot thickening.*

I laugh out loud. *But I don't want to anymore!*

I sound like a kid, protesting his bed time.

I turn to Noon Yeah.

Our faces are close.

I don't see that steel in her eyes.

Something else.

Neither do I she says.

We sit here, face to face.

She just said that.

I remind myself again.

She just said that.

She doesn't want to do this either.

We turn and watch THE THIRD.

It is as magnificent as I anticipated.

The crater glows.

The silence is wonderful.

Eventually Dill Tudd sits up and faces us.

Well then, it looks like we've got ourselves a SEVER 10!

Blank looks from both of us.

You know about this, correct? A SEVER 10?
Still blank.
You don't? Noon Yeah, they didn't tell you about this?
This is interesting.
Noon Yeah being the one in the dark.
That's usually me.
Uhhhh…she hesitates…a SEVER 10? Is that a person? Or a job? How do I not know about this?
Now Dill Tudd is the one pacing, muttering to himself. *So SILVER 8's don't know about SIGNAL 4s who haven't heard of SECTOR 6's who have no contact with SERIES 5's-*
Wait! I stop him. *Did you just say SERIES 5s?*
Dill Tudd strokes his chin. *Yes, SERIES 5s, they're a little fuzzy to me. I think they have something to do with DATA collection-SILVER 8s are clearly more bureaucratic…Then there are the SIGN 7s.* He nods to Noon Yeah. *Who don't know about SEVER 10s-*
Noon Yeah stands up and starts pacing as well.
It makes me mental.
All this pacing.
But we're getting somewhere, that's what I tell myself.
Dill Tudd, how do you know all this about who works for the CHAIRS?
He answers while he paces. *That's just it-I've been trying to piece together how it all works for laps now. It's like a giant puzzle. That just happens to run the universe. I get a little piece here from someone, another piece over there-*
I stop him. *Someone? Who?*
He stops. He sighs. He looks at us both.
They're all over.
He says this like it should answer my question. It doesn't.
Who is all over?

He sits back down, both hands on his knees.

People who used to work for the CHAIRS.

I picture myself standing on a trap door.

Someone pulls a lever.

The trap door opens.

I fall through.

You know people who USED to work for the CHAIRS?

Noon Yeah sits as well. *They're here, on Firdus?*

He has the strangest look on his face. Like he's about to spring something massive on us.

Yes, they are. They're all over. That's what you learn when you walk around all day talking to people. And that's why I ask people WHERE'D YOU PARK YOUR SPACESHIP?

I skip that last bit.

We'll get to it later.

They left? Their jobs?

Oh Heen. I do love your inquiries. Yes, sometimes it's employment. Other times it's simply participation in the system. Often they lost someone they love to a GRAINING. But if they were to officially complain, or resist, or raise a ruckus, well…the CHAIRS can't have that. So when they come across someone who knows-AND THOSE WHO KNOW, KNOW, right?-

Hold on. I gotta stop him. Noon Yeah beats me to it. *So a SEVER 10 is when you leave?*

He nods.

Without any consequences? They let you?

Dill Tudd looks at her quizzically.

You're asking me? Best I can tell, it varies. Some say they want out-they file for a SEVER 10-and they get GRAINED immediately. My guess is they know too much. The CHAIRS can't have them out with the people knowing what they know. Some stop getting a FLOOR CHECK,

others show up at their THRIVAL for some health emergency and they're told WE HAVE NO RECORD OF YOU. The CHAIRS are masters at making people's lives miserable. But what I do know is that Firdus has unexpectedly become an outpost for SEVER 10s.
Noon Yeah is tapping her foot.
So much energy, all coiled and tense next to me.
And people survive?
That's the thing, for some people the CHAIRS don't have to do anything. JUST BEING ON THEIR OWN is devastating enough for them. It's too much. The leaving. They leave the JOB but it takes a while for the JOB to leave them—know what I mean?
I do Dill Tudd, I know exactly what you mean.
I don't know why I feel the need to say that.
He has more to say.
They burn through people like you. It can take a while to reclaim yourself, to get them out of your head, to learn how to be human again. Which is where I come in.
Noon Yeah points to him. *YOU?*
Dill Tudd smiles. *Let me ask you a question: What is it like for you to find out that other people have SEVER 10'd?*
WHEEEEEEWWW I say. I don't why I make this noise.
Relief? Terror? Tension? Joy?
That noise right there Heen. That's it. You aren't the first. Feels good, doesn't it?
He's got a point. *Yes…I falter…good, but also…I'm trembling.*
Noon Yeah puts her hand on my leg.
He is. He's trembling.
I put my hand on her knee.
And you're tapping your foot.
I am.

New possibilities often do that. Dill Tudd says this with such peace and calm.

I have another question.

Why haven't more people found you here? How are we the first?

He sighs.

You can't rush these things. We usually have to be in enough pain to be ready for what's next.

Noon Yeah gasps. *Lan Zing.*

I didn't see that coming. *Lan Zing?*

Yes, her brother-

That boy in the photos in her office-

Him.

Grief on her face.

He got GRAINED, didn't he?

Probably.

I look at Dill Tudd. *So the GRAININGS…*

He picks up my sentence. *Are about way more than one life. The effects ripple outwards for generations. But most people haven't connected the dots. They haven't talked to someone else who's lost someone. So much UNGRIEVED GRIEF. That's where we start.*

Noon Yeah listens but doesn't respond.

Is this devastating for her?

To consider what she's been a part of?

I hold her close.

She lets me.

Dill Tudd returns to his pacing.

We're just getting started.

He turns to us.

You realize this don't you? We've got to reestablish BARTERING as our first economic order, eliminating all non-generative insertions. A social network is a trillion times stronger than a commercial contract-how straightforward is that? Then, of course, we have to rethink CORRECTIONS and CONFLICT-shifting all litigious activities to relational rather than punitive modes. And there WILL BE GRAININGS. And those who PROTEST the GRAININGS will be GRAINED. This is going to take a while. Healing a universe often does.

He stops, tilts his head back, and laughs.

HEALING A UNIVERSE OFTEN DOES TAKE A WHILE MY FRIENDS!!!

He stands there, staring at THE THIRD, holding Shireen. He turns to us.

Would you like to stay here tonight?

He doesn't wait for us to answer.

How about dinner in an hour? Take a stroll and pick out your house, we'll have a feast, and then tomorrow we begin…

Noon Yeah sits up. *Sounds like a plan.*

Dill Tudd heads into his house.

Noon Yeah?

Yes, Heen.

Can you tell me something about YOU? Where you're from, WHO you're from, WHO YOU ARE-something? Anything?

She looks up at me. *That might take a while.*

I run my hand through her hair.

But according to Dill Tudd we have PLENTY OF TIME.

Okay, but first…

She pauses.

Yes…?

I have no idea what's coming next.

He said we should pick out a house for tonight.

Okay-

She kisses me.
She stands up and leads me off the porch.
Let's pick out a house-
And then we'll have dinner in a crater with Dill Tudd-
And a fox-
Named Shireen-
Exactly. And then we'll becomes SEVER 10s-
We will. And maybe die in the process-
Absolutely. Or open a tea house-
And work in a Bakery-
And join an underground resistance movement-that ever so gradually alters the course of galactic history by subversively undermining the most totalizing system of power and control the universe has ever encountered-
Sounds good-
But first an hour in a little house together-
Definitely. And you'll tell me all about your life?
I will.
And you're up for doing all this with me?
I am.

Back Matter.

A thousand thanks to Caitlin Elizabeth (The roll is officially still going!), Brent French for another wonderful cover design (thewanucompany.com), Violet Bell for the cover stars, and all you friends who read various drafts: Kathy Bergman, Cody Deese, Nina Polo Wieja, Rachel Rondell, Elizabeth Gilbert, Nicole Young, Kristin Hanggi, Jonno Buckley, Andrew Morgan, Chris York, Sarah Vanderveen, Dave Vanderveen, Jeff Tkach, Bonnie Scharff, Pete Scharff, Tim Olson, Jen Wood, Phil Wood and Natalie Closner.

About the Author.

Rob Bell is the New York Times Bestselling author of fourteen books and plays which have been translated into 25 languages. His visual art can be seen on Instagram @realrobbell, his band is HUMANS ON THE FLOOR, and his podcast is called The RobCast. Rob lives with his family in Ojai, California.

robbell.com

Printed in Great Britain
by Amazon

25679042R00314